William Tegg

The Last Act

being the funeral rites of nations and individuals

William Tegg

The Last Act
being the funeral rites of nations and individuals

ISBN/EAN: 9783337335489

Printed in Europe, USA, Canada, Australia, Japan

Cover: Foto ©Andreas Hilbeck / pixelio.de

More available books at **www.hansebooks.com**

THE
LAST ACT

being

THE FUNERAL RITES OF

Nations and Individuals.

———

"Last scene of all, that ends this strange eventful history"
Shakespeare

———

COLLECTED AND ARRANGED
BY
WILLIAM TEGG,

Editor of "Wills of their own" &c.

———

LONDON,
William Tegg & Cº Pancras Lane, Cheapside, 1876.

THE

LAST ACT:

BEING THE

FUNERAL RITES OF NATIONS

AND INDIVIDUALS.

———

"Last scene of all, that ends this strange, eventful history."
—SHAKSPEARE.

———

COLLECTED AND ARRANGED

BY

WILLIAM TEGG,

Editor of "Hone's Three Trials," "Wills of their Own," &c.

———

LONDON
WILLIAM TEGG & CO.,
PANCRAS LANE, CHEAPSIDE.
1876.

M'Corquodale & Co., Printers, Glasgow and London.

PREFACE.

THE title selected for this volume, however quaint it may appear, speaks for itself—"*The Last Act:*" for it is to record "The Funeral Rites of Nations and of Individuals," who, in their last *Act*, have left special (in many cases singular and eccentric) directions for the disposal of their bodies after death, frequently evincing more care for the due celebration of these last *rites*, than in the distribution of their riches.   Montaigne remarks—

" If instructions were at all necessary in this case, I should be of opinion that, in this as in all other actions of life, the ceremony and expense should be regulated by the condition of the person deceased ; and the philosopher, Lycon, prudently ordered his executors to dispose of his body where they should think most fit, and as to his funeral, to order it to be neither superfluous nor too mean. For my part, I shall wholly refer the ordering of this ceremony to custom, and leave the whole matter to the discretion of those to whose lot it shall fall to do me that last office.   ' Totus hic locus est contemnendus in nobis, non negligendus in nostris.' *—[The place of our sepulture is wholly to be contemned by us, but not to be neglected by our friends.]   And it was a holy saying of a saint—' Curatio funeris, conditio sepulturæ, pompa exsequiarum, magis sunt vivorum salatia, quám subsidia mortuorum.' †—[The care of funerals, the place of sepulture, and the pomp of obsequies, are rather consolations to the living than any benefit to the dead.] Which made Socrates answer Criton, who, at the hour of his death, asked him, How he would be buried? ' How you will,' said he." ‡

At the present time, the subject of funerals and funeral services occupies much of the public attention. The old sombre style of English funerals, which seems to have been devised to terrify rather than to console the mourner, has, in many respects, been changed for the better, more especially by the intro-duction of wreaths of " immortelles " placed upon the coffin, or thrown into the grave, to symbolise the immortality of the soul; the great subject which should occupy the thoughts, much more than the mere return of the body to its kindred dust. The wisest of kings tells us that—

" The heart of the wise *is* in the house of mourning; but the heart of fools *is* in the house of mirth." §

* Cicero, Tusc. Quæs. 45.
† St. August de Civitate Dei. I. 12.
‡ Plato, Phædo.
§ Ecclesiastes, chap. vii. ver. 4.

I may be excused for reminding the reader of the
lines of Longfellow :—

"I like that ancient Saxon phrase, which calls
　　The burial ground God's-Acre!　It is just;
It consecrates each grave within its walls,
　　And breathes a benison o'er the sleeping dust.

"God's-Acre!　Yes, that blessed name imparts
　　Comfort to those who in the grave have sown
The seed, that they have garnered in their hearts,
　　Their bread of life—alas! no more their own.

"Into its furrows shall we all be cast,
　　In the sure faith that we shall rise again
At the great harvest, when the archangel's blast
　　Shall winnow, like a fan, the chaff and grain.

"Then shall the good stand in immortal bloom,
　　In the fair gardens of that second birth;
And each bright blossom mingle its perfume
　　With that of flowers which never bloomed on earth.

"With thy rude ploughshare, Death, turn up the sod,
　　And spread the furrow for the seed we sow;
This is the field and Acre of our God,
　　This is the place where human harvests grow!"

The curtailing of funeral pomp, and the lessening
the heavy expense of the old customary mourning,
cremation, and the introduction of wicker coffins,
have been brought prominently before the public
mind, and cannot fail to lead to considerable modi-

fication of our present funeral rites and ceremonies. The vexed question of opening the churchyards for the burial of dissenters according to their own rites, it is to be hoped, will shortly be settled, and that *" God's-Acre "* will be open to receive all, without distinction of creed, due provision being made to prevent unseemly brawls or inflammatory harangues over the grave. Mr. Osborne Morgan, in a recent speech to his constituents, has stated that—

" The churchyard was simply so much parish land, vested in the incumbent, as to the herbage or surface, for his own use, and as to the soil for the use of the entire body of the parishioners, every one of whom—nay, every person dying in the parish—had, at common law, an equal right of interment. As to the popular notion that the churchyard was Church property, because the church usually stood in the middle of it, had not even a foundation in fact, for the earliest parochial burying-grounds were entirely unconnected with, as a general rule, remote from, the church. Indeed, the practice of having churchyards encompassing or adjoining the church, is stated by Burns (a high authority on such subjects) to have originated in the superstition of praying for the dead, when the monks and priests, beginning to offer prayers for souls departed, procured leave, for their greater ease and profit, that a liberty of sepulchre might be in churches and in places adjoining to them."

A word or two in explanation of the origin of the pomp of modern funerals will be found interesting. It is but a mere caricature of the ancient baronial burials. The mutes, who stand at the doors, represent the two porters of the castle, with their staves in black; the man who heads the procession, wearing a scarf, is the herald-at-arms; the man who carries the plume of feathers on his head being an esquire who bears the shield and casque, with its plume (of feathers); the pall bearers, with batons, represent the knight companions-at-arms; and the men walking with wands, the gentlemen ushers with their wands.

By the kind permission of Messrs. Chambers, I am enabled to append the following articles from their admirable Encyclopædia on the subjects of Burials, Cemeteries, Catacombs, &c., which will give my readers much valuable information.

In selecting the different instances of curious burials, I have strictly endeavoured to avoid giving offence, or to call forth rebuke; nor have I done anything, I hope, to violate the sanctity of the grave, by recording a truthful account of the various modes of interment.

WILLIAM TEGG.

Pancras Lane, 1876.

₊ Since the above was written, the Burials Question has been brought before the House of Lords, May 15, 1876, by Lord Granville, who moved two Resolutions:—1. To give facilities for the interment of deceased persons without the burial service of the Church of England; and, 2. To enable the relatives or friends to conduct such funeral in the churchyard, "with such Christian and orderly religious observance as to them may seem fit." On the division, the numbers were, for the Resolutions, 92; against, 148; majority, 56.

THE LAST ACT.

PART I.

BURIALS.

BURIAL, a word of Teutonic origin (Ang.-Sax. *birgan,* to conceal), is applied to the prevalent method among civilised nations of disposing of the dead, by hiding them in the earth. As there is almost nothing else so deeply interesting to the living as the disposal of those whom they have loved and lost, so there is perhaps nothing else so distinctive of the condition and character of a people as the method in which they treat their dead. Hence, funeral customs associate themselves with a wide variety of sentiments, from gentle and rational sorrow, up to deification of the departed, accompanied sometimes with cruelty and ferocity towards the living. People of a low and barbarous type carelessly permit the remains of the dead to lie in the way of the living, and there are a few instances in which the object of artificial arrangements has

been to preserve a decorated portion of the body—
as, for instance, a gilded skull—among survivors.
The general tendency of mankind, however, has
always been to bury the dead out of sight of the
living; and various as the methods of accomplishing
this end have been, they have resolved themselves
into three great classifications:—1. The simple closing
up of the body in earth or stone; 2. The burning of
the body, and the entombing of the cinders; and, 3.
The embalming of the body. The first of these
seems to be the earliest form of which we have any
record, and it is the form most amply sanctioned by
the existing practice of the civilised world. It is the
method referred to in the earliest Scriptures; and all
are familiar with the touching scene in which Abraham buries Sarah in the cave in the land of Canaan
which belonged to Ephron, but was, after a solemn
and courteous negotiation, secured to Abraham for a
possession to bury his dead in (Gen. c. 23). The
horrible fate of being left unburied, either from scorn
or neglect, is powerfully told in the prophecy of
Jeremiah against Jehoiakim:—"He shall be buried
with the burial of an ass, drawn and cast forth beyond the gates of Jerusalem." There is frequent
allusion in the later Scriptures, and especially in the
New Testament, to the embalming of the body in
antiseptics and fragrant substances; and the burning
of the bodies of Saul and his sons is accounted for

by commentators on the supposition that they were too far decayed to be embalmed. The Israelites may have learned the practice of embalming from the Egyptians, among whom it was an art so greatly cultivated and extensively practised, that Egyptian corpses, as inoffensive as any article of wood or stone, are scattered over Europe in museums, and are even to be found as curiosities in private houses. The soil and climate of Upper Egypt seem to have afforded facilities for embalming unmatched in any other part of the world; and in other places the vestiges of the practice are comparatively rare, though it is usual even yet to embalm royal corpses, and in some places to preserve a series of mummies, as in the vault of the monastery of Kreuzberg, at Bonn, where the monks have been successively preserved in their costume for centuries. The practice of incremation, or of the burning of the body, and the entombing of the ashes, deserves more inquiry than it has yet obtained. In Greece, in Etruria—both before and after it came under the Romans—and in the north of Europe, the simple burial of the body, and its prior reduction to ashes, were both practised, and sometimes contemporaneously. The tombs of Etruria are rich in art, much of it going to the adornment of the urns of baked clay in which the ashes of the dead are kept. Vessels of *terra-cotta*, or cooked earth, containing human remains, have been found, often so large that they appear to have served as coffins for containing the whole body. Vessels of this kind were found in the valley of the Scamander by some British Officers while spending their leisure time after the siege of Sebastopol, upon the ground supposed to have been occupied by the besiegers of Troy. Smaller cinerary urns have been found over so extensive a portion of the world, that it is difficult to define the limits to which they belong. The Danish antiquaries say, that in their stone period, when the use of metals was unknown, the dead were all buried unburned in stone chambers, and that the burning of the bodies and the preservation of the ashes in urns came in with the age of bronze.

Some of the grandest buildings in the world have been tombs; such are the pyramids, the castle of St. Angelo, the tomb of Cæcilia Metella, and many temples scattered over Hindustan and other Eastern countries. Thus, the respect paid by the living to the dead has preserved for the world many magnificent fruits of architectural genius and labour. A notion that the dead may require the things they have been fond of in life, has also preserved to the existing world many relics of the customs of past ages. The tombs of Egypt have supplied an immense quantity of them, which have taught the present age more of the manners of ancient nations than all the learned books that have been written. It is an awful remembrance, at the same time, that inanimate things were not all that the dead were expected to take with them. Herodotus tells us of favourite horses and slaves sacrificed at the holocaust of the dead chief. The same thing has been done in our own day in Ashantee. In many countries, the wives had the doom, or privilege, as it was thought, of departing with their husbands; and down to the present generation the practice has lived in full vigour in the Hindu sutti. Among the Jews, the Greeks, the Romans, and many ancient nations, the dead were buried beyond the towns. The "stop, traveller!" was a usual memorandum on Roman tombs. In Christian countries, if the remains of the saint to whom a church was dedicated could be obtained—or anything passing for the remains— they were buried near the altar in the choir. It became a prevalent desire to be buried near these saints, and the bodies of men eminent for their piety, or high in rank, came thus to be buried in churches. The extension of the practice was the origin of churchyards. These, in crowded towns, became offensive and unhealthy. It can scarcely be said that this practice, so detrimental to the public health, as the burial within churches, was checked in this country until the whole system of intramural interment, as it was called, was attacked, about the year 1844, by Mr. Chadwick and other sanitary reformers. Measures were afterwards carried for shutting graveyards in crowded cities, and placing interments in open cemeteries under sanitary control. The first great measure was passed in 1850, when the Board of Health was made a Burial Board for the Metropolis, and power was given to the Privy Council to close the city graveyards. The act was modified two years afterwards, by transferring the duties of managing cemeteries to local boards appointed by the vestries. It was in London that the danger was most urgent and the remedy immediate. It was extended to the English provinces in 1853, and to Scotland in 1855.

In England, burial in some part of the parish churchyard is a common law right, without even paying for breaking the soil, and that right will be enforced by mandamus. But the body of a parishioner cannot be interred in an iron coffin or vault, or even in any particular part of a churchyard, as, for instance, the family vault, without the sanction of the incumbent. To acquire a *right* to be buried in a particular vault or place, a faculty must be obtained from the ordinary, as in the case of a pew in the church. But this right is at an end when the family cease to be parishioners. All such rights, by faculty or otherwise, are expressly saved by the Burial Acts.

By the canons of the Church of England, clergymen cannot refuse or delay to bury any corpse that is brought to the church or churchyard; on the other hand, a conspiracy to prevent a burial is an indictable offence, and so is the wilfully obstructing a clergyman in reading the burial-service in a parish church. It is a popular error, that a creditor can arrest or detain the body of a deceased debtor; and the doing such an act is indictable as a misdemeanour. It is also an error, that permitting a funeral procession to pass over private grounds creates a public right of way. By the 3 Geo. IV. c. 126, s. 32, the inhabitants of any parish, township, or place, when going to or returning from attending funerals of persons in England who have died and are to be buried there, are exempted from any toll within these limits. And by the 4 Geo. IV. c. 49, s. 36, the same regulation is extended to Scotland; the only difference being, that in the latter case the limitation of the district is described by the word *parish* alone. The 6 and 7 Will. IV. c. 86, regulates the registry of deaths. The 4 Geo. IV. c. 52, abolished the barbarous mode of burying persons found *felo de se*, and directs that their burial shall take place, without any marks of ignominy, privately in the parish churchyard, between the hours of nine and twelve at night, under the direction of the coroner. The burial of dead bodies cast on shore, is enforced by 48 Geo. III. c. 75. See Wharton's *Law Lexicon*.

In Scotland, the right of burial in a churchyard is an incident of property in the parish; but it is a mere right of burial, and there is not necessarily any corresponding ownership in the solum or ground of the churchyard. In Edinburgh, however, the right to special burial-places in churchyards is recognised.— *Chambers's Encyclopædia.*

CEMETERIES.

Cemetery, from the Greek, may mean any grave-yard, or other place of deposit for the dead; but it has lately acquired a special meaning, applicable to those extensive ornamental burial-grounds which have recently come into use in this and European countries, as the practice of burying within and around churches was gradually abandoned. The fine burial-grounds of the Turks, extending over large tracts adorned by cedars and other trees, may have suggested the plan to Europeans. It was first exemplified on a great scale in Paris, in which, as the largest walled town in Europe, the disposal of the dead was long a matter of extreme anxiety and difficulty. There are few considerable towns in Britain near which there is not at least one cemetery, and the legislation has rendered their establishment, to a certain extent, a legal necessity. There was at first a natural feeling of regret at the prospect of deserting places of deposit for the dead so hallowed by ancient use and recent associations as the church and churchyard. In many instances, however, the places thus professedly hallowed were in reality surrounded by degrading and disgusting circumstances. On the other hand, the new places of interment began to develop humanising and elevating influences, in beautiful trees and flowers, natural scenery, and works of monumental art. The new cemeteries are in many instances cheerful open places of recreation, and in them the place of rest for the dead has rather tended to improve than to undermine the health of the living. One of the oldest established and most celebrated of the European cemeteries is that of Père la Chaise, near Paris, the arrangements of which have been generally followed in the cemeteries of London and other English cities; with, however, this distinct difference, that the English cemeteries are divided into two portions—one consecrated for the burials of the members of the Established Church, over whose remains the funeral service is read, and one unconsecrated, for the burials of dissenters. In the Scottish cemeteries, of which those are good specimens at Edinburgh and Glasgow, no such distinctions exist. In the United States, as at Philadelphia and New York, there are cemeteries equal in point of arrangement to any in Europe.—*Chambers's Encyclopædia.*

CATACOMBS.

Catacombs (Gr. *kata*, and *kumbos*, a hollow), subterraneous chambers and passages formed generally in a rock, which is soft and easily excavated, such as *tufa*. Catacombs are to be found in almost every country in which such rocks exist, and, in most cases, probably originated in mere quarries, which afterwards came to be used either as places of sepulture for the dead, or as hiding-places for the living. The most celebrated catacombs in existence, and those which are generally understood when catacombs are spoken of, are those on the Via Appia, at a short distance from Rome. To these dreary crypts it is believed that the early Christians were in the habit of retiring, in order to celebrate their new worship, in times of persecution, and in them were buried many of the saints and martyrs of the primitive church. They consist of long narrow galleries, usually about eight feet high and five wide, which twist and turn in all directions, very much resembling mines. The graves were constructed by hollowing out a portion of the rock, at the side of the gallery, large enough to contain the body. The entrance was then built up with stones, on which usually the letters D. M. (Deo Maximo), or XP., the first two letters of the Greek name of Christ, were inscribed. Other inscriptions and marks, such as the cross, are also found. Though latterly devoted to purposes of Christian interment exclusively, it is believed that the catacombs were at one time used as burying-places by pagans also. At irregular intervals, these galleries expand into wide and lofty vaulted chambers, in which the service of the church was no doubt celebrated, and which still have the appearance of churches. The original extent of the catacombs is uncertain, the guides maintaining that they have a length of twenty miles, whereas about six only can now be ascertained to exist, and of these, many portions have either fallen in or become dangerous. When Rome was besieged by the Lombards in the eighth century, many of the catacombs were destroyed; and the popes afterwards caused the remains of many of the saints and martyrs to be removed and buried in the churches. Art found its way into the catacombs at an early period, and many remains of frescoes are still found in them. The catacombs at Naples, cut into the Cape di Monte, resemble those at Rome, and evidently were used for the same purposes, being in many parts literally covered with Christian symbols. In one of the large vaulted chambers there are paintings which have retained a freshness which is wonderful, when the influences of time and the dampness of the situation are taken into account. The palm-tree, as a memorial of Judea, is a prominent object in these pictures. At Palermo and Syracuse there are similar catacombs, the latter being of considerable extent. They are also found in Greece, in Asia Minor, in Syria, Persia, and Egypt. At Milo, one of the Cyclades, there is a hill which is honey-combed with a labyrinth of tombs running in every direction.   In these, bassirilievi and figures in *terra cotta* have been found, which prove them to be long anterior to the Christian era.   In Peru, and other parts of South America, catacombs have been discovered.   The catacombs in Paris are a species of charnel-houses, into which the contents of such burying-places as were found to be pestilential, and the bodies of some of the victims of 1792, were cast by a decree of the Government.—*Chambers's Encyclopædia.*

MAUSOLEUM.

A sepulchral monument of large size, containing a chamber in which urns or coffins are deposited. The name is derived from the tomb erected at Halicarnassus to Mausolus, king of Caria, by his disconsolate widow, Artemisia, 353 B.C.   It was one of the most magnificent monuments of the kind, and was esteemed one of the seven wonders of the world.   It was described by Pliny and other ancient writers, as late as the twelfth century, and must have been overthrown, probably by an earthquake, during the following two centuries; for all trace of it had disappeared, except some marble steps, when the Knights of St. John of Jerusalem, in 1404, took possession of the site of Halicarnassus, then occupied by a small village called Clessy.   While excavating among the ruins for building materials, the knights discovered a large chamber decorated with marble pilasters, and with richly inlaid panels. The sarcophagus of the founder was also discovered in another great hall. Excavations have been recently made by Mr. Newton, assisted by the British Government, and he has succeeded in bringing to light many of the beautiful sculptures of the mausoleum. Amongst others, the fragments of the statue of King Mausolus (now pieced together in the British Museum), and a portion of the quadriga which crowned the monument. Many fragments of lions, dogs, &c., and a beautiful sculpture of a horse, have been found. Portions of friezes of fine design and workmanship, the subjects of which invariably are Greeks in conflict with Amazons, have been also dug up.

The plan of the basement has been traced, the area being one hundred and twenty-six feet by one hundred feet; and from the fragments of columns, Ionic capitals, &c., which have been found, the description of Pliny has been verified. The mausoleum consisted of a basement sixty-five feet high, on which stood an Ionic colonnade twenty-three and a-half high, surmounted by a pyramid, rising in steps to a similar height, and on the apex of which stood a colossal group, about fourteen feet in height, of Mausolus and his wife in the quadriga. These statues are supposed to be the work of the celebrated Scopas. The above dimensions are from Mr. Newton's restoration, but they are disputed by Mr. Fergusson, and others. All agree that the total height of one hundred and forty feet given by Pliny is probably accurate.—*Chambers's Encyclopædia.*

THE EGYPTIANS.

The funeral ceremonies of the Egyptians deserve particular notice, for no people, of whom we have any account transmitted to us, ever paid so much regard to the bodies of their departed friends. Of this we have a striking instance in what still remains of their pyramids, the most stupendous buildings that ever were erected to perpetuate the memory of their princes. This ostentation, like most other customs, originated first in the courts of their kings, but in time was imitated, as far as lay in their power, by the lower ranks of people.

When any of their relations died, the whole family quitted the place of their abode, and during sixty or seventy days, according to the rank or quality of the deceased, abstained from all the comforts of life, excepting such as were necessary to support nature. They embalmed the bodies, and many persons were employed in performing this ceremony. The brains were drawn through the nostrils with an instrument, and the intestines were emptied by cutting a hole in the abdomen, or belly, with a sharp stone, after which the cavities were filled up with perfumes, and the finest odoriferous spices; but the person who made the incision in the body for this purpose, and who was commonly a slave, was obliged to run away immediately after, or the people present would have stoned him to death; but those who embalmed the body were treated with the utmost respect.

The interior parts of the body were filled with all sorts of curious spices, which they purchased from the Arabians, and after a certain number of days had expired, it was wrapped up in fine linen, glued together with gum, and then spread over with the richest perfumes. The body being thus embalmed, was delivered to the relations, and placed either in a sepulchre, or in their own houses, according to their rank and ability. It stood in a wooden chest, erect; and all those who visited the family treated it with some marks of respect. This was done, that those who knew them while alive should endeavour to imitate their conduct after death. Of this we have a striking instance in the account of the funeral of Joseph, in Egypt, and the regard that was paid to his remains long after his decease. The Egyptians would not suffer praises to be bestowed indiscriminately upon every person, let his rank be ever so elevated, for characters given to the deceased were bestowed by the judges, who represented the people at large. The judges who were to examine into the merits of the deceased met on the opposite side of a lake, of which there were many in Egypt; and while they crossed the lake, he who sat at the helm was called Charon, which gave rise to the fable among the Greeks, that Charon conducted the souls of deceased persons into the Elysian fields, or the infernal regions. When the judges met, all those who had anything to object against the deceased person were heard; and if it appeared that he had been a wicked person, then his name was condemned to perpetual infamy, nor could his dearest relations erect any monument to perpetuate his memory.

This made a deep impression on the minds of the people; for nothing operates more strongly than the fear of shame, and the consideration of our deceased relations being consigned to infamy hereafter. Kings themselves were not exempted from this inquiry; all their actions were canvassed at large by the judges, and the same impartial decision took place as if it had been upon one of the meanest of the subjects. Of this we have some instances in Scripture, where we read that wicked kings were not suffered to be interred in the sepulchres of their ancestors. Happy for mankind, if this were more attended to in our days; then wicked princes and sovereigns would learn, that notwithstanding their elevated rank in life, yet the justice of their country, which they often trample on, will scrutinize with severity their actions, while their bodies are consigned to the silent tomb.

If no objection was made to the conduct of the deceased, then a funeral oration was delivered in memory of him, reciting his most worthy actions; but no notice was taken of his birth, because every Egyptian was considered as noble. No praises were bestowed, but such as related to temporal merit; and he was applauded for having cultivated piety to the gods, and discharged his duty to his fellow-creatures. Then all the people shouted with voices of applause, and the body was honourably interred. The Egyptians, however, believed much in the doctrine of the transmigration of souls, and likewise that for some time after death the souls of the deceased hovered round the bodies; which, among many others, was one of the reasons why they deferred the interment of their relations so long.—*Burder.*

Bodies were embalmed in three different ways. The most magnificent was bestowed on persons of distinction, and the expense amounted to a talent of silver, or about £137 10s. sterling. Many hands were employed in this ceremony. Some drew the brain through the nostrils, by an instrument made for that purpose. Others emptied the bowels and intestines, by cutting a hole in the side with an Ethiopian stone as sharp as a razor; after which the cavities were filled with perfumes and odoriferous drugs. As this evacuation (which was necessarily attended with some dissections) seemed, in some measure, cruel and inhuman; the persons employed fled as soon as the operation was over, and were pursued with stones by the standers by. But those who embalmed the body were honourably treated. They filled it with myrrh, cinnamon, and all sorts of spices. After a certain time, the body was swathed in lawn fillets, which were glued together with a kind of very thin gum, and then crusted over with the most exquisite perfumes. By this means, it is said, that the entire figure of the body, the very lineaments of the face, and even the hairs on the lids and eyebrows, were preserved in their natural perfection. This shows the care the Egyptians took of their dead. Their gratitude to their deceased relations was immortal. Children, by seeing the bodies of their ancestors thus preserved, recalled to mind those virtues for which the public had honoured them; and were excited to a love of those laws which such excellent persons had left for their security. We find that part of those ceremonies was performed in the funeral honours paid to Joseph in Egypt.—*Rollin.*

THE HEBREWS.

Upon the demise of any person, the relatives and friends rent their clothes. This custom is still imitated, but with a due regard to economy, by the modern Jews, who only cut off a piece of their garment in token of affliction. It was usual to bend the dead person's thumb into the hand, and fasten it in that posture with a string, because the thumb having then the figure of the name of God, they thought the evil spirit would not dare to approach it. When they came to the burying-place, they made a speech to the dead in the following terms:—" Blessed be God, who has formed thee, fed thee, maintained thee, and taken away thy life. O dead, He knows your numbers, and shall one day restore your life;" and so on. After this they delivered the funeral oration upon the deceased, then said a prayer, called the "righteousness of judgment;" and, finally, turning the face of the dead body towards heaven, they cried out " Go in peace."—*Encyclopædia Britannica.*

If a man was found guilty of a capital offence, and condemned to be hanged, his body was not to remain after sunset on the tree; but (says the Mosaic law) " Thou shalt bury him that day, that thy land be not defiled; for he that is hanged is accursed of God."— *Burder.*

The kings of Judah were buried " with their fathers in the city of David," or Jerusalem; but some of those who had " done evil in the sight of the Lord " were not permitted to be interred in the sepulchres of the kings. Josephus gives the following account of the burial of King David. His remains were interred at Jerusalem with a magnificence of pomp, exceeding the powers of description. Solomon deposited immense treasure in his sepulchre. 1300 years after, in the time of Hyrcanus, the high priest, Jerusalem was besieged by Antiochus, the son of Demetrius, surnamed, The Pious. Antiochus offered to abandon the siege on being paid 3000 talents. Hyrcanus had no resource but in David's tomb, which he broke open, and from thence took the sum demanded. Many years after, King Herod discovered a cell, from which he took immense riches; but so deeply sunk in the earth, and so ingeniously concealed were the remains of David deposited, that both Hyrcanus and Herod were unable to effect a discovery.

ASSYRIANS, ANCIENT ARMINIANS, &C.

It is remarkable, that none of those Eastern nations burnt the bodies of their deceased relations, although they offered in sacrifice those of their living ones. They buried the dead bodies in the earth; and this they did in consequence of a tradition common among them, that the first man was buried.—*Burder.*

THE BABYLONIANS.

The Babylonians buried their dead in the same manner as the Assyrians, namely, by laying the bodies in the earth; and dark and confused as their notions were in many respects, yet they believed

in a future state of rewards and punishments.—
Burder.

THE GREEKS.

Among the Greeks and Romans great attention
was paid to the obsequies of the dead. They were
well aware of the impression that was thus made on
the minds of the living. The dead were ever held
sacred and inviolable, even amongst the most barbarous nations; to defraud them of any due respect
was a greater and more unpardonable sacrilege than
to spoil the temple of the gods; the memories of the
illustrious were preserved with a religious care and
reverence, and all their remains honoured with worship
and adoration: hatred and envy themselves were put
to silence; for it was thought a sign of a cruel and
inhuman disposition to speak evil of the dead, and
prosecute revenge beyond the grave. No provocation
was thought sufficient to warrant so foul an action,
the highest affronts from themselves whilst alive, or
afterwards from their children, were esteemed weak
pretences for disturbing their peace. Offenders of
this kind were not only branded with disgrace and
infamy, but, by Solon's laws, incurred a severe penalty.

But of all honours paid to the dead, the care of
their funeral rites was the greatest and most necessary; for these were looked upon as a debt so sacred,
that such as neglected to discharge it were thought

accursed. And no wonder that they were thus solicitous about the interment of the dead, since they were strongly possessed with an opinion that their souls could not be admitted into the Elysian shades, but were forced to wander, desolate, and without company, till their bodies were committed to the earth; and if they had never the good fortune to obtain human burial, the time of their exclusion from the common receptacle of the ghosts was no less than a hundred years.

As soon as any person had expired, they closed his eyes. The design of this custom seems to have been not only to prevent that horror, which the eyes of dead men when uncovered are apt to strike into the living, but also for the satisfaction of dying persons, who are usually desirous to die in a decent posture. For the same reason the mouth of the dead person was closed. This done, his face was covered. Almost all the offices about the dead were performed by their nearest relations; nor could a greater misfortune befal any person, than to want these last respects. All the charges expended on funerals, and the whole care and management of them, belonged also to relations, saving that persons of extraordinary worth were frequently honoured with public funerals, the expenses whereof were defrayed out of the exchequer.

Before the body was cold, they composed all the

members, stretching them out to their due length. After this the dead body was washed. This done, the body was anointed. After the body was washed and anointed, they wrapped it in a garment, which seems to have been no other than the common pallium or cloak they wore at other times, as we find the Romans made use of the toga. Then the body was adorned with a rich and splendid garment, the whole body was covered with this garment.

When persons of worth and character died in foreign countries, their remains being brought home in urns, were honoured with the ceremonies customary at other funerals.

Some time before interment a piece of money was put into the corpse's mouth, which was thought to be Charon's fare for wafting the departed soul over the Infernal River. Besides this, the corpse's mouth was furnished with a certain cake, composed of flour, honey, &c. This was designed to appease the fury of Cerberus the infernal doorkeeper, and to procure him a safe and quiet entrance.

It may further be observed, that during this time the hair of the deceased person was hung upon the door, to signify the family was in mourning; and, till the house was delivered of the corpse, there stood before the door a vessel of water. The design of this was, that such as had been concerned about the corpse might purify themselves by washing. For not the Jews only, but the greatest part of the heathen world, thought themselves polluted by the contact of a dead body.

The air proceeding from the dead body was thought to pollute all things into which it entered: whence all uncovered vessels which stood in the same room with the corpse were accounted unclean by the Jews. Hence it was customary to have the whole house purified as soon as the funeral solemnities were over.

The next thing to be observed is their carrying the corpse forth. The time of burial seems not to have been limited. The ancient burials took place on the third or fourth day after death; nor was it unusual to perform the solemnities, especially of poor persons, on the day after their death. Servius was of opinion, that the time of burning bodies was the eighth day after death—the time of burying the ninth; but this must only be understood of the funerals of great persons, which could not be duly solemnized without extraordinary preparations. In some instances it was usual to keep the bodies seventeen days and seventeen nights.

The ceremony was performed in the day, for night was looked on as a very improper time, because then furies and evil spirits, which could not endure the light, ventured abroad.

Young men only, that died in the flower of their

age, were buried in the morning twilight; for so dreadful a calamity was this accounted, that they thought it indecent, and almost impious, to reveal it in the face of the sun. The Athenians went counter to the rest of the Grecians; for their laws enjoined them to celebrate their funerals before sunrise.

The body was sometimes placed upon a bier; instead of which the Lacedæmonians commonly used their bucklers: whence that remarkable command of one of their matrons to her son—"Either bring this" (pointing to his buckler) "back, or be brought upon it." But the most ancient Grecians seem to have conveyed their dead bodies to their funerals without any support.

The persons present at funerals were the dead man's friends and relations, who thought themselves under an obligation to pay this last respect to their deceased friend. Besides these, others were frequently invited to increase the solemnity, where the laws restrained them not from it; which they did at some places, either to prevent the disorders which often happened at such promiscuous meetings, or to mitigate the excessive charges of funerals.

The habit of these persons was not always the same; for though they sometimes put on mourning, and in common funerals as frequently retained their ordinary apparel, yet the exequies of great men were commonly celebrated with expressions of joy for their reception into heaven. When the body was conveyed out of the house, they took their last farewell, saluting it in a certain form of words.

The procession was commonly made on horseback, or in coaches; but at the funerals of persons to whom a more than ordinary reverence was thought due, all went on foot. The relations went next the corpse: the rest walked some distance off. Sometimes the men went before it, with their heads uncovered—the women following it; but the ordinary way was for the body to go first, and the rest to follow; whereby the survivors were put in mind of their mortality, and bid to remember they were all following in the way the dead person was gone before. At the funerals of soldiers their fellow-soldiers attended with their spears pointed towards the ground, and the uppermost part of their bucklers turned downwards. This was not done so much because the gods were carved upon their bucklers, whose faces would have been polluted by the sight of a dead body, as that they might recede from their common custom, the method of mourning being to act quite contrary to what was usual at other times; and therefore not only their bucklers, but their spears, and the rest of their weapons were inverted.

The ceremonies by which they used to express their sorrow on the death of friends, and on other occasions, were various and uncertain; but it seems to have been a constant rule amongst them to recede as much as possible in habit, and all their behaviour, from their ordinary customs; by which change they thought it would appear that some extraordinary calamity had befallen them. Hence it was that mourners in some cities demeaned themselves in the very same manner with persons who in other places designed to express joy; for the customs of one city being contrary to those of another, it sometimes happened that what in one place passed for an expression of mirth, was in others a token of sorrow. The most ordinary ways of expressing sorrow were these that follow :—

They abstained from banquets and entertainments, and banished from their houses all musical instruments and whatever was proper to excite pleasure, or bore an air of mirth and gaiety. They frequented no public solemnities, nor appeared in places of concourse, but sequestered themselves from company, and refrained even from the comforts and conveniences of life. Wine was too great a friend to cheerfulness to gain admission into so melancholy society; the light itself was odious; and nothing courted but dark shades and lonesome retirements, which they thought bore some resemblance to their misfortunes.

They divested themselves of all ornaments, and laid aside their jewels, gold, and whatever was rich and precious in their apparel. Their mourning garments were always black, and differed not from their ordinary apparel in colour only, but likewise in value, as being of cheap and coarse stuff.

They tore, cut off, and sometimes shaved their hair. They had several ways of disposing of their hair; at times it was thrown on the dead body. It was likewise frequent to cast it into the funeral pile, to be consumed with the body of their friend. Some restrain this practice to sons, or very near relations; but it appears, by many instances, to have been common to all that thought themselves obliged to express their respect or love to the dead, insomuch that, upon the death of great men, whole cities and countries were commonly shaved. It was used partly to render the ghost of the deceased person propitious, which seems to be the reason why they threw hair into the fire to burn with him, or laid it on his body, that they might appear disfigured, and careless of their beauty. It may further be observed, that in solemn and public mournings it was common to extend this practice to their beasts, that all things might appear as deformed and ugly as might be. The Persians shaved themselves, their horses and their mules; but Alexander, as in the rest of his actions, so herein went beyond the rest of mankind; for at the death of Hephæstion, he not only cut off the manes of his horses and mules, but took down the battlements from the city walls, that even towns might seem mourners, and instead of their former beauteous appearance, look bald at the funeral.

It was frequent for persons overwhelmed with grief, and unable to bear up under it, to throw themselves upon the earth, and roll in the dust; and the more dirty the ground was, the better it served to defile them, and to express their sorrow and dejection.

They covered their heads with ashes. These customs were likewise practised in the Eastern countries, whence we find so frequent mention of penitents lying upon the ground, and putting on sackcloth and ashes.

When any occasion required their attendance abroad, their heads were muffled up.

They went softly, to express their faintness and loss of strength and spirits. Thus Ahab, king of Israel, being terrified by the judgment Elias denounced against him, fasted, and lay in sackcloth, and went softly; and Hezekiah, king of Judah, being told by the prophet that he was never to recover of a distemper he then lay under, amongst other expressions of sorrow hath this :—" I shall go softly all my years in the bitterness of my soul."

They beat their breasts and thighs, and tore their flesh, making furrows in their faces with their nails; which actions, though practised sometimes by men, were more frequent among women, whose passions are more violent and ungovernable.

> "Women with nails their breasts and faces tear,
> And thus their boundless, headstrong grief declare."

The Lacedæmonians bore the death of their private relations with great constancy and moderation; but when their kings died, they had a barbarous custom of meeting in vast numbers, where men, women, and slaves, all mixed together, and tore the flesh from their foreheads with pins and needles. The design of this was not only to testify their sorrow, but also to gratify the ghosts of the dead, who were thought to feed upon and to delight in nothing so much as blood. Nor was this the effect of extravagant passion, or practised only by persons of weaker understandings in the extremity of their sorrow, but frequently done by men of all qualities, and that in the most grave and solemn manner.

When public magistrates, or persons of note died, or any public calamity happened, all public meetings were intermitted, the schools of exercise, baths, shops, temples, and all places of concourse, were shut up, and the whole city put on a face of sorrow. Thus we find the Athenians bewailing their loss of Socrates, not long after they had sentenced him to death.

They had mourners and musicians to increase the solemnity; which custom seems to have been practised in most parts of the world.

What the design of their musical instruments was, is not agreed: some will have them intended to affright the ghosts and furies from the soul of the deceased person; others would have them to signify the soul's departure into heaven, where they fancied the motion of the spheres made a divine and eternal harmony; others say they were designed to divert the sorrow of the dead man's surviving relations: but the most probable opinion seems to be, that they were intended to excite sorrow, which was the reason that the lyra was never used at such solemnities.

Interring and burning were practised by the Grecians; yet which of these customs has the best claim to antiquity may perhaps admit of a dispute; but it seems probable, that however the later Grecians were better affected to the way of burning, yet the custom of the most primitive ages was to inter their dead. The philosophers were divided in their opinion about it; those who thought human bodies were compounded of water, earth, or the four elements, inclined to have them committed to the earth; but Heraclitus, with his followers, imagining fire to be the first principle of all things, affected burning; for every one thought it the most reasonable method, and most agreeable to nature, so to dispose of bodies, as they might soonest be reduced to their first principles.

Eustathius assigns two reasons why burning came to be of so general use in Greece: the first is, because bodies were thought to be unclean after the soul's departure, and therefore were purified by fire; the second reason is, that the soul, being separated from the gross and inactive matter, might be at liberty to take its flight to the heavenly mansions; and it seems to have been the common opinion, that fire was an admirable expedient to refine the celestial part of man by separating from it all gross and corruptible matter, with the impure qualities which attend it.

The piles whereon they burned dead bodies seem not to have been erected in any constant form, or to have consisted of the same materials, these being varied as time and place and other circumstances required. The body was placed upon the top of the pile, but was rarely burned without company; for besides the various animals they threw upon the pile, we seldom find a man of quality consumed without a number of slaves, or captives; besides these, all sorts of precious ointments and perfumes were poured into the flames.

Soldiers had usually their arms burned with them. It seems, likewise, to have been the custom for the garments they had worn in the time of their lives to be thrown into the pile. Some were so solicitous about this, that they gave orders in their last wills to have it done; and the Athenians were, as in all other observances which related any way to religion, so in this, the most profuse of all the Grecians, insomuch that some of their lawgivers were forced to restrain them by severe penalties from defrauding the living by their liberality to the dead. The pile was lighted by some of the dead person's nearest relations or friends, who made prayers and vows to the winds to assist the flames, that the body might quickly be reduced to ashes.

At the funerals of generals and great officers, the soldiers, with the rest of the company, made a solemn procession three times round the pile, to express their respect to the dead. During the time the pile was burning, the dead person's friends stood by it, pouring forth libations of wine, and calling upon the deceased. When the pile was burned down, and the flames had ceased, they extinguished the remains of the fire with wine, which being done, they collected the bones and ashes. The bones were sometimes washed with wine, and (which commonly followed washing) anointed with oil. The bones and ashes thus collected were deposited in urns. The matter they consisted of was different—either wood, stone, earth, silver, or gold, according to the quality of the deceased. When persons of eminent virtue died, their urns were frequently adorned with flowers and garlands; but the general custom seems to have been to cover them with cloths till they were deposited in the earth, that the light might not approach them.

Concerning interment, it may be observed that their bodies lay in their coffins with faces upwards; it being thought more proper, and perhaps more conducive to the welfare of the deceased, to have their faces towards heaven, the abode of the celestial gods, and fountain of light, than the dark mansions of the infernal deities.

The primitive Grecians were buried in places prepared for that purpose in their own houses; the Thebans had once a law that no person should build a house without providing a repository for his dead. It seems to have been very frequent, even in later ages, to bury within their cities, the most public and frequented places whereof seem to have been best stored with monuments; but this was a favour not ordinarily granted, except to men of great worth, and public benefactors; to such as had raised themselves above the common level, and were examples of virtue to succeeding ages, or had deserved by some eminent service to have their memories honoured by posterity.

Temples were sometimes made repositories for the dead, whereof the primitive ages afford us many instances; insomuch, that some have been of opinion that the honours paid to the dead were the first cause of erecting temples. But the general custom, in later ages especially, was to bury their dead without their cities, and chiefly by the highways, which seems to be done either to preserve themselves from the noisome smells wherewith graves might infect their cities, or to prevent the danger their houses were exposed to, when funeral piles were set on fire.

Every family was wont to have their proper burying-place, to be deprived whereof was reputed one of the greatest calamities that could befal them.

The common graves of primitive Greece were nothing but caverns dug in the earth, but those of later ages were more curiously wrought; they were commonly paved with stone, had arches built over them, and were adorned with no less art and care than the houses of the living, insomuch that mourners commonly retired into the vaults of the dead, and there lamented over their relations for many days and nights together. Kings and great men were anciently buried in mountains or at the feet of them; whence likewise appears the custom of raising a mount upon the graves of great persons.

The ornaments wherewith sepulchres were beautified were numerous. Pillars of stone were very ancient; they frequently contained inscriptions declaring the family, virtues, and whatever was remarkable in the deceased, which were commonly described in verses; nor was it unusual to omit the names of the deceased, writing instead of them some moral aphorism, or short exhortation to the living.

Isocrates' tomb was adorned with the image of a syren — Archimedes' with a sphere and cylinder; whereby the charming eloquence of the former and the mathematical studies of the latter were signified. Nor was it unusual to fix upon graves the instruments which the deceased had used. The graves of soldiers were distinguished by their weapons; those of mariners by their oars; and, in short, the tools of every art and profession accompanied their masters, and remained as monuments to preserve their memory.

It was also customary to pray for their friends, and men of piety and virtue, that the earth might lie light upon them; for their enemies, and all wicked men, that it might press heavy upon them; for they thought the ghosts that still haunted their shrouds, and were in love with their former habitations, had a very acute sense of all the accidents which befel their bodies.

Monuments were erected in honour of the dead, which, with all things belonging to the dead, were had in so great esteem, that to deface or any way violate them was a crime no less than sacrilege, and thought to entail certain ruin upon all persons guilty of it.

It has been a question whether the Cenotaphs had the same religious regard which was paid to the sepulchres where the remains of the deceased were deposited; for the resolution hereof it may be observed, that such of them as were only erected for the honour of the dead, were not held so sacred as to call for any judgment upon such as profaned them; but the rest, wherein ghosts were thought to reside, seem to have been in the same condition with sepulchres, the want whereof they were designed to supply.

Funeral orations were delivered, games instituted, and lustrations, entertainments, and consecrations, performed in honour of the illustrious dead.—*Burder.*

THE ROMANS.

The Romans paid the greatest attention to funeral rites, because they believed, like the Grecians, that the souls of the unburied were not admitted into the abodes of the dead, or at least wandered a hundred years along the river Styx before they were allowed to cross it; for which reason, if the bodies of their friends could not be found, they erected to them an empty tomb, at which they performed the usual solemnities; and if they happened to see a dead body, they always threw some earth upon it, and whoever neglected to do so was obliged to expiate his crime by sacrificing a hog to Ceres. Hence no kind of death was so much dreaded as shipwreck.

When persons were at the point of death, their nearest relation present endeavoured to catch their last breath with their mouth, for they believed that the soul, or living principle, then went out at the mouth. They now also pulled off their rings, which seem to have been put on again before they were placed on the funeral pile.

The corpse was then laid on the ground, from the ancient custom of placing sick persons at the gate, to see if any that passed had ever been ill of the same disease, and what had cured them.

The corpse was next bathed with warm water, and anointed with perfumes by slaves called Pollinctores, belonging to those who took care of funerals, and had the charge of the temple of Venus Libitina, where the things requisite for funerals were sold.

In this temple was kept an account of those who died, for each of whom a certain coin was paid.

The money paid for the liberty of burial, and other expenses, was called Arbitrium.

The body was then dressed in the best robe which the deceased had worn when alive; ordinary citizens in a white toga, magistrates in their prætexta, &c., and laid on a couch in the vestibule, with the feet outwards, as if about to take its last departure. Then a lamentation was made. The couch was sometimes decked with leaves and flowers. If the deceased had received a crown for his bravery, it was now placed on his head. A small coin was put in his mouth, which he might give to Charon, the ferryman of hell, for his freight. Hence a person who wanted this and the other funeral oblations was said — Abiisse ad Acheruntum sine viatico; for without them it was thought that souls could not purchase a lodging or place of rest.

A branch of cypress was placed at the door of the deceased, at least if he was a person of consequence, to prevent the Pontifex Maximus from entering, and thereby being polluted; for it was unlawful for him not only to touch a dead body, but even to look at it. The cypress was sacred to Pluto, because when once cut it never grows again.

The Romans, at first, usually interred their dead, which is the most ancient and most natural method. They early adopted the custom of burning from the Greeks, which is mentioned in the laws of Numa, and of the twelve tables; but it did not become general till towards the end of the republic.

Sylla was the first of the patrician branch of the Gens Cornelia that was burnt; which he is supposed to have ordered, lest any one should dig up his body, and dissipate his remains, as he did those of Marius. Pliny ascribes the first institution of burning among the Romans, to their having discovered that the bodies of those who fell in distant wars were dug up by the enemy.

Under the emperors it became almost universal, but was afterwards gradually dropped upon the introduction of Christianity; so that it had fallen into disuse about the end of the fourth century.

Children before they got teeth were not burnt, but buried in a place called Suggrundarium. So likewise persons struck with lightning were buried in the spot where they fell, called Bidental, because it was consecrated by sacrificing sheep. It was enclosed with a wall, and no one was allowed to tread upon it. To remove its bounds was esteemed sacrilege.

Of funerals there were chiefly two kinds—public and private. The public funeral was called Indictivum, because people were invited to it by a herald. Of this kind the most remarkable were, Funus Censorium; Publicum, when a person was buried at the public expense; and Collativum, by a public contribution. Augustus was very liberal in granting public funerals, as at first in conferring the honour of a triumph.

A private funeral was called Tacitum. The funeral of those who died in infancy, or under age, was called Acerbum. Infants and young men were buried sooner than grown persons, and with less pomp.

When a public funeral was intended, the corpse was kept usually for seven or eight days, with a keeper set to watch it, and sometimes boys to drive away the flies. When the funeral was private, the body was not kept so long.

On the day of the funeral, when the people were assembled, the dead body was carried out with the feet foremost, on a couch, covered with rich cloth, with gold and purple, supported commonly on the shoulders of the nearest relations of the deceased, or of his heirs—sometimes of his freedmen. Julius

Cæsar was borne by the magistrates, Augustus by the senators, and Germanicus by the tribunes and centurions. So Drusus, his father, who died in Germany, by the tribunes and centurions to the winter quarters; and then by the chief men in the different cities on the road to Rome; and Paulus Æmilius by the chief men of Macedonia, who happened to be at Rome when he died. Poor citizens and slaves were carried to the funeral pile in a plain bier or coffin.

Children who died before they were weaned, were carried to the pile by their mothers.

All funerals used anciently to be solemnised in the night time, with torches, that they might not fall in the way of magistrates and priests, who were supposed to be violated by seeing a corpse, so that they could not perform sacred rites till they were purified by an expiatory sacrifice. But in after ages public funerals were celebrated in the day time, at an early hour in the forenoon, as it is thought with torches also. Private or ordinary funerals were always at night. Torches were used both at funerals and marriages.

The order of the funeral procession was regulated, and every one's place assigned him, by a person called Designator—an undertaker, or master of ceremonies, attended by lictors, dressed in black. First went musicians of various kinds—pipers, trumpeters; then mourning women, hired to lament and to sing the funeral song, or the praises of the deceased to the sound of the flute. Boys and girls were sometimes employed for this last purpose. The flutes and trumpets used on this occasion were larger and longer than ordinary, and of a grave dismal sound. By the law of the twelve tables, the number of players on the flute at a funeral was restricted to ten.

Next came players and buffoons, who danced and sung. One of them, called Archimimus, supported the character of the deceased, imitating his words and actions while alive. These players sometimes introduced apt sayings from dramatic writers. Then followed the freedmen of the deceased, with a cap on their head. Some masters at their death freed all their slaves, from the vanity of having their funeral procession attended by a numerous train of freedmen.

Before the corpse were carried images of the deceased and of his ancestors, on long poles or frames, but not of such as had been condemned for any heinous crime, whose images were broken. The Triumviri ordained that the image of Cæsar, after his deification, should not be carried before the funeral of any of his relations. Sometimes there were a great many different couches carried before the corpse, on which it is supposed the images were placed. After the funeral, these images were again set up in the hall, where they were kept. If the deceased had distinguished himself in war, the crowns and rewards which he had received for his valour were displayed, together with the spoils and standards he had taken from the enemy. At the funerals of renowned commanders were carried images or representations of the countries they had subdued, and the cities they had taken. At the funeral of Sylla, above 2000 crowns are said to have been carried, which had been sent him by different cities on account of his victory.

The lictors attended with their fasces inverted. Sometimes also the officers and troops, with the spears pointing to the ground.

Behind the corpse walked the friends of the deceased in mourning; his sons with their head veiled, and his daughters with their head bare and their hair dishevelled, contrary to the ordinary custom cf both. The magistrates without their badges, and the nobility without their ornaments. The nearest relations sometimes tore their garments, and covered their hair with dust, or pulled it out. The women in particular, who attended the funeral, beat their breasts and tore their cheeks, although this was forbidden by the twelve tables.

At the funeral of an illustrious citizen the corpse was carried through the forum, where the procession stopped, and a funeral oration was delivered in praise of the deceased from the rostra by his son, or by some near relation or friend—sometimes by a magistrate, according to the appointment of the senate.

This custom is said to have been first introduced by Poplicola, in honour of his colleague Brutus. It was an incentive to glory and virtue, but hurtful to the authenticity of historical records.

The honour of a funeral oration was decreed by the senate also to women, for their readiness in resigning their golden ornaments to make up the sum agreed to be paid to the Gauls as a ransom for leaving the city; or, according to Plutarch, to make the golden cup which was sent to Delphi as a present to Apollo in consequence of the vow of Camillus after the taking of Veii.

But Cicero says, that Popilia was the first to whom this honour was paid, by her son Catulus, several ages after; and, according to Plutarch, Cæsar introduced the custom of praising young matrons upon the death of his wife Cornelia. But after that, both young and old, married and unmarried, were honoured with funeral orations. While the funeral oration was delivering, the corpse was placed before the rostra. The corpse of Cæsar was placed in a gilt pavilion like a small temple, with the robe in which he had been slain suspended on a pole or trophy, and his image exposed on a moveable machine, with the marks of all the wounds he had received; for the body itself was not seen—but Dio says the contrary. Under Augustus it became customary to deliver more than one funeral oration in praise of the same person, and in different places. From the forum the corpse was carried to the place of burning or burial, which the law of the twelve tables ordered to be without the city, according to the custom of other nations; the Jews, the Athenians, and others.

The ancients are said to have buried their dead at their own houses; whence, according to some, the origin of idolatry, and the worship of household gods, the fear of hobgoblins or spectres in the dark.

Augustus, in his speech to his soldiers before the battle of Actium, says that the Egyptians embalmed their dead bodies to establish an opinion of their immortality. Several of these still exist, called mummies, from mum, the Egyptian name of wax. The manner of embalming is described by Herodotus. The Persians also anointed the bodies of their dead with wax, to make them keep as long as possible.

The Romans prohibited burning or burying in the city, both from a sacred and civil consideration; that the priests might not be contaminated by seeing or touching a dead body, and that houses might not be endangered by the frequency of funeral fires, or the air infected by the stench.

The flamen of Jupiter was not allowed to touch a dead body, nor to go where there was a grave. So the high-priest among the Jews; and if the pontifex maximus had to deliver a funeral oration, a veil was laid over the corpse to keep it from his sight.

The places for burial were either private or public; the private in fields or gardens, usually near the high way, to be conspicuous, and to remind those who passed by of mortality. The public places of burial for great men were commonly in the Campus Martius or Campus Esquilinus; for poor people, without the Esquiline gate, in places called Puticulæ.

As the vast number of bones deposited in that common burying-ground rendered the places adjoining unhealthy, Augustus, with the consent of the senate and people, gave part of it to his favourite Mæcenas, who built there a magnificent house, with extensive gardens, whence it became one of the most healthy situations in Rome.

There was in the corner of the burying-ground a stone pillar, on which was marked its extent towards the road, and backwards to the fields, also who were buried in it. If a burying-ground was intended for a person and his heir, it was called Sepulchrum. If only for himself and family, Familiare. Freedmen were sometimes comprehended, and relations, when undeserving, excluded. The right of burying was sometimes purchased by those who had no burying-ground of their own.

The Vestal virgins were buried in the city; and

some illustrious men, as Poplicola, Tubertus, and Fabricius; which right their posterity retained, but did not use. To show, however, that they possessed it, when any of them died, they brought the dead body, when about to be burned, into the forum, and setting down the couch, put a burning torch under it, which they immediately removed, and carried the corpse to another place. The right of making a sepulchre for himself within the Pomærium was decreed to Julius Cæsar as a singular privilege.

When a person was burned and buried in the same place, it was called Bustum. A place where one only was burnt, Ustrina.

The funeral pile was built in the form of an altar, with four equal sides, of wood which might easily catch fire, as fir, pine, cleft oak, unpolished, according to the law of the twelve tables, but not always so; also stuffed with paper and pitch, and made higher or lower, according to the rank of the deceased, with cypress trees set around, to prevent the noisome smell, and at the distance of sixty feet from any house.

On the funeral pile was placed the corpse with the couch. The eyes of the deceased were opened. The nearest relations kissed the body with tears, and then set fire to the pile with a lighted torch, turning away their face, to show that they did it with reluctance. They prayed for a wind to assist the flames, and when that happened, it was thought fortunate.

They threw into the fire various perfumes, incense, myrrh, cassia, &c., which Cicero calls Sumptuosare-spersio, forbidden by the twelve tables; also cups of oil, and dishes, with titles marking what they contained; likewise the clothes and ornaments, not only of the deceased, but their own. Everything, in short, that was supposed to be agreeable to the deceased while alive.

If the deceased had been a soldier, they threw on the pile his arms, rewards, and spoils; and if a general, the soldiers sometimes threw in their own arms.

At the funeral of an illustrious commander, or emperor, the soldiers made a circuit three times round the pile, from right to left, with their ensigns inverted, and striking their weapons on one another to the sound of the trumpet, all present accompanying them, as at the funeral of Sylla and of Augustus; which custom seems to have been borrowed from the Greeks: used also by the Carthaginians, and sometimes performed annually at the tomb.

As the manes were supposed to be delighted with blood, various animals, especially such as the deceased had been fond of, were slaughtered at the pile, and thrown into it. In ancient times, also men, captives, or slaves. Afterwards, instead of them, gladiators, called Bustuarii, were made to fight. So among the Gauls, slaves and clients were burned on the piles of their masters; and among the Indians and Thracians, wives on the piles of their husbands. As one man had several wives, there was sometimes a contest among them about the preference, which they determined by lot. Instances are recorded of persons who came to life again on the funeral pile, after it was set on fire, so that they could not be preserved; and of others, who having revived before the pile was kindled, returned home on their feet.

The Jews, although they interred their dead, filled the couch on which the corpse was laid with sweet odours, and divers kinds of spices, and burned them.

When the pile was burned down, the fire was extinguished, and the embers soaked with wine. The bones were gathered by the nearest relations in loose robes, and sometimes barefooted. We read also of the nearest female relations gathering the bones in their bosom.

The ashes and bones of the deceased are thought to have been distinguished by their particular position. Some suppose the body to have been wrapped in a species of incombustible cloth, made of what the Greeks call asbestos. But Pliny restricts this to the kings of India, where only it was then known. The bones and ashes, besprinkled with the richest perfumes, were put into a vessel called an urn, made of earth, brass, marble, silver, or gold, according to the wealth or rank of every one. Sometimes, also, a small glass vial full of tears, called by the moderns a Lachrymatory, was put in the urn. The urn was solemnly deposited in the sepulchre.

When the body was not burned, it was put into a coffin, with all its ornaments, usually made of stone, as those of Numa and Hannibal; sometimes of Assian stone, from Assos, a town in Troas or Mysia, which consumed the body in forty days, except the teeth. Hence called Sarcophagus, which word is also put for any coffin or tomb.

The coffin was laid in the tomb on its back; in what direction among the Romans is uncertain; but among the Athenians, looking to the west. Those who died in prison were thrown out naked on the street.

When the remains of the deceased were laid in the tomb, those present were three times sprinkled by a priest with pure water from a branch of olive or laurel, to purify them, then they were dismissed by the Præfica, or some other person, pronouncing the solemn word "Ilicet," You may depart. At their departure, they used to take a last farewell, by repeating several times "Vale," expressing a wish that the earth might lie light on the person buried. This desire is found marked on several ancient monuments.

Sometimes the bones were not deposited in the earth till three days after the body was burned.

The friends, when they returned home, as a further purification, after being sprinkled with water, stepped over a fire, which was called Suffitio. The house itself also was purified, and swept with a certain kind of broom or besom, which purgation was called Exverræ, and he who performed it Everriator.

There were certain ceremonies for the purification of the family, when they buried a thumb, or some part cut off from the body before it was burned, or a bone brought home from the funeral pile; on which occasion a soldier might be absent from duty.

A place was held religious where a dead body, or any part of it, was buried, but not where it was burned. For nine days after the funeral, while the family was in mourning, and employed about certain solemnities at the tomb, it was unlawful to summon the heir, or any near relation of the deceased, to a court of justice, or in any other manner to molest them. On the ninth day a sacrifice was performed, with which the solemnities were concluded.

Oblations, or sacrifices to the dead, were afterwards made at various times, both occasionally and at stated periods, consisting of liquors, victims, and garlands; an atonement was made to their ghosts.

The sepulchre was then bespread with flowers, and covered with crowns and fillets. Before it there was a little altar, on which libations were made, and incense burned. A keeper was appointed to watch the tomb, which was frequently illuminated with lamps.

A kind of perpetual lamps are said by several authors to have been found in ancient tombs, which, however, went out on the admission of air. But this by others is reckoned a fiction. A feast was generally added, both for the dead and the living. Certain things were laid on the tomb, commonly beans, lettuces, bread, and eggs, or the like, which it was supposed the ghosts would come and eat. What remained was burned; for it was thought mean to take away anything thus consecrated, or what was thrown into the funeral pile.

After the funeral of great men, there was not only a feast for the friends of the deceased, but also a distribution of raw meat among the people, with shows of gladiators, and games, which sometimes continued for several days; sometimes celebrated also on the anniversary of the funeral. Faustus, the son of Sylla, exhibited a show of gladiators in honour of his father, several years after his death, and gave a feast to his people, according to his father's testament.

The time of mourning for departed friends was appointed by Numa, as well as funeral rites and offerings to appease the manes.

There was no limited time for men to mourn,

because none was thought most honourable. Women mourned for a husband or parent ten months, or a year, according to the computation of Romulus, but not longer.

In a public mourning for any signal calamity, the death of a prince, or the like, there was a total cessation from business, either spontaneously or by public appointment. When the courts of justice did not sit, the shops were shut. In excessive grief the temples of the gods were struck with stones, and their altars overturned.

Both public and private mourning was laid aside on account of the public games; for certain sacred rites, as those of Ceres, &c.; and for several other causes enumerated by Festus. Immoderate grief was supposed to be offensive to the manes.

The Romans in mourning kept themselves at home, avoiding every entertainment and amusement; neither cutting their hair nor beard. They dressed in black—which custom is supposed to have been borrowed from the Egyptians—and sometimes in skins, laying aside every kind of ornament; not even lighting a fire, which was esteemed an ornament to the house.

The women laid aside their gold and purple. Under the republic they dressed in black like the men; but under the emperors, when party-coloured cloths came in fashion, they wore white in mourning.

In a public mourning, the senators laid aside their latus clavus and rings; the magistrates the badges of their office; and the consuls did not sit on their usual seats in the senate, which were elevated above the rest, but on a common bench.

The Romans commonly built tombs for themselves during their lifetime. Thus, the mausoleum of Augustus, in the Campus Martius, between the via Flamina and the bank of the Tiber, with wood and walks around. If they did not live to finish them, it was done by their heirs, who were often ordered by the testament to build a tomb, and sometimes did it at their own expense. Pliny complains bitterly of the neglect of friends in this respect.

The Romans erected tombs, either for themselves alone, with their wives, or for themselves, their family, and posterity; likewise for their friends, who were buried elsewhere, or whose bodies could not be found. When a person falsely reported to have been dead returned home, he did not enter his house by the door, but was let down from the roof. The tombs of the rich were commonly built of marble, the ground inclosed with a wall, or an iron rail, and planted around with trees, as among the Greeks.

When several persons had a right to the same burying-ground, it was sometimes divided into parts, and each part assigned to its proper owner.

But common sepulchres were usually built below

ground, and called Hypogæa, many of which still exist in different parts of Italy, under the name of catacombs. There were niches cut out in the walls in which the urns were placed; these, from their resemblance to the niches in a pigeon-house, were called Columbaria.

Sepulchres were adorned with various figures in sculpture, and with statues and columns.

But what deserves particular attention is the inscription or epitaph, expressed sometimes in prose and sometimes in verse, usually beginning with these letters,—" D. M. S.—Dis manibus sacrum." Then the name of the person followed, his character, and the principal circumstances of his life.

When the body was simply interred without a tomb, an inscription was sometimes put on the stone coffin, as on that of Numa.

There was an action for violating the tombs of the dead. The punishment was a fine, the loss of a hand, working in the mines, and banishment or death.

A tomb was violated by demolition, by converting it to improper purposes, or by burying in it those who were not entitled. Tombs often served as lurking-places for the persecuted Christians.

The body was violated by handling or mutilating it, which was sometimes done for magical purposes; by stripping it of anything valuable, as gold, arms;

or by transporting it to another place, without leave obtained from the Pontifex Maximus, from the emperor, or the magistrate of the place.

Some consecrated temples to the memory of their friends. This was a very ancient custom, and perhaps is the origin of idolatry.

The highest honours were decreed to illustrious persons after death. The Romans worshipped their founder, Romulus, as a god, under the name of Quirinus. Hence, afterwards, the solemn consecration of the emperors, by a decree of the senate, who were thus said to be ranked in the number of the gods; also some empresses. Temples and priests were assigned to them. They were invoked with prayers. Men swore by their name or genius, and offered victims on their altars.

The real body was burned, and the remains buried in the usual manner. But a waxen image of the deceased was made to the life, which, after a variety of ridiculous ceremonies paid to it for seven days in the palace, was carried on a couch in solemn procession on the shoulders of young men of equestrian and patrician rank; first to the forum, where the dirge was sung by a choir of boys and girls of the most noble descent; then to the Campus Martius, where it was burned with a vast quantity of the richest odours and perfumes, on a lofty and magnificent pile, from the top of which an eagle, let loose, was

supposed to convey the prince's soul to heaven.—
Burder.

THE GOTHS AND HUNS.

The terrific honours which these ferocious nations paid to their deceased monarchs are recorded in history, by the interment of Attila, king of the Huns, and Alaric, king of the Goths.

Attila died, in 453, and was buried in the midst of a vast champaign in a coffin which was inclosed in one of gold, another of silver, and a third of iron. With the body was interred all the spoils of the enemy, harnesses embroidered with gold and studded with jewels, rich silks, and what they had taken most precious in the palaces of the kings they had pillaged; and that the place of his interment might for ever remain concealed, the Huns deprived of life all who assisted at his burial!

The Goths had done nearly the same for Alaric in 410, at Cosença, a town in Calabria. They turned aside the river Vasento; and having formed a grave in the midst of its bed where its course was most rapid, and interred this king with prodigious accumulations of riches. After having caused the river to reassume its usual course, they murdered without exception, all those who had been concerned in digging this singular grave.—*Isaac D'Israeli's Curiosities of Literature.*

THE ETHIOPIANS.

The following passage in Herodotus leads us to suppose that they placed their dead in glass coffins: "Let us next consider their sepulchres which are said to be constructed of glass. When dead, they dry the body, cover it completely with plaster, and exhibit it ornamented with pictures resembling the deceased. They then dig a grave, and cover it with glass, through which the body is visible, neither emitting a disagreeable smell, nor showing any signs of corruption." Thucydides says, in the third book of his History, "Some throw them into the river; others preserve them in their houses, after having inclosed them, as it were, in a coffin of glass." In another passage he says, "*The Ethiopians* conduct the funerals of their dead in a very singular manner. The body is first salted to keep it from putrefaction, and then placed in a grave covered with glass, that it may be seen through." But Clefias Cnidius denies this, telling us that the bodies are indeed salted, but never inclosed in glass; for the likeness of the dead could not in that way be retained, as the body would first become shrivelled, and then totally decay. A hollow statue of gold is therefore cast to contain the body, and this being placed in a conspicuous situation, and covered with glass, it may be said that a similitude is exhibited through glass. The funerals of the rich are solemnized in this manner, while persons of smaller fortune are deposited in statues of silver, and the poor in baked clay.

THE BACTRIANS.

Bactria was an ancient kingdom of Asia, now called Khorassan. The inhabitants not only suffered the dead bodies of their friends and relatives to be eaten by dogs, but kept large and savage ones to devour such as lived to an extreme age, or became enfeebled and useless through long illness.

THE ICHTHYOPHAGI.

The Ichthyophagi or Fish-Eaters, mentioned by Ptolemy, inhabited the region which lay between Carmania and Gedrosia, bordering on the Persian Gulf. They built their huts of large fish bones, the ribs of the whale serving for beams and rafters, and the jaws for doors. The mortars in which they pounded their fish, the vessels wherein they set it to bake in the sun, and the bowls which formed their dishes at table, were only the joints of the vertebræ of the same sea-monster. They invariably committed their dead to the sea; and thus fully repaid the obligations they had incurred to its inhabitants.

THE SCYTHIANS.

The Scythians had a peculiar mode of their own, in

disposing of their dead. They would neither "commit them to the earth or sea," nor destroy them by fire; but suspended the bodies in the air. Ælian records that the dead were sewn up first in skins to prevent the birds of prey from devouring them. They were then suspended on the branches of trees, and so gradually decayed.

The Colchians hung up this strange fruit amongst the foliage of their native forests. On the death of their husbands, the Heruli women hung themselves, not from great affection, but because it was fashionable; and, if they ventured to live, their neighbours would punish them by avoiding their society. In another *Scythian* district the friends and relatives of the deceased testified their grief and affection by eating him—the greater the love, the more ravenous the appetite.

THE BALCARIANS.

The Balcarians inhabited the islands now called Majorca and Minorca. They bruised the flesh and broke the bones of the corpse; then crammed them into ovens, and laid heaps of wood upon them.

THE ANCIENT CHRISTIANS

Testified their abhorrence of the Pagan custom of cremation, by depositing the entire body in the ground; and the martyrs were usually embalmed.

The body was prepared for burial by washing it with water, and dressing it in funeral attire. The carrying forth of the body was performed by near relatives, or persons of equal dignity with the deceased. Psalm singing was the chief feature in their funeral processions.—*Encyclopædia Britannica.*

THE ROMAN CATHOLIC CHURCH.

As the dissolution of the sick person approaches, the priest prepares to administer to him the Sacrament of Extreme Unction. This is done in the following manner. The priest gets ready seven balls of cotton to wipe those parts which are to be anointed with the holy oil, some crumbs of bread to rub his fingers with, water to wash them, a napkin to wipe them, and a taper to light him during the ceremony. Before he goes to the sick person he must sanctify himself by prayer; after which he must wash his hands, put on a surplice and the purple stole; he must take the vessel in which the holy oils are contained, covered with a purple vail or bag, and carry it in such a manner as not to let the oil run out. The priest is attended by the clerk, who must carry the cross without a staff, the vessel of holy water, the sprinkler, and the ritual. They must not ring the little bell by the way, but the priest is to offer up prayers, in a low voice, on behalf of the sick. On entering into the sick person's apartment, he repeats the ordinary form of words, "*Pax huic domui, et omnibus habitantibus in ea.*"—i. e., Peace be to this house, &c. After having taken off his cap and set the vessels of the holy oils upon the table, he gives the sick person the cross to kiss; afterwards takes the sprinkler, sprinkles the sick person, the apartment, and the assistants with holy water in form of a cross, at the same time repeating the anthem, "*Asperges me,*" &c. He exhorts the sick person, that he would commit the utmost sacrilege, in case he presumed to receive extreme unction without having first settled his con-science; but in case he is speechless and not sensible, the priest exhorts him to the best of his power. If the sick person discovers any tokens of contrition, the priest shall pronounce absolution, which must be fol-lowed by an exhortation, and then by a prayer. But before absolution, the sick person must either repeat the *Confiteor* himself, or, in case he be not able to do it, the clerk must pronounce it for him. The priest must then add for the sick person the "*Miseratur tui*"—i. e., May the Lord have pity on thee, &c. Before he begins to perform the ceremony of extreme unction, all the persons present must fall down upon their knees; and whilst the anointing is performed, they must repeat the penitential psalms and litanies for the sake of the sick man's soul.

The anointing is performed in this manner: the priest dips the thumb of his right hand into the oils of the infirm; he anoints in the form of a cross, and pronounces some words suitable to the anointing of each part; whilst the clerk lights him with a consecrated taper, and holds a basin in a dish in which the pieces of cotton are laid. The priest begins by anointing the right eye, observing that the eyelid is shut; then the left eye; in the mean while repeating these words: "May God, by this holy anointing, and by his most pious mercy, pardon you the sins you have committed by the eyes." If the priest be accompanied by a clergyman who is in holy orders, he must wipe the part which has been anointed, otherwise the priest must wipe it himself. He next proceeds to the ears, repeating the same form of words; then the nostrils, and afterwards the lips, the mouth being closed. He then anoints the hands; then he proceeds to the soles of the feet, and afterwards advances up to the reins, but this for men only. The anointing being ended, the priest rubs those fingers which have touched the oil, and afterwards washes his hands. The crumbs of bread with which he rubbed his fingers, and the water with which he washed them, must be thrown into the fire. The anointing being ended, the priest repeats some prayers which are followed by an exhortation to the sick; after which the priest goes away, leaving a crucifix with the sick person, in order that the representation of his dying Saviour may administer some consolation to him.

When the sick person has expired, the priest, standing uncovered, says a response in which the saints and angels are invoked to assist the soul of the deceasd: he afterwards repeats a prayer. At the same time orders are sent to toll the bell, to give notice of the sick person's death, by which every one is reminded to pray for his soul. Then the priest withdraws; and the corpse is then put in order.

The most solemn mass for the dead is that which the bishop himself celebrates. The melancholy occasion of the ceremony does not admit of any pompous decorations on the altar. All the flowers, festoons, relics, and images, are removed. Six yellow waxlights, and a cross in the middle, are the only ornaments. Two other tapers of the same kind give light to the credence-table, which is covered with a very plain small table cloth, and on which there is no other ornament than what is absolutely necessary for so mournful an occasion; such as a mass-book, a holy water-pot, a sprinkler, a thurible, a navet, and a black cloth for absolution. The acolytes spread a black cloth upon the altar, and the bishop officiates, likewise, in black. As soon as mass is over, he puts on a pluvial of the same colour; the dress of his ministers, the episcopal chair, and the pontifical books, are all black. The bishop who celebrates this melancholy mass has no crosier in his hand, no gloves on, nor his sandals upon his feet; nor does he say the *Judica*, the *Reminiscaris*, the *Quam dilecta*, nor several prayers which are said at other masses. After the *Confiteor*, he kisses the altar, but not the book; nor do the ministers kiss anything whatever during the celebration of it; for kisses on such melancholy occasions are forbidden. They do not cross themselves at the *Introite*, nor is the altar perfumed with frankincense at the beginning of this mass. In short, not to mention several other differences which are of less moment to the laity than the clergy, we shall only observe, that the person who officiates does not smite his breast at the *Agnus;* that he does not give the kiss of peace; that he concludes the mass without the usual blessing; that no indulgences are published; and that the deacon, if it be a general mass for many, says the *Requiescant in pace*, in the plural number, for the repose of the dead.

The homily follows, and the pulpit, for that purpose, is hung with black; and if it be a particular mass for any private person, remarkable for his quality or virtues, his fortune and charitable endowments, the mass for the rest and tranquility of his soul in the other world, is followed by a funeral panegyric.

A *Chapelle Ardente*, or a pompous representation of the deceased, is in the meantime erected, and adorned with branches, and illuminated with yellow wax-lights, in the middle of, or some other part of the church, or round the monuments of persons of distinction. If the deceased be not buried in that church, this *chapel* may be placed in the nave, if he be a layman; or, if a clergyman, in the choir, in case it be separated from the presbyterium, for it is never allowed to be placed there. The head of a priest and the feet of a layman are turned towards the altar. After the homily, they proceed to the absolution of the deceased, after the following manner :— The gospel of St. John being read, the person who officiates, with the deacon and sub-deacon, returns to the middle of the altar, from whence, after one genuflection, or one profound bow, in case there be no tabernacle, they go to the epistle-side. The sub-deacon, when at the bottom of the steps, takes the cross, and after he and the deacon have laid aside their maniples, all of them proceed to the place where the *Chapelle Ardente*, or representation, is erected, in the same order as if to the interment of the corpse. The incense-bearer, and he who carries the holy water, walk first; the sub-deacon follows, between the two light-bearers, with the cross; after them come the choir, with yellow tapers in their hands. The person who officiates, with the deacon on his left hand, walks last, and no one except himself is covered, unless they go out of the church, and then all are covered alike.

Being arrived at the *Chapelle Ardente*, where the celebrant is to give absolution to the deceased, the incense-bearer, and the acolyte, who is the holy water bearer, place themselves in that part of the chapel which fronts the altar, but somewhat inclining to the epistle-side, and behind the person who officiates, who has the deacon on his right hand. The sub-deacon who carries the cross, and two light-bearers, stand at the other end, at the head of the corpse, a little towards the gospel-side. When they are all placed, the person who officiates uncovers himself, and, taking the ritual out of the deacon's hands, begins the absolution of the deceased by a prayer, the first words of which are, *Non intres in judicium, &c.,*—*Enter not into judgment, &c.* We shall omit some of the responses that come afterwards, such as the *Libera nos, Domine, &c.,* to come to the benediction of the incense, after which the celebrant walks round the representation, sprinkling it with holy water, perfuming it on both sides, and making many bows and genuflections. When he has performed the great work of absolution, he says the *Pater,* and thereupon turns to the cross, repeating several verses and prayers, which are inserted in the rituals. *Lastly,* he makes the sign of the cross on the representation, and says the *Requiem* for the deceased, to which the choir answer, *Requiescat in pace,*—*Let him rest in peace.* After the absolution, the celebrant and his attendants return in the same order as they came.

The common custom among Roman Catholics is

to keep a corpse four-and-twenty hours above ground; but in some countries, it is kept five or six days, particularly in Holland, where it is often kept seven. The ceremonies ordained by the rituals to those who are allowed Christian burial vary in certain circumstances; but in general, when the time is come for the corpse to be carried to church, notice thereof must be given by the tolling of a bell to the priests, and other clergymen, whose province it is to assist at the funeral, to assemble in proper order, clothed in their sacerdotal vestments, in the church where they are to pray. After this, the rector puts his black stole and chasuble over his surplice, and they all set out to the house where the corpse lies: the exorcist, carrying the holy water, walks first; next the cross-bearer; afterwards the rest of the clergy; and last of all, the officiating priest. The corpse of the deceased must be either laid out at the street-door, or in some apartment near it, with his feet turned towards the street; the coffin being surrounded with four or six lighted tapers of yellow wax, in as many large candlesticks.

When the clergy are come to the house where the corpse lies, the cross-bearer plants himself, if possible, at the head of it; the officiating priest over-against him, at the feet; the person who carries the holy water, a little behind the officiating priest, at his right hand; and the other persons of the choir range themselves on each side, observing to stand nearer or farther off from the officiating priest, in proportion to their rank or superiority in the Church. Everything must be ordered in this manner, provided their be room for it; for it often happens, that the cross stands at the door on that side where the funeral is to go, and that the choir are obliged to range themselves on each side, in order to leave room for the officiating priest in the middle. During this interval, the tapers and torches of yellow wax are lighted, and given to those who are appointed to carry them.

The officiating priest now standing before the cross, with his face turned towards the body, the assistant who carries the holy water presents him with the sprinkler, with which the priest sprinkles the corpse thrice, without saying a word.

Then follow certain other ceremonies, after which the corpse is carried to the church, where the service for the dead is read, and also mass, if the time will permit.

Prayers now follow; the corpse is again sprinkled; after which it is carried to the grave in the same manner in which it was carried to the church.

Being come to the grave, the whole company pull off their hats, and draw up in much the same order as at church. The bearers lay the corpse near the grave, with its feet turned towards the east, it being affirmed that JESUS CHRIST was buried in that manner.

If the corpse be buried in the church, its feet must be turned towards the altar; but those of priests must have their heads turned in a contrary direction.

After the body has been laid on the brink of the grave, the officiating priest blesses it by a prayer, in which he makes the general commemoration of the dead who have been interred therein. The prayer being ended, he again sprinkles and incenses the body, and also the grave thrice. He afterwards begins this anthem, *Ego sum Resurrectio*, &c.,—*I am the resurrection and the life*, &c., and concludes with the *Requiem.* Then the officiating priest performs a third time the triple sprinkling of the corpse with holy water, but does not incense it; which is followed by another prayer, with the anthem, *Si iniquitates*, and the *De profundis.* The body being laid in the grave, the relations and friends of the deceased come, before the earth is thrown into it, and sprinkle it with holy water, in their turn. When the grave has been filled up, the company condole with the relations of the deceased, and they all return to the church, where, after the mass for the deceased is ended, the funeral sermon is preached.

Sometimes the funeral happens in a season when mass cannot be said; in which case, the ceremony is performed with much greater simplicity; for then the corpse is only sprinkled and incensed by a priest clothed in his black chasuble, and accompanied with two clerks, the one carrying the cross, and the other the sprinkler and the thurible.

When a cardinal dies, he is immediately embalmed, and the following night is carried into the church where his obsequies are to be solemnised. One of the largest churches is generally made use of for this purpose, in order that the greater concourse of people may assemble in it. The inside is hung, throughout, with black velvet, and adorned with escutcheons, on which the arms of the deceased are represented; and a great number of white tapers are lighted up on both sides of the nave.

In the middle of the church a very high and large bed of state is set, covered with black brocade, with two pillows of the same colour, which, being put one above another, are laid under the head of the deceased cardinal, whose corpse lies in the middle of the bed in such a manner that his feet point towards the great gate, and his head towards the high altar.

The corpse of the deceased cardinal is clothed in pontifical vestments, viz., the mitre; the cope, if he were a bishop; the chasuble, if a priest; and the tunic, if a deacon. The six masters of the ceremonies assist in this church, clothed in cassocks of purple serge, and all the pope's couriers, in long robes of the same colour, with silver maces in their hands. There are, likewise, two of the deceased's tall lacqueys, each holding a wand, on which are fixed purple taffety streamers, with the arms of the deceased cardinal; with these they continually fan his face, in order to keep off the flies.

On the morrow, after vespers, the religious mendicants meet together in a chapel of the same church, where they sing the matins of the dead, each order repeating alternately a *Nocturnum*, and the pope's music the *Lauds*. In the meantime the cardinals arrive, clothed in purple, and at their coming into the church they put on a cope of the same colour. They then advance towards the high altar, where the host is kept, and there offer up their prayers, and adore it upon their knees. They afterwards go, one after another, to the feet of the deceased, and repeat the *Pater Noster, &c.;* to which they add certain verses out of the Scripture, and the prayer, *Absolve, &c.,* from the office of the dead.

They, then, make the usual sprinkling with holy water, and go and seat themselves in the choir, where they hear the office of the dead sung by several monks and priests with great solemnity. Others repeat it to themselves, not stirring out of their places till it be ended; the cardinals, priests, and bishops being on the epistle-side, and the rest of the clergy in the lowest seats, which stand round the choir. The cardinals are always seated on the highest chairs or benches.

This being done, the congregation return to their respective homes, without any further ceremony. At night, the corpse is stripped, and laid in a leaden coffin, which is put in another of cypress-wood covered with black cloth. The corpse is then carried in a coach, accompanied by the rector of the parish and the chaplains of the deceased, who go by torchlight to the church, where he is to be interred.

The majority of the cardinals who die in Rome are buried in the church of their title, unless they were Romans of exalted condition, and had desired to be interred in the vaults of their ancestors; or in the case of some foreign cardinal, who chooses to be buried in the church in Rome belonging to the clergy of his nation.

Four of the cardinals are buried with greater pomp and magnificence than the rest, viz., the dean of the Apostolic College, the grand penitentiary, the vice-chancellor, and the camerlingo.

INTERMENT OF A POPE.

The Romish rituals enjoin that his holiness, finding himself on his death-bed, must recollect himself, examine his conscience, make his confession, desire his confessor to give him a plenary indulgence, make some reparation to those whom he has offended in his lifetime; afterwards receive the viaticum, assemble the sacred college, make a profession of faith before them, and beseech his eminences to forgive him for all those things in which he may have offended any of

them during his pontificate. The Roman ceremonial,
among other particulars, enjoins his holiness, when he
finds his last hour approaching, to recommend to the
cardinals the choice of a pastor worthy to be his
successor.

When the pope is at the last gasp, his nephews and
domestics strip the palace of all its furniture; for
immediately after his holiness has expired, the officers
of the Apostolic Chamber come to seize the goods;
but the pope's relations usually take care that they
find nothing but bare walls, and the corpse lying on a
*straw bed with an old wooden candlestick, in which
there is only the snuff of a taper burning.*

At the same time, the cardinal camerlingo comes,
in purple vestments, accompanied by the clerks of the
chamber in mourning, to inspect the pope's corpse.
He calls him thrice by his Christian name; and finding
he gives no answer, nor discovers the least sign of
life, he causes an instrument of his death to be drawn
up by the apostolical prothonotaries. He then takes,
from the master of the pope's chamber, the fisherman's
ring, which is the pope's seal, (made of solid gold, and
worth a hundred crowns,) and breaks it to pieces;
giving them to the masters of the ceremonies, whose
perquisite they are. The datary and secretaries, who
have the rest of the seals of the deceased pope, are
obliged to carry them to the cardinal camerlingo, who
causes them to be broken in presence of the auditor

of the chamber, the treasurer, and the apostolic clerks.

After this, the cardinal-patron and the pope's nephews are obliged to leave the palace in which he died, which is generally the Vatican, or Monte Cavallo, unless he happens to die suddenly. The cardinal camerlingo takes possession of these palaces in the name of the Apostolic Chamber; and after having entered it with the formality above mentioned, he takes a short inventory of the remaining moveables; but, as before observed, there is seldom anything left.

In the meantime, the penitentiaries of St. Peter, and the almoner of the deceased pope, after having caused the corpse to be shaved and washed, have it immediately embalmed. The dead pontiff is then clothed in his pontifical vestments, having his mitre on his head, and the chalice in his hand. The camerlingo, in the meantime, sends a body of guards to secure the gates of the city, the castle of St. Angelo, and other posts. The caporioni, or captains of the districts, likewise, patrole night and day with their guards, to prevent those who are caballing for the election of a new pope from raising any sedition.

After the camerlingo has thus provided for the security of Rome, he comes out of the apostolical palace, and goes round the city in his coach, accompanied by the Swiss guards, and the captain of the guards, who usually attended upon the deceased pope.

When this march begins, the great bell of the capitol is rung, which is never heard but at the death of the pontiff, to give notice of it to the citizens.

At this signal, the rota and all the tribunals of justice are shut up, as likewise the datary, pursuant to the bull of Pius V. *in eligendis.* No more bulls are now given out; the ordinary congregations are likewise suspended, insomuch that none but the cardinal camerlingo and the cardinal grand penitentiary continue in their employments.

As the popes have made choice of St. Peter's Church for the place of their interment, when they die at Mount Quirinal (now Monte Cavallo), or in some other of their palaces, they are carried to the Vatican in a large open litter, in the middle of which is a bed of state, on which the corpse of the pope is laid, clothed in his pontifical vestments.

The litter is preceded by a van-guard of horsemen and trumpeters, who make a mournful sound, their instruments being furled with purple and black crape: these trumpeters march at the head of the first troop, mounted on dapple horses, the housings of which are of the same colour with the streamers fixed to the trumpets; but those of the van-guard are black velvet, with gold and silver fringe. These horsemen have their lances reversed; each squadron has a standard before it, surrounded with kettle-drums, muffled, which are beaten in a mournful manner.

Several battalions of the Swiss guards advance next; one half having muskets, and the other halberds, reversed. These are followed by twenty-four grooms, each leading a horse covered with sable housings that trail upon the ground. Several of the deceased pope's tall lacqueys walk without order, between the led-horses, with lighted torches of yellow wax in their hands.

Then the twelve penitentiaries of St. Peter's advance, with each a flambeau in his hand, and surrounded with Swiss guards armed with back-swords and halberds, and having the pope's litter in the midst of them. Immediately before the litter comes the cross-bearer mounted on a tall horse, with a caparison of wire all in network, like a horse prepared for battle. Behind the bed of state, on which the pope's body lies, is seen the chief groom on a black horse, whose ears are cropped, and whose harness consists only of several stripes of linen cloth, a piece of white satin, and a grand plume of feathers, in three ranges, one above the other, on his head, and some gaudy tinsel.

Afterwards, twenty-four more grooms come forward, leading black mules with white housings, and twelve tall lacqueys with white horses covered with black velvet. After these, a troop of light horse advance, the men being all clothed in purple. Then come a troop of cuirassiers; and lastly, the remainder of the Swiss guards, whose march is closed by a troop of carabineers, who guard a few pieces of brass cannon gilt, drawn on their carriages.

In the event of the pope dying in the Vatican, his body is immediately carried, by the back stairs, into Sextus V.'s Chapel. After it has lain there twenty-four hours, it is embalmed, and on the same day is carried to St. Peter's Church, attended only by the penitentiaries, the almoners, and other ecclesiastics, who follow the pontiff's corpse as far as the portico of the great church. The canons of the church come and receive it, singing the usual prayers appointed for the dead; and afterwards carry it into the chapel of the Blessed Trinity, where it is exposed for three days, on a bed of state raised pretty high, to the sight of the people, who crowd to kiss the feet of his holiness through an iron rail, by which this chapel is inclosed.

Three days after, the corpse, being again embalmed with fresh perfumes, is laid in a leaden coffin, at the bottom of which the cardinals, whom he had promoted, lay gold and silver medals, on one side of which is the head of the deceased pope, their benefactor, and on the reverse his most remarkable actions. This coffin is afterwards inclosed in another made of cypress wood, and is deposited within the wall of some chapel, till such time as a mausoleum can be erected to his honour in St. Peter's, or any other church, in case he himself had not given any orders for the erecting of one during his lifetime; which is frequently the case. But when his holiness declares by his last will, or by word of mouth, that he chooses not to be buried in St. Peter's, but in some other church which he names, then his body must not be translated till after he has lain a whole year in some of the chapels of that church; and in this case the corpse cannot be removed till a large sum of money has been paid to the chapter of St. Peter; it sometimes costs upwards of a million of livres, in case the pope, whose corpse they are desirous of removing, was famous for his piety, and that any grounds exist to presume that he will one day be canonised.

The Apostolic Chamber defrays the expenses of the pope's burial, which are fixed at one hundred and fifty thousand livres; in which sum, not only the expenses of the funeral are included, but also those to be paid for the erection of a mausoleum in St. Peter's, and illuminating a chapel of state, where a mass of *Requiem* is to be sung every morning for a week together, in presence of the sacred college, for the repose of the soul of the deceased pontiff. The funeral obsequies end the ninth day by another solemn mass, which is sung by a cardinal bishop, assisted at the altar by four other cardinals with their mitres on, who, together with the officiating priest, at the conclusion of the office, incense the representation of the coffin, and sprinkle it in the manner enjoined in the ritual in presence of four other cardinals, and all the prelates and officers of the late pope's court, who immediately retire as soon as the last *Requiescat in pace* is pronounced, to which they answer, *Amen.*

After the pope's decease, the office of the mass is said according to the circumstances of the times; and one of the lessons is applied to the sacred college. On the first and last day of the nine days' devotion, two hundred masses are said for the soul of the deceased pontiff, the solemn mass is sung by a cardinal-bishop, and a hundred masses are sung on the other days.—*Burder.*

THE GREEK CHURCH PROPER.

On the decease of any person, the whole family appear like so many actors at the representation of a deep tragedy; all are in tears, and at the same time utter forth the most dismal groans. The body of the deceased, whether male or female, is dressed in its best apparel, and afterwards extended upon a bier, with one wax-taper at the head, and another at the feet. The wife, if the husband be the object of their sorrow, the children, servants, relations, and acquaintance, enter the apartment in which the deceased is thus laid out, with their clothes rent,

tearing their hair, beating· their breast, and disfigur-
ing their faces with their nails. When the body of
the deceased is completely dressed, and decently
extended on the bier, for the regular performance
of his last obsequies, and the hour is arrived for his
interment, the crucifix is carried in procession at the
head of the funeral train. The priests and deacons
who accompany them reciting the prayers appointed
by the church, burn incense, and implore the Divine
Majesty to receive the soul of the deceased into
his heavenly mansions. The wife follows his dear
remains, drowned in a flood of tears, and so disconsolate, that, if we might form a judgment from her
tears and the excess of her cries and lamentations,
one would imagine that she would instantly set her
soul at liberty to fly after, and overtake her husband's.
There are some women, however, to be met with,
who have no taste for these extravagant testimonies
of their grief and anguish, and yet their mourning is
not less solemn than that of their neighbours. It is
rather singular that the Greeks have women who are
mourners by profession, who weep in the widow's
stead for a certain sum, and by frequent practice of
their art, can represent to the life all the violent
emotions and gesticulations that naturally result from
the most pungent and unfeigned sorrow.

As soon as the funeral service is over, they kiss
the· crucifix, and afterwards salute the ·mouth and

forehead of the deceased. After that, each of them eats a small bit of bread, and drinks a glass of wine in the church, wishing the soul of the deceased a good repose, and the afflicted family all the consolation they can wish for. A widow who has lost her husband, a child who has lost his father or mother—in short, all persons who are in deep mourning, dress no victuals at their own houses. The friends and relations of the deceased send them in provisions for the first eight days; at the end of which they pay the disconsolate family a charitable visit, in order to condole with and comfort them under their unhappy loss, and to wait on them to the church, where prayers are read for the repose of the soul of the deceased. The men again eat and drink in the church, whilst the women renew their cries and lamentations. But those who can afford to hire professed mourners never undergo this second fatigue, but substitute proper persons in their stead, to weep over their husbands' tombs three days after their interment; at which time prayers are always read for the repose of his soul. After the ninth day, masses and prayers are again read upon the same occasion, which are repeated at the expiration of forty days; as, also, at the close of six months, and on the last day of the year. After the ceremony is concluded, they make their friends a present of some corn, boiled rice, wine, and some sweetmeats. This custom, which is generally called by the Greeks *Ta Sperna*, is looked upon by them as very ancient. They renew it with increased solemnity and devotion on the Friday immediately preceding their Lent, that before Christmas, on Good Friday, and the Friday before Whitsuntide; which days the Greek church have devoted to the service of the dead, not only of those who have departed this life according to the common course of nature, but those likewise who have unfortunately met with a sudden and untimely death.

There is no mass said for the dead on the days of their interment; but forty are said in every parish on the following day, at sevenpence per mass. As soon as they arrive in the church, the priests read aloud the service for the dead, whilst a young clerk repeats some particular psalms of David at the foot of the bier. When the service is concluded, twelve loaves, and as many bottles of wine, are distributed amongst the poor at the church door. Every priest has ten gazettas, or Venetian pence, and the bishop who accompanies the corpse three half-crowns. The grand vicar, treasurer, and keeper of the archives, who are next to the prelate in point of dignity, have three crowns, or a double fee. After this distribution, one of the priests lays a large piece of broken pot upon the breast of the deceased, on which a cross, and the usual characters I. N. R. I., being the initials of four Greek words, signifying Jesus of Nazareth, King of the Jews, are engraved with the point of a penknife, or some other tool or instrument proper for that occasion. After that they withdraw and take their leave of the deceased. The relations kiss the lips; and this is looked upon as a duty so very imperative, that the neglect of it cannot be dispensed with, although the person died with the most infectious distemper.

Nine days afterwards, the *colyva* is sent to church; which, according to the Greeks, is a large dish of boiled wheat garnished with blanched almonds, raisins, pomegranates, sesame, and strewed round with sweet basil, and other odoriferous herbs. The middle of the dish is raised in a pyramidical form, adorned at top with a large bunch of Venetian artificial flowers; large lumps of sugar, or dried sweetmeats, are ranged, like Maltese crosses, all round the borders; and this is what the Greeks call *the oblation of the colyva*, which is established amongst them, in order that the true believer may commemorate the resurrection of the dead, according to those words of our blessed Saviour, recorded in St. John—*Except a grain of wheat fall into the ground and die, it abideth alone; but if it die, it bringeth forth much fruit.* It must be acknowledged that true piety and devotion have contributed very much towards the establishment of this kind of ceremony; but it must be also allowed, that by a kind of fatality, which too frequently attends the most pious institutions, this, as well as other ceremonies of a similar nature, has degenerated into superstition. It is worthy of remark, that this ceremony of the Grecian *colyva*, which is peculiar to their funeral solemnities, their ninth day's devotion, their quarantains, their anniversaries, and the days appointed for the commemoration of their dead, is also observed on their most solemn festivals. The comfits, or sweetmeats, and other fruits, are added merely to render their boiled wheat a little more palatable. The sexton, or grave-digger, carries this dish of *colyva* upon his head, preceded by an attendant with two large flambeaux made of wood, and gilt, embellished with several rows of large ribands, and edged with lace, six inches deep. This grave-digger is followed by three other attendants, or waiters, one with two large bottles of wine in his hands, another loaded with two baskets full of fruits, and the third carrying a Turkish carpet, which is to be spread over the tomb of the deceased, and made use of as a table-cloth for their *colyva*, and their funeral entertainment.

The priest reads the service of the dead, during the time that this customary oblation is carried to the church, and he is afterwards complimented with a large proportion of it: wine is abundantly served to every person of tolerable credit or repute, and the remainder is distributed amongst the poor. As soon as the oblation is carried out of doors, the hired mourners repeat their hideous outcries, the same as on the day of the interment, and the relations, friends, and acquaintance, likewise express their sorrow by a thousand ridiculous grimaces. The whole recompense which the hired mourners receive for their flood of tears, is five loaves, two quarts of wine, half a cheese, a quarter of mutton, and fifteen pence in money. The relations are obliged, consistently with the custom of some particular places, to pay several visits to the tomb of the deceased, to weep over it, and, as an incontestible testimony of their unfeigned sorrow, they never change their clothes during the time of their mourning; the husbands never shave themselves, and the widows suffer themselves to be overrun with vermin. In some particular islands the natives mourn constantly at home, and the widowers and widows never go to church, nor frequent the sacraments, whilst they are in mourning. The bishops and priests are sometimes obliged to compel them to attend church, under pain of excommunication, of which the Greeks have a more awful apprehension than of fire and sword.

The idea which the Greeks entertain of purgatory is very dark and confused, and in general they leave the decision of eternal salvation or condemnation to the day of judgment. They are at a loss to fix and determine the place where the souls of the deceased reside till the final day of resurrection, and in this state of incertitude, they never omit to pray for them, hoping that God, in his infinite goodness, will incline his ear to their supplications.

RUSSIAN FUNERAL SOLEMNITIES.

The Russian funeral solemnities are as remarkable in all respects as their nuptial ceremonies. As soon as a sick person has expired, they send for the relations and friends of the deceased, who place themselves about the corpse, and weep over it if they can. There are women likewise who attend as mourners, and ask the deceased, "What was the cause of his death? Were his circumstances narrow and perplexed? Did he want either the necessaries or conveniences of life?" &c. The relatives of the deceased now make the priest a present of some strong beer, brandy, and metheglin, that he may pray for the repose of the soul of the deceased. In the next place, the corpse is well washed, dressed in clean linen, or wrapped in a shroud, and shod with Russia leather, and put into a coffin, the arms being laid over the stomach, in the form of a cross. The Russians make their coffins of the trunks of hollowed trees, and cover them with cloth, or at least with the great-coat of the deceased. The corpse is not carried, however, to church, till it has been kept eight or ten days at home, if the season or circumstances of the deceased will admit of such a delay; for it is a received opinion, that the longer they stay in this world, the better reception they will meet with in the next. The priest thurifies the corpse, and sprinkles it with holy water, till the very day of its interment.

The funeral procession is ranged or disposed in the following manner:—A priest marches in the front, carrying the image of the particular saint who was made choice of as patron of the deceased at the time he was baptized. Four young virgins, who are the nearest relations to the deceased, and the chief mourners, follow him; or, for want of such female friends, the same number of women are hired to attend, and to perform that melancholy office. After them comes the corpse, carried on the shoulders of six bearers. If the party deceased be a monk or a nun, the brothers or sisters of the convent to which they belonged perform this last friendly office for them. Several friends march on either side of the corpse, thurifying it, and singing as they go along, to drive away the evil spirits, and to prevent them from hovering round about it. The relations and friends bring up the rear, each having a wax-taper in his hand. As soon as they are arrived at the grave, the coffin is uncovered, and the image of the deceased's favourite saint is laid over him, whilst the priest repeats some prayers suitable to the solemn occasion, or reads some particular passages out of the liturgy. After that, the relations and friends bid their last sad adieu, either by saluting the deceased himself, or the coffin in which he is interred. The priest, in the next place, comes close to his side, and puts his *passport* or *certificate* into his hand, which is signed by the archbishop, and likewise by his father confessor, who sell it at a dearer or cheaper rate, according to the circumstances or quality of those who purchase it. This billet is a testimonial of the virtue and good actions of the deceased, or, at least, of his sincere repentance of all his sins. When a person at the point of expiring is so happy as to have the benediction of his priest, and after his decease, his passport in his hand, his immediate reception into heaven is, in their opinion, infallibly secured. The priest always recommends the deceased to the favour and protection of St. Nicholas. To conclude, the coffin is nailed up and let down into the grave, the face of the deceased being turned towards the east. The friends and relations now take their last farewell in unfeigned tears, or at least in seeming sorrow and concern, which are expressed by mourners who are hired for that purpose.

The Russians frequently distribute money and provisions amongst the poor who hover round the grave; but it is a very common custom amongst them, according to Olearius, *"to drown their sorrow and affliction in metheglin and in brandy,"* and it too often happens that they get drunk on these occasions, in commemoration of their deceased friends.

During their mourning, which continues forty days, they make three funeral entertainments, that is to say, on the third, the ninth, and the twentieth day after the interment.   A priest, who is contracted with for that purpose, must spend some time in prayer for the consolation and repose of the soul of the deceased every night and morning, for forty days successively in a tent, which is erected on that occasion over the grave of the deceased.   They commemorate their dead, likewise, once a year: this ceremony consists, principally, in mourning over their tombs, and in taking care that they be duly perfumed with incense by some of their mercenary priests, who, besides the fee or gratuity which they receive for their incense, (or more properly the small quantity of wax with which they thurify the tombs,) make an advantage likewise of the various provisions which are frequently brought to such places, or of the alms which are left there, and intended by the donors for the relief and maintenance of the poor.

We shall add in this place an interesting account of the burial of Prince Galitzin, in Moscow, taken from Dr. Clarke's Travels, who was an eye-witness of the ceremony.   This ceremony was performed in a

small church near the Mareschal bridge. The body
was laid in a superb crimson coffin, richly embossed
with silver, and placed beneath the dome of the
church. On a throne, raised at the head of the coffin,
stood the archbishop, who read the service. On each
side were ranged the inferior clergy, clothed, as usual,
in the most costly robes, bearing in their hands wax-
tapers, and burning incense. The ceremony began
at ten in the morning. Having obtained admission
to the church, we placed ourselves among the spectators, immediately behind his grace. The chanting
had a solemn and sublime effect. It seemed as if
choristers were placed in the upper part of the dome,
which, perhaps, was really the case. The words
uttered were only a constant repetition of *"Lord have
mercy upon us !"* or, in Russian, *"Ghospodi pomilui !"*
When the archbishop turned to give his benediction
to all the people, he observed us, and added in Latin,
"Pax vobiscum !" to the astonishment of the Russians;
who not comprehending the new words introduced
into the service, muttered among themselves. Incense
was then offered to the pictures and to the people;
and that ceremony ended, the archbishop read aloud
a declaration, purporting that the deceased died in
the true faith; that he had repented of his errors,
and that his sins were absolved. Then turning to us,
as the paper was placed in the coffin, he said again in
Latin: "This is what all you foreigners call *the pass-*

port; and you relate, in books of travels, that we believe no soul can go to heaven without it. Now I wish you to understand what it really is; and to explain to your countrymen upon my authority, that it is nothing more than a declaration, or certificate, concerning the death of the deceased." Then laughing, he added, "I suppose you commit all this to paper; and one day I shall see an engraving of this ceremony, with an old archbishop giving a passport to St. Peter."

The lid of the coffin being now removed, the body of the prince was exposed to view; and all the relatives, servants, slaves, and other attendants, began their loud lamentations, as is the custom among the Russians; and each person, walking round the corpse, made prostration before it, and kissed the lips of the deceased. The venerable figure of an old slave presented a most affecting spectacle. He threw himself flat on the pavement, with a degree of violence which might have cost him his life, and quite stunned by the blow, remained a few seconds insensible; afterwards, his loud sobs were heard; and we saw him tearing off and scattering his white hairs. He had, according to the custom of the country, received his liberty upon the death of the prince; but choosing rather to consign himself for the remainder of his days to a convent, he retired for ever from the world, saying, "since his dear old master was dead, there was no one living who cared for him."

A plate was handed about, containing boiled rice and raisins; a ceremony I am unable to explain. The face of the deceased was covered by linen, and the archbishop poured consecrated oil, and threw a white powder, probably lime, several times upon it, pronouncing some words in the Russian language; which supposing us not to understand, he repeated aloud in Latin: "*Dust thou art; and unto dust thou art returned!*" The lid of the coffin was then replaced; and, after a requiem, "sweet as from blest voices," a procession began from the church to a convent in the vicinity of the city, where the body was to be interred. There was nothing solemn in this part of the ceremony. It began by the slaves of the deceased on foot, all of whom were in mourning. Next came the priests, bearing tapers; then followed the body on a common droski; the whip of the driver being bound with crape; and afterwards a line of carriages, of the miserable description before observed. But, instead of that slow movement usually characteristic of funeral processions, the priests and the people ran as fast as they could; and the body was jolted along in an uncouth manner. Far behind the last rumbling vehicle were seen persons following, out of breath, unable to keep up with their companions.

The following account of the annual recollection of the dead in Russia, is taken from " The Panorama of St. Petersburg," by the celebrated German traveller Kohl :—

ANNUAL RECOLLECTION OF THE DEAD IN RUSSIA.

The Monday after Easter is called by the Russians " Pominatelnui Ponyedelnik" (Recollection Monday). When I heard this name for the first time, I asked a Russian the meaning of it, to which he replied, " Because people then remember their parents."

In the morning the people flock to the cemeteries, and after attending service in the chapels belonging to them, in memory of and honour to their departed friends, take a meal over their graves !

At a very early hour, the never-wearied holiday folks may be seen setting forth, with bag and baggage, on foot and in vehicles. The food is carried, in the first place, into the chapels, and laid upon the table in the middle. There is generally a large round loaf in the midst of a dish ; and round about it the red-painted Easter eggs, salts, gingerbread, oranges and lemons. In the midst of the loaf a lighted taper is always stuck, without which no Russian, anymore than a Gheber, can observe a religious solemnity, the clear flickering flame being to him always a symbol of the spiritual.

A Flemish pencil might produce the strangest picture in the world by a faithful representation of this oddly-furnished banquet, particularly as the taste of the purveyors varies considerably. Everyone has his loaf of a different form from the rest; one has added a dish of rice and plums, another a pot of honey, and a third some other dish, according to his means. On every loaf a little book is laid. In one I found written on one page, " This book belongs to Anna Timofeyona" (Anna, Timotheus' daughter), and on the next page, " This book is inscribed to the memory of my dear father, Fedor Paulovitch, and my good mother, Elizabeth Petrovna." They call these books " Pominatelnui Knig," or Books of Remembrance.

After the usual mass the priests approach the strangely-loaded tables and sing prayers for the dead, swinging the censers all the while. They turn over the leaves of the before-mentioned books, and introduce the names there found in the prayer. When this general prayer and consecration is over, the people disperse about the churchyard; each party seeking the graves of their friends, particularly of those lately lost, and weep over them. The greater number mourn in silence; but some, whose sorrow is yet new, cast themselves in despair upon the earth, and give it vent aloud.

The priests, in the meantime, paraded the church-yard with burning tapers and crucifixes, and performed a special service over every grave where it was desired, the "books of remembrance" being handed to them for the purpose. The priests were followed by troops of unfortunate persons, cripples, and beggars, who expected to receive part of the food in alms. I saw several whose sacks had been so abundantly stored with eggs that they might have begun trade with them. Some of the mourners gave the whole of what they had brought, and made thus a worthy offering to the departed. The majority, I am sorry to say, spread their napkins over the graves, arranged their food upon them, not forgetting the wine and brandy bottles, and set to work with as good an appetite as if the day had been preceded by seven years of Egyptian famine instead of a Russian Easter. These ghastly banqueting-tables, and the revelling groups around them, formed the strangest spectacle I ever saw in my life! The priests, of course, came in for a share, and tasted something at every grave. I approached one company, consisting of some official persons, amongst whom there was one decorated with a couple of orders. These people had covered a long grave with a large table cloth, and had loaded it abundantly from a store in their carriage, which was drawn up close by, and out of which they were continually fetching fresh supplies. Two priests were among the revellers, and were challenged more frequently than any others of the party. Not before night were the dead left in peace in their last resting-place, and many, unfortunately very many, left it in a condition which may be said to have turned the day of remembrance into one of complete forgetfulness.

WHEN a Christian dies at BAGDAD, the neighbours assemble, in order to perform his funeral obsequies. At their return from the place of interment, a handsome collation is always prepared for their refreshment at the house of the deceased, where every one is welcome without distinction, insomuch that sometimes a hundred and fifty, or more, appear at these funeral entertainments. The next day, the company meet in order to pray together over the grave of the deceased, which is likewise repeated on the third day; when there is another public entertainment provided for them, and in general the same welcome is given to all as before. These ceremonies are repeated on the seventh day, the fifteenth, the thirtieth, and the fortieth, after the decease.—*Burder.*

THE ABYSSINIANS

Commemorate their deceased friends, and have proper prayers for them. The collection of canons which they make use of, enjoins them to offer the sacrifice of the mass, and to pray for the dead, on the third and seventh day, at the month's end, and at the conclusion of the year. They have prayers, likewise, for the invocation of the saints, as well as legends, relics, and miracles, *without number.—Burder.*

THE CHURCH OF ENGLAND.

The last religious ceremony of the English Liturgy is the burial of the dead. In the order for that service, it is noted, first, " That it is not for any that die unbaptised, or excommunicated, or have laid violent hands upon themselves." The priest and clerk, meeting the corpse at the entrance of the churchyard, and going before it either into the church, or towards the grave, say, " I am the resurrection and the life," &c., (John chap. xi. v. 25,) with some other sentences of Scripture. In the church some suitable psalms are read or sung, and a lesson read, taken from that most eloquent chapter, the 15th of St. Paul's 1st Epistle to the Corinthians. When they are come to the grave, and while preparing to put the body into the earth, some appropriate sentences are said or sung, " Man that is born of a woman hath but a short time to live," &c. Earth is then cast upon the body, the priest, meanwhile, saying, " Forasmuch as it hath pleased Almighty God of His great mercy to take unto Himself the soul of our dear brother here departed, we, therefore, commit his body to the ground; earth to earth, ashes to ashes, dust to dust; in sure and certain hope of the resurrection to eternal life through our Lord Jesus Christ, who shall change our vile body, that it may be like unto His glorious body, according to the mighty working, whereby He is able to subdue all things unto Himself." A passage from the Revelation of St. John, "I heard a voice from heaven," &c., is then said or sung; some appropriate prayers follow; the whole concluding with the blessing, "The grace of our Lord," &c.

Formerly, as soon as any one had breathed his last, the minister of the parish, and persons, (usually women, called "*Searchers*,") must have notice given them. This was ordered to be done immediately after the great Plague of 1665. The corpse was then visited by the searchers, and their attestation was received by the parish clerk, and an abstract of it was printed every week (called the Bills of Mortality), by which the public were informed how many died in the week, of what distemper, or by what accident. This ineffective system was done away with by the Act for the Registration of Births and Deaths in 1837, which came into operation in January, 1838, by which registrars were appointed in every parish for the due registration of births and deaths, the whole being under the direction of a superintendent registrar at Somerset House. It is unnecessary here to give the details of this Act, its requirements being now so well known. The weekly, quarterly, and annual returns of the superintendent registrar contain invaluable information on the subject of the public health, and the duration of life.

An old Act of Parliament, made for the encouragement of the woollen manufactory, ordained that all corpses should be buried in flannel, without any allowance for linen, but the flannel might be as fine as they thought fit. As late as a hundred and eighty years ago, coffins were not in common use in England, the ordinary practice being for the corpse to be carried to the grave in an open chest or coffer, which was kept at the parish church for the purpose. The body, previously to the Act prescribing woollen, was enveloped in coarse linen, kept together by bone pins. The open burial enabled the vicar to record that it had been made in "woollen," according to the Act. "Still earlier, a couple of planks, separated at the head and foot by a turf, were used for the same purpose." *

I need not give my readers any description of preparing the body for the grave, or of the ordinary funeral procession, in this country. Most persons will be rejoiced to perceive the strong tendency of the age to curtail all unnecessary display, in committing to the grave the mortal remains of our fellow-creatures.

---

* "Earth to Earth," by Mr. F. S. Haden, M.R.C.S. From this interesting pamphlet I have gleaned much of the above information.

THE KIRK OF SCOTLAND.

The funeral ceremony is performed in total silence. The corpse is carried to the grave, and there interred without a word being spoken on the occasion.— *Burder.*

THE LUTHERAN CHURCH.

Their burials are always attended with singular testimonies of true piety and devotion; and sometimes likewise with extraordinary pomp and magnificence. Moreover, it is customary amongst them to make a funeral oration over the deceased without distinction, be the party rich or poor, of the highest or the meanest extraction. After the sermon is over, an abstract of the life of the deceased is read in public. High encomiums are given of all those who have distinguished themselves by their exemplary piety; and if any of them have led loose and profligate lives, they never fail to publish the misdemeanors of the dead, for the benefit and amendment of their surviving friends and relations. It is customary, likewise, to make funeral processions, and accompany the corpse to the grave, singing all the time some select hymns, or dirges, suitable to the solemn occasion. In some places, the principal magistrates, and other persons of respectability in the city, are invited to those processions, especially if the deceased were a person of distinction; and those who accompany the corpse to the grave receive an acknowledgment in proportion to their quality and degree.

On the day appointed for the interment of the corpse, the relations, friends, and acquaintance of the deceased, meet at his house. One or more Lutheran pastors resort likewise to the same place, attended by a train of young scholars, sometimes greater and sometimes less, with their masters at the head of them. These youth, in the first place, sing two or three hymns, or dirges, before the door of the deceased; after which they march in the front of the procession; having a large crucifix, or at least a cross, carried before them. An inferior clerk, or some young scholar appointed for that purpose, marches close by the side of the corpse with a small cross, which is afterwards fixed in that part of the churchyard where the body was interred. The relations and friends of the deceased follow the corpse; the men first, and the women after them. During the procession, the bells are generally tolled, out of respect and complaisance to the deceased, and several hymns and other dirges are sung as they march along. It is customary likewise, to open the coffin at the grave, and to take a last farewell, a last melancholy view, of their departed friend, and afterwards to nail his coffin up, singing at the same time a short hymn suitable to the occasion. After which the minister reads a proper collect, and pronounces the benediction. In the next place, the procession enters the church, where there is generally a funeral sermon, either out of respect to the deceased, at the request of his friends, or by his own immediate direction.

As soon as the corpse is let down into the grave, the minister throws a small quantity of earth upon it three times successively; at the first he says, Of the dust of the ground wast thou born; at the second, To dust shalt thou return; and at the third, Out of the dust shalt thou rise again. After that, the bearers fill up the grave. The funeral oration is pronounced immediately after the interment, if the relations be willing to defray the expense of it, or if the deceased have left any legacy or devise in his will for that purpose.—*Burder*.

BAPTISTS.

Their funerals are conducted after the model of simplicity and directness by which all their other religious ceremonies are distinguished. At the time of interment, the minister of the parish, by invitation, attends either at the house of the deceased, or at the church, where he meets the relatives and neighbours, and offers prayer suited to the occasion, after which the corpse is carried away, attended by the mourners and such of the assembly as choose, to the public burying-ground, where it is consigned to the grave.

In some places it is customary for the officiating clergyman to make a short address to the people, either before or after the body is interred.—*Burder.*

THE QUAKERS.

In a speech made by Mr. John Bright in the House of Commons in April, 1874, he said (speaking of the funerals of the Society of Friends), "We have no service—no ordered and stated service—over the dead. We don't think that necessary. But when a funeral occurs in my sect the body is borne with as much decency and solemnity as in any other sect, or in any other case, to the grave side. The coffin is laid by the side of the grave. The family and friends and mourners stand around, and they are given some time, no fixed time; it may be five minutes, or ten, or even longer—for that private and solemn meditation to which the grave invites even the most unthinking and the most frivolous. If any one there feels it his duty to offer any word of exhortation, he is at liberty to offer it. If he feels that he can bow the knee and offer a prayer to Heaven, not for the dead, but for those who stand around the grave, for comfort for the widow, or for succour and fatherly care for the fatherless children, that prayer is offered."

The Quakers do not wear mourning nor use mourning coaches in their funerals.

A. QUAKER FUNERAL IN A CHURCHYARD.

March 13th, 1876.—The interment took place at St. Ann's Church, Turton, near Bolton, of the remains of the late Mr. Thomasson, of Bolton, in the presence of a large concourse of spectators. The funeral service was conducted in accordance with the usage of the members of the Society of Friends, a dispensation having been granted by the Bishop of Manchester. Among those present were the Right Hon. John Bright, M.P., his sister (Mrs. Lucas), and Mrs. Clarke; Mr. J. K. Cross, M.P. for Bolton; Mr. F. Pennington, M.P. for Stockport; Mr. Jacob Bright, M.P. for Manchester; and Mr. Thomas Barnes, chairman of the Lancashire and Yorkshire Railway, and for sixteen years M.P. for Bolton. The Rev. S. A. Steinthal and Miss Becker were also present. On the lowering of the coffin into the vault Mr. Bright took the cord at the head, and was much moved. Wreaths of choice exotics and ferns were thrown into the vault on the wreathed coffin by the friends of the deceased. The hearse was unplumed, but at either side and at the back wreaths of flowers on a violet ground were placed. Several flags of tradesmen and the flag at the New Town Hall were at half-mast, many of the shop windows in the town being partially closed.—*Times,* March 15th, 1876.

A FUNERAL IN OULD IRELAND.

[Burial of Denis Kelly, who died from wounds received in a party fight in Ireland.]

When my brother and I entered the house, the body had just been put into the coffin; and it is usual after this takes place, and before it is nailed down, for the immediate relatives of the family to embrace the deceased, and take their last look and farewell of his remains.

Before the coffin was finally closed, Ned Corrigan came up, and repeated the "*De Profundis*" (the Psalm which in the Roman Catholic Church is repeated over the dead) in very strange Latin over the corpse. When this was finished, he got a jug of holy water, and after dipping his thumb in it, first made the sign of the cross upon his own forehead, and afterwards sprinkled it upon all present, giving my brother and myself an extra compliment, supposing, probably, that we stood most in need of it. When this was over, he sprinkled the corpse and the coffin in particular most profusely. He then placed two pebbles from Lough Derg, and a bit of holy candle, upon the breast of the corpse, and having said a *Pater* and *Ave*, in which he was joined by the people, he closed the lid, and nailed it down.

"Ned" said his brother, "are his feet and toes loose?"

"Musha, but that's more than myself knows,"
replied Ned. "Are they, Katty?" said he, inquiring
from the sister of the deceased. "Arrah! to be sure,
avourneen!" answered Katty, "do you think we
would lave him to be tied in that way, when he'd
be risin' out of his last bed at the day of judgment?
Wouldn't it be too bad to have his toes tied then,
avourneen?"

The coffin was then brought out and placed upon
four chairs before the door, to be keened; and in the
meantime, the friends and well-wishers of the deceased
were brought into the room, to get each a glass of
whiskey, as a token of respect. I observed also, that
such as had not seen any of Kelly's relations until
then, came up, and shaking hands with them, said—
"I'm sorry for your loss!" This expression of condolence was uniform, and the usual reply was, "Thank
you, Mat or Jim!" with a pluck of the skirt, accompanied by a significant nod, to follow. They then
got a due share of whiskey, and it was curious, after
they came out, their faces a little flushed, and their
eyes watery with the strong, ardent spirits, to hear
with what heartiness and alacrity they entered into
Denis's praises.

When he had been keened in the street, there
being no hearse, the coffin was placed upon two
handspikes, which were fixed across, but parallel to
each other under it. These were borne by four men,

one at the end of each, with the point of it crossing his body, a little below his stomach; in other parts of Ireland, the coffin is borne upon a bier on the shoulders, but this is more convenient and less distressing.

When we got out upon the road, the funeral was of great extent—for Kelly had been highly respected. On arriving at the merin which bounded the land he had owned, the coffin was laid down, and a loud and wailing keene took place over it. It was again raised, and the funeral proceeded in a direction which I was surprised to see it take, and it was not until an acquaintance of my brother's had explained the matter that I understood the cause of it. In Ireland when a murder is perpetrated, it is sometimes usual, as the funeral procession proceeds to the graveyard, to bring the corpse to the house of him who committed the crime, and lay it down at his door, while the relations of the deceased kneel down, and, with an appalling solemnity, utter the deepest imprecations, and invoke the justice of heaven on the head of the murderer. In cases where the crime is doubtful, or unjustly imputed, those who are thus visited come out, and laying their right hand upon the coffin, protest their innocence of the blood of the deceased, calling God to witness the truth of their asseverations; but, in cases where the crime is clearly proved against the murderer, the door is either closed, the ceremony repelled by violence, or the house abandoned by the inmates until the funeral passes.

[The coffin, amidst loud wailing, was laid opposite the door of the house of Grimes, the man who had given Kelly his death blow. And after a very exciting scene between Kelly's widow and Grimes's wife the funeral again proceeded.]

I remarked that whenever a strange passenger happened to meet it, he always turned back, and accompanied it for a short distance, after which he resumed his journey, it being considered unlucky to omit this usage on meeting a funeral. Denis's residence was not more than two miles from the churchyard, which was situated in the town where he had received the fatal blow. As soon as we had got on about the half of the way, the priest of the parish met us, and the funeral, after proceeding a few perches more, turned into a green field, in the corner of which stood a table with the apparatus for saying mass spread upon it. The coffin was then laid down once more, immediately before this temporary altar; and the priest, after having robed himself, the wrong or sable side of the vestments out, as is usual in the case of death, began to celebrate mass for the dead, the congregation all kneeling. When this was finished, the friends of the deceased approached the altar, and after some private conversation, the priest turned round, and inquired aloud—" Who will give offerings?" The people were acquainted with the manner in which this was conducted, and accordingly knew what to do. When the priest put the question, Denis's brother, who was a wealthy man, came forward, and laid down two guineas on the altar; the priest took this up, and putting it on a plate, set out among the multitude, accompanied by two or three of those who were best acquainted with the inhabitants of the parish. He thus continued putting the question, distinctly, after each man had paid; and according as the money was laid down, those who accompanied the priest pronounced the name of the person who gave it, so that all present might hear it. This is also done to enable the friends of the deceased to know not only those who show them this mark of respect, but those who neglect it, in order that they may treat them in the same manner on similar occasions. The amount of money so received is very great, for there is a kind of emulation among the people, as to who will act with most decency and spirit, that is exceedingly beneficial to the priest. In such instances the difference of religion is judiciously overlooked; for although the prayers of protestants are declined on those occasions, yet it seems the same objection does not hold good against their money, and accordingly they pay as well as the rest. When the offerings were all collected, the priest returned to the altar, repeated a few additional prayers in prime style—as rapid as lightning; and after hastily shaking the holy water on the crowd, the funeral moved on. It was now two o'clock, the day clear and frosty, and the sun unusually bright for the season. During mass, many were added to those who formed the funeral train at the outset; so that when we got out upon the road, the procession appeared very large. After this few or none joined it; for it is esteemed by no means "*dacent*" to do so *after* mass, because, in that case, the matter is ascribed to an evasion of the offerings; but those whose delay has not really been occasioned by this motive, make it a point to pay them at the grave-yard, or after the interment, and sometimes even on the following day—so jealous are the peasantry of having any degrading suspicion attached to their generosity.

The order of the funeral now was as follows:—Foremost the women—next to them the corpse, surrounded by the relations—the eldest son, in deep affliction, "led the coffin," as chief mourner, holding in his hand the corner of a sheet or piece of linen, fastened to the *mort-cloth*, called moor-cloth. After the coffin came those who were on foot, and in the rear were the equestrians. When we were a quarter of a mile from the churchyard, the funeral was met by a dozen of singing-boys, belonging to a chapel choir, which the priest, who was fond of music, had some time before formed.   They fell in, two by two, immediately behind the corpse, and commenced singing the Requiem, or Latin hymn for the dead.

The scene through which we passed at this time, though not clothed with the verdure and luxuriant beauty of summer, was, nevertheless, marked by that solemn and decaying splendour which characterises a fine country, lit up by the melancholy light of a winter setting sun.   It was, therefore, much more in character with the occasion.   Indeed I felt it altogether beautiful; and, as the " dying day-hymn stole aloft," the dim sun-beams fell, through a vista of naked motionless trees, on the coffin, which was borne with a slower and more funeral pace than before, in a manner that threw a solemn and visionary light upon the whole procession.   This, however, was raised to something dreadfully impressive, when the long train, thus proceeding with a motion so mournful, was seen, each, or at least the majority of them, covered with a profusion of crimson ribbons, to indicate that the corpse they bore owed his death to a deed of murder. The circumstance of the sun glancing his rays upon the coffin was not unobserved by the peasantry, who considered it as a good omen to the spirit of the departed.

As we went up the street which had been the scene of the quarrel that proved so fatal to Kelly, the coffin was again laid down on the spot where he received his death-blow; and, as was usual, the wild and melancholy *keene* was raised.

At length we entered the last receptacle of the dead. The coffin was now placed upon the shoulders of the son and brothers of the deceased, and borne round the churchyard; whilst the priest, with his stole upon him, preceded it, reading prayers for the eternal repose of the soul. Being then laid beside the grave, a "*Deo Profundis*" was repeated by the priest and the mass-server; after which a portion of fresh clay, carried from the fields, was brought to his reverence, who read a prayer over it, and consecrated it. This is a ceremony which is never omitted at the interment of a Roman Catholic. When it was over, the coffin was lowered into the grave, and the blessed clay shaken over it. The priest now took the shovel in his own hands, and threw in the three first shovelsful —one in the name of the Father, one in the name of the Son, and one in the name of the Holy Ghost. The sexton then took it, and in a short time Denis Kelly was fixed for ever in his narrow bed.—*Carleton's Traits and Stories of the Irish Peasantry.*

FRANCE.

We had here (Montauban), an opportunity of seeing a funeral procession; three boys preceded the priest with a bon-dieu and two flambeaux, and he was followed by four boys bearing the pall only,

with skulls, bones, &c., painted on it; next came four
men bearing the coffin, which closed the procession.
The whole number walked, chanting to and from the
church; after service in the church, which lasted half-
an-hour, the same ceremonies were observed to and
in the churchyard at a considerable distance from
the city, and the service "*De profundis*" was sung.
Some prayers used were much like ours, over the
body deposited in the grave.—*Rev. W. Pennington.*

The above may serve as a description of ordinary
funerals in France. On the occasion of the interment
of any one of note, floral wreaths are very extensively
used, and an oration is delivered over the grave. In
the earlier days of the French Revolution of 1792,
when hundreds of different ranks, and most opposite
views and parties, alike perished by the guillotine,
their bodies were deposited in the same grave, with
one layer of quick-lime (their common winding sheet
and only shroud) to consume them all together.
Religious worship was for a time abolished. The
cross and a text of scripture which stood over the
entrance gate of a cemetery were removed by Fouché,
who set up instead a statue of sleep, to intimate that
death was but an everlasting sleep. • Fouché's device
was considered pretty and poetic, and the example
was quickly followed in various parts of the country.
Where statues could not be obtained, the people
satisfied themselves with inscriptions in large black

letters, such as "Death is Sleep," "Death is an eternal Sleep," &c. All Christian emblems were removed from the cemeteries, so that their appearance was entirely changed. In 1794, however, the Atheists were out-voted, mainly through the influence of Robespierre, and these inscriptions were covered over with plaster or whitewash. At the restoration of the Bourbons in 1814, traces of these inscriptions were visible in many parts, the coating of whitewash or plaster having been washed off by the rain. In 1802, soon after Bonaparte was elected First Consul, Christian worship was resumed, and 20,000 proscribed priests returned to their duties.

A FUNERAL IN HAMBURG.

The funeral party having arranged themselves at the entrance, the ceremony commenced as follows. The Parish Clerk or Verger walked first, having a lemon in one hand, and a bunch of evergreen in the other; he was followed by six choristers or singing boys, then six men as bearers carrying the coffin, and after them the mourners and other attendants. As soon as the cavalcade moved off, the Clerk or Verger gave a strophe of some psalm or hymn, which he and the boys chanted while moving round the churchyard; and thus chanting they followed a green path, which was kept close mown for the purpose; and I observed our worthy pastor had joined the cavalcade though alone, and at some little distance from the mourners. I understood it was customary thus to move three times round, but being a very sultry afternoon, the party made two turns serve, when coming to the open grave the bearers let down the coffin into it, and then another strophe was chanted, which ended, the mourners took a last look at the coffin, and silently dropped their sprigs of evergreen upon it; the bearers then each took a spade, already provided for them, and quickly filled up the grave, and adjusted its form, when the funeral party returned silently home as they came. The attendance of the pastor did not seem to be necessary.—*Notes and Queries.*

FUNERAL CEREMONY AT ROME.

One day, in my way home, I met a funeral ceremony. A crucifix hung with black, followed by a train of priests, with lighted tapers in their hands, followed the procession. Then came a troop of figures dressed in white robes, with their faces covered with masks of the same materials. The bier followed, on which lay the corpse of a young woman arrayed in all the ornaments of dress, with her face exposed, where the bloom of life yet lingered. The members of different fraternities followed the bier, dressed in the robes of their orders, and all masked. They carried lighted tapers in their hands, and chanted out prayers in a sort of mumbling recitative. I followed the train to the church, for I had doubts whether the figure I had seen on the bier was not a figure of wax; but I was soon convinced it was indeed the corpse of a fellow creature, cut off in the pride and bloom of youthful maiden beauty. Such is the Italian mode of conducting the last scene of the tragi-comedy of life. As soon as a person dies, the relations leave the house, and fly to bury themselves and their griefs in some other retirement. The care of the funeral devolves on one of the fraternities who are associated for this purpose in every parish. They are dressed in a sort of domino and hood, which, having holes for the eyes, answers the purpose of a mask, and completely conceals the face. The funeral of the very poor is thus conducted with quite as much ceremony as need be.

As soon as the funeral service is concluded, the corpse is stripped and consigned to those who have the care of the interment. There are large vaults underneath the churches for the reception of the dead. Those who can afford it are put into a wooden shell before they are cast into one of these Golgothas; but the great mass are tossed in without a rag to cover them. When one of these caverns is full, it is bricked up, and after fifty years it is opened again, and the bones are removed to other places prepared for their reception.—*Mathews' Diary of an Invalid.*

BRAZIL.

On returning from a ramble I met the funeral procession of the Condessa de J——. A long string of chaises, followed by 20 horsemen carrying lighted candles; an elegant coach and four came next, guided by a charioteer in light livery, and in it the coffin, whose ends projected through the doors. Carriages of every style followed, some with outriders and lackeys behind; last of all a coach and four, with attendants in white and scarlet costumes, the driver and footmen sweating under enormous triangular hats with red feathers. Except the coffin and candles, there was nothing to indicate a funeral.

Soon as a person dies, the doors and windows are closed—the only occasion, it is said, when the front entrance of a Brazilian dwelling is shut. The undertaker is sent for, and as the cost of funerals is graduated to every degree of display, he is told to prepare one of so many milreis. Everything is then left to him. The corpse is always laid out in the best room, is rarely kept over 36 hours, and not often over 24—the number required by law. If the deceased was married, a festoon of black cloth and gold is hung over the street door; for unmarried, lilac and black; for children, white, or blue and gold.

Coffins for the married are invariably black, but
never for young persons; theirs are red, scarlet, or
blue. Priests are inhumed or borne to the tomb
in coffins on which a large cross is portrayed. Lay
people cannot have use of these. In fact, few persons,
rich or poor, are actually buried in coffins; their
principal use being to convey the corpse to the
cemetery; and then, like the hearse, they are returned
to the undertaker.

Fond of dress while living, Brazilians are buried
in their best, except when from religious motives
other vestments are preferred. Punctilious to the
last degree, they enforce etiquette on the dead.
These must go into the next world in becoming
attitudes and attire, married females draped in black,
with black veils, their arms folded, and their hands
resting on their opposite elbows; the unmarried, in
white robes, veils, and chaplets of white flowers,
their hands closed as in adoration, with palm branches
between them. The hands of men and boys are
crossed upon their breasts, and, if not occupied with
other symbols, a small cup is placed in them, and
removed at the tomb. Official characters are shrouded
in official vestments, priests in their robes, soldiers
in their uniforms, members of the brotherhoods in
their albs, sisters of the same societies in those
appropriate to them; *e.g.*, those of the Carmo in
black gowns, blue cloaks, and a blue slip for the

head. The lady entombed to-day was a maid of honor to the empress. Her sepulchral dress was the livery of the maids of honor—a white silk gown embroidered with gold, a train of green silk similarly decorated, a plume of ostrich feathers, necklace, bracelets, earrings, &c.

Children under ten or eleven are set out as friars, nuns, saints, and angels. When the corpse of a boy is dressed as St. John, a pen is placed in one hand, and a book in the other. When consigned to the tomb as St. José, a staff crowned with flowers takes the place of the pen, for Joseph had a rod that budded like Aaron's. If a child is named after St. Francis or Anthony, he generally has a monk's gown and cowl for his winding sheet. Of higher types, Michael the Archangel is a fashionable one. The little body wears a tunic, short skirts gathered at the waist by a belt, golden helmet (made of gilt pasteboard), and tight red boots. His right hand rests on the hilt of a sword. Girls are made to represent Madonnas and other popular characters. When supplementary locks are required the undertaker supplies them, as well as rouge for the cheeks, and pearl-powders for the neck and arms.

Formerly it was customary to carry young corpses upright in procession through the streets, when, but for the closed eyes, a stranger could hardly believe the figure before him, with ruddy cheeks, hair blowing in the wind, in silk stockings and shoes, and his raiment sparkling with jewels, grasping a palm branch in one hand, and resting the other quite naturally on some artificial support, could be a dead child. This practice is now confined chiefly to the interior.

No near relative accompanies a corpse to the cemetery. It is given at death into the hands of friends, to whom its final and respectful disposal is confided. No refreshments of any kind are furnished.

On the death of a father, mother, husband, wife, son, or daughter, the house is closed seven days, during which the survivors indulge in private grief. They wear mourning twelve months. For brothers and sisters, the house is closed four days, the period of mourning four months. On the last of the four or seven days, mourners attend mass, and then resume the business of life.

The cost of funerals ranges from $50 to $1000. Widows never lay aside their weeds unless they marry. When the corpse of a husband is laid out, custom requires his surviving partner to appear before consoling friends in a black woollen gown, train and cap, crape veil, a fan in one hand, and a handkerchief in the other.—*Ewbank's Life in Brazil.*

A FUNERAL IN THE AZORES.

Four priests, with tufts, cylindrical caps of black silk, in addition to a dress like the servitors', marched in file on each side of the street, chanting in hoarse sounds the service for the dead; and behind them, in the centre of the road, the bearers swayed from side to side, under the weight of the corpse. The priests chatted, took snuff, and blew their noses, with the natural unconcern of undertakers; the bearers talked loudly and asthmatically to one another, under the pressure of the heavy bier; children ran among the priests and bearers, blowing reed pipes and screaming, and a laden ass trotted through the procession without hindrance or observation. There were no mourners, neither was there composure, nor quiet, nor the hush of decency, nor even the outward show of grief; no single object, in fact, but the white hands of the corpse to remind you of the dead. The only solemn figure in the procession was a white-headed and bare-footed old man, much bent with years, who followed close behind the corpse, carrying his well-worn crucifix and beads, and who seemed as if he might have attended there rather to mourn his own near approach to the grave than the death of another man.—*Bullar's Winter in the Azores, &c.*

THE JEWS.

As soon as any one is dead, his eyes and mouth are closed, his body is laid upon the ground in a sheet, his face is covered, and a lighted taper is set by his head.

A pair of linen drawers is immediately provided, and some women are sent for to sew them; who, for the most part, perform this friendly office out of charity and good-will. After this, the corpse is thoroughly washed with warm water, in which camomile and dried roses have been boiled. In the next place, a shirt and drawers are put on, and over them some put a kind of surplice of fine linen, a Taled, or square cloak, and a white cap on the head.

They now bend his thumb close to the palm of the hand, and tie it with the strings of his Taled; for he goes to the other world with his veil on. The thumb thus bent stands in the form of SHADDAI, which is one of God's attributes; this is the reason which the Jews give for a custom that secures the body from the devil's clutches. The deceased, in all other respects, has his hand open, as a testimony that he relinquishes all his worldly goods. The washing of the body is intended to denote that the deceased purified himself from the pollutions of this life by a sincere repentance, and was ready and prepared to receive a better from the hands of the Almighty. Buxtorf says, that they burn wine and put an egg in it, and therewith anoint the head of the corpse. Some perform this unction at their own houses, and others at *the house of the living;* that is, in the Hebrew dialect, the churchyard. He adds, that after this ablution all the apertures of the body are stopped up.

When dressed, he is laid on his back in a coffin made on purpose, with one linen cloth under, and another over him.   If the party deceased be a person of considerable note, his coffin is made in some places with a pointed top; and if a rabbi, a considerable number of books is laid upon it.   Then the coffin is covered with black, and a small bag of earth is deposited under the head of the defunct.   The coffin is now nailed up, and conveyed to a grave as near the place as possible where the family of the deceased are interred.

All the people now crowd round about it; and since the attendance on a corpse, and the conveyance of it to the grave, is looked upon as a very meritorious action, they all carry it upon their shoulders by turns some part of the way.   In some places the mourners follow the corpse with lighted flambeaux in their hands, singing some melancholy anthem as they march along.   In others, this ceremony is omitted; the relations, however, who are in mourning, accompany the corps in tears to the grave.

In this solemn manner the dead are carried to the burial-place, which is most commonly a field set apart for that purpose, called BETH HACHAIM, or *"House of the living:"* the dead being looked upon as living, on account of their immortal souls.   When the deceased is laid in his grave, if he has been a person of any extraordinary merit, there is generally a proper person present, who makes his funeral oration. As soon as this eulogium is over, they repeat the prayer called RIDDUC ADDIN, "*the justice of the judgment,*" which begins with these words of Deuteronomy, chapter xxxii., verse 4, "He is the rock, His work is perfect; for all His ways are judgment," &c.

In some countries, when a coffin is brought within a short space of the grave, or before it is taken out of the house, ten men go in a solemn manner seven times round it, repeating a prayer for his soul; this is the practice in Holland: but in other parts this ceremony is not observed. The nearest relation now rends some part of his garments, and then the corpse is put into the grave, and covered with earth; each friend throwing a handful or spadeful in, till the grave is filled up. The coffin must be so placed in the grave, as not to touch another coffin.

The Jews account it a sin, either in man or woman, to tear their flesh, or their hair, on this melancholy occasion, either when they weep over the deceased, or at any time afterwards; for, in Deuteronomy, chapter xiv., it is written, "Ye shall not cut yourselves," &c. But as soon as the coffin is conveyed out of the house for sepulture, a brick, or broken pot, is thrown out after it, to denote that all sorrow is driven away. Those who, during the life-time of the deceased, neglected to be reconciled with him, must touch his great toe, and beg his pardon, in order that the deceased may not accuse them at God's tribunal on the day of the resurrection.

At their departure from the grave, every one tears up two or three handfuls of grass, and throws it behind him, repeating at the same time these words of the 72nd Psalm, verse 6, " They of the city shall flourish like the grass of the earth." This they do by way of acknowledgment of the resurrection. Then they wash their hands, sit down, and rise again, *nine times* successively, repeating the 91st Psalm, " He that dwelleth in the secret place of the Most High." After this, they return to their respective places of abode.

When the nearest relations of the party deceased are returned home from the burial, be they father, mother, child, husband, wife, brother, or sister, they directly seat themselves on the ground; and having pulled off their shoes, refresh themselves with bread, wine, and hard eggs, which are placed before them; according as it is written in the 31st chapter of Proverbs, verse 6, " Give strong drink unto him that is ready to perish, and wine to those that be heavy of heart," &c. He whose usual place it is to crave a blessing on their meals now introduces appropriate words of consolation. In the Levant, and in several other places, the friends of the deceased send in provisions for ten days successively, morning and night, to some of the nearest relatives, for the entertainment of such guests as they think proper to invite; and on a day appointed, they themselves partake of the feast, and condole with them.

When the dead body is conveyed from the house, his coverlet is folded double, his blankets are rolled up and laid upon a mat; afterwards, a lamp is lighted up at the bed's head, which burns for a week without intermission.

Such as are related to the deceased reside in the house for ten days together, and during all that time sit and eat upon the ground, except on the Sabbath day, on which they go with a select company of their friends and acquaintance to the synagogue, where they are more generally condoled with than at any other place. During these ten days, they are not allowed to do any manner of business; neither can the husband lie with his wife. Ten persons, at least, go every night and morning to pray with them under their confinement. Some add to their devotions on this solemn occasion, the 49th Psalm, "Hear this all ye people," &c., and afterwards pray for the soul of their deceased friend.

The Jews dress themselves in such mourning as is the fashion of the country in which they live, there being no divine direction relating thereunto. For full thirty days the mourner is not permitted to bathe, perfume, or shave his beard. Indeed, tattered clothes, sprinkled with ashes, and a general slovenly appearance, point out the mourning Jew during this period.

After the expiration of the ten days, they leave the house, and go to the synagogue, where several of them order lamps to be lighted on each side of the HECHAL or *Ark*, procure prayers to be said, and offer *charitable contributions for the soul of the deceased.* This ceremony is repeated at the close of each month, and likewise of the year: and if the person who is dead be a rabbi, or a man of worth and distinction, they make his ESPED upon those days; that is, a funeral harangue in commendation of his virtues.

A son goes daily to the synagogue, morning and night, and there repeats the prayer called CADISH, that is *Holy*, for the soul of his mother or father, for eleven months successively; in order to deliver him from purgatory; and some of them fast annually on the day of the death of their respective relatives.

In some places, they set a monument over the grave, and carve the name of the deceased upon it; also the day, month, and year of his decease, and a line or two by way of encomium.—Some Jews go, from time to time, to the tombs of their acquaintances and relatives, to say their prayers.

They seldom mourn for such as are suicides, or who die under excommunication. So far, indeed, are they from regretting the loss of them that they set a stone over the coffin, to signify that they ought to be stoned to death, if they had had their deserts.—*Burder.*

The coffins of the rich and poor are formed of four deal boards merely planed over, to free them from splinters. The shrouds are generally of wool, but some of the more wealthy are buried in fine linen.

The Jews have no walking funerals, and no difference is apparent between those of the poor and the rich, except when the relatives or friends of the latter attend them in carriages.

When any of those assembled cannot follow the corpse to the grave, a pail of water and a jug are brought, to wash each others' hands. The first takes the water, and throws it over the hands of the next three times, but he must not touch them with the vessel. This is then placed on the ground, when he who is washed takes it up, and does the same for him who washed him, and so the process of ablution is gone through by all.—*The Jew in this and other Lands.*

For an account of a modern, high-class Jewish funeral in this country, the reader is referred to an interesting report of the burial of the late Sir A. M. de Rothschild, in the second part of this work.

THE MAHOMETANS.

The mourning for the dead begins with such loud cries and lamentations made by the women, that the death soon becomes published to the most distant neighbours. The custom of making loud cries and noisy lamentations for departed friends—of rolling in the dust, or covering one's self with ashes, &c., is very ancient in the East; nor is it much altered amongst the modern inhabitants of those countries. Thevenot informs us, that these Turkish women give over crying when there are no witnesses of their tears, being hired for that purpose, which lasts several days, and is renewed at the end of the year. Previously to the burial, the corpse is washed and shaved, frankincense is burnt about it, to expel the devil and other evil spirits, which, as the Mahometans and several other nations believe, rove about the dead, no less than about the living. This ceremony being over, the body is put into a burial-dress without a seam, that it may, as they pretend, kneel with less difficulty when it is to be examined in the grave. The coffin is covered with a pall, preceded by imans, who pray, and followed by the relations and friends of the deceased, with the women, who lament and shed tears. At the grave the corpse is taken out of the coffin, and put into the ground. The women stay there to cry.

The difference betwixt the graves of the Turks and of the Christians in those countries consists in a board, which the Turks put over the corpse slanting, so that one end of it touches the bottom of the grave, and the other leans against the top of the grave. But neither the Turks nor the Christians of the East bury their dead in coffins. Moreover, the Turks place a stone at the head of the corpse, for the convenience of the angels who are to examine the deceased. This civility which is paid to them will, as the Mahometans superstitiously believe, make them more indulgent.

The palls are different, and the tombs variously adorned, according to the condition and state of life of the deceased, soldiers or churchmen, rich or poor. The burying-places of the Mahometans are by the high-road, "in order," as Thevenot says, "to put travellers in mind to offer their prayers to God for the dead, and to obtain his blessing." For which reason, those who build a bridge, or some other public fabric, from an act of charity, are likewise buried in or near them. The large stones which are erected in the churchyards are so numerous, that a town might be built with them. After the funeral, the relations and friends of the deceased come several days successively to pray on his tomb, beseeching God to rescue him from the torments inflicted by the black angels; and calling the deceased by his name, they say to him, *Fear not, but answer them bravely*. On the Friday following, victuals and drink are brought to the grave, of which whoever passes by may freely partake.

The Persian Mahometans have a strange notion, that the angel who presides at the birth of children

washing-places, there is a very large one in a back court of the Old Mosque, twenty steps under ground. This is done only to the poor, for the rich are washed at home in a basin covered with a tent, lest any one should see the corpse. When it is washed, all the openings are stopped up closely with cotton, to keep in the foul humours, which might defile it.

"This being over, the body is put into a new linen cloth, on which those who can afford it cause some passages of their holy books to be written. Some contain the *Youchen*, a book concerning the attributes of God, to the number of a thousand and one; which odd reckoning is to show the infinite perfections of God, which are not to be comprehended by a thousand ideas, more than by one. The linen about the corpse of Saroutaky, a eunuch grand vizier, who was murdered in the reign of Abas II., contained the whole Koran, written with holy earth steeped in water and gum. They call holy earth, that of those places of Arabia which the Mahometans look upon as consecrated by the bodies of the saints who died there.

"In this condition, the corpse is placed in a remote part of the house; and if it is to be carried to some distant burying-place, they put it in a wooden coffin, filled with salt, lime, and perfumes, to preserve it. No other embalming is used in the East. They do not take out the bowels, a practice apparently to them uncleanly and wicked. Persia being a hot, dry country, the bodies are soon put into their coffins, otherwise it would not be possible to accomplish it, because they swell immoderately in eight or ten hours. The funerals are not accompanied in the East with much pomp. A *molla* comes with the coffin of the next mosque, an ill-contrived, rough, unhewn, and ill-jointed box, made up of three boards, with a cover which turns by a peg; the corpse is put into it, and, if the deceased were poor, carried off without any further ceremony; only the bearers go with it, very fast, and almost running, and pronouncing slowly the words *Alla, Alla!* that is, *God, God.*

"At the funeral of a person of quality, or one who is rich, the ensigns or banners of the mosque are carried before the corpse: they are long pikes of different sorts; some have at the end a hand of brass or copper, which is called the hand of Ali; others a half-moon; others the names of Mahomet, of his daughters, and of his twelve first lawful successors, done in ciphers; the latter are called *Tcharde Massoum,* that is, the fourteen pure and holy ones. More poles are still carried, at the top of which are put some brass or iron plates, three fingers broad, and three or four feet long, but so thin that the least motion makes them bend; to them are tied long slips of taffety, which hang down to the ground. These banners are followed by five or six led-horses, with the arms and turban of the deceased: next to them comes the *Sirpare*, or the Koran, divided into thirty *guisve* or parts, written in large characters, each letter being an inch in size. The chief mosques have a similar one; thirty *talebelme*, or students, carry each one part, and read it, so that the whole is read over, before the body be put into the grave. At the burial of a woman, the *tcharchadour*, that is, a pall supported on four long sticks, is placed over the coffin. This is the greatest funeral pomp, which the friends and relations cannot exceed, unless by an addition of each sort of standards, &c.

"The neighbours or servants of the deceased carry the corpse, no bearers being appointed to perform that last duty; but the Mahometan law teaches its followers to grant their assistance, and carry the coffin at least ten steps. Persons of note alight when they meet a funeral, comply with that pious custom, and then remount and proceed on their journey. They do not bury any one in their mosques, because, though the corpse be purified, yet whatever it touches, or the place in which it is put, is looked upon as defiled.

"In small towns, the burying-places are on the road-side, without the gates, as a moral instruction to the living: but in great towns, which are situate in a dry air, several churchyards are to be seen. The graves are smaller in Persia than in other countries, only two feet broad, six in length, and four in depth. On that side of them which is towards Mecca, they dig a slanting vault, which is as long and broad as the first grave; they thrust the corpse into it without a coffin, the face towards Mecca, and place two tiles to cover the head from the earth, when the grave is filled up. If the deceased were rich, or a warrior, his turban, sword, bow, and quiver full of arrows, are set by him, and the vault is plastered up with tiles. The *Sahieds*, who pretend to be the descendants of Mahomet, have no earth thrown upon them; their grave is covered only with a stone or brick, or that sort of hard brown marble which is common in Persia.

"Stones are erected at the end of each tomb, with a turban, if it be a man's grave; but plain, if a woman's. These tomb-stones ought not to exceed the height of four feet; commonly they are but two feet high; the inscription on them does not declare the name nor praises of the deceased—it only contains some passages of the Koran. The common people begin to visit the grave at the end of eight or ten days; the women particularly never fail: the church-yards are full of them, morning and evening, and on some particular festivals; they bring their children with them, and lament the loss of their friends with tears and cries, beating their breasts, tearing their hair, scratching their faces, repeating the several dialogues and long discourses which they heretofore held with the deceased; every now and then saying, *Rouh, Rouh, soul, spirit, whither are you gone? Why do you not animate this body? And you, corpse, what occasion had you to die? Did you want gold, silver, clothes, pleasures, or tender treatment?* They are then comforted, and led away by their friends: sometimes they leave behind them cakes, fruits, sweetmeats, as an offering to the angels, guardians of the grave, to engage them to be favourable to the deceased.

"People of quality generally order their corpse to be buried near some great saint of their sect. They are seldom carried to Mecca or Medina, these places being at too great a distance; but either to Negef, a town in the country, called Kerbela, where Ali, the grand saint of Persia, lies interred; or to Metched, near the grave of Iman Reza, or to Com near Fatime (both were descendants of Ali), or to Ardevil, near Cheik Sephy, at the distance of two or three months' journey. Whilst they prepare themselves for this long voyage, the coffin is put in some great mosque, where vaults are made for that purpose, which are walled up to keep the body from being seen; and they do not take it out till everything be ready to carry it off. The Persians fancy that corpses, under these circumstances, suffer no alteration; for, they say, before they putrify, they must give an account to the angels, who stay at the grave to examine them. The funeral convoy never goes through a town; this, as they think, would be a bad omen; *the dead must go out, but not come in*, is a common saying amongst the Persians.

"The mourning lasts forty days at most; it does not consist in wearing black clothes (that colour is looked upon in the East as the devil's colour, and a hellish dress), but in loud cries and lamentations, in sitting without motion, half-clad with a brown gown or one of a pale colour; in fasting for eight days, as if they were resolved to live no longer. Other friends send or come themselves to comfort the mourners. On the ninth day, the men go to the bagnio, have their head and beard shaved, put on new clothes, return their visits, and the mourning ceases abroad; but at home the cries are renewed now and then, twice or thrice a week, chiefly at the hour of the death. These cries diminish gradually till the fortieth day; after which, no further mention is made of the deceased. The women are not so easily comforted, for the state of widowhood is generally for life in the East.

"The motives of consolation alleged in Persia on the death of friends and relations are rational, and grounded on solid philosophy. They compare this life to a caravan, or a company of travellers; all come at last to the caravansary or inn; yet some arrive sooner, some later."—*Burder.*

MAHOMET'S CREED.

We must truly and firmly believe, and hold as certain and assured, the interrogation of the sepulchre, which will after death be administered to every one of us by two angels upon these four important questions:—1. Who was our Lord and our God? 2. Who was our prophet? 3. Which was our religion? 4. On what side was our Keblah? He who shall be in a condition to make answer, that God was his only Lord, and Mahomet his prophet, shall find a great illumination in his tomb, and shall himself rest in glory. But he who shall not make a proper answer to these questions, shall be involved in darkness until the day of judgment.

We must heartily believe and hold as certain, that not only shall all things one day perish and be annihilated,—viz., angels, men, and devils,—but likewise this shall come to pass at the end of the world, when the angel Israfil shall blow the trumpet in such sort—that, except the sovereign God, none of the universal creation shall remain alive immediately after the dreadful noise, which shall cause the mountains to tremble, the earth to sink, and the sea to be changed to the colour of blood. In this total extinction, the last who shall die will be Azrael, the angel of death; and the power of the Most High God will be evidently manifested.—*Burder.*

THE CHINESE.

The Chinese in their mourning lay aside yellow and blue, which in their opinion are gay colours, and dress themselves only in white, a colour destined by them to express their sorrow from the earliest times. No one, from the prince to the meanest mechanic, ever deviates from this established custom. In general they wear girdles made of hemp. Their mourning for all their relations is of longer or shorter duration, according to proximity of blood.

As soon as ever a person has expired, some relation or friend immediately takes his coat, ascends to the top of the house, and turning his face towards the north, calls as loudly as possible upon the soul of the deceased three times successively. He addresses himself to the heaven, the earth, and the mid region of the air. After which, he folds the coat up, and turns his face towards the south; then he unfolds the coat again, and spreads it over the deceased, there to remain three days untouched, in expectation that his soul will resume its former state. The same ceremony is observed out of their cities, for a person who has unfortunately been killed.

When a Chinese dies, an altar is immediately erected in some particular room in the house, which in general is hung with mourning. An image or representation of the deceased is laid upon the altar,

with all the decorations before mentioned, and the
corpse behind it in a coffin. All who approach it,
to testify their concern, or pay their compliments of
condolence, bow the knee four times before the image,
and prostrate themselves to the very ground: but
before these genuflections, they make their oblations
of perfumes. The children of the deceased, if there
be any who survive him, stand dressed in mourning
close by the coffin; and his wives and relations weep
aloud, with the female mourners who are hired, behind
a curtain which conceals them. It is to be observed,
that according to the Chinese ritual, as soon as the
corpse of the deceased is laid in the coffin, there must
be as much corn, rice, silver, and gold put into his
mouth as his circumstances will admit of. They put,
likewise, a quantity of nails, and several scissors tied
up in purses, and laid at each corner of the coffin,
that he may cut them as occasion shall require.

The day on which the funeral is to be solemnised,
all the relations and friends meet at the house of the
deceased, dressed in mourning, who, together with the
priests, form the funeral procession, which is attended
with the images or pictures of men, women, elephants,
tigers, &c., all destined to be burned for the benefit of
the party deceased. The priests, and those who are
hired to read prayers or make a funeral panegyric
over the grave, bring up the rear. Several persons
march in the front, with brazen censers of a consider-

able size on their shoulders. The children of the deceased march directly after the corpse, on foot, leaning upon sticks, which is an expression—at least, an external one—of sorrow and concern.

After the children come the wives and the more distant relations of the deceased, in a close litter. A great variety of ceremonies attend this procession; but we shall only take notice, that it is accompanied with the sound of cymbals, drums, flutes, and other instrumental music. As soon as the coffin has advanced about thirty yards from the house, a considerable quantity of red sand is thrown upon it.

Each family has a sepulchre belonging to it, which is erected on some little hill, or place adjacent, embellished with figures and other decorations, like those at the procession. Epitaphs and other inscriptions are also in use among them.—*Burder*.

There is no business in the life of a Chinese, so important to him as his funeral, and no object of art or science in which he is so interested as his coffin. A wealthy man will expend 1,000 crowns upon this piece of vanity; a poor man will give all he is worth; and a son is frequently known to sell himself for a slave, that he may purchase a rich coffin for his father.

The following curious particulars are taken from the Work on China, by the eminent Missionary, Medhurst :—

"Amongst the Taou Sect death is considered peculiarly unclean, and, wherever it occurs, brings a number of evil influences into the dwelling, and which are only to be expelled by the sacrifices and prayers of the priest of Taou. This is termed, cleansing the house; and, as it is attended with some expense, many prefer turning lodgers and strangers in dying circumstances, out of doors, rather than have the house haunted with ghosts for years afterwards. According to the precepts of Confucius, children are bound to sacrifice to their deceased ancestors; and at the anniversary of their parents death, as well as at the feast of the tombs, all persons must present offerings to the manes of their progenitors. These sacrifices are not offered as an atonement or propitiation, but merely the support of the departed individual. The ghosts are supposed to feed upon the provisions offered up, and, in consequence, forbear to annoy their descendants; or, it may be, exert some influence in their favour. As the food, however, does not decrease in bulk, after being feasted on by the spirits; the Chinese imagine that the flavour only is taken away, while the substance remains. Thus those who leave children and grandchildren are well provided for by their descendants, but alas! for those who happen to die without posterity. Deprived of all sustenance, they wander about in the invisible regions cold, hungry, and destitute. The Buddhists have grounded on this prevailing sentiment, many super-stitious services. They induce survivors to call in their aid at almost every funeral, that the souls of their deceased relatives may be released out of purgatory. They have also got up public services for the wretched ghosts, who have no posterity to provide for them. This they put forth as an entirely benevolent undertaking, and a committee is appointed to collect the funds, and lay in the necessary pro-visions. On the day fixed for the ceremony, stages are erected, one for the priests, the other for the provisions. Flags and lanterns are displayed near, gongs and drums beaten to give notice to the forlorn ghosts, that a rich feast is provided for them; and then the priests set to work to repeat their prayers, and move their fingers in a peculiar way, by which means they believe the gates of hell are opened, and the hungry ghosts come forth to receive the boon. Some of the spectators profess to be able to see through the open portals, and the scampering demons, pale and wan, with hair standing on end, and every rib discernible, hurrying up to the high table, and shouldering away the baskets of fruit and pots of rice, or whole hogs and goats, as the case may be, and returning with satisfied looks, as if they had enough to last them till the next anniversary. When the priests have gone through the service, the rabble come forward, and scramble for what the spirits have left."

THE JAPANESE.

The Japanese burn their dead. If the deceased be a person of distinction, all his friends and relations, dressed in mourning, repair to the place appointed for burning the corpse, about an hour before the funeral procession. They are preceded by several companies of bonzes. The deceased, seated in a coffin, is carried by four men; his head is somewhat inclined forwards, and his hands closed, as if in a praying posture. The spot where the body is burned is surrounded with four walls, covered with white cloth, the four gates only excepted, through which they are to enter. These gates front the four cardinal points of the compass. They dig a deep grave in the middle, which is filled with wood, and on each side a table is placed, covered with all manner of provisions. On one of them stands a little chafing dish, like a censer, full of live coals and sweet wood. As soon as the corpse is brought to the brink of the grave, they fasten a long cord to the coffin, which is made like a little bed for the deceased to lie on. After they have carried the little bed in form thrice round the grave, they lay it on the funeral pile, whilst the bonzes and relations of the deceased call incessantly on the name of his tutelary idol. After this, the superior bonze, that is, he who marched at the head of the procession, walks three times round the corpse with his lighted taper, waving it three times over his head, and pronouncing some mystic words, to the meaning of which the assistants themselves are perfect strangers. The last action denotes that the soul exists from all eternity, and will never cease to be; but this emblem seems forced and very obscure. After this he throws away his taper, and two of the nearest relations to the deceased taking it up, wave it thrice over the corpse, and then toss it into the grave. But, according to Crasset, the bonze gives it to the youngest son of the deceased, who, after there has been a considerable quantity of oils, perfumes, and aromatic drugs poured into the grave, throws his torch into it. During the time that the body is consuming in the flames, the children, or nearest relations of the deceased, advance towards the censer that stands upon the table, put perfumes into it, and then worship and adore it. This ceremony being concluded, the friends and relations of the deceased withdraw, leaving none but the populace and the poor behind them, who either eat or carry home the entertainment provided for the deceased.—*Burder*.

THE HINDOOS.

The following account of the burning of a Gentoo woman on the funeral pile of her deceased husband is taken from the Voyages of Stavorinus, who was an eye-witness to the ceremony:—" We found," says M. Stavorinus, "the body of the deceased lying upon a couch, covered with a piece of white cotton, and strewed with betel leaves. The woman who was to be the victim sat upon the couch, with her face turned to that of the deceased. She was richly adorned, and held a little green branch in her right hand, with which she drove away the flies from the body. She seemed like one buried in the most profound meditation, yet betrayed no signs of fear. Many of her relations attended upon her, who, at stated intervals, struck up various kinds of music.

"The pile was made by driving green bamboo stakes into the earth, between which was first laid fire-wood, very dry and combustible; upon this was put a quantity of dry straw, or reeds, besmeared with grease: this was done alternately, till the pile was five feet in height, and the whole was then strewed with rosin finely powdered.—A white cotton sheet, which had been washed in the Ganges, was then spread over the pile, and the whole was ready for the reception of the victim.

"The widow was now admonished by a priest, that it was time to begin the rites. She was then surrounded by women, who offered her betel, and besought her to supplicate favours for them when she joined her husband in the presence of Ram, or their highest god; and, above all, that she would salute their deceased friends whom she might meet in the celestial mansions.

"In the meantime, the body of the husband was taken and washed in the river. The woman was also led to the Ganges for ablution, where she divested herself of all her ornaments. Her head was covered with a piece of silk, and a cloth was tied round her body, in which the priests put some parched rice.

"She then took a farewell of her friends, and was conducted by two of her female relations to the pile. When she came to it, she scattered flowers and parched rice upon the spectators, and put some into the mouth of the corpse. Two priests next led her three times round it, while she threw rice among the bystanders, who gathered it up with great eagerness. The last time she went round, she placed a little earthen burning-lamp to each of the four corners of the pile, then laid herself down on the right side, next to the body, which she embraced with both her arms, a piece of white cotton was spread over them both, they were bound together with two easy bandages, and a quantity of fire-wood, straw, and rosin, was laid upon them. In the last place, her nearest relations, to whom, on the banks of the river, she had given her nose-jewels, came with a burning torch, and set the straw on fire, and in a moment the whole was in a flame. The noise of the drums, and the shouts of the spectators, were such, that the shrieks of the unfortunate woman, if she uttered any, could not have been heard."

Voluntary suicide is considered an act of great merit. The person who is about to offer himself, is directed first to offer an atonement for all his sins, by making a present of gold to Bramins, and honouring them with a feast; afterwards, putting on new apparel, and adorning himself with garlands of flowers, he is accompanied to the river by a band of music. If he has any property, he gives it to whom he pleases: then, sitting down by the side of the river, he repeats the name of his idol, and proclaims, that he is now about to renounce his life in this place, in order to obtain such or such a benefit. After this, he and his friends proceed in a boat, and fastening pans of water to his body, he plunges into the stream. The spectators cry out, "Huree bul! Huree bul! Huzza! Huzza!" and then retire. Sometimes a person of property kindly interferes, and offers to relieve the wants of the victim if he will abstain from drowning himself; but the deluded man replies, that he wants nothing, as he is going to heaven.

People in some parts of India, particularly the inhabitants of Orissa, and of the eastern parts of Bengal, frequently offer their children to the goddess Gunga. The following reason is assigned for this practice: when a woman has been long married, and has no children, it is common for the man, or his wife, or both of them, to make a vow to the goddess Gunga, that if she will bestow the blessing of children upon them, they will devote the first-born to her. If after this vow they have children, the eldest is nourished till a proper age, which may be three, four, or more years, according to circumstances, when, on a particular day, appointed for bathing in any holy part of the river, they take the child with them, and offer it to this goddess: the child is encouraged to go farther and farther into the water, till it is carried away by the stream, or is pushed off by its inhuman parents. Sometimes a stranger seizes the child, and brings it up, but it is abandoned by its parents from the moment it floats in the water, and if no one be found more humane than they it infallibly perishes. The principal places in Bengal where this species of murder is practised, are Gunga-Saguru, where the river Hoogley disembogues itself into the sea; Voidyuvatee, a town about fourteen miles to the north of Calcutta; Trivenee, Nudeeya, Chakduh, and Pruyagu.

A sick person after his removal to the banks of the Ganges, if he possesses sufficient strength, directs quantities of food, garments, &c., to be presented to the bramins. That he may not be compelled to cross, Voiturunee, whose waters are hot, in his way to the seat of judgment, he presents to a bramin a black cow. When about to expire, the relations place the body up to the middle in the river, and direct the dying man to call aloud on the gods to assist him in doing so.*

The burning of the body is one of the first ceremonies which the Hindoos perform for the help of the dead in a future state. If this ceremony have not been attended to, the shraddhu, or rites for the repose of the dead, cannot be performed. If a person be unable to provide wood, cloth, clarified butter, rice, water pans, and other things, beside the fee to the priest, he must beg among his neighbours. If the body be thrown into the river, or burned without the accustomed ceremonies (as is sometimes the case), the ceremonies may be performed over an image of the deceased, made of kooshu grass.

Immediately after death, the attendants lay out the body on a sheet, placing two pieces of wood under the head and feet; after which they anoint the corpse with clarified butter, bathe it with the water of the Ganges, put round the loins a new garment, and another over the left shoulder, and then draw the sheet on which the body lies over the whole. The heir-at-law next bathes himself, puts on new garments

---

* The burning of widows, as well as the horrible customs detailed in these last three paragraphs, have been suppressed, as far as possible, by the British Government throughout our Indian Empire.

and boils some rice, a ball of which, and a lighted brand, he puts to the mouth of the deceased, repeating incantations. The pile having been prepared, he sets fire to it, and occasionally throws on it clarified butter and other combustibles. When the body is consumed, he washes the ashes into the river; the attendants bathe, and, presenting a drink-offering to the deceased, return home; before they enter the house, however, each one touches fire, and chews some bitter leaves, to signify that parting with relations by death is an unpleasant task.

CUSTOMS OBSERVED DURING THE SICKNESS, OR AT THE DEATH OF THE BRAMINS, AND OF THEIR BURIAL.

When a Bramin falls sick, though the vessels of the body be ever so much overcharged with blood, they yet always prefer abstinence to bleeding; but then they frequently make him fast so long, that he quite loses the habit of eating; by which means he is unable to swallow, when they afterwards think proper to give him sustenance.

When the symptoms of death appear, a Bramin is sent for to pray with the sick person, and alms are given to the poor. In the meantime, the sick person is repeating continually the name of God; and when he is no longer able to do it, his friends ring it incessantly in his ears.

The Vedam declares, that as God has promised to

and boils some rice, a ball of which, and a lighted brand, he puts to the mouth of the deceased, repeating incantations. The pile having been prepared, he sets fire to it, and occasionally throws on it clarified butter and other combustibles. When the body is consumed, he washes the ashes into the river; the attendants bathe, and, presenting a drink-offering to the deceased, return home; before they enter the house, however, each one touches fire, and chews some bitter leaves, to signify that parting with relations by death is an unpleasant task.

CUSTOMS OBSERVED DURING THE SICKNESS, OR AT THE DEATH OF THE BRAMINS, AND OF THEIR BURIAL.

When a Bramin falls sick, though the vessels of the body be ever so much overcharged with blood, they yet always prefer abstinence to bleeding; but then they frequently make him fast so long, that he quite loses the habit of eating; by which means he is unable to swallow, when they afterwards think proper to give him sustenance.

When the symptoms of death appear, a Bramin is sent for to pray with the sick person, and alms are given to the poor. In the meantime, the sick person is repeating continually the name of God; and when he is no longer able to do it, his friends ring it incessantly in his ears.

The Vedam declares, that as God has promised to

THE JAPANESE.

The Japanese burn their dead. If the deceased be a person of distinction, all his friends and relations, dressed in mourning, repair to the place appointed for burning the corpse, about an hour before the funeral procession. They are preceded by several companies of bonzes. The deceased, seated in a coffin, is carried by four men; his head is somewhat inclined forwards, and his hands closed, as if in a praying posture. The spot where the body is burned is surrounded with four walls, covered with white cloth, the four gates only excepted, through which they are to enter. These gates front the four cardinal points of the compass. They dig a deep grave in the middle, which is filled with wood, and on each side a table is placed, covered with all manner of provisions. On one of them stands a little chafing dish, like a censer, full of live coals and sweet wood. As soon as the corpse is brought to the brink of the grave, they fasten a long cord to the coffin, which is made like a little bed for the deceased to lie on. After they have carried the little bed in form thrice round the grave, they lay it on the funeral pile, whilst the bonzes and relations of the deceased call incessantly on the name of his tutelary idol. After this, the superior bonze, that is, he who marched at the head of the procession, walks three times round the corpse with his lighted taper, waving it three times over his head, and pronouncing some mystic words, to the meaning of which the assistants themselves are perfect strangers. The last action denotes that the soul exists from all eternity, and will never cease to be; but this emblem seems forced and very obscure. After this he throws away his taper, and two of the nearest relations to the deceased taking it up, wave it thrice over the corpse, and then toss it into the grave. But, according to Crasset, the bonze gives it to the youngest son of the deceased, who, after there has been a considerable quantity of oils, perfumes, and aromatic drugs poured into the grave, throws his torch into it. During the time that the body is consuming in the flames, the children, or nearest relations of the deceased, advance towards the censer that stands upon the table, put perfumes into it, and then worship and adore it. This ceremony being concluded, the friends and relations of the deceased withdraw, leaving none but the populace and the poor behind them, who either eat or carry home the entertainment provided for the deceased.—*Burder.*

THE HINDOOS.

The following account of the burning of a Gentoo woman on the funeral pile of her deceased husband is taken from the Voyages of Stavorinus, who was an eye-witness to the ceremony:—" We found," assist those who think on his name, and repeat it, he is obliged to succour them in this extreme; but in case their speech fails them, and their friends do this office for them, it is the same thing as if they themselves had performed it. If the sick person be married, and his senses are not yet gone, he asks his wife whether she will be burned, or buried with him. If she answers in the affirmative, she is obliged to adhere to her promise, and it then becomes her duty, because of the oath by which she bound herself at her marriage, in presence of the Bramin and the fire Homam. She then took an oath that her soul should not be separated from that of her husband, and she could not, without being guilty of a great sin, violate an oath which the presence of the Bramin and the fire had made sacred. In case she has any children, and loves them better than she did her deceased husband, then she is at liberty either to live with them or die with him. If she dreads the fire, she must not be forced to throw herself into it; but the general opinion is, that no virtuous woman will refuse to make herself a sacrifice on this occasion; for, according to the Vedam, the duty of a wife consists in the three following particulars:—The first is, a blind and implicit compliance in all the desires and wishes of her husband.

The second duty of a virtuous wife is to observe a great modesty and simplicity in her dress, and not to prevails among them, that though they have served Vishnu ever so faithfully they yet contract certain impurities, which are thoroughly purged by fire. On the contrary, the Seivias and Sansjasiis maintain, that their sins will not be imputed to them, though they have not exactly filled up all the duties of life; consequently, that they have no occasion for this purification, and therefore may be quietly laid in the ground. The former have an eye chiefly to God's justice; the latter rely more on his mercy.

OF WOMEN WHO ARE BURNT OR BURIED WITH THEIR HUSBANDS.

When a woman has promised to follow her husband, either to the funeral pile or the grave, he is no sooner dead than preparation is immediately made for the interment of both; nor can she retract nor suspend the performance of her promise. She must be consumed on the same day, and in the same fire in which her husband's body is burnt. The Bramins and Veinsjas are extremely rigorous on this article; but the Settreas allow their wives to burn themselves at different times, and in different places, when their husbands either die in a foreign country, or many years before.

Notice being given of the husband's death, the woman is seated in a chair before the door, splendidly dressed after the manner of the country. Then the instruments begin to strike up; the drums beat; upon which betel is given her to chew, and she is entertained by conversation, for fear lest by thinking too intensely on her impending fate, she should repent of her choice. The Settreas and the Sondras mix something with the betel, which has the property of benumbing all the senses, and locking up all the faculties of the soul; but the Bramins never do this, because they would have this sacrifice a voluntary one.

At her leaving the house she bids her friends farewell, having a citron or lemon in one hand, and a looking-glass in the other, and all the time repeating the name of God incessantly; some use the word Naraina, others Ramma, or some other name. If she be of the caste of the Bramins, or of the Veinsjas, she then, instead of a lemon and a looking-glass, holds some of those red flowers in her hand which are strewed in the temple and before the idols, and it is necessary that these flowers should have been presented to it. An idol is also hung about her neck.

The woman being thus equipped, walks on foot to the place where the corpse of her husband was burnt; and if she be of the caste of the Settreas, or that of the Sondras, she is accompanied by her relations, who employ a great many exhortations, and cheer up her spirits; but if she be the wife of a Bramin, she is drawn on a kind of sledge. Not far from the funeral pile is a pond, where she goes and washes herself. They take off her jewels and other ornaments, when a Bramin prays by her, and alms are distributed among the Bramins. On coming out of the water, she wraps herself up in a yellow shroud, and draws near to the pile. It is raised in a pretty deep hole, the earth of which being all thrown on one side, forms by that means an eminence, on which she ascends. The wood with which the corpse of her husband had been consumed, is half burnt, and casts a dreadful blaze; but to prevent this sight from terrifying her, they place a mat betwixt her and the fire, so that she does not see it. It is on this eminence that she takes the last farewell of her relations, who all exhort her to behave with great bravery on this occasion. She then takes some kitchen utensils, such as a pilang, or a pestle to pound rice, a soup, or little fan to winnow it after it be pounded, and tosses them into the fire over the mat. She afterwards takes a pot full of oil, part of which she pours on her head, repeating incessantly the name of God; when at last, the mat being taken away, she throws herself into the fire with the pot of oil. She then is immediately covered with wood five or six feet deep, while others pour oil and butter on the fire to make it blaze the more. Sometimes, when the female slaves find their mistress is greatly afflicted at the loss of her husband, they promise her, in case she be resolved not to survive him, to burn themselves along with her, and are always as good as their words. There is less ceremony used upon their account; they dance near the funeral pile, and throw themselves into it, one after another.

The burning of the women of the first caste is accompanied with still more barbarous circumstances. These ascend the funeral pile, and lay themselves down by the corpse of their husbands, as if they were going to sleep with them. Being thus placed, the funeral pile is raised over them, when the fire is set to that part of it that is nearest their heads, on which oil and other unctuous substances have been poured, in order to make the fire sooner catch the funeral pile, the wood of which is of a coarser or more precious kind, according to the condition and circumstances of the deceased. Some of them use a wood called aquila-brava, a sort of aloe, which grows in the island of Ceylon, and on the coasts of Coromandel; and others employ sandal-wood on these occasions.

At Surat, over the funeral pile a small hut is raised, made of thick millet-straw, entwined with small wood; the woman goes into this hut, sits down on the funeral pile, takes her husband's head into her lap, and puts fire to it with a torch, which she holds in her hand; while a great number of Bramins, with pokers in their hands, stir up the fire, which they also light on the outward part, and even push the woman forward, in case the dread of the fire should make her attempt to leap out of it; but this does not any way correspond with the liberty which they pretend to indulge the women in on this occasion.

The same preparations are made, whether the woman is to be burned or buried; but the circumstances of the burial are different. When she is come to the grave where the corpse of her husband lies, she goes down into it, and seats herself on a bench made of earth, which is made under a kind of vault dug in the earth. Having seated herself, she takes the corpse in her arms, throws incense into a fire that is just by her, and perfumes her body. This being done, they begin to fill the grave gently, and the woman draws the earth to her, and disposes it about her with her hands. When she is up to the neck in it, two of those who fill up the grave take a carpet, and hold it before the grave, to prevent her seeing what they are going to do. After this they give her poison in a shell, which, as soon as she has swallowed, they twist her neck round so very dexterously, that it is impossible for any of the spectators to perceive it, unless they happen to stand very near her. Both these infernal tragedies are exhibited to the sound of instruments, the noise of drums, and the shouts of all the people present, which drown the cries of the unhappy victims; some of them devote themselves to death with inexpressible resolution.

Any woman who should refuse to die with her husband, would be looked upon as a most infamous wretch. Their hair is cut off; they are not allowed to touch any betel, to wear precious stones, or marry again, but are exposed to insults of every kind; for which reason, those among them who are gifted with heroic sentiments, prefer death to so wretched a life. As they are incapacitated from enjoying the most inconsiderable trifle, and are not allowed to have the least honours paid them, they do not inherit the smallest portion of their husband's estate, but lie at the mercy of their eldest son, who succeeds to it, and has an absolute empire over them. If such a woman has only daughters, the inheritance devolves on her husband's brother, who is obliged only barely to maintain her and her daughters; but they never fail to reproach her with it so long as she lives; and are often reproaching her with not loving her husband, since she had not the courage to die with him. To this may be added their artful insinuations, in assuring them that if they either burn or bury themselves with their husbands, they will save their souls from hell, and that all those who thus submit to death out of pure love and affection feel none of those torments which the fire causes on other occasions. These things considered, we may easily account for their devoting themselves to death in this manner.

OF MOURNING AND THE PRAYERS FOR THE DEAD.

The Bramins have various methods of expressing their sorrow for the death of their relations. At the death of one older than themselves, they shave their beards, and cut off their whiskers, abstain from betel ten days, and eat but one meal a day during that term, which is precisely the time that his soul may possibly be condemned to skip up and down the world. But in case the deceased were younger, they do not impose on themselves this penance; as their wives are always younger, they are consequently never obliged to mourn in this manner for them, much less for their children. The Sondras do not make this distinction, for they mourn for the young as well as the old, and not only shave their beards, but also their heads, leaving only a tuft on the crown of it, and wrap the rest with a punger instead of a piece of linen, which they commonly use for that purpose, and likewise abstain from betel for three or four days. When a Sondra loses a child, he neither has his beard nor head shaved, but deprives himself of betel for the first three days, and puts a punger about his head.

When any person in a house dies, all the bearded slaves shave themselves; and if the deceased were a ploughman, of the family of the Vettalas, or of that of the Ambrias, which are the two principal among the Sondras, twelve sorts of persons are to pay him the last duties,—viz., 1. The Bramins, who serve the pagods. 2. The Beteanis, or Perreas, who beat the drum. 3. The Pannejevas, who play on long horn flutes. 4. The goldsmiths. 5. The carpenters. 6. The locksmiths. 7. The Vasseris. 8. The barbers. 9. The Poumaliandes, who scatter flowers round the dead. 10. The Canapules, who are writers or secretaries. 11. The Salevadis. 12. The Kaicules, or courtesans. The Bramins, the Canapules, and Poumaliandes, do not at this time practise this custom. A certain tax or duty is paid to all those who come on this occasion, and a Vasseri gives to each person present a punger, which they fix on their heads, so as to let it hang half an ell down their backs. They prostrate themselves in the place where the alms called Nili, or rice that has not been winnowed, are bestowed.

The fire of the pile being out, they gather up the remnants of the bones which are not consumed, and throw them into the Ganges; for the waters of that river being reputed very holy, are therefore of great comfort to the soul of the deceased. They also think to procure him a superlative degree of felicity, by building, pursuant to his last will, Tampandals, or huts, in the highways, in which all these passengers who are thirsty have cold and warm water given.

them, or Canje,—*i. e.*, water in which rice has been boiled, and sometimes a few beans.

They often build pagods over the graves of the dead; but as they are considered impure, no religious act is therefore ever performed in them. Some figures are indeed to be met with; but these are not the object of any religious worship, and are no more than merely the images of those persons who were either burned or buried in that place. If they pay them any honours, such as the presenting them victuals, or incensing them, it is only with this view,—to engage the soul of the deceased, in case it be a Ratsjasja, or devil, not to do them any harm, nor frighten them in any manner. They also dig wells and tanks for the service of the public, and imagine that the benefit which will thereby accrue to every individual will be of advantage to the departed soul.—*Burder.*

THE PARSEES.

The following very interesting account of the Parsees and their funeral rites, appeared in "The Times," on the 28th January, 1876:—

THE TOWERS OF SILENCE.

Mr. Monier Williams, Boden Professor of Sanskrit, writing under date Belvedere, Calcutta, favours us with the following highly interesting account of what may be called, though the expression scarcely applies, the Parsee "Cemetery" in Bombay :—

"At a time when the attention of the British public is attracted irresistibly towards the Queen's Indian Empire a short account of a visit I have lately paid to the Parsee 'Towers of Silence' may possibly be read with interest. Your columns have probably already contained a record of the Prince of Wales's visit to the same locality, and through the kindness of Sir Jamsetjee Jejeebhoy the very same privileges of inspection which his Royal Highness enjoyed were accorded to me.

"Your readers are doubtless aware that the Parsees are descendants of the ancient Persians who were expelled from Persia by the Muhammedan conquerors, and who first settled at Surat about 1,100 years ago. According to the last Census they do not number more than 70,000 souls, of whom about 50,000 are found in the city of Bombay, the remaining 20,000 in different parts of India, but chiefly in Guzerat and the Bombay Presidency. Though a mere drop in the ocean of 240 million inhabitants, they form a most important and influential body of men, emulating Europeans in energy and enterprise, rivalling them in opulence, and imitating them in many of their habits. Their vernacular language is Guzeráti, but nearly every adult speaks English with fluency, and English is now taught in all their schools.

Their benevolent institution for the education of at least 1,000 boys and girls is in a noble building, and is a model of good management. Their religion, as delivered in its original purity by their prophet Zoroaster, and as propounded in the Zend-Avestá, is monotheistic, or, perhaps, rather pantheistic, in spite of its philosophical dualism and in spite of the apparent worship of fire and the elements, regarded as visible representations of the Deity. Its morality is summed up in three precepts of two words each— 'good thoughts,' 'good words,' 'good deeds;' of which the Parsee is constantly reminded by the triple coil of his white cotton girdle. In its origin the Parsee system is allied to that of the Hindú Aryans—as represented in the Veda—and has much in common with the more recent Bráhmanism. Neither religion can make proselytes.

"A man must be born a Bráhman or a Parsee; no power can convert him into either one or the other. One notable peculiarity, however, distinguishes Parseeism. Nothing similar to its funeral rites prevails among other nations; though the practice of exposing bodies on the tops of rocks is not unusual among the Buddhists of Bhotan.

"The Dakhmas, or Parsee Towers of Silence, are erected in a garden, on the highest point of Malabar-hill, a beautiful rising ground on one side of Black Bay, noted for the bungalows and compounds of the

European and wealthier inhabitants of Bombay scattered in every direction over its surface.

"The garden is approached by a well-constructed private road, all access to which, except to Parsees, is barred by strong iron gates. Thanks to the omnipotent Sir Jamsetjee, no obstacles impeded my advance. The massive gates flew open before me as if by magic. I drove rapidly through a park-like enclosure, and found the courteous Secretary of the Parsee Puncháyal, Mr. Nusserwanjee Byramjee, awaiting my arrival at the entrance to the garden. He took me at once to the highest point in the consecrated ground, and we stood together on the terrace of the largest of the three *Sagrís*, or Houses of Prayer, which overlook the five Towers of Silence. This principal *Sagrí* contains the sacred fire, which, when once kindled and consecrated by solemn ceremonial, is fed day and night with incense and fragrant sandal, and never extinguished. The view from this spot can scarcely be surpassed by any in the world. Beneath us lay the city of Bombay, partially hidden by cocoanut groves, with its beautiful bay and harbour glittering in the brilliant December light. Beyond stretched the magnificent ranges of the ghauts, while immediately around us extended a garden, such as can only be seen in tropical countries. No English nobleman's garden could be better kept, and no pen could do justice to the glories of its flowering shrubs, cypresses, and palms. It seemed the very ideal, not only of a place of sacred silence, but of peaceful rest.

"But what are those five circular structures which appear at intervals rising mysteriously out of the foliage? They are simply masses of masonry, massive enough to last for centuries, built of the hardest black granite, and covered with white chunam, the purity and smoothness of which are disfigured by patches of black fungus-like incrustations. Towers they scarcely deserve to be called; for the height of each is quite out of proportion to its diameter. The largest of the five, built with such solid granite that the cost of erection was three lacs of rupees, seemed about 40 feet in diameter and not more than 25 feet in height. The oldest and smallest of the five was constructed 200 years ago, when the Parsees first settled in Bombay, and is now only used by the Modi family, whose forefathers built it, and here the bones of many kindred generations are commingled. The next oldest was erected in 1756, and the other three during the succeeding century. A sixth tower stands quite apart from the others. It is square in shape, and only used for persons who have suffered death for heinous crimes. The bones of convicted criminals are never allowed to mingle with those of the rest of the community.

M

"But the strangest feature in these strange, unsightly structures, so incongruously intermixed with graceful cypresses and palms, exquisite shrubs, and gorgeous flowers, remains to be described. Though wholly destitute of ornament, and even of the simplest moulding, the parapet of each tower possesses an extraordinary coping, which instantly attracts and fascinates the gaze. It is a coping formed, not of dead stone, but of living vultures. These birds on the occasion of my visit had settled themselves side by side in perfect order and in a complete circle around the parapets of the towers, with their heads pointed inwards, and so lazily did they sit there and so motionless was their whole mien that, except for their colour, they might have been carved out of the stonework. So much for the external aspect of the celebrated Towers of Silence. After they have been once consecrated by solemn ceremonies no one except the corpse-bearers is allowed to enter; nor is any one, not even a Parsee High Priest, permitted to approach within 30 feet of the immediate precincts. An exact model of the interior was, however, shown to me.

"Imagine a round column or massive cylinder 12 or 14 feet high, and at least 40 feet in diameter, built throughout of solid stone, except in the centre; where a well 5 or 6 feet across leads down to an excavation under the masonry, containing four drains at right angles to each other, terminated by holes filled with charcoal. Round the upper surface of this solid circular cylinder and completely hiding the interior from view is a stone parapet, 10 or 12 feet in height. This it is which, when viewed from the outside, appears to form one piece with the solid stonework, and being, like it, covered with chunam, gives the whole the appearance of a low tower. The upper surface of the solid stone column is divided into 72 compartments, or open receptacles, radiating like the spokes of a wheel from the central well, and arranged in three concentric rings, separated from each other by narrow ridges of stone, which are grooved to act as channels for conveying all moisture from the receptacles into the well and into the lower drains. It should be noted, by the by, that the number '3' is emblematical of Zoroaster's three precepts, and the number '72' of the chapters of his Yasna,— a portion of the Zend-Avestá.

"Each circle of open stone coffins is divided from the next by a pathway, so that there are three circular pathways, the last encircling the central well, and these three pathways are crossed by another pathway conducting from the solitary door which admits the corpse-bearers from the exterior. In the outermost circle of the stone coffins are placed the bodies of males, in the middle those of females, and in the inner and smallest circle, nearest the well, those of children.

"While I was engaged with the Secretary in examining the model, a sudden stir among the vultures made us raise our heads. At least a hundred birds collected round one of the towers began to show symptoms of excitement, while others swooped down from neighbouring trees. The cause of this sudden abandonment of their previous apathy soon revealed itself. A funeral was seen to be approaching. However distant the house of a deceased person, and whether he be rich or poor, high or low in rank, his body is always carried to the towers by the official corpse-bearers, called *Nasasalár*, who form a distinct class, the mourners walking behind. As the bearers are supposed to contract impurity in the discharge of their duty, they are forced to live quite apart from the rest of the community, and are, therefore, highly paid.

"Before they remove the body from the house where the relatives are assembled funeral prayers are recited, and the corpse is exposed to the gaze of a dog, regarded by the Parsees as a sacred animal. This latter ceremony is called *Sagdid*.

"Then the body, swathed in a white sheet, is placed on a curved metal trough, open at both ends, and the corpse-bearers, dressed in pure white garments, proceed with it towards the towers. They are followed by the mourners at a distance of at least 30 feet, in pairs, also dressed in white, and each couple joined by holding a white handkerchief between them. The particular funeral I witnessed was that of a child. When the two corpse-bearers reached the path leading by a steep incline to the door of the tower, the mourners, about eight in number, turned back and entered one of the prayer houses. 'There,' said the Secretary, 'they repeat certain Gáthás, and pray that the spirit of the deceased may be safely transported on the fourth day after death to its final resting-place.'

"The tower selected for the present funeral was one in which other members of the same family had before been laid. The two bearers speedily unlocked the door, reverently conveyed the body of the child into the interior, and, unseen by any one, laid it uncovered in one of the open stone receptacles nearest the central well. In two minutes they re-appeared with the empty bier and white cloth; and scarcely had they closed the door when a dozen vultures swooped down upon the body, and were rapidly followed by others. In five minutes more we saw the satiated birds fly back and lazily settle down again upon the parapet. They had left nothing behind but a skeleton. Meanwhile the bearers were seen to enter a building shaped like a huge barrel. There, as the Secretary informed me, they changed their clothes and washed themselves. Shortly afterwards we saw them come out and deposit their cast-off funeral garments on a stone receptacle near at hand. Not a thread leaves the garden, lest it should carry defilement into the city. Perfectly new garments are supplied at each funeral. In a fortnight, or at most four weeks, the same bearers return, and with gloved hands and implements resembling tongs place the dry skeleton in the central well. There the bones find their last resting-place, and there the dust of whole generations of Parsees commingling is left undisturbed for centuries.

"The revolting sight of the gorged vultures made me turn my back on the towers with ill-concealed abhorrence. I asked the Secretary how it was possible to become reconciled to such a usage. His reply was nearly in the following words:—'Our Prophet, Zoroaster, who lived 6,000 years ago, taught us to regard the elements as symbols of the Deity. Earth, fire, water, he said, ought never, under any circumstances, to be defiled by contact with putrefying flesh. Naked, he said, we came into the world, and naked we ought to leave it. But the decaying particles of our bodies should be dissipated as rapidly as possible, and in such a way that neither Mother Earth nor the beings she supports should be contaminated in the slightest degree. In fact, our Prophet was the greatest of health officers, and, following his sanitary laws, we build our towers on the tops of the hills, above all human habitations. We spare no expense in constructing them of the hardest materials, and we expose our putrescent bodies in open stone receptacles, resting on fourteen feet of solid granite, not necessarily to be consumed by vultures, but to be dissipated in the speediest possible manner, and without the possibility of polluting the earth or contaminating a single living being dwelling thereon. God indeed sends the vultures, and, as a matter of fact, these birds do their appointed work much more expeditiously than millions of insects would do if we committed our bodies to the ground. In a sanitary point of view nothing can be more perfect than our plan. Even the rain water which washes our skeletons is conducted by channels into purifying charcoal. Here in these five towers rest the bones of all the Parsees that have lived in Bombay for the last 200 years. We form a united body in life, and we are united in death. Even our leader, Sir Jamsetjee, likes to feel that when he dies he will be reduced to perfect equality with the poorest and humblest of the Parsee community.'

" When the Secretary had finished his defence of the Towers of Silence, I could not help thinking that however much such a system may shock our European feelings and ideas, yet our own method of interment, if regarded from a Parsee point of view, may possibly be equally revolting to Parsee sensibilities.

"The exposure of the decaying body to the assaults of innumerable worms may have no terrors for us, because our survivors do not see the assailants; but let it be borne in mind that neither are the Parsee survivors permitted to look at the swoop of the Heaven-sent birds. Why, then, should we be surprised if they prefer the more rapid to the more lingering operation? and which of the two systems, they may reasonably ask, is more defensible on sanitary grounds?"

THE TARTARS.

It is the custom among some of the Tartar nations to burn their dead, and inter their ashes on an eminence, upon which they raise a heap of stones, and place on it little banners; but the greater part of the Pagan Tartars bury their dead, and with each man his best horse and moveables, for his use in the other world. Others, however, throw their dead into open fields, to be devoured by the dogs, of which many run wild, and some are kept for this purpose. If the bodies are thus devoured by any number exceeding six, they think honourably of the deceased; otherwise he is a disgrace to his relations.

On some of the skirts of the villages are seen tombs, which are larger and better built than the houses:

each of them encloses three, four, or five biers, of a neat workmanship, ornamented with Chinese stuffs, some pieces of which are brocade. Bows, arrows, lines, and, in general, the most valuable articles belonging to these people, are suspended in the interior of the monuments, the wooden door of which is closed with a bar, supported at its extremities by two props.

Although no external distinction seems to exist between the living inhabitants, yet the same cannot be said of the dead, whose ashes repose in a style of greater or less magnificence, according to their wealth; it is probable that the labour of a long life, would scarcely defray the expense of one of these sumptuous mausolea; which, however, bear no comparison with the monuments of more civilised people. The bodies of the poorest inhabitants are exposed in the open air, on a bier, placed upon a stage, supported by stakes. They all appear to hold their dead in great veneration, and to employ the whole of their industry and ingenuity in procuring them an honourable burial. They are interred with their clothes on, and the arms and implements that they made use of when alive; and it would probably be esteemed sacrilege to take any of these away.—*Burder.*

THE JUKOGAIES AND THE JUKUTZES.

The Jukogaies, who are inhabitants of the parts

adjacent to Lena, pay divine honours to their dead, after they have hung up and dried their skeletons in the air, and adorned them with necklaces made of glass. The Jukutzes seem to acknowledge the existence of a god, who is their creator and preserver, and the all-wise disposer of good and evil. They have an annual festival, which they celebrate every spring with a great degree of solemnity—that is, by kindling a large bonfire, which must be kept up as long as the festival lasts, and abstaining the whole time from all kinds of liquors, they being destined only for libations, which consist in pouring their common drink eastward into the fire. In this ceremony there seems to be a kind of religious adoration paid to that element.

The mourning of children for their parents, amongst the Tartars, consists generally in weeping over them for several days successively; and during all that time they are obliged to abstain from all manner of amusements, and from the society of women for several months. The child must inter his father or mother with all the funeral pomp and solemnity of which his circumstances will admit, and pay his annual respects to their respective tombs, which must be attended not only with tears but loud lamentations. These people, as well as the Indians, Chinese, &c., make provision for their dead, and supply them with variety of apparel. The Tunguses hang their dead upon some particular trees, and there leave them till they have nothing but skin and bone remaining; then they inter them. The Jukogaies, likewise, hang up their deceased relations in the very same manner, and when their skeletons are perfectly dry, adorn them with coral and little pieces of painted glass. Afterwards they carry them in solemn procession round their houses, and revere them as idols.

THE OSTIACS either bury their dead, or hide both them and their bows, arrows, implements of household, and provisions, in the snow, from the very same principle which actuates others, who are habituated to these customs. A widow, to testify her unfeigned sorrow for the loss of her dearly beloved husband, takes an idol, dresses it up in the good man's clothes, lays it in the bed with her, and affects to have it always before her eyes, in order to aggravate her grief, and bring her departed husband to her remembrance. The widows of the Ostiacs kiss the idols of their deceased husbands, and honour them as partners of their beds during a whole year, and then they are looked upon as incumbrances, and thrown neglected into some corner of the house; no more mention is then made of their old bedfellows, for the time of their mourning is then accomplished.

THE SAMOIDES hang their deceased infants, who have not attained the age of one year, upon trees; but they inter between two boards those who are of a more advanced age. They drown or otherwise make away with those relations who are superannuated, infirm, and who have become a burden to themselves and all about them. Near the place where they bury their dead, they hang up their fire-arms, their hatchets, their hammers, and, in short, all the other implements which they made use of during their lives.

All these people in general acknowledge the doctrine of the metempsychosis, but in two different acceptations. Some are of opinion, that the very souls transmigrate from one body into another; others, that there is no other transmigration than that of the operations and faculties belonging to the soul of the deceased. These last, in all probability, imagine, that there is only an emanation of virtues, because they confound the body and the soul together.—*Burder.*

THE CIRCASSIAN TARTARS.

The Circassian Tartars are reckoned as Mahometans and Greeks, there being several of both those persuasions amongst them; idolatry, nevertheless, has a prevailing power over them. When any person of distinction amongst them dies, they sacrifice a he-goat, hang up his skin upon a high pole in the middle of the town, and come one after another to pay it divine adoration. This skin is never taken down till some other person of distinction dies; and then they put a fresh one in its place. John de Luca, in his account informs us, that they sacrifice rams, and call those victims Curbans; and, moreover, that the places where the sacrifices are made are deemed so sacred, that the most determined thief amongst them will never venture to touch the least thing that is carried to them. He adds likewise, "that there are bows, arrows, and scimitars hung on the trees in these sacred places, as public testimonies that they have performed their vows."

GEORGIA.

Through the rapacity of the clergy, who receive enormous fees from both the dead and the living, the burials in this country are very expensive to the family.

THE LAPLANDERS.

The funerals of the Laplanders are conducted with little ceremony. The body, slightly wrapped in a coarse cloth, is carried to the grave by the friends and relatives, who are entertained with a slight repast, and a small portion of metheglin. In former times, it was the custom to raise a heap of stones over the grave; but an old sledge, turned with its bottom upwards, is now the only monument placed over the spot of interment. Before the conversion of the Laplanders to Christianity, they placed an axe and tinder-box beside the corpse of a man; and beside that of a woman, her needle and scissors, supposing them to require these implements in the other world. They likewise interred a quantity of provisions along with the dead body; and, during the first three years after the decease of a relative, were accustomed, from time to time, to deposit, in holes dug beside the grave, small quantities of tobacco, or of whatever was most agreeable to their departed friend during his lifetime.

MEXICO.

As soon as any person died, certain masters of funeral ceremonies were called, who were generally men advanced in years. They cut a number of pieces of paper, with which they dressed the dead body, and took a glass of water with which they sprinkled the head, saying, that that was the water used in the time of their life. They then dressed it in a habit suitable to the rank, the wealth, and the circumstances attending the death of the party. If the deceased had been a warrior, they clothed him in the habit of Huitzilopochtli;* if a merchant, in that of Jacatuetli;† if an artist, in that of the protecting god of his art or trade: one who had been drowned was dressed in the habit of Tlaloc;‡ one

* The God of War.
† The God of Commerce.
‡ God of Water.

who had been executed for adultery, in that of Tlazolteotl ;* and a drunkard in the habit of Tezcatzoncatl, god of wine. In short, as Gomara has well observed, they wore more garments after they were dead, than while they were living.

With the habit they gave the dead a jug of water, which was to serve on the journey to the other world, and also at successive different times, different pieces of paper mentioning the use of each. On consigning the first piece to the dead, they said :—By means of this you will pass without danger between the two mountains which fight against each other. With the second they said: By means of this you will walk without obstruction along the road which is defended by the great serpent. With the third: By this you will go securely through the place where there is the Crocodile Xochitonal. The fourth was a safe passport through the eight deserts; the fifth through the eight hills; and the sixth was given in order to pass without hurt through the sharp wind; for they pretended that it was necessary to pass a place called Itzehecajan, where a wind blew so violently as to tear up rocks, and so sharp that it cut like a knife; on which account they burned all the habits which the deceased had worn during life, their arms, and some household

* Was the god whom the Mexicans invoked to obtain pardon of their sins, and to be freed from the disgrace to which the guilty are exposed.

goods, in order that the heat of this fire might defend them from the cold of that terrible wind.

One of the chief and most ridiculous ceremonies at funerals was the killing a techichi, a domestic quadruped, resembling a little dog, to accompany the deceased in their journey to the other world. They fixed a string about its neck, believing that necessary to enable it to pass the deep river of Chiuhnahuapan, or New Waters. They buried the techichi, or burned it along with the body of its master, according to the kind of death of which he died. While the masters of the ceremonies were lighting up the fire in which the body was to be burned, the other priests kept singing in a melancholy strain. After burning the body, they gathered the ashes in an earthen pot, amongst which, according to the circumstances of the deceased, they put a gem of more or less value; which they said would serve him in the place of a heart in the other world. They buried this earthen pot in a deep ditch, and fourscore days after made oblations of bread and wine over it.

Such were the funeral rites of the common people; but at the death of kings, and that of lords, or persons of high rank, some peculiar forms were observed that are worthy to be mentioned. When the king fell sick, says Gomara, they put a mask on the idol of Huitzilopochtli, and also one on the idol of Tezcatlipoca, which they never took off until the king was either dead or recovered; but it is certain, that the idol of Huitzilopochtli had always two masks, not one. As soon as a king of Mexico happened to die, his death was published in great form, and all the lords who resided at Court, and also those who were but a little distant from it were informed of the event, in order that they might be present at the funeral. In the meantime they laid the royal corpse upon beautiful curiously wrought mats, which was attended and watched by his domestics. Upon the fourth or fifth day after, when the lords were arrived, who brought with them rich dresses, beautiful feathers and slaves to be presented, to add to the pomp of the funeral they clothed the corpse in fifteen, or more, very fine habits of cotton of various colors, ornamented it with gold, silver and gems, hung an emerald at the under lip, which was to serve in place of a heart, covered the face with a mask and over the habits were placed the ensigns of that god in whose temple or area the ashes were to be buried. They cut off some of the hair which, together with some more which had been cut off in the infancy of the king, they preserved in a little box, in order to perpetuate, as they said, the memory of the deceased. Upon the box they laid an image of the deceased made of wood or of stone. Then they killed the slave who was his chaplain, who had the care of his oratory, and all that belonged to the private worship of his gods, in order that he might serve him in the same office in the other world.

The funeral procession came next, accompanied by all the relations of the deceased, the whole of the nobility, and the wives of the late king, who testified their sorrow by tears and other demonstrations of grief. The nobles carried a great standard of paper and the royal arms and ensigns. The priests continued singing, but without any musical instrument. Upon their arrival at the lower area of the temple, the high priest, together with their servants, came out to meet the royal corpse, which, without delay, they placed upon the funeral pile, which was prepared there for that purpose of odoriferous resinous woods, together with a large quantity of copal and other aromatic substances. While the royal corpse, and all its habits, the arms and ensigns were burning, they sacrificed at the bottom of the stairs of the temple a great number of slaves of those which belonged to the deceased, and also of those which had been presented by the lords. Along with the slaves, they likewise sacrificed some of the irregularly formed men, whom the king had collected in his palaces for his entertainment, in order that they might give him the same pleasure in the other world, and for the same reason they used also to sacrifice some of his wives.

The number of the victims was proportioned to the

grandeur of the funeral, and amounted sometimes as several historians affirm to two hundred. Among the other sacrifices the techichi was not omitted; they were firmly persuaded, that without such a guide it would be impossible to get through some dangerous ways which led to the other world.

The day following the ashes were gathered and the teeth which remained entire; they sought carefully for the emerald which had been hung to the under lip and the whole were put into the box with the hair; and they deposited the box in the place defined for his sepulchre. The four following days they made oblations of eatables over the sepulchre; on the fifth, they sacrificed some slaves and also some others on the twentieth, fortieth, sixtieth and eightieth day after. From that time forward, they sacrificed no more human victims, but every year they celebrated the day of the funeral with sacrifices of rabbits, butterflies, quails and other birds, and with oblations of bread, wine, copal, flowers, and certain little reeds filled with aromatic substances, which they called Acajetl. This anniversary was held for four years.

The bodies of the dead were in general burned; they buried the bodies entire of those only who had been drowned, or had died of dropsy, and some other diseases, but what was the reason of these exceptions we know not.

There was no fixed place for burials. Many ordered their ashes to be buried near to some temple or altar, some in the fields, and others in those sacred places of the mountains where sacrifices used to be made. The ashes of the kings and lords, were, for the most part, deposited in the towers of the temples especially in those of the greater temple. Close to Teotihuacan, where there were many temples, there were also innumerable sepulchres. The tombs of those whose bodies had been buried entire, agreeable to the testimony of the anonymous conqueror who saw them, were deep ditches, formed with stone and lime, within which they placed the bodies in a sitting posture upon icpalli, or low seats, together with the instruments of their art or profession. If it was the sepulchre of any military person, they laid a shield and sword by him; if of a woman, a spindle, a weaver's shuttle, and a xicalli, which was a certain naturally formed vessel. In the tombs of the rich they put gold and jewels; but all were provided with eatables for the long journey which they had to make. The Spanish Conquerors, knowing of the gold which was buried with the Mexican lords in their tombs, dug up several and found considerable quantities of that precious metal. Cortes says in his letters, that at one entry which he made into the Capital, when it was besieged by his army, his soldiers found fifteen hundred Castellanos,* that is, two hundred and forty ounces of gold, in one sepulchre, which was in the tower of a temple. The famous conqueror says also, that he was present at the digging up of another sepulchre, from which they took about three thousand Castellanos.

The caves of the mountains were the sepulchres of the ancient Chechemecas; but as they grew more civilized, they adopted in this and other rites, the customs of the Acolhuan Nation which were nearly the same with those of the Mexicans.

The Mixtecas retained in part the ancient usage of the Chechemecas, but in some things they were singular in their customs. When any of their lords fell sick, they offered prayers, vows and sacrifices for the recovery of his health. If it was restored they made great rejoicings. If he died, they continued to speak of him as if he was still alive and conducted one of his slaves to the corpse, dressed him in the habits of his master, put a mask upon his face, and for one whole day, paid him all the honours which they had used to render to the deceased. At midnight, four priests carried the corpse to be buried in a wood, or in some cavern, particularly in that one where they believed the gate of paradise was, and at their return

---

* The Spanish goldsmiths divide the pound weight of gold into two Marchi or into sixteen ounces or a hundred Castellanos; consequently, an ounce contains six and a quarter Castellanos.

they sacrificed the slave, and laid him, with all the ornaments of his transitory dignity, in a ditch, but without covering him with earth.

Every year they held a festival in honour of their lost lord on which they celebrated his birth, not his death, for of it they never spoke.

The Zopotecas, their neighbours, embalmed the body of the principal lord of their Nation. Even from the time of the first Chechemecan kings . aromatic preparations were in use among those nations to preserve dead bodies from speedy corruption; but we do not know that these were very frequent.

HOTTENTOTS.

A Hottentot is taken to some cave or cleft in a neighbouring rock, and there left; the entrance being carefully closed up with stones, to prevent the body being devoured by wild beasts.

GUINEA.

When a native of Guinea expires his wives and relations commence howling hideously. They next proceed to shave their heads, and smear a chalky substance over their bodies, as outward tokens of their despair. The body is dressed in its best attire, with its most valuable coral ornaments, scimitar, and other articles of personal adornment, then laid in a coffin, with its fetiches beside it.

THE TONQUINESE.

The Tonquinese burn the body, and deposit the ashes in cinerary urns.

THE CONGOESE.

The Congoese kindle fires round the body at a sufficient distance to preserve it from ignition, and as fast as the moisture is absorbed by the clothes, they renew them till the body is completely dried. It is then buried with great pomp.

MADAGASCAR.

The Afana is performed at the grave of a person lately buried, and consists of slaughtering cattle and feasting, accompanied with firing of muskets or cannon. The skulls of the slaughtered cattle are fixed on poles at the head of the tomb. This is done to take evil from the dead, that he may repose in peace. The Malagasy (the inhabitants of Madagascar) believe that when the body dies the mind becomes "*levona*," *i.e.*, varnished, invisible, and that the life becomes "*rivotra*," air, or wind, a mere breeze. Chicanery, lying, and cheating, are considered but very light offences, compared to trampling on a grave.

AMERICAN INDIANS.

The Indians use the same ceremonies to the bones

of their dead, as if they were covered with their former skin, flesh, and ligaments. The bones of their people who have been killed in battle, are tied in white deer skins separately, and laid before their houses, the female relatives weeping over them for about half-an-hour. They are then carried to their graves and buried. The chieftains carry twelve small sticks, tied together in the form of a quadrangle, each square consisting of three. The sticks are peeled, not painted, and swan feathers tied to each corner. They call this frame the White Circle, and place it over the door while the women weep over the bones. Adair, who was present at one of their funerals, says: "They laid the corpse in his tomb in a sitting posture, with his feet towards the east, his head anointed with bear's oil, and his face painted red; but not streaked with black, because that is a constant emblem of war and death. He was dressed in his finest apparel, having his gun and pouch, and trusty hiccory bow, with a young panther's skin full of arrows, alongside of him, and every other useful thing he had been possessed of, that when he rises again they may serve him in that track of land which pleased him best before he went to take his long sleep. His tomb was firm and clean inside; they covered it with thick logs, so as to bear several tiers of cypress bark, and such a quantity of clay, as would confine the putrid smell, and be on a level with the rest of the floor. They often sleep over these tombs, which, with the loud wailing of the women at the dusk of the evening, and dawn of the day, on benches close by the tombs, must awake the memory of their relations very often; and if they were killed by an enemy, it helps to irritate, and set on such revengeful tempers to retaliate blood for blood."

The MOSQUITO INDIANS are buried in their houses, and the very spot they lay over when alive, their hatchet, harpoon, lances with *mushelaw*, and other necessaries being buried with them. If the deceased left a gun, some friend preserves that from the earth, as it would spoil the powder, and render it unserviceable in that strange journey. His boat is cut in pieces, and laid over his grave, with the rest of his household goods.

The Tribes of OONALASKA and NOOTKA SOUND inter their dead on the tops of hills, and place a little tumulus over the grave, which soon becomes a large size, as every passer-by adds a stone to it.

THE POLYNESIANS.

When a person deceased, the first object was to ascertain the *cause* of his death, as the ceremonies which followed varied accordingly. These ceremonies being performed, the body was to be disposed of. In case of a chief, or person of rank, the body was preserved; but all others were buried. When about to be interred, the corpse was placed in a sitting posture, with the knees elevated, the face pressed down between the knees, the hands fastened under the legs, and the whole body tied with a cord. The interment usually took place on the day the person deceased, or the day following. During the interval which elapsed between death and burial, the surviving friends watched the corpse, indulging their grief in loud and bitter lamentations, and cutting themselves with a shark's tooth. The bodies of their chiefs were embalmed, and afterwards preserved in houses erected for that purpose.

The Rarotongans represented their paradise as a very long house, encircled with beautiful shrubs and flowers, which never lost their bloom or fragrance, and whose inmates enjoyed unwithering beauty and perpetual youth. These passed their days without weariness or alloy, in dancing, festivity, and merriment. The hell of the Rarotongans consisted in their being compelled to crawl round this house, observing the pleasures of its inmates, while racked with intense but vain desires of admittance and enjoyment. The heaven of the Samoa islanders seems to have nearly resembled that of the Rarotongans.

In order to secure the admission of a departed spirit to future joys, the corpse was dressed in the best attire the relatives could provide; the head was wreathed with flowers, and other decorations were added. A pig was then baked whole, and placed upon the body of the deceased, surrounded by a pile of vegetable food. After this, the father would thus address the corpse:—"My son, when you were alive, I treated you with kindness, and when you were taken ill, I did my best to restore you to health; and now you are dead, there's your momoe o, or property of admission. Go, my son, and with that gain an entrance into the palace of Tiki, and do not come to this world again to disturb and alarm us." The whole would then be buried; and if they received no intimation to the contrary within a few days of the interment, the relatives believed that the pig and the other food had obtained for him the desired admittance. If, however, a cricket was heard on the premises, it was considered an ill omen. They would utter dismal howlings, and exclaim, "Oh, our brother! his spirit has not entered the paradise; he is suffering from hunger; he is shivering with cold!" Forthwith the grave would be opened, and the offering repeated. This was generally successful.

THE FIJI ISLANDERS present most costly sacrifices. Their chiefs have from twenty to a hundred wives, according to their rank. At the interment of a principal chief, the body is laid in state upon a spacious lawn, in the presence of an immense concourse of spectators. The principal wife, after the utmost ingenuity of the natives has been exercised in adorning her person, then walks out, and takes her seat near the body of her husband. A rope is passed round her neck, which eight or ten powerful men pull with all their strength, until she is strangled, and dies. Her body is then laid by that of the chief. In this manner four wives are sacrificed, and all of them are then interred in a common grave, one above, one below, and one on either side of the husband. This is done, that the spirit of the chief may not be lonely in its passage to the invisible world; and that, by such an offering, its happiness may be at once secured.—*Burder.*

OTAHEITE.

About this time died an old woman of some rank, who was related to Tomir, which gave us an opportunity to see how they disposed of the body, and confirmed us in our opinion that these people, contrary to the present custom of all other nations now known, never bury their dead. In the middle of a small square, neatly railed in with bamboo, the awning of a canoe was raised upon two posts, and under this the body was deposited upon a frame; it was covered with fine cloth, and near it was placed bread-fruit, fish, and other provisions; we suppose that the food was placed there for the spirit of the deceased, and, consequently, that these Indians had some confused notion of a separate state; but upon our applying for further information to Tubourai Tamaide, he told us that the food was placed there as an offering to their gods. They do not, however, suppose that the gods eat, any more than the Jews suppose that Jehovah could dwell in a house: the offering is made here on the same principle as the Temple was built at Jerusalem, as an expression of reverence and gratitude, and a solicitation of the more immediate presence of the Deity. In the front of the area was a kind of stile, where the relations of the deceased stood to pay the tribute of their sorrow; and under the awning were innumerable small pieces of cloth, on which the tears and blood of the mourners had been shed; for, in their paroxysms of grief it is a universal custom to wound themselves with the shark's tooth. Within a few yards two occasional houses were set up, in one of which some relations of the deceased constantly resided, and in the other the chief mourner, who is always a man, and who keeps there a very singular dress, in which a ceremony is performed. Near the place where the dead are thus set up to rot, the bones are afterwards buried.

What can have introduced among these people the custom of exposing their dead above ground till the flesh is consumed by putrefaction, and then burying the bones, it is, perhaps, impossible to guess; but it is remarkable, that Ælian and Apollonius Rhodius impute a similar practice to the ancient inhabitants of Colchis, a country near Pontus, in Asia, now called Mingrelia; except that among them this manner of disposing of the dead did not extend to both sexes: the women they buried; but the men they wrapped in a hide, and hung up in the air by a chain. This practice among the Colchians is referred to a religious cause. The principal objects of their worship were the earth and the air; and it is supposed that in consequence of some superstitious notion, they devoted their dead to both. Whether the natives of Otaheite had any notion of the same kind, we were never able certainly to determine; but we soon discovered, that the repositories of their dead were also places of worship. Upon this occasion it may be observed, that nothing can be more absurd than the notion that the happiness or misery of a future life depends, in any degree, upon the disposition of the body when the state of probation is past; yet that nothing is more general than a solicitude about it. However cheap we may hold any funeral rites which custom has not familiarised, or superstition rendered sacred, most men gravely deliberate how to prevent their body from being broken by the mattock and devoured by the worm when it is no longer capable of sensation; and purchase a place for it in holy ground when they believe the lot of its future existence to be irrevocably determined. So strong is the association of pleasing or painful ideas with certain opinions and actions which affect us while we live, that we involuntarily act as if it was equally certain that they would affect us in the same manner when we are dead, though this is an opinion that nobody will maintain. Thus it happens, that the desire of preserving from reproach even the name that we leave behind us, or of procuring it honour, is one of the most powerful principles of action among the inhabitants of the most speculative and enlightened nations. Posthumous reputation, upon every principle, must be acknowledged to have no influence upon the dead; yet the desire of obtaining and securing it, no force of reason, no habits of thinking can subdue, except in those whom habitual baseness and guilt have rendered indifferent to honour and shame while they lived. This, indeed, seems to be among the happy imperfections of our nature, upon which the general good of society in a certain measure depends; for as some crimes are supposed to be prevented by hanging the body of the criminal in chains after he is dead, so in consequence of the same association of ideas, much good is procured to society, and much evil prevented, by a desire of preventing disgrace or procuring honour to a name, when nothing but a name remains.

Perhaps no better use can be made of reading an account of manners altogether new, by which the follies and absurdities of mankind are taken out of that particular connection in which habit has reconciled them to us, than to consider in how many instances they are essentially the same. When an honest devotee of the Church of Rome reads, that there are Indians on the banks of the Ganges who believe that they shall secure the happiness of a future state by dying with a cow's tail in their hands, he laughs at their folly and superstition; and if these Indians were to be told, that there are people on the continent of Europe who imagine that they shall derive the same advantage from dying with the slipper of St. Francis upon their foot, they would laugh in their turn. But if, when the Indian heard the account of the Catholic and the Catholic that of the Indian, each was to reflect that there was no difference between the absurdity of the slipper and of the tail, but that the veil of prejudice and custom, which covered it in their own case, was withdrawn in the other, they would turn their knowledge to a profitable purpose.—*Captain Cook's First Voyage.*

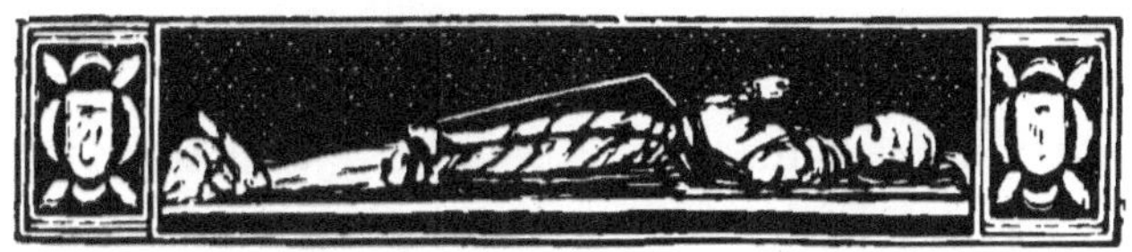

PART II.

MOURNING COSTUME IN VARIOUS NATIONS.

Wearing mourning is one of the most ancient customs in the history of the world. Abraham mourned for Sarah, Isaac for his father, the Egyptians, for Jacob, threescore and ten days, and the Children of Israel, for Moses and Aaron, thirty days. In most European Countries, black is deemed the most appropriate colour. This was also the colour in vogue in most of the ancient Greek States. The Romans and Spartans wore white (as do the Chinese), emblematical of their friends being in Paradise, clad in robes of pure white. This accords with many of the passages in the Book of the Revelation of St. John. At the marriage of the Lamb, to the Wife it was granted that she should be "arrayed in fine linen, clean and *white;* for the fine linen is the righteousness of Saints," c. xix. 8. "He that overcometh, the same shall be clothed in white raiment," c. iii. 5. White robes were given to "the souls of those who were slain for the word of God, and for the testimony which they held," c. vi. 9-11, and the "great multitude, which no man could number," that stood before the throne, and came out of great tribulation, had "washed their robes, and made them *white* in the blood of the Lamb," c. vii. 9-14. The Egyptians wear yellow, in allusion to the fall and decay of the leaf. The Ethiopian colour is brown, symbolising the return of the body to its native brown earth. The Peruvians, at the time of the Spanish conquest, mourned in mouse coloured attire. The Turks wear violet, in allusion to that early spring flower, or hope on one side, and sorrow on the other. The French kings also wore violet, as did formerly the sovereigns of England, but who, till recently, mourned in purple. The Pacific Islanders wear grey, implying that grey hairs go down to the grave in sorrow. In Poland, when a woman of rank mourns, she wears a coarse black stuff; and the higher the rank of the deceased, the coarser are the mourning weeds. In Spain, a widow passed the first year of mourning in a chamber hung with black, and from which daylight was entirely excluded. At the expiration of that time, she removed to a chamber hung with grey, occasionally enlivened by a sunbeam. After the execution of Charles the First, many of the royalists suffered their beards to grow, without being cut, for the remainder of their lives. When a Japanese monarch dies, fifteen or twenty of his subjects, to show their loyalty, rip themselves open, and follow him to the other world; he who inflicts upon himself the deepest wound, acquiring the greatest glory.

MOURNING ON THE DEATH OF THE KING OF SERINDIB.

In the Isle of Serindib, when the king dies, his body is placed upon a chariot in such a situation, that, being laid back, his head hangs down to the ground and his hair drags in the dust. The chariot is followed by a woman, who with a besom casts dust upon the head of the corpse. At the same time proclamation is made with a loud voice, "O men, behold your king! he was your master yesterday; but the empire which he possessed over you is now past away. He is reduced to the state in which you now behold him, having quitted the world, and the Dispenser of death has summoned his soul. Depend not upon the uncertain hopes of life." During three days this cry is made, and others of a like import; after which time the body is embalmed with sandal wood, camphire and saffron; it is then burnt, and the ashes scattered to the wind.—*Ancienne Relations des Indes et de la Chine, Paris*, 1718.

FUNERALS SOLEMNIZED WITHIN THE CHURCH PORCH.

Audry, who died of the pestilence in 669, and Chad, who did not outlive the year 672, with others of that era, of extraordinary reputed sanctity, being anxious to creep near the church, were the first placed there. There is an old legend that St. Swithin's corpse not being allowed to enter the Church, was placed in the porch, where it remained forty days, during which time it rained incessantly. This account agrees in some measure with the Latin legend which William of Malmesbury has given us as a proof of St. Swithin's great humility. "For when he was about to bid farewell to this life, he gave orders to be buried outside the church, exposed to the rain dropping from the skies, and the treading of the passers by," and so he continued for some time; but the ecclesiastics, not liking that a person of his sanctity should be exposed, dug him up, when it is possible that, agreeably to his desire to be buried outside the church, they placed him in the porch.

There are the following curious items in the Church-wardens' Accounts of Banwell, Somersetshire:—"1521. Recd. of Robert Cabell, for lying of his wyffe in the *porch*, 3s. 4d.   Recd. of Robert Blundon, for lying of his wyffe in the church, 6s. 8d."   So that the fee was twice as much for burying in the church as in the porch.

FUNERAL OF HECTOR.

The Trojan train
Their mules and oxen harness to the wain,
Pour through their gates, and fell'd from Ida's crown,
Roll back the gather'd forests to the town.

These toils continued nine succeeding days,
And high in air a sylvan structure raise.
But when the tenth fair morn began to shine,
Forth to the pile was borne the man divine
And plac'd aloft: while all, with streaming eyes,
Beheld the flames and rolling smokes arise.
Soon as Aurora, daughter of the dawn,
With rosy lustre streak'd the dewy lawn,
Again the mournful crowds surround the pyre,
And quench with wine the yet remaining fire.
The snowy bones his friends and brothers place
(With tears collected) in a golden vase;
The golden vase in purple palls they roll'd,
Of softest texture, and inwrought with gold.
Last o'er the urn the sacred earth they spread
And raised the tomb, memorial of the dead
(Strong guards and spies, till all the rites were done,
Watch'd from the rising to the setting sun).
All Troy then moves to Priam's court again,
A solemn, silent, melancholy train;
Assembled there, from pious toil they rest,
And sadly shar'd the last sepulchral feast.
Such honours Ilion to her hero paid,
And peaceful slept the mighty Hector's shade.

Pope's Homer's Iliad.

THE FUNERAL OF ALEXANDER THE GREAT.

Ante J. C. 321.—Much about this time the funeral

obsequies of Alexander were performed.   Aridœus having been deputed by all the governors and grandees of the kingdom to take upon himself the care of that solemnity, had employed two years in preparing every thing that could possibly render it the most pompous and splendid funeral that had ever been seen.   When all things were ready for the celebration of this mournful but superb ceremonial, orders were given for the procession to begin.   This was preceded by a great number of pioneers and other workmen, whose office was to make all the ways practicable through which the procession was to pass. As soon as these were levelled, that magnificent chariot, the invention and design of which raised as much admiration as the immense riches that glittered all over it, set out from Babylon.   The body of the chariot rested upon two axletrees, that were inserted into four wheels, made after the Persian manner, the naves and spokes of which were covered with gold, and the felloes plated over with iron.   The extremities of the axletrees were made of gold, representing the muzzles of lions biting a dart.   The chariot had four poles, to each of which were harnessed four sets of mules, each set consisting of four of those animals; so that this chariot was drawn by sixty-four mules.   The strongest of those creatures, and the largest, were chosen on this occasion.   They were adorned with crowns of gold, and collars enriched with precious stones and golden bells. On this chariot was erected a pavilion of entire gold, twelve feet wide and eighteen in length, supported by columns of the Ionic order, embellished with the leaves of acanthus. The inside was adorned with jewels, disposed in the forms of shells. The circumference was beautified with a fringe of golden net work: the threads that compassed the texture were an inch in thickness, and to these were fastened large bells, whose sound was heard to a great distance. The external decorations consisted of four groups in basso relievo. The first represented Alexander seated in a military chariot, with a splendid sceptre in his hand, and surrounded on one side with a troop of Macedonians in arms; and the other, with an equal number of Persians armed in their own manner. These were preceded by the king's equerries. In the second were seen elephants completely har-nessed, with a band of Indians seated on the forepart of their bodies; and on their hinder another band of Macedonians, armed as in the day of battle. The third exhibited to the view several squadrons of horse arranged in military array. The fourth represented ships preparing for a battle. At the entrance into the pavilion were golden lions, that seemed to guard the passage. The four corners were adorned with statues of massy gold, representing victories, with trophies of arms in their hands. Under the pavilion was placed a throne of gold of a square form, adorned with the heads of animals, whose necks were encompassed with circlets of gold a foot and a half in breadth; to these were hung crowns that glittered with the liveliest colours, such as were carried in procession at the celebration of sacred solemnities. At the foot of the throne was placed the coffin of Alexander, formed of beaten gold, and half filled with aromatic spices and perfumes, as well to exhale an agreeable odour, as for the preservation of the corpse. A pall of purple, brocaded with gold, covered the coffin. Between this and the throne, the arms of that monarch were disposed in the manner he wore them when living. The outside of the pavilion was likewise covered with purple flowered with gold. The top ended in a very large crown of the same metal, which seemed to be a composition of olive-branches. The beams of the sun which darted on this diadem, in conjunction with the motion of the chariot, caused it to emit a kind of rays like those of lightning. It may easily be imagined, that in so long a procession, the motion of a chariot, laden like this, would be liable to great inconveniences. In order, therefore, that the pavilion, with all its appendages, might, when the chariot moved in any uneven ways, constantly continue in the same situation, notwithstanding the inequality of the ground and the shocks that would be frequently unavoidable, a cylinder was raised from the middle of each axletree, to support the pavilion; by which expedient the whole machine was preserved steady.   The chariot was followed by the royal guards, all in arms, and magnificently arrayed.   The multitude of spectators in this solemnity is hardly credible; but they were drawn together as well by their veneration for the memory of Alexander, as by the magnificence of this funeral pomp, which had never been equalled in the world.   There was a current prediction, that the place where Alexander should be interred would be rendered the most happy and flourishing part of the earth. The governors contested with each other for the disposal of a body that was to be attended with such a glorious prerogative.   The affection Perdiccas entertained for his country, made him desirous that the corpse should be conveyed to Ægæ in Macedonia, where the remains of its kings were usually deposited. Other places were likewise proposed, but the preference was given to Egypt.   Ptolemy, who had such extraordinary and recent obligations to the king of Macœdonia, was determined to signalise his gratitude on this occasion.   He accordingly set out with a numerous guard of his best troops, in order to meet the procession, and advanced as far as Syria.   When he had joined the attendants on the funeral, he prevented them from interring the corpse in the temple of Jupiter Ammon, as they had proposed.   It was therefore deposited first in the City of Memphis, and from thence was conveyed to Alexandria.

Ptolemy raised a magnificent temple to the memory of this monarch, and rendered him all the honours which were usually paid to demi-gods and heroes by Pagan antiquity.—*Rollin.*

THE LEGEND OF ST. CUTHBERT.

St. Cuthbert died in the Farne Islands, and his body was brought to Lindisfarne, where it remained until a descent of the Danes about 763, when the monks fled to Scotland, with his reliques: they paraded him through Scotland for several years, and came as far west as Whithorn in Galloway, whence they attempted to sail for Ireland, but were driven back by tempests. He at length made a halt at Norham; thence he went to Melrose, where he remained stationary for a short time, and then caused himself to be launched upon the Tweed in a stone coffin, which landed him at Tillmouth in Northumberland. From Tillmouth, Cuthbert wandered into Yorkshire; and at length made a long stay at Chester le Street, to which the Bishop's See was transferred. At length, the Danes continuing to infest the country, the monks removed to Ripon for a season; and it was in return from thence to Chester le Street, that passing through a forest called Dunholme, the Saint and his carriage became immovable at a place named Wardlaw, or Wardilaw. The Saint, we are told, appeared in a vision to Alfred, when lurking in the marshes of

Glastonbury, and promised him assistance and victory over his heathen enemies. As to William the Conqueror, having intimated an indiscreet curiosity to view the Saint's body, he was, while in the act of commanding the shrine to be opened, seized with heat, sickness, and such a panic terror, that he fled, and never drew bridle till he got to the River Tees. St. Cuthbert, since his death, has acquired the reputation of forging those *Entrochi* which are found among the rocks of Holy Island, and pass there by the name of St. Cuthbert's beads. While at this task he is supposed to sit during the night upon a certain rock, and use another for his anvil.—*Notes to "Marmion," Canto II.*

A ROMAN BURIAL AT YORK.

At the monthly meeting of the Newcastle Society of Antiquaries, Mr. R. Carr-Ellison presiding, the following paper was read by Dr. Bruce:—I have been directed by the Rev. Canon Raine of York to present to the society a photograph of the back hair of a young Roman lady, who, judging from a coin which was lying under her coffin, and the style of the coffin itself, probably lived about the time of Constantine. The hair is of an auburn colour; after being slightly twisted, it had been laid in a circular form on the back of her head, and secured in position by two jet pins of two or three inches long. The heads of the pins are neatly ornamented. I have here a small lock of the hair, which, however, was not connected with the main mass. When first discovered the hair was darker than it now is, in consequence probably of its being in a damp condition. The hair is that of a young lady of about fifteen years of age. It is curious how the sight of a simple and inanimate object like this brings near far distant ages, and sets vividly before us scenes long past. Though fifteen or sixteen centuries have rolled away since this young lady breathed our air, we fancy we see her in the flush of her early youth, adorning her locks, and admiring the charms with which she was endowed. It seems so strange that she and the youths who sought her society should express their merry thoughts in the words which Tacitus and Terence used. We can fancy, too, that she was not a stranger to the Celtic tongue. The slaves of her father's household were probably the inhabitants of the land. Her nurse would most likely be a native Briton, and with her she would converse in the tongue of our Celtic forefathers. Sickness seizes her; how would her bright eyes be clouded; how would her parents' breast swell with deep anxiety. The healing truths of the gospel had been brought to our island long before her time. Had she heard them? Had she received them? And before she closed her eyes in death were they brightened up by the blissful apprehension of coming glory? I looked upon her empty eye-sockets, but could get no answer to my question. Being much interested in this strange specimen of Roman humanity, I went to York the other day to see it. Canon Raine kindly accompanied me to the museum, and supplied me with much information respecting the recent discoveries in that city, which was during several centuries the stronghold of Roman power in the North of England. The results of my inquiries I shall endeavour to convey to you. The facts, so far as they are correctly told, are Mr. Raine's; should I fall into any mis-statements, these are my own. In digging the foundations for the walls of the new station at York, it was found that the site had in Roman days formed a large burial ground outside the walls of the city. Very many ancient graves were disturbed, in which were found numerous articles of great interest and beauty which had been interred with the deceased. Little children had their pretty necklaces round their bony throats, their toys were by their sides; women still wore their rings and their splendidly carved jet armlets; numerous vessels of glass and earthenware of peculiar patterns and exquisite workmanship were enclosed in the coffins. In some of these vessels were the remains of unguents, which, on being treated with hot water, gave forth powerful and fragrant odours. As the ground was disturbed only in places where the walls of the building are being reared, it may be conceived what a mass of treasure remains behind, unseen, unmoved. The coffin of the young lady whose hair I have shown you was found under one of the walls of the new booking office. The number of interments which have from time to time been discovered at York is quite extraordinary. They amount on a rough calculation to about three thousand. Other large graveyards have been found beside the one I have been speaking of, and on the sides of some of the roads leading out of York tombs have been planted for a considerable distance on each side of them. The place must have been very populous. One extraordinary fact has come under Mr. Raine's notice during the recent excavations. It is well known that at Rome the dead bodies of slaves and of obscure persons who had no one to care for them, were cast without covering into old quarries and sand pits; there they were left to decay, to the great annoyance and injury of the living who occupied the neighbourhood. Horace tells us of one of these *puteoli* on the Esquiline Hill, which was acquired by Mecænas, who turned it into a garden. Mr. Raine noticed one or two pits at York which had been filled with human bodies promiscuously thrown in; some of the skeletons had the feet uppermost. It is humbling to think that such things should have taken place in this land of ours, even sixteen hundred years ago.

Amongst so many graves numerous skulls have been found, many of them in a perfect state. There is a noble collection of them in one of the underground chambers of the Museum. Most of them have a fine intellectual development; one of them has been pronounced by Professor Rolleston to be the finest he had ever seen. Several specimens of the fir-cone ornament have been found in the burial ground. These, as I have elsewhere endeavoured to show, are supposed to be emblematic of a resuscitated existence. We now return to our own young lady. Her remains were enclosed externally in a large stone coffin, formed of a rough sandstone, resembling mill stone grit, very roughly carved, and destitute of inscription or ornament. This, as well as most of the coffins, if I remember rightly, was lying south and north. Within the stone coffin was another of lead, which contained the body. The lead of this coffin has been cast in sheets and not rolled. The lid was tightly fastened to the coffin; it had to be forced off by violence. We shall presently return to this subject. The lid of the lead coffin bore a simple ornament. It was divided into three compartments by an upright line representing a slender twig, round which was loosely twisted a fillet of ribbon. These compartments were occupied by two similar lines, crossing each other in the centre and terminating in the angles of the compartments. There was no inscription.

The body seems to have been deposited in its resting-place in the following manner.   After being enveloped in some coarse cloth, a quantity of fluid plaster of Paris was poured into the coffin, in the midst of which, whilst still soft, the body was laid; after which the rest of the coffin was filled in with more plaster of Paris.   In this particular case it seems as if the head had been made to repose upon a pillow so that it rose above the gypsum which entirely covered the rest of the young lady's person.   On opening the coffin the jaws, the bones of the face, and the frontal bones of the skull were found to have fallen forward, and were seen resting upon the covering of gypsum; the back hair being deprived of its bony support, had also fallen down, and was resting in the place where these bones should have been.   One other singular circumstance is yet to be named.   The lid of the stone coffin was found to be cracked not far from its middle; immediately under this crack, and in the lid of the leaden shell, was a round jagged hole of about the size of your fist; a corresponding hollow penetrated the gypsum, and the bottom of the stone coffin was cracked.   What had caused these appearances?   Possibly after death had done his worst by this young lady her narrow house had been stricken by the lightning's flash, or, to carry out the figure more correctly, by a thunderbolt.   No other probable solution of the difficulty has been suggested.   Before leaving our young lady I must mention that there is a record of hair having been found upon the head of another Roman subject found in York, but it has long been lost sight of. These, so far as I can learn, are the only known instances. Roman antiquaries are but slowly awakening to the fact that the Romans used leaden cases in the burial of their dead. At the present moment there are not less than twelve leaden coffins in the Museum at York, all derived from the graveyards of the city. If my memory does not deceive me, the late Mr. Denham of Pierse Bridge met with a leaden coffin in a Roman burying-ground near that station. In 1844 a leaden coffin was found on the site of a Roman burial place at Stratford-le-Bow. The coffin had been run in with lime. Mr. Roach Smith published an account of it in the "Archæologia," voL xxxi., p. 308. In that gentleman's "Collectanea Antidua," vol. iii., is a record of the finding of many others, from which I make a few extracts. "In 1739 a leaden coffin was ploughed up near Stilton, with Roman coins and a cinerary urn. At Colchester several Roman leaden coffins have been found from time to time, consisting each of two pieces of lead. At Southfleet, in Kent, in 1801, was found a tomb of stone, covered with two very large stones. The tomb contained two leaden coffins of the most simple construction; the bottom pieces being turned up, formed the sides of each, and the top pieces being turned down at each end and a little over at the sides, formed the tops and ends of the coffins." In London several cases have occurred besides that at Stratford-le-Bow already mentioned. In 1811, one was dug up in the Old Kent Road. On the lid were two figures of Minerva. In 1844, a small leaden coffin, containing the remains of a child, was found in Mansell Street, Whitechapel. Several foreign examples are on record. Near the village of Savigny-sous-Beaune a leaden coffin was found in 1819. Other interments of the ordinary character had taken place near it, amongst which were four jet pins worked in facets, and twelve small brass coins of Maximinus, Constans, and Constantius II. In 1828 two leaden coffins were found at Rouen; one contained a coin of Postumus, the other, which was that of a child, contained the playthings of the deceased and four Roman coins, the effigies on which could not be determined. In 1835 one was found at Evreux; it inclosed a coin of Constantine. Others have been found near Nismes and at Amiens. Mr. Roach Smith, in a letter which I had from him the other day, says, "I could cite some fifty or sixty examples, the latest being one at Ilchester." A question occurs to me in reference to these leaden coffins which I find it difficult to answer. What end had the Romans in view in making use of them? We employ them in order hermetically to

seal up the dead. So far as I have observed the
Roman coffins were not air tight. Some of those
at York have been very clumsily put together. In
every case the lead has been cast, and the sheets are
thick and heavy. In some cases the pieces of which
the coffin is composed are nailed together. In one
instance the lead has been held in position by being
nailed to a strong external covering of wood, and this
in turn has been strongly braced together by bars
of iron. In the case of our young lady, Mr. Raine
thinks the lid of the coffin was fastened on with
cement. I may be wrong, but I do not think that
the Romans used solder. Their leaden pipes were
formed of long, flat strips of metal, twisted into shape
and fastened at the edges. The fastening, so far as
I have observed, was not effected by the intervention
of easily fusible metal such as our solder. A jet of
ignited hydrogen gas made to play upon the edges
would partially melt them, so as to allow of their
being brought into permanent union. In this way,
possibly, the Roman pipes were formed. The process,
however, is one which could not easily be applied to
coffins. If the object had been simply to provide an
imperishable ark in which to deposit the precious
remains of the departed one, why not rest satisfied
with a stone sarcophagus? In the instance before us,
both stone and lead were used. Perhaps it was to
make security doubly secure. And yet, after all, in

this particular case, the effort was vain; first of all, the lightning invaded the carefully guarded precinct, and then the modern navvy fairly bore the whole away. We are much obliged to the navvy for the information which he has afforded us.

FUNERAL OF ELEANORA OF CASTILE, QUEEN OF EDWARD THE FIRST.

Edward had not entered Scotland when the fatal news reached him that Eleanora, the faithful companion of his life, in travelling through Lincolnshire to join him previously to his entering Scotland, had been seized with an autumnal fever at Herdby, near Grantham. It seems, by existing documents, that the queen's illness was lingering, but did not take a fatal character until a few days before the king was summoned. Ambition, at the strong call of conjugal love, for once released its grasp on the mighty heart of Edward. In comparison with Eleanora, dead or dying, the coveted crown of Scotland was nothing in his estimation. He turned southward instantly when the fatal news of her danger reached him; but though he travelled with the utmost speed, he arrived too late to see her living once more. His admirable queen had expired, November 29th, 1290, at the house of a gentleman named Weston. She died, according to our calculation, in the forty-seventh year of her age.

The whole affairs of Scotland, however pressing they might be, were obliterated for a time from the mind of the great Edward, by the acute sorrow he suffered for the death of Eleanora; nor, till he had paid the duties he considered due to her breathless clay, would he attend to the slightest temporal business. In the bitterest grief he followed her corpse in person, during thirteen days, in the progress of the royal funeral from Grantham to Westminster.   At the end of every stage the royal bier rested, surrounded by its attendants, in some central part of a great town, till the neighbouring ecclesiastics came to meet it in solemn procession, and to place it before the high altar of the principal church.   At every one of these resting-places the royal mourner vowed to erect a cross in memory of the *chère reine*, as he passionately called his lost Eleanora.   Thirteen of these splendid monuments of his affection once existed; those of Northampton and Waltham still remain, models of architectural beauty. *

The ceremony of making the sites for these crosses is thus described by the chronicler of Dunstable:

* The places where the body remained for the night have been numbered at fifteen, but probably only twelve of the so-called Eleanora's crosses were erected, namely, Lincoln, Grantham, Stamford, Geddington, Northampton, Stony-Stratford, Woburn, Dunstable, St. Albans, Waltham, Westcheep, and Charing.— *Editor.*

"Her body passed through Dunstable and rested one night, and two precious cloths were given us, and eighty pounds of wax. And when the body of the queen was departing from Dunstable, her bier rested in the centre of the market-place, till the king's chancellor and the great men then and there present had marked a fitting place where they might afterwards erect, at the royal expense, a cross of wonderful size,—our prior being there present, and sprinkling holy water."

The principal citizens of London, with their magistrates, came several miles on the north road, clad in black hoods and mourning cloaks, to meet the royal corpse and join the solemn procession. The hearse rested, previously to its admission into Westminster Abbey, at the spot now occupied by the statue of Charles I., which commanded a grand view of the Abbey, the hall, and palace of Westminster. The king, in his letter to the abbot of Cluny, desires prayers for the soul of her "whom living he loved, and whom dead he shall never cease to love." Yet, as the great expenses of crosses erected, her funeral, and her beautiful tomb and statue, were paid by her executors, there is some reason to suppose her own funds discharged the costs. It is needful to explain the use of these crosses: they were places of the field or out-door preaching of the ancient church; likewise, sustenance for the poor was distributed from them,

according to the means of several endowments.
They buried queen Eleanora at the feet of her
father-in-law, December 10th, 1290. Her heart was
enclosed in an urn, and deposited in the church of
the Black Friars, London: round it a rich picture
was painted or enamelled. Her elegant statue,
reclining on an altar-shaped tomb, was cast in bronze
by an artist patronized by Henry III. and Edward I.
He was supposed to be the celebrated Pietro Caval-
lini, but his name is now certified as Master William
Torch, a native statuary. He built his furnace to
cast the queen's statue in St. Margaret's churchyard.
The nine beautiful crosses were erected by artists
who were of English descent. As to Torch, he
certainly produced a work of which any modern
artist might be justly proud. We feel, while gazing
upon it, that it possesses all the reality of individual
resemblance. The countenance of Eleanora is
serenely smiling; the delicate features are perfect,
both in form and expression. The right hand held
a sceptre, now broken away; the left is closed
over something pendant from the neck by a string,
supposed to be a crucifix, likewise destroyed. Her
head is crowned with a magnificent circlet, from
which her hair falls in elegant waves on her shoulders.
The queen of Edward I. must have been a model of
feminine beauty. No wonder that the united influence
of loveliness, virtue and sweet temper should have

inspired in the heart of her renowned lord an attachment so deep and true.—*Strickland's Lives of the Queens of England.*

JOHN OF GAUNT.

He directed that his body be kept above ground 40 days, and on each day 40 marks of silver distributed to the poor, on the eve of burial 300, and on day of burial. His will also contains the following clause :—" Item. I desire to be burnt round my body on the day of my burial—first, ten great tapers in the name of the 10 commandments of our Lord, which I have too wickedly transgressed; and besides these 10, that there be placed 7 great tapers in memory of the 7 works of charity which I have neglected, and for the 7 mortal sins: I will that there be 5 great tapers in honour of the 5 principal wounds of our Lord Jesus, and for my 5 senses which I have very negligently wasted, for which I pray God's mercy; and, in addition to all the aforesaid tapers, I will there be 3 in honour of the blessed Trinity." Died 1399.

CHEERFUL FUNERAL.

Lodovick Cortusius, an eminent lawyer, who died at Padua on the 15th of July, 1518, when upon his death-bed forbad his relations to shed tears at his funeral, and even put his heir under a heavy penalty if he neglected to perform his orders. On the other hand, he ordered musicians, singers, pipers, and fiddlers, of all kinds, to supply the place of mourners, and directed that fifty of them should walk before his corpse with the clergymen, playing upon their several instruments; for this service he ordered each of them half a ducat. He likewise appointed twelve maids in green habits to carry his corpse to the church of St. Sophia, where he was buried, and that they too as they went along should sing aloud, having each of them, as a recompense, a handsome sum of money allotted for a portion. All the clergy of Padua marched before in long procession, together with all the monks of the convent, except those wearing black habits, whom he expressly excluded by his will, lest the blackness of their hoods should throw a gloom upon the cheerfulness of the procession.

"SERAPHIC INTERMENT."

1535. Albert Pio, prince of Carpi, was buried with extraordinary pomp in the church of the Cordeliers at Paris. He had been deprived of his principality by the duke of Ferara, became an author, and finally a fanatic. Entering one day into one of the churches at Madrid, he presented holy water to a lady who had a very thin hand ornamented by a most beautiful and valuable ring. He exclaimed in a loud voice as she reached the water, "Madam, I admire the ring more than the hand." The lady instantly exclaimed with reference to the cordon with which he was decorated, "And for my part, I admire the halter more than I do the ass." He was buried in the habit of a Cordelier, and Erasmus made a satire upon the circumstance, entitled the "Seraphic Interment."

DEATH BELLS.

An old homily for Trinity Sunday declares that the form of the Trinity was found in man: that Adam, our forefather of the earth, was the first person; that Eve, of Adam, was the second person; and that of them both was the third person: further, that at the death of a man three bells were to be rung as his knell in worship of the Trinity, and two bells for a woman, as the second person of the Trinity.—*Hone on Ancient Mysteries.*

CHARLES THE FIFTH CELEBRATING HIS OWN FUNERAL.

A short time before his death he resolved to celebrate his own obsequies. He ordered his tomb to be erected in the Chapel of the Monastery. His domestics marched thither in funeral procession, with black tapers in their hands. He himself followed in his shroud. He was laid in his coffin with much solemnity. The service for the dead was chanted, and Charles joined in the prayers which were offered up for the rest of his soul, mingling his tears with those which his attendants shed, as if they had been celebrating a real funeral. The ceremony closed with sprinkling holy water on the coffin in the usual form, and all the assistants retiring, the doors of the chapel were shut. Then Charles rose out of his coffin, and withdrew to his apartments, full of those awful sentiments, which such a singular solemnity was calculated to inspire. Died 21st Sept., 1558.—*Robertson.*

LORD EDWARD BRUCE

Was killed in a duel in 1613. His body was interred at Bergen, in Holland; where he died: and a monument was there erected to his memory. The tradition long handed down in the family was, that his heart had been conveyed to Scotland, and deposited in the burial ground adjoining the old Abbey Church of Culross in Perthshire. But this being at length discredited as simply a legendary tale, in 1806, in order to settle the matter, a search was made. Two flat stones, strongly clasped together with iron, were discovered about two feet beneath the level of the pavement, and partly under an old projection in the wall. These stones had on them no inscription, but the singularity of their being thus braced together, induced the searchers to separate them; when a silver case shaped like a heart, was found in a cavity between the stones. The case, which was engraved with the arms and name of Lord Edward Bruce, had hinges and clasps: on being opened, it was found to contain a heart carefully embalmed in a brownishly coloured liquid. After drawings of it had been taken it was carefully restored to its former position. In another cavity was a small leaden box, which had probably contained some other portion of his body; but, if so, they had become resolved into dust.

THE REV. DR. DONNE AND HIS EFFIGY.

This Divine, who was formerly Dean of St. Paul's, among other preparations for his death, ordered an urn to be cut in wood, on which was to be placed a board, of the exact height of his body. He then caused himself to be tied up in a winding-sheet. Thus shrouded, and standing with his eyes shut, and with just so much of the sheet put aside, as might discover his death-like face, he caused his portrait to be taken, which, when finished, was placed near his bedside, and there remained to the hour of his death, March 31, 1631. He was buried in St. Paul's Cathedral, where a monument was erected over him, composed of white marble, and carved from the above-mentioned picture, by order of his dearest friend and executor, Dr. King, Bishop of Chichester.

BURIALS DURING THE PLAGUE OF LONDON, 1665.

The number of burials in London in this eventful year, according to the Bills of Mortality, amounted to no less than 97,306, of which 68,596 were of persons who died of the plague. But this number was considered by many authorities living at the time, to be considerably under the mark. Lord Clarendon says, " The frequent deaths of the Clerks and Sextons of Parishes, hindered the exact account of every week; but that which left it without any certainty, was the vast number that was buried in the fields, of which no account was kept. Then, of the Anabaptists and other Sectaries, who abounded in the City, very few left their habitations; and multitudes of them died, whereof no churchwarden or other officer ·had notice; but they found burials according to their own fancies, in small gardens, or the next fields." Defoe is probably not exaggerating, in placing the number carried off by this awful scourge at 100,000. At the commencement of the plague, when the numbers who died were comparatively small, the burials took place in the ordinary churchyards, and the service read as usual. The following were the regulations made by the Lord Mayor and Aldermen:—" That the burial of the dead by this visitation be at most convenient hours, always either before sun-rising, or after sun-setting, with the privity of the Churchwardens or Constables, and not otherwise; and that no neighbours or friends be suffered to accompany the corpse to church, or to enter the house visited, upon pain of having his house shut up, or being imprisoned. And that no corpse dying of infection shall be buried or remain in any church in time of common prayer, sermon or lecture. And that no children be suffered at time of burial of any corpse in any church, churchyard, or burying-place, to come near the corpse, coffin or grave. And that all the graves shall be at least six feet deep. And farther, all public assemblies at other burials are to be forborne during the continuance of this visitation." As the numbers of the dead increased, the service was dispensed with, and tolling the bells ceased. Great pits were dug in the churchyards for the reception of the corpses; one in Aldgate was forty feet long, fifteen or sixteen feet broad, and in one part twenty feet deep. Into this pit, between the 6th and 20th September, 1,114 bodies were thrown, when it was obliged to be filled up, the bodies being within six feet of the surface. Into these pits some of the infected, in a state of delirium, threw themselves, and expired before any earth was thrown upon them. One large pit was in Finsbury, in the Parish of Cripplegate, then open to the fields. The authorities were soon compelled to provide new burial grounds in Bunhill Fields, in the neighbourhood of Goswell Street, in Shoreditch, at the end of Holywell Lane, at the upper end of Hand Alley, in Bishopsgate Street, which was then a green field, and lastly in Moorfields. When the plague was at its height, the nights were not long enough to bury the dead, which were collected in carts. Pepys, under date August the 12th, says, "The people die so, that now it seems they are fain to carry the dead to be buried by daylight, the nights not sufficing to do it in."

One word as to the meaning of the term "Bills of Mortality" may be inserted here. The Parish Registers in England for Births, Marriages and Deaths were commenced in 1538, in consequence of an injunction set forth in that year in the name of King Henry VIII., by the Lord Thomas Cromwell, his vicegerent in ecclesiastical matters; and the weekly *Bills of Mortality*, containing an account of Christenings as well as Burials, taken by the Company of Parish Clerks of London, had their rise, 21st December, 1592. In 1594 the particular or weekly account of both Christenings and Burials was first made public, as also was the general or yearly account. For a fuller account, the reader is referred to "Defoe's History of the Great Plague."

MIDNIGHT FUNERALS, 1667.

"When I think to ease myself at night, by sleep, as last night, about 11 or 12 o'clock, at a solemn funeral, the bells set out. That men should be such owls to keep five thousand people awake, with ringing a peal to him that does not hear it." [This passage is taken from Shadwell's " Sullen Lovers," from which it appears that midnight funerals were not uncommon at the above date.]

A QUAKER BURIED ERECT.

In Oliver Heywood's Register is the following entry:—" Oct. 28, 1684. Captain Taylor's wife, of Brighouse, buried in her garden, with head upwards, standing upright, by her husband, daughter, &c. Quakers."—*Watson's History of Halifax, p. 233.*

BISHOP SVEDBERG

(Father of the celebrated Emanuel Swedenborg) died 1735. So far back as 1718 he had written out precise directions for his funeral:—" There is to be no fuss made about my corpse: the Masters of Arts and the Clergy of the vicinity are to bear it from my house to the grave, and if they grow tired the parishioners will relieve them. The funeral will take place by daylight, so that there may be no need for flambeaux or torches; the funeral sermon will be taken from the text, 'I believe in the communion of Saints, the remission of sins, the resurrection of the body, and life everlasting. Amen.' Music and organ will be silent, and only the hymn 'I know I shall again arise' sung at the end. Meat and drink will be provided abundantly for the guests, and the remnants distributed among the poor of Asaka and Saranaka. The funeral memoirs written by myself will be read before the sermon."—*White's Life and Writings of Emanuel Swedenborg.*

DANCING ON HIS GRAVE.

The following curious entry is in the register of Lymington Church, under the year 1736 :—

"Samuel Baldwin, esq., sojourner in this parish, was *immersed*, without the Needles, *sans cérémonie,* May 20."

This was performed in consequence of an earnest wish the deceased had expressed, a little before his dissolution, in order to disappoint the intention of his wife, who had repeatedly assured him, in their domestic squabbles, (which were very frequent,) that if she survived him, she would revenge her conjugal sufferings, by dancing on his grave.

WATERY GRAVE.

The late Dr. Clarke mentions in his "Travels," that as he was "one day leaning out of the cabin window, by the side of an officer who was employed in fishing, the corpse of a man, newly sewed in a hammock, started half out of the water, and continued its course, with the current, towards the shore. Nothing could be more horrible: its head and shoulders were visible, turning first to one side, then to the other, with a solemn and awful movement, as if impressed with some dreadful secret of the deep, which, from its watery grave, it came upwards to reveal." Dr. Ferriar observes, that "in a certain stage of putrefaction, the bodies of persons which have been immersed in water, rise to the surface, and in deep water are supported in an erect posture, to the terror of uninstructed spectators. Menacing looks and gestures, and even words, are supplied by the affrighted imagination, with infinite facility, and referred to the horrible apparition." This is perfectly natural; and it is easy to imagine the excessive terror of extreme ignorance at such appearances.

MODE OF BURIAL IN THE BASTILE—EIGHTEENTH CENTURY.

As soon as the breath was out of the body, a notice was sent to the minister of the home department and the lieutenant-general of police. The king's commissary then visited the prison, to minute down the circumstances. This being done, orders were issued to inter the body. In the gloom of evening it was conveyed to the burying-ground of St. Paul's; two persons belonging to the Bastile attended it to sign the parish register; and the name under which the deceased was *entered*, and the description of the rank which he held, were fictitious, that all trace of him might be obliterated. Another register, containing his real name and station, was in truth kept at the Bastile, but it was almost inaccessible, a sight of it, for the purpose of making an extract, being never allowed, without a strict inquiry into the reason why the application was made.   His family and friends meanwhile remained in profound ignorance of his having been released from his troubles.   No mourning mother, wife, or child, followed his remains to their last abode; and even the poor consolation was denied them of knowing the spot where he reposed, that they might water it with their tears.   Thus, in death, as in life, oppression and malice triumphantly asserted their absolute dominion over the captives of the Bastile.— *History of the Bastile, Tegg's Edition.*

WIFE OF TWO HUSBANDS.

Account of the Earl of Roseberry's Son, and a Clergyman's Wife, in Essex.

In the Cambridge Journal of October, 1752, is the following Article:—

Extract of a Letter from Colchester, August 18.

"Perhaps you have heard that a chest was seized by the Custom-house officers, which was landed near this place about a fortnight ago: they took it for smuggled goods, though the person with it produced the king of France's signature to Mr. Williams, as a Hamburgh merchant: but people not satisfied with the account Mr. Williams gave, opened the chest, and one of them was going to run his hanger in, when the person to whom it belonged clapt his hand upon his sword, and desired him to desist (in French), for it was the corpse of his dear wife. Not content with this, the officers plucked off the embalming, and found it as he had said. The man, who appeared to be a person of consequence, was in the utmost agonies, while they made a spectacle of the lady. They sat her in the high church, where anybody might come and look on her, and would not suffer him to bury her, till he gave a further account of himself. There were other chests of fine clothes, jewels, &c., &c., belonging to the deceased. He acknowledged at last that he was a person of quality, that his name was not Williams, that he was born at Florence, and the lady was a native of England, whom he married, and she desired to be buried in Essex: that he had brought her from Verona, in Italy, to France, by land, there hired a vessel for Dover, discharged the vessel there, and took another for Harwich, but was drove hither by contrary winds. This account was not enough to satisfy the people: he must tell her name and condition, in order to clear himself of a suspicion of murder. He was continually in tears, and had a key of the vestry, where he sat every day with the corpse: my brother went to see him there, and the scene so shocked him he could hardly bear it, he said it was so like Romeo and Juliet.

"He was much pleased with my brother, as he talked both Latin and French, and to his great surprise, told him who the lady was: which proving to be a person he knew, he could not help uncovering the face. In short, the gentleman confessed he was the Earl of Roseberry's son, (the name is Primrose,) and his title Lord Delamere, [Dalmeny,] that he was born and educated in Italy, and never was in England till two or three years ago, when he came to London, and was in company with this lady, with whom he fell passionately in love, and prevailed on her to quit the kingdom, and marry him: that having bad health, he had travelled with her all over Europe; and when she was dying, she asked for pen and paper, and wrote, 'I am the wife of the rev. Mr. G.—, rector of Th—, in Essex: my maiden name was C. Cannom; and my last request is to be buried at Th—.'

"The poor gentleman, who last married her, protests he never knew, (till this confession on her death-bed,) that she was another's wife: but in compliance with her desire, he brought her over, and should have buried her at Th— (if the corpse had not been stopped) without making any stir about it. After the nobleman had made this confession, they sent to Mr. G—, who put himself in a passion, and threatened to run her last husband through the body; however, he was prevailed on to be calm: it was represented to him, that this gentleman had been at great expense and trouble to fulfil her desire; and, Mr. G— consented to see him. They say the meeting was very moving, and that they addressed each other civilly. The stranger protested his affection to the lady was so strong, that it was his earnest wish, not only to attend her to the grave, but to be shut up for ever with her there.

"Nothing in romance ever came up to the passion of this man. He had a very fine coffin made for her, with six large silver plates over it: and at last, was very loth to part with her, to have her buried: he put himself in the most solemn mourning, and on Sunday last in a coach, attended the corpse to Th—, where Mr. G— met it in solemn mourning likewise.

"The Florentine is a genteel person of a man, seems about twenty-five years of age, and they say, a sensible man: but there was never any thing like his behaviour to his dear, dear wife, for so he would call her to the last. Mr. G— attended him to London yesterday, and they were very civil to each other; but my lord is inconsolable: he says he must fly England, which he can never see more. I have heard this account from many hands, and can assure you it is fact. Kitty Cannom is, I believe, the first woman in England that had two husbands attended her to the grave together. You may remember her to be sure: her life would appear more romantic than a novel."

BURIED ALIVE.

A remarkable instance of premature interment, is related in the case of the Rev. Mr. Richards, parson of the Hay, in Herefordshire, who, in December, 1751, was supposed to have died suddenly. His friends seeing his body and limbs did not stiffen, after twenty-four hours, sent for a surgeon, who, upon bleeding him, and not being able to stop the blood, told them that he was not dead, but in a sort of trance, and ordered them not to bury him. They paid no attention to the injunction, but committed the body to the grave the next day. A person walking along the churchyard, hearing a noise in the grave, ran and prevailed with the clerk to have the grave opened, where they found a great bleeding at the nose, and the body in a profuse sweat; whence it was conjectured that he was buried alive. They were now, however, obliged to let him remain, as all appearance of further recovery had been precluded by his interment.

A writer in the "Gentleman's Magazine" some years before, observes, "I have undoubted authority for saying, a man was lately (and I believe is still) living at Hustley, near Winchester, December, 1747, who, after lying dead for two days and two nights, was committed to the grave, and rescued from it by some boys luckily playing in the churchyard!"

THE FUNERAL OF EMANUEL SWEDENBORG.

Charles Lindegren, a Swedish merchant, settled in the city, directed his obsequies. He found in Swedenborg's pocket-book a bill for £400, drawn on Hope of Amsterdam. He had the corpse conveyed to the shop of Robinson, an undertaker in Ratcliff Highway, and there laid in state.*

The funeral took place on the 5th of April, 1772, with all the ceremonies of the Lutheran religion. Ferelius officiated—the last service he performed previous to his return to Sweden. The body was deposited in the vault of the Swedish Church in Prince's Square, a short way to the east of the Tower of London.

In 1790, Swedenborg's remains suffered an almost incredible violation. A Rosicrucian in debate with a party of Swedenborgians, maintained that Swedenborg must have possessed the elixir of life, that he was not dead, and that his funeral was a sham. To settle the question, the company set off for Prince's Square, and with the sexton descended into the vault, raised the lid of the outer coffin, and sawed the leaden one across the breast. The corpse was exposed, and the Rosicrucian confuted.

A few days after a second party of Swedenborgians

* The custom of lying in state was common a hundred years ago. The corpse or coffin was surrounded with black velvet hangings, day-light was excluded, and wax candles lit, and the doors were thrown open for the public to enter and view. When it was not convenient to have this dismal ceremony at home, it came off at the undertaker's. The funeral usually took place in the evening by torch-light.

visited the vault.   The features of Swedenborg were perfect, and answered to his portrait.   Various relics were carried off: Dr. Spurgin told me he possessed the cartilage of an ear.   Exposed to the air, the flesh quickly fell to dust, and a skeleton was all that remained for subsequent visitors.

Even worse was to follow.   At a funeral in 1817, Granholm, an officer in the Swedish navy, seeing the lid of Swedenborg's coffin loose, abstracted the skull, and hawked it about amongst London Swedenborgians, but none would buy.   Dr. Wählin, pastor of the Swedish Church, recovered what he supposed to be the stolen skull, had a cast of it taken, and placed it in the coffin in 1819.   The cast, which is sometimes seen in phrenological collections, is obviously not Swedenborg's; it is thought to be that of a small female skull.   In 1857 a marble slab was fixed in the south wall of the Church in Prince's Square, with this inscription :—

IN THE VAULT BENEATH THIS CHURCH ARE

DEPOSITED THE MORTAL REMAINS

OF

EMANUEL SWEDENBORG,

THE SWEDISH PHILOSOPHER AND THEOLOGIAN.

HE WAS BORN AT STOCKHOLM, JAN. 29TH, 1688,

AND DIED IN LONDON, MARCH 29TH, 1772.

—*White's Life and Writings of Emanuel Swedenborg.*

BURIAL WITHOUT SERVICE.

Baskerville the eminent Printer died at Birmingham, but was not interred, and his corpse was kept in the house in which he had lived. After a time this house was sold, and the purchaser of it became embarrassed by the unexpected discovery that he was in possession of the old printer's mortal remains. He applied to the Clergyman of the Parish for release from his difficulty; and this gentleman, being a man of the world, said that he was the last person who ought to have been consulted, but since it was so, the churchyard and the shades of evening afforded a remedy. Died 1775.—*Notes and Queries.*

THE REV. JOHN WESLEY.

On the day preceding his interment, his remains were, according to his own direction, placed in the Chapel near his dwelling house in London; and the crowds that went to see them were so great, that business was generally suspended in the City Road. His funeral took place early in the morning, lest any accident should occur in consequence of the vast concourse of people which was otherwise expected to attend. When the officiating clergyman at the grave-side pronounced the words "Forasmuch as it hath pleased Almighty God to take unto himself our dear *Father* here departed," the people who nearly filled the burying ground, burst into loud weeping; and it is believed that scarcely a dry eye was to be seen in the entire assembly. When the funeral sermon was preached at the City Road Chapel, the men occupied one side of it, and the women the other; and with one solitary exception, it is said that not a coloured riband was to be seen in the vast congregation. One lady with a blue riband in her beaver hat found her way into the gallery, and observing her singularity, she instantly tore it from her head. His Will contained the following characteristic item:—"I give six pounds to be divided among the six poor men who shall carry my body to the grave; for I particularly desire that there may be no hearse, no coach, no escutcheon, no pomp, except the tears of them that loved me, and are following me to Abraham's bosom. I solemnly adjure my Executors, in the name of God, punctually to observe this." Died March 2nd, 1791.

WOLFGANG AMADEUS MOZART. *

"The funeral, with the arrangements for which Baron von Swieten charged himself, was unostentatious to meanness, and far from such as befitted the obsequies of so great a man. The mortal remains of the composer were deposited in the cemetery of St. Marxer Linie, near Vienna; the same in which his

* Died December 5th, 1791, aged thirty-five years.

intimate friends Albrechtsberger and Joseph Haydn were afterwards buried. A common undistinguished grave received the coffin, which was then left without memorial—almost forgotten—for nearly twenty years; and when, in 1808, some inquiries were made as to the precise spot of the interment, all that the sexton could tell was that, at the latter end of 1791, the space about the third and fourth row from the cross was being occupied with graves; but the contents of these graves being from time to time exhumed, nothing could be determined concerning that which was once Mozart."—*Home's Life of Mozart.*

FREDERICK THE SECOND OF PRUSSIA, AND HIS GREYHOUNDS.

The king had always about him several small English greyhounds; but of these only one was in favour at a time, the others being taken merely as companions and playmates to the fondling. As these greyhounds died they were buried on the Terrace of Sans Souci, with the name of each on a gravestone; and Frederick, in his Will, expressed his desire that his own remains might be interred by their side— a parting token of his attachment to them, and of his contempt for mankind! On this point, however, his wishes have not been complied with. Frederick the Second died November 16th, 1797.—*Lord Mahon's Historical Essays.*

IN THE FENS OF ESSEX AND KENT.

And, first, as to this "grave" custom on the London side of the Thames, we have the epistolary testimony of a writer in the year 1773, viz. :—

Nothing but that unaccountable variety of life, which my stars have imposed upon me, could have apologised for my taking a journey to the fens of Essex. Few strangers go into those scenes of desolation, and fewer still (I find) return from thence—as you shall hear.

When I was walking one morning between two of the banks which restrain the waters in their proper bounds, I met one of the inhabitants, a tall and emaciated figure, with whom I entered into conversation. We talked concerning the manners and peculiarities of the place, and I condoled with him very pathetically on his forlorn and meagre appearance. He gave me to understand, however, that his case was far from being so desperate as I seemed to apprehend it, for that he had never looked better since he buried the first of his last nine wives.

"Nine wives!" rejoined I, eager and astonished, "have you buried nine wives?"

"Yes," replied the fen-man, "and I hope to bury nine more."

"Bravissimo!"—This was so far from allaying my astonishment, that it increased it. I then begged him to explain the miraculous matter, which he did in the following words :—

" Lord ! master," said he, "we people in the fens here be such strange creatures, that there be no creatures like us; we be like fish, or water-fowl, or others, for we be able to live where other folks would die sure enough."

He then informed me, that to reside in the fens was a certain and quick death to people who had not been bred among them; that therefore when any of the fen-men wanted a wife, they went into the upland country for one, and that, after they carried her down among the fens, she never survived long: that after her death they went to the uplands for another, who also died; then " another, and another, and another," for they all followed each other as regular as the change of the moon; that by these means some "poor fellows" had picked up a good living, and collected together from the whole a little snug fortune; that he himself had made more money this way than he ever could do by his labour, for that he was now at his tenth wife, and she could not possibly stand it out above three weeks longer; that these proceedings were very equitable, for such girls as were born among themselves they sent into the uplands to get husbands, and that, in exchange, they took their young women as wives; that he never knew a better custom in his life, and that the only comfort he ever found against the ill-nature and caprice of women was. the fens.   This woman-killer then concluded with desiring me, if I had a wife with whom I was not over head and ears in love, to bring her to his house, and it would kill her as effectually as any doctor in Christendom could do.   This offer I waived; for you know, sir, that (thank God) I am not married.

This strange conversation of my friend, the fen-man, I could not pass over without many reflections; and I thought it my duty to give notice to my countrymen concerning a place which may be converted in so peculiar a manner to their advantage.

[So far is from the narrative of a traveller into *Essex*, who, be it observed, "speaks for himself," and whose account is given "without note or comment;" it being certain that every rightly affected reader will form a correct opinion of such a narrator, and of the "fearful estate" of "upland women" who marry "lowland men."]

"HERE YOU LIE, OLD CROP!"

During the siege of Acre, Daniel Bryan, an old seaman and captain of the fore-top, who had been turned over from the Blanche into Sir Sidney Smith's ship Le Tigré, repeatedly applied to be employed on shore; but, being an elderly man and rather deaf, his request was not acceded to.   At the first storming of the breach by the French, one of their generals fell.

among the multitude of the slain, and the Turks, in triumph, struck off his head, and, after mangling the body with their sabres, left it a prey to the dogs, which in that country are of great ferocity, and rove in herds. In a few days it became a shocking spectacle, and when any of the sailors who had been on shore returned to their ship, inquiries were constantly made respecting the state of the French general. To Dan's frequent demands of his messmates why they had not buried him, the only answer he received was, "Go and do it yourself." One morning having obtained leave to go and see the town, he dressed himself as though for an excursion of pleasure, and went ashore with the surgeon in the jolly-boat. About an hour or two after, while the surgeon was dressing the wounded Turks in the hospital, in came honest Dan, who, in his rough, good-natured manner, exclaimed, "I've been burying the general, sir, and now I'm come to see the sick!" Not particularly attending to the tar's salute, but fearing that he might catch the plague, which was making great ravages among the wounded Turks, the surgeon immediately ordered him out. Returning on board, the cockswain asked of the surgeon if he had seen old Dan? It was then that Dan's words in the hospital first occurred, and on further inquiry of the boat's crew they related the following circumstances:—

The old man procured a pick-axe, a shovel, and a rope, and insisted on being let down out of a porthole, close to the breach. Some of his more juvenile companions offered to attend him. "No!" he replied, "you are too young to be shot yet; as for me, I am old and deaf, and *my* loss would be no great matter." Persisting in his adventure, in the midst of the firing, Dan was slung and lowered down, with his implements of action on his shoulder. His first difficulty was to beat away the dogs. The French levelled their pieces—they were on the instant of firing at the hero!—but an officer, perceiving the friendly intentions of the sailor, was seen to throw himself across the file: instantaneously the din of military thunder ceased, a dead, solemn silence prevailed, and the worthy fellow consigned the corpse to its parent earth. He covered it with mould and stones, placing a large stone at its head and another at its feet. The unostentatious grave was formed, but no inscription recorded the fate or character of its possessor. Dan, with the peculiar air of a British sailor, took a piece of chalk from his pocket, and attempted to write

" HERE YOU LIE, OLD CROP!"

He was then, with his pick-axe and shovel, hoisted into the town, and the hostile firing immediately recommenced.

A few days afterwards, Sir Sidney, having been informed of the circumstance, ordered old Dan to

R

called into the cabin.—"Well, Dan, I hear you have buried the French general."—"Yes, your honour."—"Had you any body with you?"—"Yes, your honour."—"Why, Mr. —— says you had not."—"But I had, your honour."—"Ah! who had you?"—"God Almighty, sir."—"A very good assistant, indeed. Give old Dan a glass of grog."—"Thank your honour." Dan drank the grog, and left the cabin highly gratified.—*Hone's Every Day Book.*

JEREMY BENTHAM.

This celebrated political Philosopher left his body to Dr. Southwood Smith, who was to ascertain by appropriate experiment that no life remained. He then gives the following directions:—"It is my request that he will take my body under his charge, and take the requisite and appropriate measures for the disposal and preservation of the several parts of my bodily frame, in the manner expressed in the Paper annexed to this my Will, and at the top of which I have written "*Auto Icon.*" The skeleton he will cause to be put together in such manner as that the whole figure may be seated in a chair usually occupied by me when living, in the attitude in which I am sitting when engaged in thought in the course of the time employed in writing. I direct that the body thus prepared shall be transferred to my executor, and that he will cause the skeleton to be clothed in one of

the suits of black usually worn by me. The body so
clothed, together with the chair and the staff in my
later years borne by me he will take charge of, and
for containing the whole apparatus he will cause to be
prepared an appropriate box or case, and will cause
to be engraved in conspicuous characters on a plate
to be affixed thereon, and also on the glass cases in
which the preparations of the soft parts of my body
shall be contained, as, for example, in the manner
used in the case of wine decanters; my name at
length with the letters ob: followed by the day of my
decease. If it should so happen that my personal
friends and other disciples should be disposed to meet
together on some day or days of the year for the purpose of commemorating the founder of the Greatest
Happiness System of Morals and Legislation, my
Executor will, from time to time, cause to be conveyed to the room in which they meet the said box or
case, with the contents, there to be stationed in such
part of the room as to the assembled company shall
seem meet."

The directions given in the Paper entitled "Auto
Icon" are:—The head to be prepared according to a
specimen seen and approved by Mr. Bentham. The
body to be used as the means of illustrating a series
of lectures; the lecturer to expound the situation,
structure and functions of the different organs. The
object of the lectures was two-fold: to show that the

prevailing terror at dissection originates in ignorance, and is kept up by misconception; and, that the human body, when dissected, instead of being an object of disgust, is as much more beautiful than any other piece of mechanism, as it is more curious and wonderful.

Jeremy Bentham's remains have for some years past been deposited in University College, Gower Street. Died 1832.

O'BRIEN, THE IRISH GIANT.

I have been reading the account of the great giant O'Brien, and the discussion as to whether the bones of this huge man rest peacefully in his grave, or are standing in the attitude of Mr. Pitt in the Hunterian Museum. Five-and-thirty years ago I was pupil to Mr. Richard Smith, the senior surgeon of the Bristol Infirmary. Mr. Smith at that time was the oldest hospital surgeon in England. Mr. Smith knew Patrick Coller O'Brien well, and not long before he died, about the year 1843, he told me the following story. I will give it you as nearly as I can in Mr. Smith's own words:—" They tell you in London that they have got the skeleton of O'Brien in the College Museum, but they have not. They have got O'Brien a smaller man. Why, O'Brien was 8 ft. 2 in. If anybody could have got out his body it would have been myself. He was buried, sir, in the porch of the Roman Catholic Church in Trenchard Street. He had a great horror of being dissected, but I was determined to have him, and took a house (or intended to take a house) on the other side of the street, that we might dig a tunnel under the road, and remove him quietly. But we found he was buried in a grave sunk deep in the red rock, and the stone over him secured by strong iron bars, so that we could not run a mine to him without blasting him with gunpowder, so we gave the plan up. And there he lies; and if anybody ever tells you that they have got him in London, you tell them that he would have been in Richard Smith's Museum if in any museum at all."—*George Pycroft, in "Land and Water."*

FUNERAL OF THE WIFE OF ANDREW DUCROW.

At the close of the season, the company went to Newcastle-on-Tyne, and here a sad affair and a memorable turning-point in Andrew's career occurred. His excellent wife, who, as I have formerly remarked, was indeed a helpmeet for him, caught a severe cold, on which inflammation of the lungs supervened, of which she died after three weeks' illness, on the 10th of November, 1835. I was in London at the time, and received a letter from Ducrow to meet him on a certain day at Barnet, the first stage out of London, on the great north road. I did so, and found him with the dead body of his wife, which he had brought 280 miles by road in a hearse, following it himself in his own carriage. He was terribly cut up, and could scarcely speak coherently to me. We had some breakfast together, and then he said we should start together for Kensal Green Cemetery, to get a piece of ground and arrange about the interment. We did so, and on arriving there he selected a site 20 feet square, for which he paid down one hundred pounds, and forty pounds more for the construction of a vault, which was to be ready for the funeral on the ensuing Thursday, this being Saturday forenoon. We then returned to the Plough Hotel, near the cemetery gate, where it was agreed that I should hasten on to London, and have the large room in his house, the one over the portico at Astley's,* hung with black, and other arrangements made for receiving the body, with which he would follow as soon as dusk had set in, as he did not want to bring it through the streets of London during daylight. I did so, and sent word also to his mother to come to the house and meet her heart-broken son on his arrival. At seven o'clock the cortège arrived; and when the coffin had been laid on the table prepared for it, Ducrow leant over it, and wept like a child. From this night up till the day of the funeral we passed a dreary time of it; Andrew taking no regular rest, and going about like one distraught. The weather too was dull, wet and gloomy, thorough November in fact, and served additionally to depress one's spirits. At last the

* Amphitheatre, Westminster Road.

Thursday came round, and we started on our melancholy four-mile journey to Kensal Green, amid a heavy and persistent fall of sleety rain. When the body was taken into the chapel at the cemetery, I went round to see if the vault was all right, and found that there were some two or three feet of water in it, the ground around it, moreover, being a deep puddle of clay and water. At the conclusion of the service, I whispered to Ducrow that it would be impossible to complete our mission to-day, as the vault was unfinished and full of water. At this he broke out into a towering passion on the spot, and would not be restrained. Turning to the clergyman, he called him "a swindling old humbug," for taking £150 from him, and then not having the vault ready, and demanded his money back again. He would take the body home with him, he said, and find some other place to bury it in to-morrow. At last, on the strong remonstrances of several friends, he was induced to consent that the body should remain in the chapel until the next day, he being allowed to take the key of the place away with him. When we reached his house that night, he told the one or two intimate friends who accompanied him, that he was determined now that his poor wife should be buried either in St. Paul's Churchyard or that of Westminster Abbey. Not only did he say this in all seriousness, but nothing would satisfy him short of

my immediately going to make inquiries as to having
it carried out. I went accordingly to please him,
and in a short time had found the proper official for
St. Paul's at the office in Doctors' Commons. He
was palpably tickled with the idea when I told him
my business, and stated that the lowest terms on
which permission could be obtained for an interment
at St. Paul's, without room for any monument, would
be about £130. I then went to Westminster Abbey,
where they would not entertain the proposal at all,
and so I returned to the house. He was much
disappointed at the result of my mission, but ultimately he was persuaded to agree to having the
coffin deposited in the Catacombs at Kensal Green,
until the tomb for which he had contracted could be
fittingly prepared. This was done, and in the course
of the ensuing summer was erected the well-known
monument, in the Egyptian style, which every one
who has visited Kensal Green will remember, from
a design by Mr. Dawson. On the 24th August, in
presence of a few friends, the body was removed
from the Catacombs and laid in this its last resting-
place. I may just mention that this tomb cost
Ducrow altogether over £3,000, and that by his will
he left a sum of £500, the interest of which goes
towards keeping the monument, ground and railing,
in good repair, and for the purchase of flowers to
deck it.—*Stage Reminiscences by an Old Stager.*

THREE TIMES MAYOR OF KINGSTON, SURREY.

Mr. John Williams has thus expressed his wishes: his spelling does not agree with Dr. Johnson's:—I wish to be buried in Kingston Ceme*try*, in the ground I purchased some time ago, & a head & foot stone to be ere*uc*ted with the following inscription: 'In Remembrance of John Williams, last surviving child of John & Salley Skellet Williams born at Gillingham in Kent July 19. 1806   Died ——   The above was 3 times Mayor of Kingston, a Mag*astrat* of the Borough, & one of the first to establi*est* the 12 Surrey Volunteers of *wich* he died a Lieu*tant*.'   Whatever may be the wish of the Corporation, by all means let them do so. I served them over 20 years; but I could wish the 12 Surrey would shoulder me to my last home.

SURGEON-MAJOR JOHN WYATT, C.B.

The following are his testamentary directions as to the disposal of his remains :—

I desire that the outer coffin may be covered with a simple black pall enveloped in the Union Jack; but whether buried as a soldier or civilian, I desire to be buried at Kensal Green, and to have the Bible which was given to me by my wife buried with me. I desire that the horses which may be used at my funeral may not be decorated in any manner, and that the hired attendants may not wear any hatbands or scarves. I desire that each person who may attend my funeral shall wear only a plain black band of medium width, (of crape for relations, of cloth for friends,) around his hat, black gloves, and a white rose or camellia, or other white flower, in the button hole of his coat. I wish the ceremony to be as much as possible free from all gloomy associations, and that it should be considered more an occasion for rejoicing than mourning in accordance with Holy Scripture. Especially do I desire that no description of widow's cap or crape on her dresses be worn by my wife; also that no particle of crape be worn upon the clothes of any of my relations.

HOW TO HAVE A CORPSE CONVEYED CHEAPLY BY RAIL.

Mrs. Kitty Jenkyn Packe, of Reading, who died in 1870, directed that if she died away from Branksome, she wished her remains "to be duly placed in the proper coffins, and enclosed in a plain deal box, (so that no one may know the contents,) and conveyed by a goods train to Poole, *which will cost no more than any other package of the same weight.*" From Poole Station the box was to be conveyed in a cart to Branksome Tower. [The railway charges for conveying a corpse are from 6d. to 1s. per mile.]

JOYFUL RESURRECTION.

An old man died and was buried in a piece of ground attached to a dissenting place of worship at Woolhope, a village about eight miles from Hereford.

Shortly afterwards, some one, it is said, "got the ear" of one of the old man's sons, and persuaded him, first, that his father's spirit could not rest in the ground where his body was; secondly, that there was no hope of a "*joyful resurrection*" from such a place; thirdly, that he and his family would never have peaceful possession of the old man's property until his body was in more comfortable quarters; and, fourthly, that those quarters were only to be found in the duly consecrated ground of the parish churchyard. Accordingly, in the dead of night, with crowbar, pick and shovel, this son of sons, with assistance, repaired, it is said, to the chapel burial ground, opened the grave, and, not without great difficulty, took the coffin out of it, the body being in a dreadfully advanced state of decomposition, and conveyed it to the Woolhope churchyard, where a new grave had been prepared, and where, it is alleged, the clergyman of the parish performed the burial service over the body on its reinterment.

CHARLES DICKENS.*

Directions in his Will as to funeral:—"I emphatically direct that I be buried in an inexpensive, unostentatious, and strictly private manner; that no

* Buried in Westminster Abbey. The stone placed upon his grave is inscribed—
CHARLES DICKENS,
Born February the Seventh, 1812. Died June the Ninth, 1870.

public announcement be made of the time or place of my burial; that at the utmost not more than three plain mourning coaches be employed; and that those who attend my funeral wear no scarf, cloak, black bow, long hat-band, or other such revolting absurdity. I direct that my name be inscribed in plain English letters on my tomb, without the addition of Mr. or Esquire. I conjure my friends on no account to make me the subject of any monument, memorial, or testimonial whatever."

LORD LYTTON.

The following are his directions as to the disposal of his body:—"I desire that it may not be disturbed from the bed in which it may be lying, nor prepared for burial, nor, above all, be placed in a coffin, till three medical men of high standing and reputation shall have inspected it separately, and not in the presence of each other, and shall have declared in writing, to be signed by them respectively, that the signs of decomposition have unmistakably commenced. And I desire that two, out of the three medical men, shall be other than the medical men who have attended me in my last illness. I forbid all dissection or autopsy of my remains, unless there be a suspicion in the mind of my executor that I have not died a natural death, but earnestly request that the most approved means, (short of mangling the body) may

.be used for restoring my life in case there be any
doubt of my decease, or I appear to be in a catalepsy
-or trance."

His Lordship directs his body to be buried in the
family mausoleum at Knebworth, his epitaph, (if any,)
to be in the English language, and the funeral to be
limited to the modest expense usual in the funeral of
a private gentleman.*

A KING'S FUNERAL IN SCYTHIA.

When a king died in Scythia, we are told by
Herodotus that the undertakers who attended him
cut off one ear, shaved their heads, wounded themselves on the arms, forehead, and nose, and pierced

---

* Lord Lytton was buried in Westminster Abbey with the following epitaph, written by his son, the present lord:—

EDWARD GEORGE EARLE LYTTON BULWER LYTTON

Born 25. May 1803—Died 18. January 1873

1831-1841 Member of Parliament for St. Ives and for Lincoln
1838 Baronet of the United Kingdom
1852-1866 Knight of the Shire for the County of Hertford
1858 One of Her Majesty's Principal Secretaries of State
Knight Grand Cross of St. Michael and St. George
1866 Baron Lytton of Knebworth

Laborious and Distinguished in all fields of intellectual activity
Indefatigable and Ardent in the cultivation and love of Letters
His genius as an Author was displayed in the most varied forms
Which have connected indissolubly
With every department of the Literature of his time
The name of EDWARD BULWER LYTTON.

the left hand with an arrow.   Furthermore, at a royal funeral the undertakers had to furnish a concubine to be strangled, together with a cup-bearer, a cook, a groom, a waiter, a messenger, and a certain number of horses.   The historian goes on to say, in his description of a king's funeral, that, not content with the above list, "they took the king's ministers, fifty in number, and strangled them; and with them the king's stud, fifty beautiful horses, and after they have emptied and cleansed their bellies (the king's ministers, they having been supposed to have filled them extraordinarily) they fill them with straw and sew them up again.   Then they lay two planks of a semicircular form upon four pieces of timber, placed at a convenient distance, with the half circle upwards; and when they have erected a sufficient number of these machines, they set the horses upon them, spitted with a long pole, quite through the body to the neck; and thus one semicircle supports the shoulders of the horse, the other his flank, and his legs are suspended in the air.   After this they bridle the horses, and, hanging the reins at full length upon posts erected to that end, mount one of the fifty they have strangled upon each horse, and fix him in the seat by driving a straight stick upwards from the end of the back-bone to his head, and fastening the lowest part of that stick in an. aperture of the beam that spits the horses. Then, placing these horsemen quite round the monument, they all depart; and this is the manner of the King's Funeral."

THE DEATH CLUB OF CLASSIC TIMES.

Strange and melancholy are the stories which have come down to us concerning a band of young men of Greece who formed themselves into a kind of club, in accordance with certain philosophic teaching. "Let us eat and drink for to-morrow we die" was emphatically their maxim, and they called themselves "Those about to die together," or as it runs in Greek, οἱ συναποθανούμενοι. We have historical evidence of their existence, and weird tales are told of their feasts in a darkened chamber hung round with black draperies, having no outlet save a door of brass and dimly lighted with lamps. There these ghastly *viveurs* met, and in flasks of red Chian wine they toasted death and sang Anacreon's songs. And on the centre table, as the genius and the demon of the scene, lay the enshrouded corpse of one of their number who had died of the plague; and his eyes, in which death had but half extinguished the fire of the pestilence, seemed to take such interest in the hideous revelry as might be taken in the merriment of those about to die. Surely a terrible club this, and even in our age of many clubs one not likely to be revived at the present day.

ATTENDING HIS OWN FUNERAL.

It was generally supposed that Sir Giles ————, the sceptic of ———— Park, died abroad, but he did no such thing, and a few years after the occurrences to be here related, the truth oozed out. After living a very retired life for some years, shunning society and only going out after nightfall, Sir Giles, just as his woods were putting on their fairest spring verdure, retired to the Continent, taking with him one old and faithful servant. To this domestic he declared his scheme, which was to give out that he was dead and to procure a mock funeral. The old servant had never in all his life dreamed of disputing his master's wishes and did not do so now, while to secure his fidelity, Sir Giles showed him a very beneficial codicil to his Will, not available except in case of his real or supposed death. The old domestic then becomes acquainted with some of the attendants at a hospital and under the pretence that his master is a Professor of Anatomy, procures a body, conveys it to the lodgings, and all minor matters prepared for the deception, tells the people of the house that a friend of his master's had died suddenly while paying him a morning visit. The body, under the real name of his master, is coffined, and magnificent orders given for the interment. Things being in this state the domestic writes to the next heir an account of his master's sudden death, states that he was obliged to deposit the body in lead and that he awaits "further orders." The heir arrives with little show of sorrow, which, strange to say, rather amused than offended old Sir Giles, who, now disguised with a red wig and otherwise metamorphosed, has contrived to become one of the official attendants at his own funeral: the servant having recommended him to the undertaker. Everything was magnificently ordered as becoming the rank of so important a man. In his capacity as assistant undertaker he was initiated into all the mysteries of the craft, and felt a new joy in his misanthropy. For the first time in his life he was not miserable. Happy to him was the day of his death, but far happier that of his burial. He looked upon his heir as the fool who had taken the burden of his station and property off his shoulders; and as he would only have hated him the more had he shown any feeling on the occasion, he was quite indifferent as to his attitude. After his own funeral Sir Giles walked away, no one ever knew whither, bequeathing as he fully believed all the miseries of unalloyed prosperity to his heir. His epitaph was found among his papers, written by himself and was duly inscribed on his supposed tomb. After some years the old domestic died bequeathing his money to a chapel, but before his dissolution he relieved his conscience by disclosing this strange story.

PICKLING A WIFE.

The celebrated Van Butchel was notorious not only for his beard and spotted horse, but on account of the ingenuity with which he disappointed "the black fraternity," *i. e.* the undertakers, of their unreasonable expectations. He was at no sumptuous cost for *his* wife. It has been said that an annuity had been bequeathed to her "so long as she should be above ground." Be that, however, as it may. He did preserve her above ground, and above ground she may be to this day. For he was the inventor of a new pickle, and in the experiment the great Hunter was coadjutor. It is quite pleasant, says an old writer, to think that one human being in the great city could escape the hands of the Black Harpies. The old woman in Horace was to be carried oiled, to see if it was possible for her to slip through the hands of her heir and the undertakers. But the pickle of Madame Van Butchel was a happier thing, for through it she was never carried out at all, but preserved at home. Her epitaph declared that she had no share in the tomb, but was kept whole and incorruptible, to the delight of her affectionate husband.

FUNERAL OF THE LATE SIR ANTHONY DE ROTHSCHILD.

Sir Anthony de Rothschild was followed to his grave at the Willesden Cemetery of the United

Synagogue by a larger number of persons than the funeral of any English Jew had hitherto drawn together. At Grosvenor Place, Count Beust, the Austrian Ambassador, Lord Hardwicke, the Hon. Eliot Yorke, M.P., the Hon. Alexander Yorke, were some among those collected. Baron Lionel de Rothschild was unable, on account of illness, to be present. Baron Alphonse de Rothschild of Paris, Baron Ferdinand de Rothschild, Baron Albert de Rothschild of Vienna, Mr. Nathaniel M. de Rothschild, M.P., Mr. Alfred de Rothschild, Mr. Leopold de Rothschild, were the members of the family of the deceased who took part in the religious service. The Russian Ambassador, the Duke of Wellington, the Lord Mayor, the Governor of the Bank of England, Sir Moses Montefiore, were a few of those who sent their carriages. The Council of the United Synagogue, of which the late baronet was President, attended in a body, and so did representative members of all the principal Jewish institutions, and a few pupils, with most of the teachers, from each of the Jewish schools, the Free School, the Gates of Hope School, the Western School, Stepney School, the Jews' College, the Jews' Hospital, and many others. According to invariable custom, no ladies were present at the ceremonial.

The funeral began to leave Grosvenor Place at half-past 10. The number of mourning coaches (61) and of private carriages was so great that a long time elapsed before it was fully formed. Policemen stood at the corners of all the streets, but the day chosen for the funeral being Sunday, little or no interference with traffic occurred. Willesden was reached by noon, and the plain oak coffin, covered with cloth, but without any plate or ornament, as the funeral horses were likewise without plumes, was carried into the chapel of the burial ground, and placed upon the bier. Violets and camellias on the walls adorned the homely building (too small for any but a selection from those present on the ground). The Rev. B. H. Ascher, the Rabbi of the Burial Society of the United Synagogue, recited in Hebrew solemnly and slowly, but abstaining, as in the service throughout, from the use of the chant or half-chant common in the ordinary liturgy of the Synagogue, a prayer, the leading note of which was perfect resignation to the Divine will. The bearers raised the coffin and carried it forward towards the place of burial. Midway they set it down again and the minister praised God, "the Supreme King, who orders death and restoreth life and causeth salvation to spring forth; who also, in His great mercy, reviveth the dead."

Then the Chief Rabbi, Dr. N. M. Adler, whose great age adds to the veneration for him which his office inspires, standing in the open air, pronounced a short funeral discourse, such as is only delivered among the Jews in exceptional cases. Quoting at the commencement of his brief address the words of King David on the death of Abner—"Know you not that a Prince and a great man hath fallen in Israel?"—the Chief Rabbi said that he whom they deplored was great in being truly good. He followed the traditions of his noble family to shed lustre upon Israel. His beneficence was unlimited, dispensed without distinction of creed or nationality, intelligently and judiciously. Though one of the heads of the great firm which had its agents in every city, he yet devoted himself heart and soul to the two great institutions over which he presided. For 20 years he was the presiding warder of the Great Synagogue, and when nearly all the metropolitan congregations were united into one body, he was unanimously chosen President of the United Synagogue. He imparted dignity to its deliberations by the prestige of his name, and assisted to weld together its elements by his genial presence. They all knew the important part he took in the administration of his favourite institution—the Free School. By his unwearied zeal he aided it to attain its present gigantic dimensions, and the school would ever remain a perpetual memorial of the love for his race which fired his soul. His survivors would be consoled by their belief in the immortality of his soul and the blessed certainty of a reunion hereafter, even as the earth, which is now clad with its wintry garb, will be renewed in the perennial beauty of spring. He who was in every sense the head of that august family would (the speaker confidently expected) be blessed with strength to labour, as before, with ardent love for his people, this Heaven-favoured country, and humanity, and the heir of the title would inherit his zeal and love in every good work. He quoted the words of the Ethics of the Fathers—"Those who work for the public good will be aided by the merits of their forefathers; their righteousness will follow them to the grave; yea, it will endure for ever"—and concluded with a prayer that the Ruler over Life and Death would grant their departed brother to enjoy the heavenly abode. "Send," he continued, "Thy comfort, O Lord, into the hearts of the mourners, and hasten the time foretold by Thy Holy Prophet when Thou wilt destroy death for ever and wipe off the tears from every face."

The coffin was slowly borne forward to a place close beside the tomb of Baron Meyer de Rothschild, who was laid there two years ago. The spot is only marked by wreaths continually renewed till a fitting memorial of the departed and the affection of the survivors shall have been completed. The near relatives of the deceased, standing close by, placed upon the coffin wreaths of white camellias, and it was lowered into the grave, the officiating Rabbi standing beside in silent prayer, and at the end exclaiming, "May he come to his appointed end in peace." The near bystanders then, as the affecting custom is, took each in turn the spade; and the thud of the earth cast three times by each into the grave was heard. Then the mourners went back to the chapel; some of them repeating in Hebrew the pious sentence, "They shall blossom forth from the tomb as the grass of the earth."

Some of those present began to visit the tombs of their own relations, but a larger number than were before admitted now gathered in the chapel again, where the Rabbi read the beautiful 91st Psalm, in which occurs the reference to him who dwells in the shadow of the Almighty, and the verses, "He shall give his angels charge over thee, to keep thee in all thy ways. . . . Because he hath set his love upon me, therefore will I deliver him; I will set him on high, because he hath known my name." The officiating Rabbi then said the ancient prayer in the Chaldean language, called Sanctification, or Kadish, which survives from the time when this dialect was the vernacular of the Jews. When children are left behind, they say the prayer every day during the year of mourning, as well as on each anniversary of the death. Its words glorify the Creator as the reviver of the dead, and implore the speedy coming of His Kingdom. When the minister had recited

this prayer, those present responded with " Amen;"
and the dismissing words of the Rabbi were, " May
He who establisheth peace in His high Heavens
grant peace unto us and all Israel."

During the week after the funeral it is customary
among the Israelites for prayers to be said and a
discourse to be preached at the house of the departed.
—*The Times, Jany. 10th, 1876.*

WHAT NEXT?

It seems that a Mr. Mahrenholz, an American,
has devised a plan for utilising the remains of his
deceased fellow-creatures by converting their skins
into leather. He has lately tanned the hide of a
respectable working man who lost his life by a
lamentable accident, and the value of whose skin was
an immense boon to his disconsolate widow and
children. A pair of boots manufactured from the
skin of this ill-fated labourer have been deposited in
the Smithsonian Institution at Washington, where
they excite much interest and attention. It is proposed by the inventor to exhibit the boots at the
Centennial Exhibition at Philadelphia. The leather
is remarkable for its softness and pliancy, and takes
a good polish, but its wearing qualities have yet to
be proved. The general impression appears to be
that it is hardly adapted for rough work, such as that
of sportsmen or pedestrian tourists, but for evening

wear at the theatre or in the ball-room it will be found far more comfortable than boots and shoes made of ordinary leather. Some little prejudice, it is expected, will have to be overcome before the new leather is taken into general use.*

GETTING READY.

The Church has lost an eccentric luminary in the person of the vicar of St. Petrock Minor, Cornwall, who lately advertised that he would reject all letters addressed to him as " Reverend," and would only be styled " G. W. Manning." He had his coffin made years ago, and has slept either upon it or in it for many months. It was fitted with mattress and pillow, and lately he employed a carpenter to alter it so as to make it more comfortable. For several weeks he had slept in the coffin. The walls of his bed-room were papered with letters received respecting his rejection of title, and with notices of the steps to be taken in the event of his being seized with illness. Among other eccentricities he from the pulpit one Sunday gave his domestic servant notice to leave his employ.

* During the first French Revolution it is said that a tannery was established at Mendon, near Paris, for utilising the skins of the victims of the guillotine.

SOMEWHAT PECULIAR.

The funeral of the Countess of Essex, who was buried at Watford, Herts, was somewhat peculiar. The Earl some time ago had a hearse constructed somewhat in the shape of a waggonette, surmounted by a canopy supported from each angle by a simple iron bar, and trimmed with heavy purple and white worsted fringe. The body of the vehicle was painted purple, pricked out in white, and bore a coronet on the panels, and was drawn by a pair of his lordship's horses, driven by his coachman. The Earl's private carriage formed the chief mourning coach, and the coffin was of deal wood, and perforated.

GRAVE PHOTOGRAPHS.

A custom seems to be common in Cemeteries on the Continent of placing a photograph of the deceased upon the stone or cross that marks the remains. At the Montmartre Cemetery in Paris, and in some of the German graveyards, there are to be seen neat iron crosses with portraits, framed and glazed to protect them from the weather, let into the metal; so that not only the name of the deceased and the dates of birth and death are given, but also a trace of the features when living. Even in this country, at Shrewsbury, for instance, the custom is to be found, and there seems no doubt that now imperishable photographs can be produced, burnt upon enamel, the practice will become more and more general. Whatever may be said of such a custom, it is certainly far preferable to having roughly painted pictures produced by the village artist upon the iron and wooden monuments, as is the case in many Swiss villages, such as the Lungern graveyard at the foot of the Brünig pass. Horrible daubs like these staring at one from every corner of the churchyard render the place perfectly gruesome, and wind and weather beating against such monstrosities only render the pale faces and unkempt hair the more hideous. If neat photographic portraits are allowed to take the place of these primitive paintings, it will certainly be matter for congratulation.

FORETELLING THE HOUR OF DEATH.

Dr. Woodville, the author of a work on medical botany, lived in lodgings at a carpenter's house in Ely Place, London; and a few days before he died Dr. Adams brought about his removal, for better attendance, to the Small-pox Hospital. The carpenter with whom he lodged had not been always on the best terms with him. Woodville said he should like to let the man see that he died at peace with him, and, as he never had had much occasion to employ him, desired that he might be sent for to come and measure him for his coffin. This was done; the carpenter came, and took measure of the Doctor, who begged him not to be more than two days about it, "for," said he, "I shall not live beyond that time;" and he actually did die just before the end of the next day. A contemporary and friend of his, Dr. George Fordyce, also expired under similar circumstances. He desired his youngest daughter, who was sitting by his bedside, to take up a book and read to him; she read for about twenty minutes when the Doctor said "stop, go out of the room; I am going to die." She put down the book, and went out of the room to call the attendant, who immediately went into the bedroom and found that her father had breathed his last.

AN ADDRESS DELIVERED BY VICTOR HUGO AT THE TOMB OF MADAME LOUIS BLANC, PARIS.

"What Louis Blanc did for me two years ago I do for him to-day. In his name I bid the last adieu to a beloved being. The friend who has yet strength to speak stands here on behalf of the friend who does not know whether he has strength remaining to live. These sad reunions upon the brink of the tomb form part of the human destiny. Madame Louis Blanc was the humble companion of an illustrious exile. The proscribed Louis Blanc met with this loving soul. Providence reserves such meetings to good men. The double life is the happy life. Madame Louis Blanc was a serene and calm figure appearing upon one of those stormy scenes which now-a-days make part of the life of great men. Madame Blanc paled before the lustre of her glorious husband. She was more ready to pale before his light than he to radiate it. He was her glory, she his joy. She fulfilled the great mysterious function of woman, which is to love. Man pushes forward, invents, creates, and sows and reaps, destroys and constructs, thinks, combats, contemplates. Woman loves. And what does her love produce? Man's strength. The worker has need of a life side by side with his own. The greater the worker, the gentler should his life's companion be; and Madame Louis Blanc was gentle. Louis Blanc is an apostle of the ideal, the philosopher, and the tribune in one, the great orator, the great citizen, the honest combatant, the historian who digs out of the past the furrow of the future. Hence a life insulted, tormented. Louis Blanc, in his struggle for the past and the true, the prey to all hatred and outrage, had well employed his day and borne nobly through the storm the standard of his undaunted and invincible determination. He turned to this woman, at once humble and noble, and found refuge in her loving smile. Alas! she is dead. Let us sanctify her. Let us glorify her. In the wife and in wifely influence one contemplates humanity from its tranquil side. In the wife one sees the hearth, the home, the centre of all peaceable and loving thought. It is the tender prompting of an innocent voice in the midst of all that obstructs, distracts, and annoys. Around us all is hostile. The wife is love itself. Ah! let us protect this sentiment. Let us render to it its due. Let us give it in law the place which it holds in right. Let us honour, O citizens, this mother, this sister, this spouse! In the wife is centered the social problem and the human mystery. She seems the embodiment of weakness; she is the soul of strength. The man on whom a people rely must needs rely upon the wife of his bosom. And should the day come when she fails us, all else fails. It is we who are dead; it is she who is living still. Her memory takes possession of us, and when we stand before her tomb it appears that it is our own heart which goes down there to burial; hers which rises again to life. (Marked sensation.) And you are alone, Louis Blanc. O, beloved exile, it is now that the veritable period of exile begins! But I have faith in your indomitable courage. I have faith in your illustrious mind. You will triumph in will, triumph even over grief; you will know what is your duty towards truth, right, the Republic, and Liberty. You well know that you possess within yourself that imperative law which no other law can override—the law of conscience. You will delegate to your beloved one dead the heroic efforts which yet remain to you to achieve. You will feel that she is watching you.

Oh, my friend, live, weep, persevere.   Men like you
are privileged in the highest sense of the word; they
accept and cherish within themselves the depth of
human grief; fate places them in a harmony of sensi-
bility with those whom it behoves them to protect and
to defend.   Their lot has taught them to feel the
bitterness of that calumny which they resent when it
falls upon others; their fate has acquainted them with
internal struggles, even as they stand up for those
who combat with a never-ending mourning, even as
they array themselves upon the side of those who
suffer as though, indeed, some mysterious destiny
intended by this constant appeal to individual human
feeling to measure the height of the sufferer's duty by
the depth of the sufferer's woe.   And as for you, for
us, O people! O citizens! let us forget our sorrows:
let us think only of our country.   She, too, this
august France, she is cruelly woe-stricken; she has
her enemies, alas! even among her children.   While
some mourn over her past, others cherish revengeful
thoughts concerning her future.   But she needs light
—that is to say, education.   She needs unity—that is
to say, universal reconciliation.   Let us give her
what she needs; let us enlighten her; let us pacify
her; let us take up her watchword even from this
point.   For there is a new life in everything, even in
death, which is but another life.   Yes; let us seek
out of this situation of to-day those gifts for our

country which our country needs. Let us seek it in the presence of the grave at our feet, as of the sun which shines upon us from above, for what the sun gives is light and what the tomb gives is peace. Peace and light; herein is life! (Profound sensation. Cries of '*Vive Victor Hugo!*' '*Vive Louis Blanc!*')"— *Times, April 27, 1876.*

THE FUNERAL OF FRANCIS DEAK.

Buda-Pesth, Feb. 4, 1876.

Yesterday Deak was buried. The Legislature had passed the resolution that it considered Deak the dead of the nation, and it was indeed the nation who buried its dead. "In the name of the Diet we notify with deep patriotic grief that Francis Deak died on the 28th of January, and that he will be buried on the 3rd of February"—thus ran the notice signed by the Presidents of both Houses. No one was asked, and every one came. If in the first days of national mourning it was chiefly the population of the capital which stood at the coffin of Deak, on the last day before the funeral it was so to say the whole country who had come up for a pilgrimage to the mortuary chamber in the hall of the palace of the Academy. From the furthest points of the kingdom of St. Stephan the pilgrims had come up. Counties, towns, corporations, associations of every kind—literary, benevolent, industrial, commercial—

had sent up representatives. Few of them had come without bringing with them a wreath, and there you saw them going one after another in a body to lay down this their tribute on the coffin, so that what with these and those offered by private persons there lay round the coffin some 150. Last of all came the wreath of oak leaves taken there in the dusk of the evening, when access had already been closed to the general public, by the members of the Liberal Club of the Diet, in which now, besides the original followers, are gathered those who for seven years had so energetically opposed the policy of Deak. It was perhaps the greatest triumph of that policy to see the Minister President, once the leader of that Opposition, laying down that wreath in the name of the now united Parties.

So great had been the preparations, so great the manifestation of national mourning before the funeral itself, that there might have been almost an apprehension lest the last and chief act should not be equal to the occasion. Days before the town looked like a city in mourning. There was scarcely a house that had not a mourning flag. Most of the houses and shops in the chief parts of the town were decorated in black. Almost in every shop window you could see a picture or bust of the deceased surrounded by wreaths and mortuary emblems, and in this gloomy framework moved about thousands and thousands all

in black and crape. It was in itself a permanent
funeral procession for some days which wound its
way to and from the palace of the Academy, so that
you had considerable difficulty to make your way
through it.   It was as if every one of the 300,000
people of the sister towns had been bent on seeing
once more the face which was so familiar to most of
them, and mingled with these one could recognise
at a glance other thousands which had been pouring
in from all parts of the country. All this was in
itself a demonstration which it seemed almost impossible to surpass; and yet all this has become faint
and insignificant in face of the grand and imposing
demonstration of the funeral. All that had passed
before one's eyes for several days was concentrated
in one grand picture during the funeral. Since the
funeral of your Iron Duke* I do not believe that
an equally grand demonstration has been made by
any nation in honour of the mighty dead. Indeed,
proportionately, that of yesterday was perhaps the
grander.

Opposite the suspension bridge over the Danube
spreads out the large square of Francis Joseph, some
400 yards in length and about 150 in width, with the
Coronation Mound in the centre formed of earth
brought from every county in the kingdom, and on
which, according to old custom, the newly-crowned

* The late Duke of Wellington.

King in 1868, as your readers will well remember, drew his sword, waving it as a symbol that he would defend the country against all comers. All round the square stand palace-like buildings, the finest of them being that of the Hungarian Academy on the north side. The entrance hall of it, where the body had been lying in state, and where the religious ceremony was to be performed, was far too small to admit all those who had, as it were, a right to be there, and the idea arose to hold the ceremony in the open square, where, besides those on duty, thousands of spectators might have participated in what was, in reality, a public act; but the frosty winter weather, with the chances of a snowstorm, deterred the managers from adopting this idea. Except, therefore, the members of both Houses, who were there in a body, only single representatives of the deputations could be admitted, the rest remaining outside, either on the space kept open for them before the Academy building or else already marshalled up in procession to march in front of the *cortége*.

The hour of meeting was fixed for 10 a.m., and even before that the mortuary hall was filled with the privileged hundreds. So perfect were the arrangements that, in spite of the crowds which had already taken up their position on the line or were hastening to do so, there was not the slightest difficulty in getting to the place. A number of volunteers from among the members of both Houses had taken upon themselves to superintend the arrangements made by the police and military to keep order, and to act as mediators to prevent any collision between these latter and the public. They had enlisted under them a number of students of the University and high schools to assist them, each of them provided with a sash in black and white as an emblem of his office.

Long before 11 a.m., the time fixed for the ceremony, every one had taken up his place in the hall. On the broad corridor, raised a few steps above the hall, were the members of both Houses, with their Presidents at their heads; below, the representatives of the various deputations and corporations; and alongside the coffin, now closed, the relations of the deceased. On the other side were ranged the whole Consular body, the deputation of both Houses of the Austrian Reichsrath, with Dr. Rechbauer, the President of the Lower House, a friend of Hungary from olden times. They had brought a laurel wreath in the name of the Reichsrath. The Polish Club had sent three members. Soon after Count Andrassy came General Mondel as representative of His Majesty, and Baron Moster, of Her Majesty's Household, as her representative; and shortly before the ceremony began there came Archduke Joseph, with the Archduchess Clotilde, and her brother, the Prince of Coburg, with his wife, the

Royal daughter of Belgium. Almost to the minute, at 11 a.m., appeared the clergy in full ornaments. Although himself suffering, the Cardinal Primate of Hungary, assisted by nine Bishops and the Archbishop of Erlau, performed the service. Amid the most impressive silence the clear voice of the Primate intoned the *De profundis*, which was taken up by the choir, and rarely did that simple choral, massively executed, produce a deeper effect than on this occasion; the fumes of incense filled the dimly-lighted hall, and when the Primate, sprinkling over the coffin holy water, began the Lord's Prayer, there was not a heart that remained unmoved and not a lip that did not follow him.

The religious ceremony over, the President of the Lower House of the Diet addressed the audience in a short speech; and the hearse, with six black horses, drew up before the door. The coffin, on which only the wreaths of their Majesties lay, was brought down and placed on the hearse, which was decorated with some of the wreaths, the rest having been laid on a special carriage, which was in charge of the deputations of the Hungarian students of the Vienna University. The sight outside was one never to be forgotten—the large square draped with black, and filled with a dense crowd equally in black; every window and balcony occupied, almost without exception, by ladies in deep mourning, and through the winter's haze you could see across the Danube, the mourning flag half-mast up, hanging on the flagstaff of the Royal Palace. Not a breath of wind stirred, not a sound was heard until, at a given signal, all the bells of the town were set ringing, and from afar, towards the head of the *cortége*, the dim sounds of Beethoven's "Funeral March" were heard. It was about an English mile off, for so far did the *cortége* extend in front. With the exception of a few prevented by illness, every one was in the *cortége* who has a name in Hungary, or is of any account in Hungary in any sphere of life—political, social, literary, scientific, commercial, industrial. In front of the *cortége* marched a military band, behind it the secretaries of the Lower Houses; behind them were arrayed, as forming the first part of the *cortége*, the inmates of the Asylum of Invalided Honveds of 1848. Then came the students of the University and Polytechnic School, some 120 guilds and associations with their flags, and a number of scientific and other corporations of engineers, railway officials; miners from Schemnitz and sailors and pilots from Fiume; freemasons, fire brigades, athletic clubs—in fact, almost every corporation known. The second part of the *cortége* consisted of the deputations sent by the counties and towns; 52 counties and 56 towns were represented there. After them came the corporation of the Capital, the professors of the University and

High Schools, the members of the Supreme Tribunal, the Hungarian Academy, and lastly, the whole body of officers of the Garrison not on duty, and of the Honveds. They marched according to their rank, the generals, with Archduke Joseph, and the commander of the troops in Hungary closing the long line. After them came the funeral *cortége* proper. In front was the carriage drawn by two white horses, on which the wreaths were placed ; then the clergy, with the Archbishop of Erlau, who was now officiating instead of the Primate, who, being unwell, could not venture to officiate at more than the ceremony in the hall. At starting the pall was borne by the Presidents of the two Houses, the Minister, Count Andrassy, the Bann of Croatia, and the Governor of Fiume. All along the road the members of both Houses, which followed the hearse immediately after the relations of the deceased, passed forward one after another to take their turn in carrying the pall. It was a *cortége* only a sovereign could command, and it had come not by command but spontaneously, all vying with each other in paying the last honours to the great man.

But, numerous as this *cortége* was, and comprising as it did all that is prominent in Hungary, as a demonstration it was nothing compared with what the people at large offered. The measured distance from the palace of the Academy to the Cemetery is

6,100 yards, or above 3½ English miles, and along that whole distance on every side the line was marked by soldiers six and eight deep. Wherever a cross street or an open square afforded room, hundreds were congregated in a body on tribunes and other temporary constructions. The line of road chosen is flanked almost all along by houses three and four storeys high, and every one of the thousands of windows and numerous balconies was crowded with people, mostly ladies in black, while in some places people stood on the roofs and had taken out the tiles so as to make an opening. Every one of that crowd looked and behaved as if he felt the earnestness and solemnity of the moment. Not a sound was heard along the long line while the convoy passed. This silent reverence was the greatest tribute that could be paid by a crowd. The roughs seemed to have left the place, or else so to have been cowed down that there was not even an attempt all the time to break through the line. The line of soldiers standing a couple of yards distant from each other, and the body of police accompanying the *cortége* seemed to be there more for show than work. Not only was there no interruption, except now and then for a minute or two at the turnings, when the long line came necessarily to a standstill, but you saw nowhere any pushing forward or other signs of disorder, and the *cortége* could march at so regular a pace that,

in spite of its unwieldiness, it reached the entrance
of the cemetery, 3½ miles distant, in two hours.
Instead of diminishing, if anything the crowd right
and left had increased, and at the gate it stood in a
compact mass. As a precaution at the rather awk-
ward turnings the Volunteer Fire Brigade had been
posted three deep on each side, but even this seemed
almost superfluous, so orderly and well-behaved were
the people.

The chapel in which the body was to be deposited
until a fitting place for a monument can be selected
and prepared is about half an English mile from the
entrance. A broad road covered with sand led up
to it. On both sides of it the guilds, corporations
and deputations selected arrayed themselves each
under their flag, and this last reception was not the
last or least in impressiveness. All round the ground
was white with snow, and the trees and shrubs
glittered with hoar-frost, as if covered with white
flowers. The gloomy haze which lay upon the town
seemed to have cleared away, and a reddish tinge
from the west lent a warmer light to the whole scene.
As the convoy passed along there rose on the left
the mound with the monument erected to the memory
of the unfortunate Count Louis Batthyanyi, Hungary's first Prime Minister in 1848. It is but a
couple of hundred yards from the chapel in which
Deak's body was to be deposited. Involuntarily you

thought of the well-intentioned man who attempted, but failed, and paid for the failure with his life, and the man now brought out, to lie close by, who accomplished the deed successfully.

Before the chapel door the carriage stopped. Deak had reached his last resting-place. The coffin and wreaths were taken down, and once more the chant resounded; the priests again blessed the body, and with them those present sent a silent blessing on the man to whom Hungary owes so much. The last sound of the chant died away, and it was all over. The man is dust, but his name will live as long as Hungary or a Hungarian will live.—*Times, February 10, 1876.*

THE FUNERAL OF PRINCE DORIA.

The *Times'* Correspondent at Rome, writing under date March 22, 1876, describes the funeral of Prince Doria, husband of the late Lady Mary Talbot :—

"About 4 o'clock yesterday afternoon an unpretending funeral procession was seen making its way along part of the Corso, and through the streets leading to the Piazza Navona. First there walked some 30 or 40 of the confraternity of the *Sacconi*, dressed in sackcloth of the coarsest kind, girt round their waists with thick knotted cords, sandals on their naked feet, and their cowls drawn down over their faces, completely hiding the features, except where, through two holes, the eyes could be distinguished but not recognized. They were followed by a few Capuchins, a single priest, with the customary cross-bearer, and then others of the *Sacconi* bearing a bier upon their shoulders.

"The streets along which the procession passed were crowded with people lining the way on either side. The marked contrast between the unobtrusive character of the funeral and the great amount of attention it attracted might well cause a stranger to ask, 'Who is it?' for even the very poor contrive to obtain the hire of a rich pall to cover their dead for the last time, and over this coffin there was nothing but coarse sackcloth; all can pay for a dozen or more candles, but around this bier the number was limited to four; few are so absolutely unknown that some conveyance, however modest, is not sent to pay them honour, but after this corpse not even a hack cab followed. One thing was especially noticeable— the bare feet and ankles of the closely-cowled brotherhood were white and scrupulously clean.

"The procession entered the Church of St. Agnes, in the Piazza Navona. There were no armorial bearings over the door, or other indications of any kind that a funeral service was to be solemnized there, nor were there any hangings or other preparations within the church. The bier was laid down upon the floor, a few common benches placed around it. The ordinary service for the dead was performed in the simplest manner; the *Sacconi* knelt for some time in silent prayer, and then with one single taper burning at the head and another at the feet, they left—in the solitude of his own church, where lie buried many members of his family, and with the figure of Innocent X. looking down on the sackcloth pall which covered his remains—all that is mortal of Filippo Andrea, until two days ago representative of the great Houses of Doria and Pamphili.

"It was the will of this Prince, so well known to many of your readers, that his funeral obsequies should be performed *more pauperrimo* by the members of the confraternity of the *Sacconi*, to which he belonged. There are few who have been in Rome who have not seen the weird-looking figures of the *Sacconi* flitting hurriedly from shop to shop, rattling a money-box, which at times, also, they would urgently but silently present to a passer-by, who seldom failed to drop a coin within. On Fridays in Lent they were to be met with, and on special occasions of public suffering they were to be seen in numbers. The chief of the Roman patriciate are members of this brotherhood; it is essentially an aristocratic Order, bound together for works of penitence and charity, particularly towards the very indigent, the dying, and the dead. Its head-quarters are attached to the little round church of St. Theodore, commonly called St. Toto, near the Forum, and there each member has a cupboard where he keeps his sackcloth dress and hempen girdle, together with a knotted scourge of many cords for penitential use there upon himself, and which, I am told, is often lustily applied.

"This morning the Requiem Mass was said, and the '*Dies iræ*' simply recited, with the same entire absence of pomp, excepting only that those who, out of respect for the Prince's wishes, refrained yesterday from taking, either directly or indirectly, any part in the funeral, to-day attended in numbers; the side of the Piazza Navona on which the church stands was lined with carriages two and three deep throughout the entire length. But no preparation had been made for any one; the coffin, covered with its sackcloth pall, lay on its bier in the middle of the church, and around it crowded rich and poor, noble and plebeian, Princesses and beggar women, without the slightest distinction of rank and station. To send you the names of the many distinguished persons present would be simply to give a list of the noble Roman Houses, with Prince and Princess, Marchese and Marchesa, and so on, attached; the difficulty would be to say what Roman lady or gentleman of rank was absent, or what station of life was unrepresented, from the Heir to the Throne to the halt, the lame, and the blind, indiscriminately mixed together.

"On Saturday evening, the 19th, Prince Doria was at the Opera. It was the benefit of the *prima donna*, Borghi-Mamo. He retired as usual on returning home, but at half-past four he awoke and called to his servant to bring him some broth. While drinking it he noticed how heavily it was hailing. He then turned to go to sleep again. Something, however, in his manner alarmed his attendant; assistance was called, but by six o'clock he had expired. Prince Doria was born on the 28th of September, 1813. On the 4th of April, 1839, he married Lady Mary Talbot, daughter of the Earl of Shrewsbury and sister of Lady Gwendoline Talbot, who married Prince Borghese. He became a widower on the 18th of December, 1858. His high social qualities are too extensively known to need any setting forth by me. In politics he belonged to that number of men who rejoiced to see Italy made one, while remaining faithful and devoted spiritual subjects of the Pope. In 1847 he filled for a short time the office of Minister of War in that Constitutional Government which Pius IX. attempted at the commencement of his reign. Shortly after Rome became the capital of Italy he filled the office of Pro-Syndic until Prince Pallavicini was appointed Syndic. It was he who signed the Note announcing to foreign Governments that the Court and seat of Government of His Majesty King Victor Emmanuel was established in Rome, the capital of Italy. On the removal of the Court here he was created a Senator and appointed Prefect of the Royal Palace; but matters of administrative detail, with which he found it difficult to deal, caused him to resign the latter office a few months afterwards. It has been stated that he also resigned his seat in the Senate, but if he ever expressed such an intention it was never carried into effect.

" He leaves five children—Donna Teresa, married to the Duke of Rignano; Don Gian Andrea, who succeeds to the title; Donna Guendalina, married to the Marchese Somaglia; Don Alfonso Maria, and Donna Olympia, unmarried.

" As the law now prohibits intramural burial in Rome, his remains could not be placed in the family vaults beside those of his wife. They were removed this afternoon to the Villa Pamphilo-Doria, outside the Porta San Pancrazio, and interred in the chapel there, in accordance with directions he had given some time before his death. After a sufficient lapse of time, which is fixed at ten years, they will finally be brought in again and laid among those of his family in the church of St. Agnes, in the Piazza Navona.

" Utterly devoid of pomp and ceremonial as the arrangements connected with Prince Doria's funeral were, there was, after all, no ostentation of humility, and no indication whatever of a return under priestly influence beyond its legitimate claims. Every one in Rome knows who the *Sacconi* are—they are nobles, many of them of the highest rank, and by the number attending the rank of the deceased may be judged. In desiring to be buried by the *Sacconi* Prince Doria acted in full accordance with that practice of the dead being carried or accompanied to the grave by the members of their own order, profession, or trade which has become general since the change of Government. In olden times the Religious Orders only accompanied the dead—it was a right, involving, also, a very heavy tax, which the Church reserved to herself. The only exceptions were when the troops attended and his brother officers followed the remains of a military man, or the wealthy sent their empty carriages to close the procession. By the funeral arrangements being left in the hands of the *Sacconi* Prince Doria was carried to the grave on the shoulders of the members of his own order, exactly as may be seen any day in the case of a carpenter, blacksmith, or other artisan, and with no further ecclesiastical interference than was necessary for the performance of the funeral rites prescribed by the Church. The strict humility of the form observed was in simple accordance with the rigid rules of the Order. The only signs of wealth manifested were two enormous bundles of great wax candles laid on the ground at the head and foot of the coffin this morning, and the incessant masses going on at each of the seven chapels in St. Agnese during the whole day."

REFUSAL OF A PRIEST TO BURY.

A man, who died on Christmas-day, 1875, in the city of Armagh from an overdose of whisky, as proved at the coroner's inquest, was buried in the Roman Catholic cemetery at early dawn on Monday morning. There was no priest present to perform the funeral service, and it is understood that there was a difference of opinion between the primate and priests on the subject. His grace is said to have been favourable to the service being performed at the dead man's grave, but the priest who was sent for was of a different opinion.

GOD'S ACRE.

An extraordinary funeral took place on Sunday, February 20th, 1876, at Eltham, in Kent. A few days previously the son of Mr. Thomas Chester Haworth, parish surveyor, died, and his father decided to bury him upon a waste piece of building land, the freehold of Mr. Haworth, situated at the side of the turnpike road. Three o'clock on Sunday afternoon was the time fixed for the interment, and at that hour a very large number of persons congregated on the spot. They found a brick building about 14 feet square and 8 feet high bearing the inscription, "The family mausoleum of Thomas Chester Haworth, of Eltham." An opening in front showed that another son of Mr. Haworth's had been already interred there. The funeral rites, which lasted about an hour, were performed by the Rev. B. Price, Congregational Minister of Eltham, who, in the course of an address, stated that the ground upon which they stood was "God's acre," and that he, with the friends of the deceased young man, preferred it as a burial place for their dead to the "Priest's acre."

NO NONSENSE.

The late DOWAGER COUNTESS OF SANDWICH in her Will, written by herself at the age of 80, expressed a wish to be buried decently and quietly—no under-taker's frauds or cheating—no scarfs, hatbands, OR NONSENSE.

ALL PLAIN.

The late philanthropic and humorous Deputy Assistant Judge, MR. JOSEPH PAYNE, desired that he should be buried "in a *plain* way, in a *plain* grave, and covered with a *plain* stone."

A BETHNAL GREEN BIRD FANCIER.

A few years ago, might have been witnessed in the Bethnal Green Road, a walking funeral, which differed from the ordinary working men's funeral in one singular respect only. On the velvet pall which covered the coffin, was a large white cotton handkerchief, on which rested two small cages, each containing a beautiful canary. On inquiry, it was ascertained that it was the funeral of a well-known bird fancier, who made his wife promise before he died, that his two pet canaries should accompany his coffin to the grave. Little bits of crape were tied round the cages, the woodwork had also been stained a dark colour, which gave them a peculiar appearance. No coarse jokes or light remarks were made by the crowd which followed the mourners. "Poor man," said a great muscular fishwoman, "he lov'd his birds." "An' he might 'a lov'd summat wuss," was the reply of her swarthy mate.

A SPITALFIELDS DOG FANCIER.

The death of a famous dog fancier in this locality was followed by a funeral, in which each of the human mourners led by a string some favourite animal belonging to the deceased. The dogs behaved as if they really understood the nature of the sad ceremony in which they took part.

A WHITECHAPEL FUNERAL PROCESSION.

Several years ago there was a funeral in which a large number of artisans in working dress took part.

This was from no want of respect towards their fellow-workman, but was occasioned by the refusal of their employer to grant them leave of absence to attend the obsequies of a man whom he disliked. They, however, baffled him in the following manner:—The funeral was arranged to take place during the dinner hour of the men, who, instead of adjourning to different coffee houses and public houses for their usual meal, formed themselves into a funeral procession behind the coffin of their old comrade.

FLORAL FUNERALS.

At the funeral of the wife of the son of Sir Charles Locock, Bart., the outer coffin was polished, and covered with costly flowers, and floral festoons entwined around it. The mourners each carried a bouquet of white flowers, and did not wear the usual habiliments of mourning. A muffled peal was rung before and after the interment, and also as the body was being borne from the church to the grave, and after the coffin had been lowered to its last resting place, the mourners threw their bouquets upon it, so that nothing was visible but a mass of flowers.

BOUQUETS.

About twenty years ago, when dahlias were much cultivated by the Bethnal Green and Spitalfields weavers, a well-known grower was followed to the grave by a number of weavers, carrying bouquets of his favourite flowers in their hands, the coffin being covered with an immense number of the same flowers.

"WHITE FUNERALS"

Were formerly common at the East-end of London, the coffin being invariably followed by a number of young women, dressed in white, and carrying funeral bouquets.

RESPECT TO AN OLD SERVANT.

Mr. William Bishop, of Notting Hill, who died 1875, directed his body to be buried in Godalming Churchyard or vaults—the vault or grave to be sufficiently large for two coffins, the other space being intended for his female servant. "I think," he says, in his Will, "this respect due to her for her long, and, I hope and believe, faithful services to me." His name and date of birth, 17th July, 1784, was to be inscribed on one side of the superstructure of the grave, and that of his servant on the other.

SHAKSPEARE'S JEST BOOK.

Under this title a book was reprinted in 1815, from one lately discovered bearing the title of

¶ A. C. Mery Talys.

Referring to the preface of the reprint for its value in support of the opinion corroborated by other

reprints, that Shakspeare was destitute of the learning attributed to him by some writers, an extract (with the spelling modernised) is taken from it as a specimen of the wit and morals which amused our ancestors :—

Of the woman that followed her fourth husband's bier and wept.

A woman there was which had four husbands. It fortuned also that her fourth husband died and was brought to church upon the bier, whom this woman followed, and made great moan, and waxed very sorry, insomuch that her neighbours thought she would swoon and die for sorrow; wherefore one of her gossips came to her and spake to her in her ear, and bade her for God's sake comfort herself and refrain that lamentation, or else it would hurt her, and peradventure put her in jeopardy of her life. To whom this woman answered and said, "I wys good gossip I have great cause to mourn if ye knew all, for I have buried three husbands besides this man, but I was never in the case that I am now, for there was not one of them but when that I followed the corse to church, yet I was sure of another husband, before the corse came out of my house; and now I am sure of no other husband, and therefore ye may be sure I have great cause to be sad and heavy."

By this tale ye may see, that the old proverb is
true, that it is as great a pity to see a woman weep,
as a goose to go barefoot.

CURIOUS ENGLISH PROVINCIAL CUSTOMS.

At Hatherleigh, in Devonshire, the church bells
ring out a lively peal after the funeral; and to this
custom the parishioners are perfectly reconciled by
the consideration that the deceased has been removed
from a scene of trouble to a state of peace.

AT HEXHAM, IN NORTHUMBERLAND,

An invitation to a funeral is, or was, a few years
since, proclaimed by the public bellman to the inhabitants in the following terms :—" Blessed are the dead
which die in the Lord; Edwin Holmes is departed,
son of Robert Holmes who was. Their company is
desired to-morrow at three o'clock, and at four he is
to be buried. For him and all faithful people give
God most hearty thanks."

IN HIS OWN GROUNDS, WITHOUT SERVICE.

Mr. Richard Christopher Carrington, of Churt,
near Farnham, Surrey, Astronomer, (died Nov., 1875)
desired that if he died in England, (which he did,) he
might be buried at a depth of between 10 and 12
feet in the grounds surrounding his own freehold
house at Churt, at an expense not exceeding £5,

and without any service being read over his grave, or any memorial erected to his memory; and that after his death, neither his chin should be shaved nor his shirt changed.

IMMURED ALIVE!

The monks and nuns, who broke their vows of chastity, suffered the same penalty as the Roman vestals in a similar case. A small niche, sufficient to enclose their bodies, was made in the massive wall of the convent; a slender pittance of food and water was deposited in it, and the awful words "*Vade in Pacem*" (Depart in peace), were the signal for immuring the criminal. (Read the glowing description of this frightful punishment in Scott's "Marmion," Canto II.)

BURIED IN FULL HUNTING COSTUME.

An eccentric character, named Pilkington, but generally known in the neighbourhood as Squire Hawley, was buried very recently at Hatfield, near Doncaster, in his own garden, in the centre of the graves of his cattle which died during the rinderpest. He was laid out in full hunting costume, including spurs and whip, and was carried from the house on a coffin board, when he was placed in a stone coffin, which weighing upwards of a ton, had to be lowered by means of a crane. His old pony was shot, and buried at his feet in bridle and saddle, and his dog and an old fox were buried at his head.   The deceased left the whole of his estate to his groom, John Vickers, on condition that the funeral, &c., be conducted according to his expressed wish, and should he fail in doing this the property was to revert to the priest of Doncaster, for the benefit of the Roman Catholic religion.

HOWLING AT FUNERALS.

This custom originated with the Irish, who make a great outcry upon the death of their friends, hoping thus to awaken the soul, which they suppose might otherwise be inactive.   It was also practised by the Arabs, Greeks, and Romans.   The latter nation had officers called *Præficæ*, whose special duty it was to superintend the manner and form of the lamentation.

WAKES.

All through Ireland the ceremonial of wakes and funerals is most punctually attended to, and it requires some *savoir faire* to carry through the arrangement in a masterly manner.   A great adept at the business, who had been the prime manager at all the wakes in the neighbourhood for many years, was at last called away from the death-beds of his friends to his own.   Shortly before he died he gave minute directions to his people as to the mode of waking him in proper style. " Recollect," says he, " to put three candles at the head of the bed, after you lay me out, and two at the foot, and one at each side. Mind now, and put a plate with the salt on it just a top of my breast. And, do you hear? have plenty of tobacco and pipes enough; and remember to make the punch strong. And—but what the devil is the use of talking to you? sure I know you'll be sure to botch it, as I won't be there myself."

DENIAL OF FUNERAL RITES AS A CURE FOR DUELLING.

Perhaps the most celebrated social problem presented for solution in the last days of the last century and the beginning of the present was the question how to suppress duelling. It can hardly be said with certainty what was the cause of its rather sudden extinction in this country; but probably public opinion had a great deal more to do with the result than any judicial or legislative methods. Some of the continental nations are still troubled with the fashionable pest, and still engaged in devising expedients to eradicate it from their territories. Hitherto all such attempts have been aimed at that one of the duellists who had the best of it in the field. The loser was possibly supposed to have paid a sufficient penalty in the sufferings entailed upon him by his wounds, or, if actually killed, escaped, as a matter of course, the vengeance of the law.   But a Government has at last hit upon the very original and novel plan of inflicting a vindictive punishment upon the body of the slain.   This is the Bavarian Government, which has carried out a signally severe sentence upon a certain Count killed in a duel, close to Munich, by an officer of the Royal Army.   The old laws of the country recognise in duels only a sort of suicide, and condemn the persons killed in them to all the penalties attaching to suicidal acts.   One of these consists in the denial to the defunct of the rights of burial.   Accordingly, the body of the deceased Count was carried off from the hands of those relations and friends who were about to perform the funeral rites and handed over to the dissecting room of the Munich Hospital. Great efforts are, it seems, being made to secure the remains from this ignominious fate, and from an inglorious interment in the common burial-ground. But if these attempts fail, it is expected that a death blow will be given to duelling in Bavaria.   Should it be so, it will be strange how far more powerful the dread of humiliation after death has proved than the fear of judicial vengeance while alive.

GIPSY FUNERAL.

The following account of a "Gipsy Funeral" is curious :—

The mortal remains of an aged female, belonging

to this singular race of people, were after death consigned to the earth in Highworth Churchyard, attended by a great concourse of spectators, attracted to the spot by the novelty of the spectacle. The interment was conducted with the greatest decorum, the interest of the scene being heightened, instead of damped, by the incessant rain, which fell in torrents on the venerable uncovered locks of the husband. He acted as chief mourner on the occasion, and, with his numerous offspring forming the procession was by "the pitiless storm assailed, unmoved." They appeared fully impressed with the awful solemnity of the last duty they were about to perform for one who had been a wife and a mother for nearly three-score years and ten. When living, she was a perfect "Meg Merrilies" in appearance, and it is even said that she was the identical person whom Walter Scott had in view when he wrote that inimitable character in Guy Mannering. Be this as it may, for considerably more than half a century she exercised her oracular powers in propounding the "good or bad fortune" of all the fair-going damsels of the country round. She had inspired many a love-lorn maid, not merely with hope, but with a "dead certainty" that the joys of Hymen should be hers in less than one fleeting year; and the Delphic oracle never imparted half the satisfaction to its anxious enquirers that our aged sybil invariably did to hers. True it is, however,

that her powers of divining good fortune in some
measure depended on the generosity of her applicants;
and while, for a shilling, or less, some *poor* maidens
were constrained to put up with the promise merely
of "a gentleman with a one-horse shay,"—the boon
of half-a-crown would purchase a "lord with a coach
and six." Often at "fair time" she was seen to retire
with some expecting lass to a remote corner of Highworth Churchyard, when, like a second Cassandra,
"big with the mysteries of fate," she would unfold
her anxious enquirer's future destiny; her predictions
might not "always" come true to the exact letter,
still while there was life there was hope, and who
would not purchase a year of *such* hopes for the
trifling sum of half-a-crown?—besides, even in this
case, the verifications of her predictions were only
in unison with those of our great High Priest of
Astrologers, Francis Moore, who wonderfully contrives
that every thing shall come to pass "the day before,
or the day after." It should have been stated before,
that she made her mortal exit in a lane in the vicinity
of Highworth, and that, in the coffin with her remains,
were enclosed a knife and fork, and plate; and five
tapers (not wax we presume) were placed on the lid,
and kept constantly burning till her removal for
interment; after which ceremony, the whole of her
wardrobe was burnt; and her donkey and dog were
slaughtered by her nearest relatives, in conformity

to a superstitious custom remaining among her tribe, derived, perhaps, from the east, where, on the demise of a person of distinction, the whole of their appendages both living and dead, are destroyed, in order that the defunct may have the benefit of their services in the next world. It is said that a memorial was erected to her memory with the following simple epitaph :—

> " Being dead yet speaketh."
> Beneath lies one—they say could tell
> By the magic of her spell,
> By the most unerring signs,
> By the hand's mysterious signs,
> What our earthly lot should be,
> What our future destiny.
> But the dust that lies below
> Speaks more truly, for e'en now,
> It bids the proud, ere life is past,
> Contemplate their lot at last,
> When this world's gaudy vision's gone,
> When high and low shall be as one,
> When rich and poor, and vile and just,
> Shall mingle in one common dust.

A FUNERAL AT SEA.

A funeral at sea is a very affecting scene ; and many a sunburnt, hardy and brave man, have I known who could not restrain the tear of sorrow and sympathy for his departed companion and messmate.

The funeral is conducted in the following manner :—

As soon as a seaman dies, the surgeon reports it to the officer of the watch; and, at whatever time of the night or day it happens, the captain is immediately made acquainted with it.

The deceased is prepared by his messmates for his "deep sea grave;" who, with the assistance of the sailmaker, in presence of the master-at-arms, sew him up in his hammock, putting a couple of shot at his feet. The body is then carried aft, and placed upon the after-hatchway, or on the half-deck, with the Union Jack (flag) thrown over all.

Next day, at about eleven o'clock, the bell is tolled for the funeral; and all who choose to attend, assemble on the gangway and around the mainmast, whilst the fore part of the quarter-deck is occupied by the officers.

While the people are repairing to the quarter-deck, the body is moved by the messmates of the deceased, and placed upon the lee-gangway, where an opening is made large enough to allow the body to pass. (It is still covered with the Union Jack.) While the messmates arrange themselves around, a rope, which is kept out of sight, is made fast to the grating upon which the body rests.

When all is ready, the chaplain (or, if there is not one on board, the captain or any of the officers may officiate) reads the service for the dead. On coming to the passage, "we therefore commit his body to the deep," &c., one of the sailors disengages the flag, and the others launch the grating overboard; when the body, loaded with the shot at one end, glances off the grating, and plunges at once into the ocean, where it must remain until earth and ocean give up their dead at the dread summons of the Creator.

After the funeral the grating is hauled on deck, and all hands return to their duties.

RURAL FUNERALS.

Among the beautiful and simple-hearted customs of rural life which still linger in some parts of England, are those of strewing flowers before the funerals, and planting them at the graves, of departed friends. These, it is said, are the remains of some of the rites of the primitive church; but they are of still higher antiquity, having been observed among the Greeks and Romans, and frequently mentioned by their writers, and were, no doubt, the spontaneous tributes of unlettered affection, originating long before art had tasked itself to modulate sorrow into song, or story it on the monument.

In Glamorganshire, we are told, the bed whereon the corpse lies is covered with flowers, a custom alluded to in one of the wild and plaintive ditties of Ophelia:

> White his shroud as the mountain snow,
> Larded all with sweet flowers:
> Which be-wept to the grave did go,
> With true love showers.

There is also a most delicate and beautiful rite observed in some of the remote villages of the south, at the funeral of a female who has died young and unmarried. A chaplet of white flowers is borne before the corpse by a young girl nearest in age, size, and resemblance, and is afterwards hung up in the church over the accustomed seat of the deceased. These chaplets are sometimes made of white paper, in imitation of flowers, and inside of them is generally a pair of white gloves. They are intended as emblems of the purity of the deceased, and the crown of glory which she has received in heaven.

In some parts of the country, also, the dead are carried to the grave with the singing of psalms and hymns: a kind of triumph, "to show," says Bourne, "that they have finished their course with joy, and are become conquerors." This, I am informed, is observed in some of the northern counties, particularly in Northumberland, and it has a pleasing, though melancholy effect, to hear, of a still evening, in some lonely country scene, the mournful melody of a funeral dirge swelling from a distance, and to see the train slowly moving along the landscape.

The custom of decorating graves was once universally prevalent: osiers were carefully bent over them to keep the turf uninjured, and about them were planted evergreens and flowers. "We adorn their graves," says Evelyn, in his Sylva, "with flowers and redolent plants, just emblems of the life of man, which has been compared in Holy Scriptures to those fading beauties, whose roots being buried in dishonour, rise again in glory." This usage has now become extremely rare in England; but it may still be met with in the churchyards of retired villages among the Welsh mountains; and I recollect an instance of it at the small town of Ruthven, which lies at the head of the beautiful vale of Clewyd. I have been told also by a friend, who was present at the funeral of a young girl in Glamorganshire, that the female attendants had their aprons full of flowers, which, as soon as the body was interred, they stuck about the grave.

He noticed several graves which had been decorated in the same manner. As the flowers had been merely stuck in the ground, and not planted, they had soon withered, and might be seen in various states of decay; some drooping, others quite perished. They were afterwards to be supplanted by holly, rosemary, and other evergreens; which on some graves had grown to great luxuriance, and overshadowed the tombstones.

There was formerly a melancholy fancifulness in the arrangement of these rustic offerings, that had something in it truly poetical. The rose was sometimes blended with the lily, to form a general emblem of frail mortality. "This sweet flower," said Evelyn, "borne on a branch set with thorns, and accompanied with the lily, are natural hieroglyphics of our fugitive, umbratile, anxious, and transitory life, which, making so fair a show for a time, is not yet without its thorns and crosses." The nature and colour of the flowers, and of the ribands with which they were tied, had often a particular reference to the qualities or story of the deceased, or were expressive of the feelings of the mourner.

The white rose, we are told, was planted at the grave of a virgin: her chaplet was tied with white ribands, in token of her spotless innocence; though sometimes black ribands were intermingled, to bespeak the grief of the survivors. The red rose was occasionally used in remembrance of such as had been remarkable for benevolence; but roses in general were appropriated to the graves of lovers.

When the deceased had been unhappy in their loves, emblems of a more gloomy character were used, such as the yew and cypress; and if flowers were strewn, they were of the most melancholy colours.

The natural effect of sorrow over the dead is to refine and elevate the mind; and we have a proof of it in the purity of sentiment and the unaffected elegance of thought which pervaded the whole of these funeral observances. Thus, it was an especial precaution, that none but sweet-scented evergreens and flowers should be employed. The intention seems to have been to soften the horrors of the tomb, to beguile the mind from brooding over the disgraces of perishing mortality, and to associate the memory of the deceased with the most delicate and beautiful objects in nature. There is a dismal process going on in the grave, ere dust can return to its kindred dust, which the imagination shrinks from contemplating; and we seek still to think of the form we have loved, with those refined associations which it awakened when blooming before us in youth and beauty.

There is certainly something more affecting in these prompt and spontaneous offerings of nature, than in the most costly monuments of art: the hand strews the flower while the heart is warm, and the tear falls on the grave as affection is binding the osier round the sod; but pathos expires under the slow labour of the chisel, and is chilled among the cold conceits of sculptured marble.

It is greatly to be regretted, that a custom so truly elegant and touching has disappeared from general use, and exists only in the most remote and insignificant villages. But it seems as if poetical custom always shuns the walks of cultivated society. In proportion as people grow polite they cease to be poetical. They talk of poetry, but they have learnt to check its free impulses, to distrust its sallying emotions, and to supply its most affecting and picturesque usages, by studied form and pompous ceremonial. Few pageants can be more stately and frigid than an English funeral in town. It is made up of show and gloomy parade; mourning carriages, mourning horses, mourning plumes, and hireling mourners, who make a mockery of grief. "There is a grave digged," says Jeremy Taylor, " and a solemn mourning, and a great talk in the neighbourhood, and when the daies are finished, they shall be, and they shall be remembered no more." The associate in the gay and crowded city is soon forgotten; the hurrying succession of new intimates and new pleasures effaces him from our minds, and the very scenes and circles in which he moved are incessantly fluctuating. But funerals in the country are solemnly impressive. The stroke of death makes a wider space in the village circle, and is an awful event in the tranquil uniformity of rural life. The passing-bell tolls its knell in every ear; it steals with its pervading melancholy over every hill and vale, and saddens all the landscape.

The fixed and unchanging features of the country also perpetuate the memory of the friend with whom we once enjoyed them; who was the companion of our most retired walks, and gave animation to every lonely scene. His idea is associated with every charm of nature; we hear his voice in the echo which he once delighted to awaken; his spirit haunts every grove which he once frequented; we think of him in the wild upland solitude, or amidst the pensive beauty of the valley. In the freshness of joyous morning, we remember his beaming smiles and bounding gaiety; and when sober evening returns with its gathering shadows and subduing quiet, we call to mind many a twilight hour of gentle talk and sweet-souled melancholy.

> Each lonely place shall him restore,
> For him the tear be duly shed;
> Beloved, till life can charm no more;
> And mourn'd till pity's self be dead.

Another cause that perpetuates the memory of the deceased in the country, is, that the grave is more immediately in sight of the survivors. They pass it on their way to prayer; it meets their eyes when their hearts are softened by the exercises of devotion; they linger about it on the Sabbath, when the mind is disengaged from worldly cares, and most disposed to turn aside from present pleasures and present loves, and to sit down among the solemn mementos of the past. In North Wales the peasantry kneel and pray over the graves of their deceased friends for several Sundays after the interment; and where the tender rite of strewing and planting flowers is still practised, it is always renewed on Easter, Whitsun-tide, and other festivals, when the season brings the companion of former festivity more vividly to mind. It is also invariably performed by the nearest relatives and friends; no menials nor hirelings are employed; and if a neighbour yields assistance, it would be deemed an insult to offer compensation.

I have dwelt upon this beautiful rural custom, because, as it is one of the last, so it is one of the holiest offices of love. The grave is the ordeal of true affection. It is there that the divine passion of the soul manifests its superiority to the instinctive impulse of mere animal attachment. The latter must be continually refreshed and kept alive by the presence of its object; but the love that is seated in the soul can live on long remembrance. The mere inclinations of sense languish and decline with the charms which excited them, and turn with shuddering disgust from the dismal precincts of the tomb; but it is thence that truly spiritual affection rises purified from every sensual desire, and returns like a holy flame to illumine and sanctify the heart of the survivor.

The sorrow for the dead is the only sorrow from which we refuse to be divorced. Every other wound we seek to heal—every other affliction to forget; but this wound we consider it a duty to keep open—this affliction we cherish and brood over in solitude. Where is the mother who would willingly forget the infant that perished like a blossom from her arms, though every recollection is a pang? Where is the child that would willingly forget the most tender of parents, though to remember be but to lament? Who, even in the hour of agony, would forget the friend over whom he mourns? Who, even when the tomb is closing upon the remains of her he most loved; when he feels his heart, as it were, crushed in the closing of its portal; would accept of consolation that must be bought by forgetfulness?—No, the love which survives the tomb is one of the noblest attributes of the soul. If it has its woes, it has likewise its delights; and when the overwhelming burst of grief is calmed into the gentle tear of recollection; when the sudden anguish and the convulsive agony over the present ruins of all that we most loved is softened away into pensive meditation on all that it was in the days of its loveliness—who would root out such a sorrow from the heart? Though it may sometimes throw a passing cloud over the bright hour of gaiety; or spread a deeper sadness over the hour of gloom; yet who would exchange it, even for the song of pleasure, or the burst of revelry? No, there is a voice from the tomb sweeter than song. There is a remembrance of the dead to which we turn even from the charms of the living. Oh, the grave!—the grave!—It buries every error—covers every defect—extinguishes every resentment! From its peaceful bosom spring none but fond regrets and tender recollections. Who can look down upon the grave even of an enemy, and not feel a compunctious throb, that he should ever have warred with the poor handful of earth, that lies mouldering before him?

But the grave of those we loved—what a place for meditation! There it is that we call up in long review the whole history of virtue and gentleness, and the thousand endearments lavished upon us almost unheeded in the daily intercourse of intimacy —there it is that we dwell upon the tenderness, the solemn, awful tenderness of the parting scene. The bed of death, with all its stifled griefs—its noiseless attendance—its mute, watchful assiduities. The last testimonies of expiring love! The feeble, fluttering, thrilling—oh, how thrilling!—pressure of the hand. The last fond look of the glazing eye turning upon us even from the threshold of existence! The faint, faltering accents, struggling in death to give one more assurance of affection!

Ay, go to the grave of buried love, and meditate! There settle the account with thy conscience for every past benefit unrequited—every past endearment unregarded, of that departed being, who can never—never—never return to be soothed by thy contrition!

If thou art a child, and hast ever added a sorrow to the soul, or a furrow to the silvered brow of an affectionate parent—if thou art a husband, and hast ever caused the fond bosom that ventured its whole happiness in thy arms to doubt one moment of thy kindness or thy truth—if thou art a friend, and hast ever wronged, in thought, or word, or deed, the spirit that generously confided in thee—if thou art a lover, and hast ever given one unmerited pang to that true heart which now lies cold and still beneath thy feet;—then be sure that every unkind look, every ungracious word, every ungentle action, will come thronging back upon thy memory, and knocking dolefully at thy soul—then be sure that thou wilt lie down sorrowing and repentant on the grave, and utter the unheard groan, and pour the unavailing tear; more deep, more bitter, because unheard and unavailing.

Then weave thy chaplet of flowers, and strew the beauties of nature about the grave; console thy broken spirit, if thou canst, with these tender, yet futile tributes of regret; but take warning by the bitterness of this thy contrite affliction over the dead, and henceforth be more faithful and affectionate in the discharge of thy duties to the living.—*Washington Irving.*

THE GRANDEST TOMB IN THE WORLD.

The afternoon was devoted to an excursion in open carriages to what is perhaps the grandest tomb in the world, as the Taj is certainly the most beautiful—Secundra, where lie the remains of Akber (or Akhbar, or however else his name may be spelt), to whom India—Hindoo and Mussulman—accords the title of "Great"—apparently with every reason. The road still shows the coshminars (round stone pillars) which were put up at the distance of every two miles along Imperial Mogul routes, and which it is said were erected along the highway, extending for more than 700 miles, from Agra to Lahore. Near each end was a watch-tower, and there were halting-places and serais and wells for travellers in the olden time. So imperiously impatient were Great Moguls in those days that, if the legend be true, trees of full growth, thirty years old, were carried on elephants from the forests and planted along the road to shade the way-farer. Some six miles from camp the modern tourist sees before him a grand gateway in a quadrangle enclosure, with octagon minarets at each angle. This gives access to a garden, in the centre of which is the mausoleum, a square of noble masonry of red sand-stone, 300 feet a side, built in five stories, each diminishing in area from the base, which measures 300 feet, to the screen work of marble which surrounds the marble story at the summit at the height of 100 feet from the bottom. Every terrace is ornamented with an arched gallery and cupolas, and these were said to bear relation to the divisions of the vast Empire over which he who now rests below once ruled in dignity and power. This grand pile is approached by a causeway from each of the four gateways—one in each of the lofty battlemented walls surrounding the garden.   Without going so far as Mr. Bayard Taylor, who considers Secundra nobler in conception and more successful in embodiment of Saracenic art than the Alcazar or Alhambra, it may be admitted that this work stands among the grandest ever reared by man. Two hundred and sixty-three years have elapsed since the tomb was finished.   The son of the Queen of that England which was then represented in this land by a few adventurous merchants and mariners and one or two wandering travellers, whose greatest wonder was that they were there at all, now stood before the Sarcophagus within which lie the bones of the fourth descendant of Tamerlane, grandson of Baber, grand-father of Shah Jehan—stood there acknowledged heir to the sceptre, which had been wielded with such grandeur and might—successor to the throne of Akber the Great, whose titles one might read in the exquisitely-carved inscriptions, ascribing to him majesty and glory for ever.   Secundra stands amid ruins, some ascribed to Lake's army, others to the Jats, others to 1857-8.   It is a fitting scene for a sermon on the rise and fall of Empire and on the vanity of human wishes.—*Times' Special Correspondent in India, 1876.*

FUNERALS OF THE FRENCH AND GERMAN CONSULS
AT SALONICA,

(Who were cruelly murdered in a Mosque there by the Turks, May, 1876), from the *Times'* Correspondent's Letter, dated May 23, 1876.

The funeral ceremonies yesterday, when the body of the late French Consul, M. Moulin, was conveyed on board the French frigate Gaulois, for passage to France, and that of the late German Consul, Mr. Abbott, who was interred in the European cemetery in Salonica, were calculated to show the Turks that if the Christian nations will so easily and readily assemble so large a force as is here to pay a last tribute of respect to their late countrymen, when only two are concerned, they will quickly take measures to resent any hostilities of a more extended nature, should the Turks contemplate them.

Owing to the difference of religion between the two late Consuls, also to their different destinations, there had to be two distinct ceremonials. The first body, that of the French Consul, had to be brought from the French Roman Catholic chapel to the Quay for embarkation; the second, from the Greek Church through almost every street in the Greek quarter to the cemetery. The processions, which were conducted by the Viceroy (or Pasha) in person, attended by the Second Commissioner and Turkish Admiral, were protected on either side by a guard of about 60 or 70 men from the different men-of-war, consisting of English Marines, French, German, Russian, Austrian, Italian, Greek, and Turkish sailors, each vessel furnishing about 15 men, except the French and Germans, who furnished more. The coffins, preceded by the Pasha and clergy, were followed by the families of the deceased. The German senior officer and French Admiral, the Captains of the men-of-war, the delegates from Constantinople (on the Commission), and a large number of officers from all the ships, including the whole of those of the French and German. After them came a party of seamen, who were followed by all the residents who wished to take part. The two processions only differed in the fact that the French were on the right in the French funeral and the Germans on the right in the other one. The guards, consisting of picked men from the ships, among which the Marines were, by their red tunics and beautifully polished arms, very conspicuous, looked most imposing as they marched in two lines with swords fixed and rifles at the "slope," and the different variety of uniforms of the officers, who were in full dress, added to the effect. The Pasha had taken every precaution to insure the safety of the procession, it having been reported that the Turks intended to make an attack. The Turkish troops were guarding every street and byway leading into those through which it would have to pass, sometimes three deep. Moreover, the Turkish quarter was completely isolated by a cordon of troops, and no Turk was allowed to leave his own quarter of the town; and, in addition, the procession was provided with a strong advanced and rear guard of Turkish soldiers.. Each funeral occupied about two hours. The body of the French Consul was taken to the Quay and was conveyed to the Gaulois under a salute of seven guns from the fleet. That of the German Consul, according to the Greek custom, was carried in procession, after a long service in the church, through the Greek quarter, the body being exposed the whole time. The wisdom of parading the body of a man murdered under such circumstances, with the marks of violence plainly visible about him, is open to question at any time, and on this occasion, especially, is likely to embitter to a very great degree the hatred which already exists between the Greeks and Turks. The houses, windows, &c., were densely crowded. Just before interment the family, clergy, and friends of the deceased came forward and kissed the forehead of the deceased. At the moment of interment the fleet, for the second time, thundered forth a salute of seven guns, and all the ensigns, which have been half-mast high since the affair, were simultaneously hoisted quite up. It must have been somewhat galling to the Pasha, who

is by no means so young as he used to be, to have
to march slowly for four hours at the head of a
Christian procession, besides having to go into the
Christian church during the service. It is supposed
that it was the French who requested his presence.
In any case it must have been a deep humiliation
to him.

REMOVAL FROM ENGLAND, AND RE-INTERMENT IN FRANCE OF THE BODIES OF MEMBERS OF THE ORLEANS FAMILY.

The President of the French Republic* having
consented to the mortal remains of the late King
Louis Philippe, his Queen Marie Amelie, and other
members of the Orleans family, until now buried
at Weybridge, being interred in the family burying-
place at Dreux, in Normandy, the Comte de Paris
came over from France for the purpose of superin-
tending their removal, accompanied by his Secretary
and the Abbé Berthe, a French Roman Catholic
priest. The Royal remains were taken from the
vaults of the Roman Catholic Chapel at Weybridge,
on the 8th June, 1876, at 3 o'clock in the morning.
The remains of the Duchess of Orleans, the only
Protestant among the number, were first taken out
of the vault. A short Mass was afterwards said over
the bodies of all the others, who were Roman Catholics,

* Marshal Macmahon.

and a special train, with the Comte de Paris and his attendants, left Weybridge at 6.10 a.m.

On arrival at Southampton, the train was taken alongside the Dock-quay, where was berthed one of the London, Chatham, and Dover Company's steamships, the Samphire, commanded by Captain Pittock, which had been chartered and sent round for the purpose. The several coffins were immediately transferred from the railway carriages to the steamer.

There were in all ten coffins, the first to be removed, as at Weybridge, being that containing the remains of the Duchess of Orleans. Then followed in succession those of King Louis Philippe, the Queen Marie Amelie, the Duchesse d'Aumale, the Prince de Condé, and five of the Royal children, one bearing the name of the young Duc de Guise, and the others having no names on them. An eleventh case contained the heart of the Prince de Condé embalmed in an urn. The whole proceedings had been kept so strictly private that, beyond the officials and those concerned, not a score of persons witnessed what may with propriety be termed an interesting historical incident. The after-part of the Samphire, where the coffins were arranged in rows, that of the Duchess of Orleans being a little apart from the rest, was draped with black cloth. The British ensign floated from the peak halyards, and the French tricolor from the mainmast, both at half-mast. The Dock Company's flag was also hoisted half-mast high at the dock entrance until the steamer had left, and beyond these simple symbols of mourning not the slightest indication was given of anything out of the usual course. All the coffins were perfectly sound and in an excellent state of preservation, with the sole exception of that of the Prince de Condé, the wood of which was so decayed that the coffin was placed in a stout black case prepared for the purpose before being lowered into the vessel. The Comte de Paris, with his Secretary and the Abbé Berthe, proceeded in the Samphire.

The remains of the Duchesse de Nemours, now the only member of the Orleans family whose body reposes at Weybridge, were not removed with the others transferred to France yesterday.

Dreux, June 9th, 1876.

Yesterday evening at 9 o'clock the exhumed remains of those members of the Orleans family who died in exile in England arrived at Honfleur, in charge of the Comte de Paris. He brought them on at once to Paris, where they arrived at an early hour this morning, and a special train left shortly afterwards for Dreux, the Comte being joined by the Duc and Duchesse de Montpensier, the Prince and Princess de Joinville, the Duc d'Aumale, the Duc de Nemours, the Comte de Flandres, the Duc de

Chartres, the Duc and Duchesse de Saxe Coburg, the Comtesse de Paris, and several other members of the family. The train was exclusively occupied by them, not even the intimate friends of the Princes being permitted to accompany the mourners.

As the hour at which the special train was to arrive was long before the time of the arrival of the regular train from Paris, I came here yesterday evening, and thus had the advantage of a preparatory glance at the town. It is a place of some seven thousand inhabitants, with the tall houses and narrow streets characteristic of old French towns, its Hôtel de Ville and market-place dating unmistakably from a time when notions of convenience had not yet been developed to the detriment of elegance. At a short distance from the town is the Mausoleum of the Orleans family. There is no castle or other dwelling place belonging to them in the neighbourhood, except a lodge which goes by the name of the *Eveché*, because, I was told, at one time a Bishop connected with the chapel occasionally stayed there. The chapel is an almost even cross with a central illuminated dome and ·richly stained windows. It is situated on an ascent overlooking the town. Close to it, surrounded by a dense shrubbery, are the ruins of an old tower, of whose history my informants knew nothing. The chapel, as well as the grounds, are open to the public, and full service is held there every

Sunday. Unfortunately, the incessant rain which has been falling since yesterday afternoon was calculated to render gloomier than ever the already gloomy aspect of the whole place. The town was, as one might expect, talking of nothing but the event of to-day, and of the phenomenon of forty horses and six hearses which had that afternoon arrived; but I noticed no stronger feeling than simple curiosity. The Princes having no residence in the town are, of course, hardly known to the inhabitants except by name.

This morning, at 7 o'clock, the mourners and the bodies arrived, and with them a troop of porters and several priests. It was some time before all was in readiness to start; then it was raining heavily, and we were all bare-headed. Everybody stood patiently, for there was a certain fascination in the spectacle of this return to France of those who had left it so mournfully. The Orleans Princes, it is said, have lately sold most of their property in England, and have now brought back to France all that could embitter any recollections of the past. The bodies they brought this morning were those of King Louis Philippe, Queen Marie Amelie, the Duchesse d'Orleans, the Duchesse d'Aumale, the Prince de Condé, and five of the royal children. At about 8 o'clock the six hearses were in motion, and the mourners, headed by the Duc de Montpensier, the

Duc de Nemours, and the Prince de Joinville, followed bare-headed and on foot through the rain and dirt. The whole town had apparently turned into the streets, and I was surprised to see so large a crowd assembled where I had previously seen such desolation. There was, however, no demonstration. Many remained covered as the *hautes personnages* proceeded on their route through the town. This was curious, because the Princes are almost without exception tall, and have that rigid commanding expression which generally produces so much awe among French lower classes. But, as I have already said, it was simple curiosity which had brought them into the streets. Thus, the grand hearses, each drawn by four horses, and the brilliant *Fleur de Lys*, were so novel to them and absorbed them so completely, that the mourners were hardly remarked. Gradually the line of bystanders came to an end, and in the last part of our course we were merely followed by a few of the more curious townspeople. At the gate of the grounds surrounding the chapel one hearse detached itself from the others and went by another part to the ruin I have already referred to. This hearse contained the body of the Duchesse d'Orleans, who, having been a Protestant, will be provisionally placed in the Tower; that is, I suppose, till arrangements are made for interring her remains with a Protestant service. In the chapel a magnificent catafalque had been erected for the immediate reception of the coffins. The front seats were occupied by the members of the family, the aisles only being open to the few strangers who had followed in the rear of the mourners. Here I stationed myself during the long ceremony, the monotonous chanting and the grating of the bass viol in the responses being occasionally broken by very sweet music from the organ, which is hidden away in the west corner. Under the chapel are the burial vaults. Thither, after the chapel service was concluded, the coffins were borne, the last rites being performed in strict privacy. The Comte de Paris, I have since been told, keeps the key of the tomb, and never opens it but for the interment of a member of the family, so that it is only a rare occasion on which it can be viewed. After the coffins had been finally deposited, the family quitted the chapel for the Lodge, and are, I understand, to return to Paris this evening.

The whole ceremony was strictly private, the most faithful political adherents of the Orleans family having been requested to abstain from attending. Nobody can have witnessed it without being struck by the contrast it presented to the return of Napoleon's remains from St. Helena. The latter were brought back with all imaginable pomp to the capital which had exulted over his triumphs, the many years during

which they had lain in a foreign soil having only
effaced the recollection of his faults and rekindled
the admiration of his achievements.   Louis Philippe's
ashes, after a still more prolonged exile, are brought
over by his family like those of a private individual,
and interred, not in St. Dénis or in the capital of the
nation over which he reigned, but in an obscure
Norman town, escorted only by his descendants, and
amid the mere curiosity or positive apathy of the
population along the route.—*The Times, June,
1876.*

THE CATACOMBS, SYRACUSE.

The Church of St. Marcian, said to be the first
structure in Europe appropriated to Christian worship,
is now a subterranean crypt, over which the modern
church of S. Giovanni has been erected.   Opposite
the tomb of this Saint Marcian, the protomartyr, the
first bishop of Syracuse, stands a block of red granite,
to which he is said to have been tied at the time of
his decapitation; and which, in the opinion of all
good Catholics, owes its colour to the blood with
which it was bespattered on that and similar tragical
occasions.

The Catacombs, contiguous to this crypt, are vast
excavations of uncertain date, forming extensive
subterranean streets of tombs cut out of the solid
rock.   The entrance to them is by a passage six

feet high, eight broad—expanding afterwards to twenty—and carried on in a right line, so as to form the principal street, with an aperture in the roof for the admission of air. From this master-line other streets branch off in different directions, all of them bordered with columbaria, and oblong sepulchral niches of various sizes. Here and there are found little squares and circular openings, formed by different convergent avenues, and ventilated by the external air, admitted through conical apertures. From the marks of gates and locks still remaining, it has been conjectured that some of the recesses were private property. The walls of many of them are decorated with rude paintings on a vermilion ground, representing palm-branches, doves, circles, inclosing crosses, and other religious emblems, Pagan as well as Christian. Lamps, urns, vases, crucifixes, and monumental tablets have here been found in great abundance; many of which are now deposited in the public museum.

These Catacombs, which consists of two stories, have been referred to very different ages, and assigned to very different objects; but the most plausible opinion seems to be that which ascribes them to the Romans, during the period between the colonization of Syracuse by Augustus, and the division of the Empire. That they were merely the quarries from which the Syracusan Greeks drew materials for building the city, seems very improbable; for we can hardly suppose that ingenious people to have been so indifferent to the waste of time and labour, as to have cut their quarries into such precise and inconvenient shapes, and still less that they would have formed them into two distinct tiers or stories. Nor is it at all more probable that the Greeks would provide such extensive receptacles for their dead; and for this plain reason, that, as the bodies of their dead were generally burnt, small niches for cinerary urns were all that was required.

It should be remembered, too, that no example of such a cemetery exists in any Grecian city which was not a Roman colony; whereas, at Rome itself, as well as at Naples—which was colonized by Romans— we meet with catacombs the very counterpart of those at Syracuse.—*Evans' " Classic and Connoisseur."*

THE CATACOMBS OF THE CAPUCHINS, PALERMO.

Beneath the old Monastery of the Capuchins at Palermo, where there is a college for the education of young priests, and is situated in the environs about two miles from the city. These vaults are entered by a flight of steps, and are open to the public till four o'clock each day, though visited by very few people. The air is admitted with the light through open iron bars, which makes a draught, causing the remains to swing their heads and hands a little, and look alive. They are dried bodies, not skeletons, and are prepared by being placed in a kneeling position in a room where the air has full play round them till the bowels drop out. This takes six months with a man and nine or twelve with a woman, so the monk in charge said. The remains of monks have a card on the breast, stating name and age and date of death. Many of them have been there fifty years, some are recent. On the more recent additions the hair and beard were quite perfect and the face black and swollen. Many had one side only of the beard remaining, the opposite having fallen off, which gave the poor face a grotesque look. There are also priests in their full vestments, and two boys in surplices on each side of them, just as they appear in the churches when "celebrating mass." The coffins or boxes have in many cases glass fronts or tops, and contain lay men and women, dressed in their every-day apparel. I have seen ladies open with a key the lid of one of those boxes, and cry over the remains of a female child about ten years old, dressed in evening costume, in others they were gentlemen in evening dress, with a boy or girl of eight or ten years laid in beside them, also nicely dressed. The flags contain only the names, &c., of those in the trunks. It is only lay people of the highest class, who must also belong to a certain religious confraternity, who have the "privilege" of being placed in those trunks or boxes.   There are on the shelves also monks, those which from age fall to pieces are placed on them. Cats may be met with asleep here and there through the place.   They have attached to the monastery a regular ordinary cemetery, containing a number of first-class busts and statues of the occupants of the graves."—*The Graphic.*

THE CATACOMBS OF PARIS.

The Catacombs are a vast excavated place containing the skulls and bones of many thousands of persons, brought from different burial grounds in Paris, and deposited here after the Revolution, when the churchyards were ransacked for the dead.   They are placed in regular piles, on each side as you walk: and the frequent solemn and appropriate inscriptions, taken from the classic authors, add not a little to the solemnity of the scene.—*Rev. T. Pennington.*

* CEMETERY OF PERE LA CHAISE.

The approach to it (a little way out of Paris) is literally "garlanded with flowers."   You imagine yourself in the neighbourhood of a wedding, a fair, or some holiday-festival.   Women are sitting by the road side or at their own doors, making chaplets of a sort of yellow flowers, which are gathered in the

* Formerly the garden of Pere La Chaise, the Father Confessor of Louis XIV.

fields, baked, and will then last a French " For ever."
They have taken "the lean abhorred monster" Death
and strewed him o'er and o'er with sweets; they
have made the grave a garden, a flower bed where
all Paris reposes, the rich and the poor, the mean and
the mighty, gay and laughing, and putting on a fair
outside as in their lifetime. Death here seems life's
play-fellow, and grief and smiling content sit at one
tomb together. Roses grow out of the clayey ground,
there is the urn for tears, the slender cross for faith
to twine round; the neat marble monument, the
painted wreaths thrown upon it to freshen memory
and mark the hand of friendship. No black and
melancholic yew-trees darken the scene, and add a
studied gloom to it—no ugly death's heads or carved
skeletons shock the sight. On the contrary, some
pretty Ophelia, as general mourner, appears to have
been playing her fancies over a nation's bier, to
have been scattering "pansies for thoughts, rue for
remembrances." . . · . . . . . Here is the
tomb of Abelard and Heloise—immortal monument,
immortal as the human heart and poet's verse can
make it ! But it is slight, fantastic, of the olden time,
and seems to shrink from the glare of daylight, or as
if it would like to totter back to the old walls of the
Paraclete, and bury its quaint devices and its hallowed
inscriptions in shadowy twilight. It is, however, an
affecting sight, and many a votive garment is

sprinkled over it.   Here is the tomb of Ney (the double traitor), worthy of his fate and of his executioner;—and of Massena and Kellerman.   There are many others of great note, and some of the greatest names—Molière, Fontaine, De Lille, chancellors and *charbottiers* [charcoal burners] lie mixed together, and announce themselves with equal pomp.   These people have as good an opinion of themselves after death as before it.   You see a bust with a wreath or crown round its head—a strange piece of masquerade—and other tombs with a print or miniature of the deceased hanging to them !   Frequently a plain marble slab is laid down for the surviving relatives of the deceased, waiting its prey in expressive silence.   This is making too free with death, and acknowledging a claim which requires no kind of light to be thrown upon it.   We should visit the tombs of our friends with more soothing feelings, without marking out our own places beside them.   But every French thought or sentiment must have an external emblem.   The inscriptions are in general, however, simple and appropriate.   I only remarked one to which any exception could be taken; it was a plain tribute of affection to some individual by his family, who professed to have "erected this *modest* monument to preserve his memory *for ever*."   What a singular idea of modesty and eternity !—*W. Hazlitt.*

COFFINS AND CEMETERIES IN BRAZIL.

The coffins are of the same width and depth throughout, and so shallow that the face, folded hands, and feet of the corpse appear above the edge. The covers are peaked, like the roofs of houses, consisting of two boards meeting in the middle at an angle. Hinged at both sides, they open along the ridge, so that either one half or both may be thrown back. When finally closed, the only fastening is a small padlock.

The cemeteries of Rio adjoin the rear or sides of their respective churches. They are not seen from any street, not opening directly into any. At first I wondered where they were, and when I found them, I wondered more at their limited dimensions. The dead are not interred in graves, nor concealed below the surface; instead of extensive burial grounds or subterraneous excavations, room for four thick walls, of which the side of a church commonly answers for one, is found sufficient. As these places are on one plan, a description of this of St. Francisco de Paula will give a general idea of all.

Passing out through a side door, we entered a quadrangular area bounded by four high walls, with a contiguous shed or roof projecting inward, leaving a central space open to the sky, occupied by a few marble tombstones. The niches for the dead, wrought in the walls, were a little over six feet by two and a-half, eighteen inches high at the ends, and two feet at the middle, the roof forming a low arch. All are plastered and whitewashed. In hot weather they would be no bad resting places for the living. I was no longer surprised that people here are mostly buried without coffins, and especially as all are entombed in their clothes.

Here were three tiers of niches, each continued round the place. Those that are occupied have the fronts bricked up and plastered over. All are numbered; no other mark or lettering. Their tenants occupy them too short a time for inscriptions or eulogies to remain.

The coffin was placed on a temporary platform close to a niche in the middle tier, into which it was slid with the covers open. A handkerchief was spread over the face of the deceased by one of his friends; then, in succession, priests and friends stepped up, one at a time, and, with a silver sprinkler, handed by the sacristan, threw holy water on the body, and emptied a small scoop of powdered quick-lime, which an attendant held ready, upon it. A bushel or more of lime was thus disposed of, until it entirely concealed the body, and was heaped over the trunk. A priest used the silver sprinkler once more, poured something out of a small perforated box, and the church ceremonies were over.

A gentleman now drew a paper from his bosom, and for half-an-hour read a eulogy on the dead. A second, third, and even a fourth oration was thus delivered; at the close of which the president of the institute closed the coffin lids, locked them, and handed the minute key to a relative of the defunct. In half-an-hour the front of the niche was bricked up, and covered with a coat of white plaster.

In this mode of inhumation nothing like corruption takes place. The lime consumes the flesh, and in two years the bones are taken out and placed in a rosewood or marble vase, or burned, and the ashes preserved. The niche will then be whitewashed, and ready for another tenant.

The cemeteries of Rio are literal copies, on a smaller scale, of the sepulchral structures of the Greeks and Romans. The form of coffins here is also of remote antiquity. Originally of stone, and placed in the open air, their roofs were formed after those of houses, and with the same view—to allow rain to run off. Stone sarcophagi of this description are counted among the oldest of ecclesiastical monuments in Europe.—*Ewbank's " Life in Brazil."*

THE BURYING-GROUND OF HERETICS IN BRAZIL.

The British burying-ground is an irregular plot, part of a mountain slope, opposite the little bay of Gamboa, and the last resting-place of heretics that die here. The broad path leading through it is necessarily steep and crooked. Half way up a spot has been levelled for a little structure in which the burial service is read. The graves are generally level with the surface, and marked by narrow plates of cast iron thrust into the grave and numbered. The prevailing monuments are horizontal slabs. Foreign officers lie here, who might at this moment have been the pride of their parents and ornaments of their country—victims of a false sentiment of honour, that has consigned them to corruption and oblivion in their bloom.

One monumental souvenir above all others engaged my attention. A low stucco fence incloses it, leaving room for lilies, rose bushes, sandacles, and purple flowering vines, while at the corners, young cypresses shoot up. It is the grave of Alfred ———, an affectionate and precocious child, whose departure has torn his parent's heart-strings.

A more auspicious resting-place for the dead can hardly be found on earth. Located on the declivity of a tropical mount, clothed in perpetual verdure, its walks and tombs bordered with flowers, and its area dotted with Indian walnut-trees, mangoes, cinnamon, African corn, and the sweet mandioca; with araças, cajus, and the cardamonia, with its rose-coloured clustres; pinheiros, pitangas, and calabash-trees with both rounded and elongated fruit—what Christian could desire a fitter sepulchre, or where find one more abounding with emblems of innocence and immortality! The blights of winter invade it not; ranges of everlasting hills surround it, and earth's brightest skies smile over it.—*Ewbank's "Life in Brazil."*

SALT.

According to Moresin, *salt* not being liable to putrefaction, and preserving things seasoned with it from decay, was the emblem of eternity and immortality, and mightily abhorred by infernal spirits. "In reference to this symbolical explication, how beautiful," says Mr. Brand, "is that expression applied to the righteous, 'Ye are the *salt* of the earth!'"

On the custom in Ireland of placing a plate of *salt* over the heart of a dead person, Dr. Campbell supposes, in agreement with Moresin's remark, that the salt was considered the emblem of the incorruptible part; "the body itself," says he, "being the type of corruption."

It likewise appears from Mr. Pennant, that, on the death of a highlander, the friends laid on the breast of the deceased a wooden platter, containing a small quantity of *salt* and earth, separate and unmixed; the earth an emblem of the corruptible body—the salt an emblem of the immortal spirit.

The body's *salt* the soul is, which when gone
The flesh soone sucks in putrefaction.

Herrick.

The custom of placing a plate of *salt* upon the dead, Mr. Douce says, is still retained in many parts of England, and particularly in Leicestershire; but the pewter plate and salt are laid with an intent to hinder air from getting into the body and distending it, so as to occasion bursting or inconvenience in closing the coffin. Though this be the reason for the usage at present, yet it is doubtful whether the practice is not a vulgar continuation of the ancient symbolical usage; otherwise, why is *salt* selected?

To these instances of the relation that *salt* bore to the dead, should be annexed Bodin's affirmation, cited by Reginald Scot; namely, that as *salt* "is a sign of eternity, and used by divine commandment in all sacrifices," so "*the devil loveth no* SALT *in his meat.*"—This saying is of itself, perhaps, sufficient to account for the sudden flight of the spectre, and the vanishing of the feast in the churchyard of Kirby Malhamdale on the call for the *salt.—Hone's "Every Day Book."*

SALTIN' 'EM !

An unemblematical, but practical, use of salt in connection with dead bodies seems to have been in vogue, half a century ago, in remote parts of Devonshire. A traveller, it is related, finding himself unable to proceed with his journey, on account of a heavy fall of snow, was forced to take refuge at a lone cottage, inhabited by a woman and her son of a very forbidding aspect. He was, however, hospitably treated, and the son gave him up his bed, which was situated in a loft above. Before retiring to rest he observed a box, bearing a very strong resemblance to a coffin, and his fear and curiosity being aroused, he peeped in, and was horrified to find in it a dead body. He lay down, but was resolved not to go to sleep, not knowing whether they might attempt to murder him in the night. In the morning he rose early, but he found the old woman and her son were astir before him; but their aspect seemed more forbidding than before. He was invited to breakfast; and he summoned up courage to ask the son the meaning of this dead body being in the loft. "Oh!" said he, "it's only *fayther*. You see the snow's very deep, and we shan't be able to bury him till its gone; so mother's salted him. She's a capital hand at *saltin' 'em!*"

CREMATION.

A work of this character would not be complete without a few words on the subject of cremation, or the burning of the dead. The word is derived from the Latin *cremare*, [to burn.] It is a practice of very great antiquity, reaching as far back as the Theban

war, where we are told of the great solemnity that
accompanied this ceremony at the pyre of Menœacus
and Archemorus, who were contemporary with Jair,
the 8th Judge of Israel. In the interior of Asia it is
also of very ancient date, and equally so in the
western parts of the world. The custom seems to
have arisen out of friendship to the deceased, whose
ashes were preserved, as we do a lock of hair, a
ring, or other token of a departed relative or friend.
The bodies of kings were burnt in cloth made of
asbestos, to preserve the ashes, and prevent them
mixing with the fuel, or other matter, of the funeral
pile. Artemesia, wife of Mausolus, king of Caria, to
mitigate her grief at his loss, drank some of his ashes,
mingled with wine. The first mention of cremation
in the Bible is in the First Book of Samuel xxxi.
12, 13, where the Jews having taken the bodies of
Saul and his sons from the wall of Beth-shan, to
which the Philistines had fastened them, brought
them to Jabesh, where they burnt them. The bones
were afterwards buried under a tree. The bodies of
some of the kings of Judah were also subjected to
cremation. Of its practice amongst the Greeks and
Romans, a detailed account has already been given.
Amongst the latter nation it fell into disuse about
the fourth century. In the East, the Hindoos still
adopt it, and the Prince of Wales recently visited the
Hindoo burning-ground at Back Bay, Sonapore, near

Bombay, the fire of which is continually fed by dead bodies, which are collected from various places, and brought down in boats.

Cremation has been strongly advocated by some very influential men in various quarters. In 1856 Professor Richter, of Dresden, drew attention to the subject. In Germany, however, at present, it has made but little progress. It was in that country that Lady Dilke's remains, last year, were submitted to the fiery process. Italy seems to take the lead, where many experiments have been made by some eminent physicists. Brunetti, Professor of Anatomy at Padua, has invented a furnace in the shape of a long square chest. His method, however, turns the bodies into burned coal.

Signor Alberto Keller, having left 50,000 francs for the construction of a temple of cremation in Milan Cemetery, in which his remains were to be burnt, the rite was performed on the 22nd of last January, the first anniversary of his death. The process occupied about an hour, during which time speeches were delivered on the advantages of cremation.

The best plan appears to be that of Messrs. Siemens,* which consists of (1) a gasometer for the manufacture of the gas necessary to heat the furnace; (2) the furnace, with regulator, and a space for

* See Frontispiece.

burning; (3) a chimney to carry off smoke, &c. The process of cremation is effected by means of heated air. The gasometer is put in action by an enormous consumption of coal, charcoal, peat and wood. The gas is conducted through a pipe, provided with a regulating valve, where, meeting with a stream of air, it is converted into flame. The flame extends through the room, which has the regulator, so that the brick material, which is piled up there is heated and kept up to white heat. The flame still continuing supplies heat till the furnace or place for the reception of the body is heated to a weak red heat, when the flame escapes through a pipe into the chimney. As soon as the furnace is in this condition, the process of cremation goes on. The covering of the furnace is removed by the man who superintends the operation. It is put back again, and the body subjected to the action of the red heat for a longer or shorter time, according to its physical condition. After this is done, the gas-valve is closed, and the air in consequence goes through the regulator into the place for burning. It is here heated in the furnace nearly to red heat, in which condition it comes to the bodies already, in some measure, dried, so that decomposition soon follows. The bones are decomposed by the action of the heat, while the carbonate dissolves, and the lime remains as dust. An instrument is provided to collect this dust (which weighs from 6 to 10 lbs.) and place it in a jar, or other vessel, for preservation by the relatives of the deceased. Sir Henry Thompson, who has so recently drawn attention to the subject, by his letters and articles in the "Contemporary Review," has made experiments with this apparatus on the bodies of swine, and has found it entirely successful.

A Cremation Society has been formed in this country, by whom a suitable site has been secured, but £1,000 only, towards the £3,000, required to commence operations, has, at present, been raised— a proof that it has not met with much popular support. There have been some isolated instances of testators recently deceased having expressed a wish in favour of this method of disposing of their remains; one gentleman having, it is said, given private instructions for his body to be burnt on the top of a hill in Wales, but his relatives did not carry out his wishes. I do not venture to express any opinion upon this subject myself; sufficient time not having yet elapsed for an impartial judgment either for or against its adoption.

SIR HENRY THOMPSON AND CREMATION.

A reply to critics and an exposition of the process by Sir H. Thompson, was published in the "Contemporary Review" of March, 1874. After replying to his opponents, and expressing a very strong opinion in favour of the furnaces invented by Dr. Wm. Siemens, (described above,) he sums up the arguments in these words:—

"For the purposes of cremation nothing is required but an apparatus of a suitable kind, the construction of which is well understood, and easy to accomplish. With such apparatus the process is rapid and inoffensive, and the result is perfect. The space necessary for the purpose is small, and but little skilled labour is wanted.

"Not only is its employment compatible with religious rites, but it enables them to be conducted with far greater ease and with far greater safety to the attendants than at a cemetery. For example, burial takes place in the open air, and necessitates exposure to all weathers, while cremation is necessarily conducted within a building, which may be constructed to meet the requirements of mourners and attendants in relation to comfort and taste.

"Cremation destroys instantly all infectious qualities in the body submitted to the process, and effectually prevents the possibility of other injury to the living from the remains at any future time. All care to prevent such evil is obviously unnecessary, and ceases from the moment the process commences. The aim of cremation is to prevent the process of putrefaction.

"On the other hand, burial cannot be conducted

without serious risks to the living, and great care is required to render them inconsiderable with our present population. Costly cemeteries also are necessary, with ample space for all possible demands upon it, and complete isolation from the vicinity of the living, to ensure, as far as possible, the absence of danger to them.

"It is a process designed essentially to prolong decay and putrefaction with all its attendant mischief; and the best that can be affirmed of it is, that in the course of many years it arrives, by a process which is antagonistic to the health of survivors, at results similar to, but less complete, than cremation produces in an hour, without injury to any."

CREMATION ILLEGAL.

The question of the legality of cremation has again been brought before the Saxon Diet by the death of Professor Richter, a physician of great repute in that country, but of rather advanced views, whose wish, as expressed in his last WILL, was to be cremated. The Government refused its sanction to the execution of that rite. When questioned in the Chamber, the Home Minister, Herr Von Nostitz-Wallwitz, declared CREMATION to be ILLEGAL, a statute of 1850 distinctly ordering that the body of every person dying in Saxony shall be buried.

FIRE-BURIAL AMONG OUR GERMANIC FOREFATHERS.

This is the title of an article by Karl Blind, which appeared in "Fraser's Magazine," and has been republished by Messrs. Longmans. It contains a very interesting account of the Poetry and History of Teutonic Cremation. From the testimony of Tacitus he infers the universal practice of cremation among the Germans of old. Among the Scandinavians, it was said to have arisen from a law given by Odin, who, on falling sick, ordered a pyre to be raised for himself. Odin was "the governor of a people originally settled near the Don, who later migrated as conquering warriors towards the north, driven forward as they were by the progress of Roman rule." "He ordained that the dead should be burnt, and that everything that had been their own should be carried to the pyre. He said every one should go up to Walhalla with as many riches as would be heaped upon his pyre, and that he should enjoy in Walhalla also those things which he had hidden away in the earth. The ashes should be thrown into the sea, or be buried deep in the soil; but for illustrious men a mound should be raised as a token of remembrance." The dog of the Norse warrior was buried with him. Among the Northmen abroad cremation was continued till the 10th century; and, in Orkney and Shetland, the heathen Northmen, for at least a century and a-half, practised the fire-burial customs which they had brought with them from Norway. "A striking picture of those Germanic cremation rites in Russia has been handed down to us by Ahmed Ibn Fozlan, an Arab ambassador from the Khalife Al Moktador, who, in 921, wrote a report of his journey. 'You Arabs'—said one of the Northmen in Russia to Ahmed Ibn Fozlan—'are fools! You take the man whom you must have loved and honoured, and put him down in the earth, where vermin and worms devour him. We, on the contrary, burn him up in a twinkling; and he goes straight to Paradise.'" An idea of Anglo-Saxon cremation may be gathered from *Beowulf*. Before dying he asked his warriors to raise for him, after the funeral fire, a mound upon the cliffy height at Hronesnaess, so that it might stand as a lasting memorial before the eyes of his people, and sailors, tossed on ocean's dark waves, might point to it and say, "This is Beo-Wulf's mound!" Ten days were spent in raising over the burnt corpse a tumulus and monument. Precious stones and ornaments were buried with it. Twelve noble warriors rode round the hillock, with words of grief and songs of praise, lauding Beo-Wulf's bravery and his glorious deeds. After cremation, the Scandinavians buried the ashes of the dead in the open fields or in groves, where flowers and herbs were planted on the tomb. Graves were held in high estimation among them; and the runic inscriptions on the gravestones were only a plain unadorned sign of remembrance. The Germanic nations believed in the sacredness of flame, as a means even of appeasing and purifying the soul; a view also found among the Greeks and Romans. Hence the idea of Purgatory in the Roman Catholic Church.

The Germanic belief in the resurrection of the flesh was very strong, and Karl Blind ridicules the assertion of Dr. Wordsworth, Bishop of Lincoln, that cremation must injure the belief in bodily resurrection. He asks "How could the strictly orthodox reconcile their theory with the fact of many people losing their lives accidentally by fire? Are those who have the misfortune of being burnt also excluded from continued existence in another world?" He also asks if martyrs at the stake were "effectually disposed of to all eternity?"

Finally, as to men of a scientific way of thinking, "the question resolves itself into one of public health, to be settled in the public interest, though with every due regard for the memory of the dead."

GASES FROM THE GRAVEYARD

Dr. Lyon Playfair, M.P., in 1849, estimated for the 52,000* annual interments of the metropolis, no less

* Now increased to 80,000.

a quantity than 2,572,580 cubic feet of gases are emitted, "the whole of which, beyond what is absorbed by the soil, must pass into the water below, or the atmosphere above."

EITHER WAY.

A testator, a few years ago, desired that his body should be burnt in a gas retort, but if that could not be done it was to be buried, "*to poison the living!*"

" EARTH TO EARTH."

Under this title, Mr. Francis Seymour Haden, F.R.C.S., addressed three very important letters on the subject of burials to " The Times," and which he had subsequently reprinted in the form of a pamphlet. I shall take the liberty of laying a short outline of these letters before my readers, for they advocate a reform in the present mode of interments, which is of the very highest importance to the health of the living. Mr. Haden starts with these propositions :—

" 1. That the natural destination of all organised bodies that have lived, and that die, on the earth's surface, is the earth.

" 2. That the evils which the Cremationists would have us to believe to be inseparable from the principle of interment are independent of that principle, and wholly of our own creation.

" 3. That the source of these evils is to be found, not in the burial of the dead, but in the unreasoning sentiment which prompts us to keep them unburied as long as possible, and then to bury them in such a way that the earth can have no access to them.

" 4. That the burial of the body supposes its resolution by the direct agency of the earth to which we commit it, and that the earth is fully competent to effect that resolution.

" 5. That the remedy for such evils is not in cremation, but in a sensible recognition of, and a timely submission to, a well-defined law of nature, and in legislative action to enforce the provisions of that law."

Mr. Haden then proceeds to show that the body when enclosed in an air-tight coffin putrifies, and may be found fifty years afterwards in a state of " advanced but unprogressive putrefaction ;" whereas, if it is exposed to the action of the earth, at the end of five or six years we shall not find it, or only the inorganic part of it—the organic, resolved into its constituent elements, having re-entered the atmosphere.

Mr. Haden gives the following illustrations as aptly representing the two conditions described :—

On Christmas Day, 1870, he buried a dog, and on the 1st November, 1874, he dug down and recovered all that was recoverable, which consisted of a few bones with a little friable matter loosely attached to them which had all the physical characters of common earth, without the slightest odour. In 1868 he visited the burial ground of St. Andrew's, Holborn, the contents of which were being removed to make way for the new Viaduct. " The ground about the church had become raised 15 or 18 feet above its original level, and perpendicular sections had been made in it, here and there, from its surface to a depth varying from 10 to 30 feet or more. The face of these sections represented the interments of three centuries and a half. All the burials, except those in the Plague-pit and one or two others to be presently mentioned, had been made in leaden or wooden coffins, some of which were still intact, and some broken in. Little difference as to condition could be perceived between the coffins of Charles II.'s time and those recently used, or between the coffins which were of lead and those which were of wood. In the coffins which were intact were their contents, also intact but putrid, unrecognizable. In those which had been broken in nothing was to be found but a little ordinary earth, corresponding chiefly to the extraneous matters which had accompanied the interment, and, occasionally, not always, a few bones. Nothing more. The body itself had disappeared, and *'earth to earth'* had been accomplished. Here and there in other parts of the ground, were graves lined with brick and filled with water, in which the coffins of those who had been buried in peculiar honour still floated, some head, some feet uppermost, as their gaseous contents determined. Here, again, a few fetters indicated the spot where some evil-doer had undergone what was intended, no doubt, to be the last sentence of degradation, but whose poor body, having had the advantage of being buried without a coffin, had disappeared — as had also, for the same reason, the tenants of the Plague-pit."

Mr. Haden then proceeds to give us his plan for a new kind of coffin "(if we must have coffins)," which will not prevent the resolution of the body. It should be of the thinnest substance,

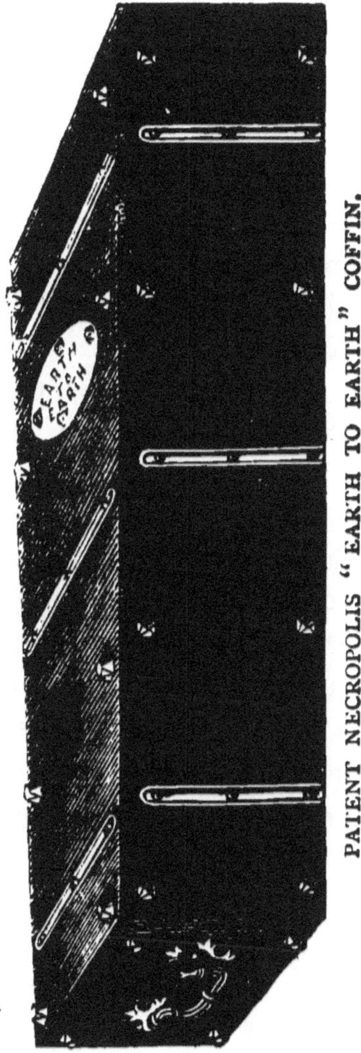

PATENT NECROPOLIS "EARTH TO EARTH" COFFIN.

or the top and sides should admit of removal after the body had been lowered into the grave, or a coffin of wicker or lattice work, open at the top, and filled-in with fragrant herbs. " A layer of ferns or mosses for a bed, a bundle of sweet herbs for a pillow, and as much as it would still contain, after the body had been gently laid in it, of any aromatic or flowering plant for a coverlet—such a covering,. in short, as while it protected the body from the immediate pressure of the earth as effectually as the stoutest oak, would not yet prevent its resolution." The body is to be sponged, the eyes closed, the chin supported, the limbs composed, and the hands crossed upon the breast. In cases of infectious disease, rather finely divided charcoal is to be substituted for the herbs. Models of these wicker coffins were, by the courtesy of the Duke of Sutherland, exhibited at Stafford House, and excited much public interest.

The ingenious author disclaims any intention "to disturb the national sentiment which prompts us to an exceptional treatment of the bodies of the great. Princes, since they are few, may still find rest in marble, and great men, since they are fewer, among the shadows of our glorious Abbey. All that is necessary in such cases is that a certain period — a year or more — should be allowed to elapse between the death and the final entomb-ment during which time the body might lie imbedded in charcoal, in a crypt to which the air has free ingress."

Mr. Haden would dispense with all the ordinary cavalcade and accessories of a funeral. The body being conveyed privately by rail or water to the cemetery, the mourners and friends assembling in the chapel. There is to be "no reunion at the house of death. The conventional feast will not be spread." He points to the lowlands on the Essex bank of the river about Rainham, Purfleet and Grays, or to the Kentish bank, east of Erith, as the most suitable ground for a cemetery. "A thousand acres would bury 100,000 bodies a year for ever; . . . . and adopting, say 200,000 as a probable mean of the prospective annual mortality of Greater London, a total of 2,000 acres of cemetery space, once obtained, would, without entailing upon us any further outlay at any future time, bury the whole of the mortality for ever."

Of the number of dead bodies that may be crowded into one small space of ground, the following startling statement is made from a Report of the Directors of the Kensal Green Cemetery:—"It has been found that seven acres will contain 133,500 graves; each grave will contain 10 coffins: thus accommodation will be found for 1,335,000 bodies!" Nothing need be added to shew the importance of a reformation in our present mode of burials, and that, ere long, the subject must be seriously taken in hand by the legislature. The London Necropolis Company are carrying out the plan recommended by Mr. Haden, where the friends choose to do so, by the use of their " Earth to Earth " coffins, of which an illustration is given above. They have the advantage of being closed up coffins, but the material of which they are principally made is such that, on being placed in the soil, it speedily becomes disintegrated, and allows the body to be resolved into its constituent elements. Thus both the reverential feelings of the mourners are duly consulted, and the requirements of health are satisfied. They are free from the objections which attach to the use of wicker coffins, whilst, at the same time, they most effectually carry out the principle of " *earth to earth* " advocated by Mr. Seymour Haden. They may be seen at the Office of the Company, 2 Lancaster Place, Strand. The Cemetery of this Company at Woking contains more than 500 acres of gravelly soil (the most appropriate for the purpose). Each body is interred in a separate grave, and it has been commended by Dr. Sutherland, the late Government Inspector, as the only cemetery where a proper regard to public health and public decency is observed.

DEAD SULTANS.

A correspondent at Constantinople reports a conversation with one who has long been resident there, and who has an intimate acquaintance with Turkish life and manners. He says:—"And how are the Sultans buried?" I asked. "I will tell you," was the reply, "what was told me by a Turk among Turks— one who knew, and would tell the truth. The dead Sultans have always been buried like dogs. The great thing is to get rid altogether of the idea of a dead Sultan; for never was there a people among whom is so literally carried out the idea that 'Le Roi ne meurt pas.' When it is quite certain that a Sultan is about to die, those round him hardly wait for the breath to leave the body. Most of them run away to be ready to do homage to the new occupant of the throne. Then follows an odd arrangement: All homage is due to the living Sovereign; nothing must interfere with that, not even the corpse of the late Sovereign. So one or two of his old servants only remain with the body, and when it is quite dead they roll it up in straw matting and prop it up behind the door of his room, to be as much out of sight as possible, and when night falls it is carried out of the palace and buried very quietly. No train of mourning coaches here, you see—but, then, they never are used in Turkey; no elaborate preparation for the last resting-place of one all-powerful a few hours before. With us, in fact, a dead Sultan is nobody—his sacredness has descended to his successor. To him we turn our thoughts. We Osmanlis could not do as you Franks do—have a grand lying-in-state. We should bewail at the sight, and that would be incongruous with the rejoicing demanded of us on the accession of our new Sovereign, and would be displeasing to him. Therefore, the custom of burying the Sultans in this manner has never been interfered with; and it is best so." "But how are grandees buried in Turkey?" I continued. "Ah!" was the reply, "I myself saw the funerals of Ali Pasha, Fuad Pasha, and Djemil Pasha, so I can make you understand what the ordinary ceremony is at the burial of a person of rank. Neither Turkish ladies nor Turks ever wear mourning. That they dispense with. Let me tell you about the late Fuad Pasha's funeral, Minister for Foreign Affairs. Well, he, you know, died in Italy, and his body was brought back to Stamboul for burial. They dug three different graves for him, because in preparing the first they came upon some animal (a scorpion, I believe), and it was thought that Turkish ground (sacred in the eyes of Turks) would not receive the body of him who had died among unbelievers. The second grave was not completed when they found water, and again it was believed the earth in this way refused to let the body lie there. But the third time no such impediments appeared, and the grave was dug on a hill within Stamboul, in a desolate place on a site once occupied by houses, and belonging to a mosque ; but this waste place had been devastated by one of the great fires so common in Constantinople, and there were the ruins standing out like pillars on the burnt-up ground." "But about the *cortége* to the burial-place?" asked I. "Well, this is the manner of it. First of all the body is taken to a mosque. Over the simple coffin of cypress wood which contains the body magnificent shawls are thrown, many sent by friends of the dead Pasha, some provided by his own household. These shawls are very costly. Several Pashas help to carry the body to the grave, and as the procession goes on, every one rushes forward to help to bear the coffin for a moment, as this is thought to be holy work. Imaums wearing blue, green, or violet turbans according to the school to which they belong, walk before and after the body. At Fuad Pasha's funeral they walked four abreast in green turbans, to escort the body to the mosque, chanting verses from the Koran. The dead are always taken to a mosque before burial, and there, after prayers recited by the imaums, the Pashas present spoke of the virtues of the deceased over his bier, as is the custom, and then the funeral party started for the grave. The route to it lay through the beautiful new street of Constantinople, called the Yeni Sokak. There were lines of carriages filled with Turkish ladies in bright coloured feridgees, these ladies having waited there since 9 o'clock that morning to see the sight. Among that multitude I mingled, dressed as a Turk, and, as I understood the Turkish language, I overheard much of the conversation and remarks of the crowd. A wooden railing only was placed at first round the grave. You see that a Pasha has the respect paid him of a ceremonious burial; but, as for the Sultans, you may depend on me when I assure you that a dead Sultan is got out of sight as speedily and quietly as possible."—*Pall Mall Gazette, June, 1876.*

CHURCHYARDS AND CEMETERIES IN ENGLAND AND WALES.

According to a Parliamentary return recently issued, the number of churchyards in England and Wales now open is 9,989, while the number closed amounts to 794, or, (according to a later return,) 843. 7,369 parishes, with a population of 20,503,870, only, however, had sent in a return. 2,332 parishes, with a population of 2,208,396, in other words, one quarter of the parishes in England and Wales, have supplied no information whatever.

The closing of churchyards is proceeding very slowly, for though in 1854-5, just after the earlier Burial Acts had been passed, as many as 541 consecrated burial grounds were wholly, and 345 partially closed; in the following years down to 1875, only 119 were wholly closed, and 700 partially, giving an average of about 6 a year wholly closed, and 35 partially.   The metropolis is not included in these returns.

The number of cemeteries containing unconsecrated ground is 539.

In Wales and Monmouthshire together, the number of churchyards open is 788; churchyards closed, 25; cemeteries, 21.   (The returns appear to be very incomplete, 4 cemeteries having been omitted in Anglesey, and some in other parts.)

The number of unconsecrated burial grounds in England and Wales attached to chapels is 2,833 to 14,000 chapels.—*Mr. G. O. Morgan's Speech in the House of Commons, March 3, 1876.*

CONDITION OF IRISH CHURCHYARDS.

The Times, 1876, draws attention to the bad state of burial-grounds in England, in but too many places.   In Ireland the case is as bad, and, if possible, worse, and, as in the country parts at least the poor people are unable to help themselves out of their difficulty, it is full time that something should be done by those in authority.   In many places the people may be said to be without the means of decent burial, and have to use the family grave in a way quite opposed to decency or the requirements of law.   The burial-grounds throughout Ireland are small, old, and full as a rule.   If it were not for emigration on the one hand, and longevity on the other, burials in such grounds would long before this have become impossible. Even as it is, some graves are used so frequently that it is only by resorting to the savage act of breaking up the previous coffin and its only partially decomposed contents that some space is made for the coming coffin. Often this space is but too near the surface. Another practice is to take up the old coffin and put the new one under it. Again, the plan is sometimes followed of merely piling a lot of earth over the coffin. There being no person in charge of these grounds there is no control, and the people do as they like; and but too often on the occasion of country burials there is a great deal of intoxicating liquor consumed before hand, which does not tend to add much to the decency or solemnity of the affair. To counteract all such is certainly the duty as well as the interest of society. We require proper cemeteries at convenient distances throughout Ireland, under efficient control, and I believe that if the subject is taken properly in hand by the authorities there will be little difficulty in getting sites of, say, five acres each, say every ten miles distant. Landholders, if properly invited to give such land, will do so.

STRIKE OF GRAVEDIGGERS.

The operations of the Toxteth Burial Board, Liverpool, have been somewhat impeded by a strike of gravediggers, and some of the men have been summoned for practising intimidation towards substitutes who have been engaged.—*Times, May 22, 1876.*

VICTORIA PARK CEMETERY.

Questions concerning burials and burial rights are likely to occupy public attention for some time to come, but there is one which deserves special notice. Where are the dead of this great Metropolis buried? Our readers will be "surprised to find" that, at the present time, about one seventh of the whole number (or, 200 per week) are interred in a small private cemetery of eleven acres in extent, which is called "The Victoria Park Cemetery," in the neighbourhood of Morpeth-street, Green-street, Bethnal-green. It was originally established in 1845 by the late Mr. Charles Salisbury Butler, many years one of the members for the Tower Hamlets, and who was defeated, when a candidate for the new borough of Hackney, owing mainly, it was supposed, to having incurred the displeasure of the lower order of electors, by having raised the burial fees on Sundays, with a view to decrease the number on that day, at one time ranging as high as 110 or 120, and which, for some years past, have been put a stop to altogether. To Mr. Butler's family the cemetery still belongs, and has been, and still no doubt is, a source of considerable profit. It is bounded on two sides by narrow streets of houses, and, on the other sides, by the Great Eastern Railway and goods station, and some factories and workshops, the smoke from which, in bygone years, has tended to give a more than usually grimy appearance to the few tombstones to be found in it. There is something very dismal and sombre in the aspect of the place, materially increased by two tall, ugly, dilapidated, obelisks in the middle of the ground, which have nearly lost their centre of gravity, and which it would be a mercy for the proprietors to bury out of sight to prevent an accident to the living, and to remove a reproach from the memory of the dead whose relatives have long ceased to care for them. Shells appear to be a favourite ornament for graves in this locality, and look certainly better than blackened, half-rotted wreaths of so-called immortelles. Some "rude memorials" are to be seen here and there on the graves, such as a framed card, or even the name scratched on a small piece of wood. The grass is lank and poor, and some wretched shrubs, with their dead branches unremoved, and a few trees do not tend to relieve the sombreness of the landscape. A small building on the right-hand side of the entrance gates is used as a chapel, where the "Desk Service" of the Church of England is read for a fee of two shillings by somebody in a surplice, who probably does not affect the "courteous epithet" of Reverend whilst living, or will be honoured by its being inscribed on his gravestone when dead. There is a broad carriage-way down the centre of the ground, but at a short distance from the entrance gates part of it on each side is being appropriated for graves, so fully occupied is the cemetery already. Most of the interments are what are called "common," as many as six coffins at least being placed in one grave. We shall be within the mark if we say that more than 300,000 bodies are buried in this small piece of ground, situated in a close and poor neighbourhood. Should anyone ask, how is it that it has not been closed long ago, the answer may be read in large white letters on a black board at the entrance, "All rights preserved by Act of Parliament." Such is the inefficient state of our burial laws that all the large parishes at the East-end of London are unprovided with cemeteries of their own, the Act to authorise their construction being only permissive. Efforts have been made in some of these parishes to carry out the intentions of the Act, but they have been defeated by a joint combination of Radicalism and Dissent. In the event of a severe outbreak of any epidemic in the Metropolis the burials in this ground would be increased to a frightful extent. Government inspection amounts to little more than a sham; the Home Secretary (as he recently lamented in the House) having only one inspector for all the burial grounds in England and Wales. Who is to see that the foot of earth is placed between each coffin, and that there are four feet of it above the uppermost one? Timely steps ought to be taken to close this ground and to purchase it, to prevent its being ultimately built over, or appropriated for a railway goods station—a not improbable fate. If private rights have been preserved, we presume they must be compensated for when taken away. Our local self-government is incomplete indeed which still permits the dead to be buried among the living, and allows, six days out of the seven, in a most crowded part of London, a constant stream of "long funerals, which blacken all the way." The Metropolitan Board of Works ought certainly seriously to consider whether it would not be advisable to take steps to have all the suburban cemeteries placed under its charge, and that new ones should be provided where the most humble might have (as in the Necropolis at Woking) a separate private grave, neatly turfed, where the relatives might place the name of the departed and plant a flower or two in fond remembrance. The wretched appearance of the ground where the poor are interred in many of our cemeteries is a disgrace to our boasted civilisation. It may be a question well worthy of attention whether a general register of burials should not be kept, and that the proprietors of cemeteries and the parochial authorities

should not be compelled to send up a weekly return
of burials to the general registry, from which conclu-
sions might be drawn as to the proper time for closing
any churchyard or cemetery. It is also to be wished
that wicker or "earth to earth" coffins should
come into general use, the admission of earth to
the body causing a much more speedy resolution
into its original elements, and preventing any bad
consequences to general health.—*The Hour, 1876.*

LIFETIME OF MAN.

A hundred years is fixed by Dr. Farr as the natural
lifetime of man. In other words, if all children were
born in perfect health and were to live afterwards
under the most favourable sanitary conditions, a
hundred years would be the age to which every one
of them would attain. As a matter of fact this
extreme limit is reached by scarcely one English
child in a hundred thousand. The average duration
of life in England is only forty-one years, and even
in the most healthy districts of the country it scarcely
amounts to fifty years. But in spite of all drawbacks,
the sanitary progress we have already made has
been by no means inconsiderable. Two hundred
years ago the yearly mortality of London was not
less than 8 per cent. A hundred years ago it had
been reduced to 5 per cent. It is now 2·4. The
more carefully, too, that we look into the causes

of the mortality which exists among us, the more certainly shall we feel convinced that it can be still further reduced. Impure air, impure water, accidents by negligence, and mischief done in a thousand preventable ways, all number their yearly victims. There are, too, no less than 54 large tracts of the country where the yearly mortality for each thousand of the inhabitants is less by five than the average mortality, and less by twenty-two than the mortality of Liverpool. Even in these there are faults in such abundance that we need not anywhere despair of attaining to their standard. In other words, the yearly death-rate of England—or the death-toll, as Dr. Farr very graphically terms it—ought not to be suffered to exceed 17 per 1,000, and all who die in excess of that number must be considered simply as sacrificed to the ignorance or carelessness of society. Nor does the evil of a high death-rate end with the mere loss of life which it implies. It is found by experience that for each annual death there are at least two cases of severe sickness, and that whatever causes influence the one order of events influence the other, too, in the same proportion. A diminution of the year's deaths means, therefore, a better chance of good health to the survivors. This will be to many persons the most attractive side of the picture.

It is unfortunate that our returns of sickness are much less complete than those of death. Dr. Farr can tell his readers the chances that any named disease will prove fatal to any one of them; he can give much less certain information of the chance that they will be attacked by it, or of the length of time that the attack will last. If the clinical history of civilians could be as carefully recorded as that of soldiers, the deficiency would be soon supplied. We find, however, that there is by no means the same staff of skilled reporters in the former case as in the latter. The difference is very considerable. Every 202 soldiers have one medical man to look after them, and to record their sanitary condition. Among civilians there is but one medical man to every 1,276 men, women, and children.

Let us look now at what Dr. Farr calls the march of an English generation through life. Let us follow the physical fortune any million of our countrymen and countrywomen may expect. The first thing we will say is that their number has been made up of 511,745 boys, and of only 488,255 girls, a disproportion which will by and by be redressed by the undue mortality of the boys, and will be reversed before the scene is ended. We will add next that more than a quarter of them will die before they are five years old, or, in exact numbers, 141,387 boys and 121,795 girls. The two sexes are now not far from an exact level. The next five years will be very much less fatal to either sex. The survivors have gone through risks which will never recur. They have probably all suffered from some one or more of the many diseases of childhood; and whooping cough or measles or scarlet fever, which have claimed from them already their thousands and tens of thousands of victims, will have no further terrors for the rest. In the next five years—*i. e.*, from 10 to 15—the mortality will be still more reduced. This is, indeed, the most healthy period of life, the period of which the death-rate is lowest for both sexes, but lower for boys than for girls. There will be some advance of deaths in the next five years, and still more in the five that follow, but 634,045 may confidently expect to enter on their 26th year. Before the end of the next ten years two-thirds of the women will have been married. The deaths will be 62,052, of which not less than 27,134 will be caused by consumption. Between 35 and 45 a still larger "death-toll" will be paid. In spite of the diminished numbers, the deaths will become more frequent, and only a little more than half the original band, or in exact numbers 502,915, will pass on into the next decade of years. Each succeeding decade up to 75 will now become more fatal. At the age of 55 the new deaths will have been 81,800; at 65 they will have been 112,086; at 75, 147,905. The numbers have now shrunk terribly. Only 161,124 still remain to be struck down, and of these 122,559 will have passed away by the eighty-fifth year of the march. The 38,565 that remain, the forlorn hope of well-tried veterans, are now not far from the end. 2,153 of them will live to be 95, and 223 to be 100 years old. Finally, in the 108th year of the course, the last solitary life will flicker out.

This, then, is the average lot of a million Englishmen and Englishwomen. There are, as we have said, some specially favoured districts where the chances of a long life will be much greater, and there are some dark spots, notably in and about Liverpool, where the step of death will be much more rapid. If the rest of England were as healthy as Hampstead the deaths before five years would be reduced by more than 80,000. Each succeeding period would be less fatal than it has been shown actually to be, and there would be nearly double the number of survivors up to 85 years. In Liverpool— or rather in old Liverpool before 1870, for it is down to that year only Dr. Farr's tables extend—the infants which died were not much fewer than half of the entire number born, and, if the conditions of life had everywhere been as unfavourable, of the whole million of lives with which we started there would have been found at 85 to be only 6,003 survivors.—*" Supplement to the Thirty-fifth Annual Report of the Registrar-General of Births, Deaths, and Marriages in England."*

THE HEALTH OF LONDON.

(From the Registrar-General's Annual Summary of births, deaths, and causes of death in London, and other large Cities, for 1875.)

"London is still growing. Its estimated population in the middle of the year was 3,445,160. The increase over the numbers in the previous year was 44,459. This increase is a balance. There is a continual addition to the population by births, and a continual diminution by deaths; and the registered births (122,871) exceeded the deaths (81,513) by 41,358. Then people flock to London from every county, from every part of the Empire, and Londoners by birth flow beyond its limits in great numbers. The extent of this interchange of population is unknown; but the difference in the inflow and outflow probably does not exceed 3,101, that being all of the increase of population that remains unaccounted for by the excess of births over deaths.

"The births of males exceeded the births of females by 2,477; and, upon the other hand, the deaths of males exceeded the deaths of females by 2,321, thus redressing the inequality at birth. It is evident, therefore, that if there is any great inequality in the living population of the two sexes, it is due to the movements of migration. Now the females exceeded the males by 220,158. At the Census of 1871, of the 1,731,109 women and girls, 226,393, or more than one in eight, were domestics, for whose services there is a demand greater than the demand, not only for men servants, but for men in any other occupation. The milliners, dressmakers, and sempstresses amounted to 102,359, the latter probably being as unhealthy as the servants are healthy.

" *Density*.—The estimated increase of population after the Census of 1871 was 190,900; so the density of population then expressed by 42 persons to an acre has risen to 44 persons to an acre. The increase in the years 1861-71 was chiefly in the outlying districts of Kensington, Hampstead, Islington, Hackney, Mile-end Old Town, Poplar, St. Olave, Southwark, Lambeth, Wandsworth, Camberwell, Greenwich, and Lewisham. The population decreased in all the central districts; in the City of London, Holborn, the Strand, and St. Giles; in Marylebone, Westminster, and St. George's, Hanover-square; in Shoreditch, St. George-in-the-East, and Whitechapel. The same process, for the same reasons, has gone on since 1871, so the population in the aggregate has increased at a decreasing rate.

" It has been shown in the supplement to the 35th Report that by a general law under the existing sanitary conditions of England the mortality increases with the density of the population, and in such a way as to make the increased rate of mortality equivalent to nearly the eighth root of the increase of density. Now there were 25 persons to an acre in London in 1841, and 42 persons to an acre in 1871; the mortality in the years 1840-4 was 24·4, and by the increase of density it should have been 26·0 in 1871; but it was on an average 23·5 in the five years, of which 1871 is the middle. So it is a fair inference that the health of London, instead of getting worse by reason of increased density, has grown better by countervailing sanitary measures.

"*Mortality.*—The mortality in the year was at the rate of 23·7 to 1,000 living, which is higher by 1·2 than in the preceding year, and higher than the average of the preceding five years. The increase was very much due to the combination of epidemics of scarlet fever and whooping cough. Mesentric disease also increased. Bronchitis and pneumonia were raised above the average by the weeks of very low temperature.

"It is worthy of remark that the number of deaths to be dealt with in the year 1840 was 46,281, while in the year 1875 the number was 81,513, both being average years, and this is mainly due to increase of population, for the mortality was at the rate of 25·0 in the first, and 23·7 in the last year. The weekly deaths to be abstracted were 890 in 1840, and 1,568 in 1875.

"The mortality in the west districts was at the rate of 22·1 per 1,000, of the north districts 22·3, of the south districts 24·0, of the east districts 25·5, of the central districts 26·0. The density of the same groups of districts expressed by the number of persons to an acre in 1871 was 52, 56, 21, 107, and 150. The south districts, even allowing for their rapid increase since 1871, are out of their order of mortality. They suffered excessively both from the epidemics of scarlet fever and whooping cough.

"South London was formerly supplied by waters contaminated by sewage and it was undrained. So the districts suffered exceptionally from the cholera epidemics of 1849 and 1854, the mortality per 1,000 being 37·6 and 34·8, whereas when the water was purer it was only 24·1 in the epidemic of 1866. The mortality of South London was 24·9 in 1840-4, and only 22·4 in 1870-4. But the density of the population is rapidly increasing, and especial vigilance is required to sustain the advantages South London derived from the drainage, as it now has a population exceeding a million. The periodical tidal floods are fraught with danger.

"The mortality of the central districts remains

high and stationary; nor is it likely to be much reduced until the many rookeries still subsisting are cleared under the new Act, as they are unfit for the habitation of civilized men. The east districts, as the population is growing denser (there were 66 and are 107 persons to an acre) every year, exhibit no diminution in the rates of mortality. In the west and north districts, although the number of persons to an acre is nearly double what it was in 1841, the mortality—all along below the average of the other groups of districts—is lower than it was in the first five years (1840-4).

" *Violent Deaths.*—The violent deaths were 2,852, or more by 82 than in 1874. Homicide is declining; the average annual number in the ten preceding years was 124, whereas the deaths by homicide in the last two years were 97 and 70. The 298 deaths from suicide are the average number; they were much less frequent in October, November, and December, than in the first three months of the year. The chief increase was in the deaths from negligence and accident. Accidental deaths by poison were below, by drowning above, the average. The deaths by suffocation have recently shown a remarkable increase; the annual numbers were on an average 407 during the six years 1865-70; in the last four years the numbers were 496, 534, 540, and 555.

This increase deserves the attention of the coroners. Nearly all the victims were children.

" Two hundred and thirty-one men, women, and children died of injuries by horses and vehicles in the streets of London. It is the highest number yet recorded in a year. The vans, waggons, and drays killed 82, carts killed 55, cabs 39, omnibuses 18, carriages 15, horses 11. Tram-cars are driven now with more care than they were; the deaths they caused in the last three years declined from 17 to 14, and to 9. The vans, waggons, and carts are evidently not driven so skilfully as the other vehicles, and they have no efficient brakes. Some of the victims were probably infirm and a few might have been intoxicated; but this was not the case with the majority. The numbers injured reported to the police, exclusive of 93 killed on the spot, were 2,926. So in this battle of the streets, going on daily, 231 were killed and more than 2,926 were wounded. Can nothing more be done to diminish these injuries and deaths?

" GREATER LONDON.

" Greater London extends over the City and over the Metropolitan Police District. It is a circle including all parishes of which any part is within a radius of 12 miles, and all parishes which are entirely within a circle struck with a radius of 15 miles from Charing-cross. The area is 698 square miles, equivalent to that of a circle of 14·9 miles radius. It includes, south of the Thames, Carshalton, Epsom, Croydon, Richmond, Kingston, in Surrey; Bromley, in Kent; north of the Thames, Chiswick, Brentford, Twickenham, Hampton, Staines, Uxbridge, Harrow, Barnet, Hornsey, in Middlesex; Cheshunt, in Hertfordshire; Stratford, Walthamstow, and Barking Town, in Essex. With a wise foresight these bounds were fixed by the late Sir Robert Peel.

"The population was 3,885,641 in 1871; and it was estimated for 1875, by a satisfactory method, at 4,207,167; the births exceeded the deaths by 51,903; but the increase going on by this and by excess of immigration over emigration together was at the rate of about 80,000 a year. The mean density of population was between eight and nine persons to an acre. The inhabited houses in 1871 amounted to 528,804; and the rateable annual value to £23,177,380.

"The rate of mortality in the Greater London was 22·7, of which 3·7 was by zymotic diseases. The mortality in the Outer Ring is still at the corrected annual rate of 17·9. Fever, however, had become more fatal in the Outer Ring than in Inner London.

" ENGLISH CITIES.

" *Eighteen Great English Cities or Towns.*—Excluding London, the estimated population was 3,236,873. Nearly all these cities present the same problems for solution as London. Each has in its different degrees its outer ring, now healthier than the inner city of these returns, but more destitute of sewerage, water supply, and cheap light, and thus owing its relative superiority mainly to the lesser density of its population, which is every year increasing. The mortality of some of the cities is decreasing, and among them may be named Liverpool, Manchester, Sheffield, Sunderland, and Newcastle-upon-Tyne. Bristol, Birmingham, Nottingham, Salford, Oldham, Bradford, Hull experienced higher rates of mortality in 1875 than in 1871. The salubrity fluctuates from year to year; but in the year 1875 the towns, including London, stood in the following order :—Portsmouth, 19·5; Sunderland, 22·4; London, 23·7; Norwich, 24·5; Wolverhampton, 24·7; Sheffield, 24·8; Newcastle-upon-Tyne, 26·1; Leeds, 26·4; Birmingham, 26·5; Leicester, 26·6; Bristol, 26·8; Bradford, 27·1; Hull, 27·4; Liverpool, 27·5; Nottingham, 27·7; Oldham, 29·6; Manchester, 29·9; and the borough of Salford, 31·5.

" Fifty other large town districts, with an estimated population of 2,724,784, offer some interesting facts. Table 8 shows their birth-rates, as well as death-rates from all causes, and from seven zymotic diseases. In this year the mortality was at rates below 20 per 1,000 in Dover (16·4), Chatham, Maidstone, Hastings, Reading (18·7), Colchester, Devonport (18·5), and

Cheltenham (18·8). The mortality exceeded 26 in Exeter, Stockport (31·6), Wigan (30·3), Bolton, Bury, Ashton-under-Lyne (33·2), Preston (31·8), Gateshead, and Carlisle.

"INDIAN, EUROPEAN, AND AMERICAN CITIES.

"*Eighteen Great Cities Abroad.*—The Registrar-General has been able fortunately to induce the enlightened authorities of more than twenty great cities in India, Europe, and America to supply him with weekly returns in correspondence with those of England. They are all continuations, with the extensions modern science demands, of the old London bills of mortality which were commenced at the close of Elizabeth's reign. The only cities of great States now in default—and that, we may hope, only for a time — are Stockholm (this defect is now being supplied), St. Petersburg, and Moscow. In the year the mortality was lowest in Philadelphia and Christiania (23), and highest in Munich (37·4). Cholera augmented the mortality in Calcutta, Bombay, and Madras. Diphtheria and typhus were very fatal in Berlin; typhus in Munich; smallpox in Vienna; fever in Rome and Naples; diphtheria and small-pox in New York and Brooklyn; scarlet fever in Philadelphia."

INDEX.

————

PART I.

PART II.

9 783337 335489